Praise for the novels of

Lora Leigh

"Leigh draws readers in to her stories and takes them on a sensual roller coaster." —*Love Romances*

"Leigh writes wonderfully straightforward and emotional stories with characters that jump off the page." —*The Road to Romance*

"Fraught with tension from the first page to the last . . . a love story of the deepest kind with a very emotional and sensual base. Combine all these elements together, and [you're] guaranteed an intriguing story that will have you glued to the edge of your seat."
—*Fallen Angel Reviews*

"Blistering sexuality and eroticism . . . bursting with passion and drama . . . enthralls and excites from beginning to end."
—*Romance Reviews Today*

"A scorcher with sex scenes that blister the pages."
—*A Romance Review*

"Thrilling . . . explosive . . . a perfect blend of sexual tension and suspense." —*Sensual Romance*

"An emotional read." —*The Best Reviews*

"Hot sex, snappy dialogue, and kick-butt action add up to outstanding entertainment." —*Romantic Times* (Top Pick)

"Ms. Leigh is one of my favorite authors because she creates new worlds that I want to visit and would move to if only I could."
—*Erotic-Escapades*

"The writing of Lora Leigh continues to amaze me . . . electrically charged, erotic, and just a sinfully good read!"

—JoyfullyReviewed.com

"Wow! This was one hot . . . romance. The lovemaking is scorching." —*Just Erotic Romance Reviews*

Nauti
Dreams

Lora Leigh

BERKLEY SENSATION, NEW YORK

THE BERKLEY PUBLISHING GROUP
Published by the Penguin Group
Penguin Group (USA) Inc.
375 Hudson Street, New York, New York 10014, USA
Penguin Group (Canada), 90 Eglinton Avenue East, Suite 700, Toronto, Ontario M4P 2Y3, Canada
(a division of Pearson Penguin Canada Inc.)
Penguin Books Ltd., 80 Strand, London WC2R 0RL, England
Penguin Group Ireland, 25 St. Stephen's Green, Dublin 2, Ireland (a division of Penguin Books Ltd.)
Penguin Group (Australia), 250 Camberwell Road, Camberwell, Victoria 3124, Australia
(a division of Pearson Australia Group Pty. Ltd.)
Penguin Books India Pvt. Ltd., 11 Community Centre, Panchsheel Park, New Delhi—110 017, India
Penguin Group (NZ), 67 Apollo Drive, Rosedale, North Shore 0632, New Zealand
(a division of Pearson New Zealand Ltd.)
Penguin Books (South Africa) (Pty.) Ltd., 24 Sturdee Avenue, Rosebank, Johannesburg 2196,
South Africa

Penguin Books Ltd., Registered Offices: 80 Strand, London WC2R 0RL, England

This is an original publication of The Berkley Publishing Group.

This is a work of fiction. Names, characters, places, and incidents either are the product of the author's imagination or are used fictitiously, and any resemblance to actual persons, living or dead, business establishments, events, or locales is entirely coincidental. The publisher does not have any control over and does not assume any responsibility for author or third-party websites or their content.

First edition: August 2008

Library of Congress Cataloging-in-Publication Data

Leigh, Lora.
    Nauti dreams / Lora Leigh.—1st ed.
        p. cm.
    ISBN 978-0-425-21951-5
    I. Title.

PS3612.E357N384 2008
813'.6—dc22
                        2008019357

PRINTED IN THE UNITED STATES OF AMERICA

10 9 8 7 6 5 4 3 2 1

Tippytoes, for everything you've done,
thank you.

PROLOGUE 1

Iraq

Five Years Ago

"Little American whore." The kick was harder this time, aimed at the tender flesh of Chaya's stomach, driving the breath out of her and causing her to send a tortured cry through the small cell she had been tossed into.

Her cry. She knew it was her scream, strangled and agonized, but it no longer sounded familiar to her. Reality had receded the day before, and it hadn't yet returned.

She had been dragged from her car just outside Baghdad, blindfolded, and shoved into a van. And that had been a walk in the park compared to the hours since.

"How much easier would it be, whore, to simply give us what we need?" The muzzle of a handgun caressed her cheek. "You could die then. Quickly. There would be no more pain. Wouldn't that be nice? No more clamps attached to tender parts of your body. No more electricity. No more kicks. All you need to do is tell us who contacted you. Tell us the information they have."

The voice was an insidious whisper inside her head as she felt herself crying. Curled in on herself, shuddering with sobs.

Oh God, please don't let them hurt her anymore. She could feel the bruises along her body now, the swollen tenderness of her nipples, the fragility of bones that couldn't take much more abuse without breaking.

They hadn't broken her yet. Had she managed to convince them she didn't know? That she was unaware of the illegal weapons pipeline they were buying their guns and explosives through? That she knew nothing of the information she had been sent to retrieve about the spy within Army Intelligence providing access to those weapons?

And what did she do with the information that only one person had known where she was headed and why?

"So easy," a voice crooned, and she focused on the accent. It wasn't Iraqi, she knew Iraqi. It wasn't Afghani. There were tonal differences in the voices, even when speaking the same language. She knew the difference. This voice was a whisper of something else. Someone else. She knew this voice.

Another blow landed and a scream tore from her as the toe of the boot connected with her ribs. Terror washed through her like an oily, dark wave of suffocating heat. They would break them next. If her ribs broke she wouldn't have a chance of escape. Naked, bruised, and hurting, hell yeah. She could escape given half a chance. But if they broke her ribs? If they caused internal bleeding? She would never make it.

"Maybe we will get to keep this one awhile," the voice mused, laughter filling the tone. "I think maybe she enjoys our caresses, yes?"

No. No. She shook her head, dry heaves shaking through her, torturing her as the spasms ripped through her body.

"You do not like our touch?" False sympathy filled the voice as he bent to her again. "Maybe we use you and fill your belly with seed: We take your brat then and place it in a pretty stroller filled with explosives and park it in front of your White House. Who can resist a baby's cries, eh?"

She fought to breathe.

Reality. Reality was birth control that had been administered before this mission. Reality was backup, somewhere. Her team didn't want to lose her or the information she had, but they could only rescue her if they knew she was missing. If the officer she had discussed the trip with had reported that she hadn't returned.

Reality was, she was beginning to suspect that officer may well be the leak they had been searching for in Army Intelligence.

Reality. She had to hold on, just a little bit longer. She had to find a way to escape, a way to get that information back to her superiors despite the disillusionment and the betrayal that seared her soul.

She felt a hand on her thigh, moving along the back of her leg, fingers touching her, probing.

Rage and terror blazed through her mind. Kicking out she fought to avoid the touch, tried to hurt or to maim, to piss him off enough to keep him away from her. She would prefer to be kicked. She would prefer the broken bones.

"Tell us, Greta." The voice sighed then, resignation in his tone as she heard the shuffling around her. "Raping you would not be a pleasant experience for some reason. And raping you broken and unable to fight holds even less appeal. But if you do not give me what I need, I will spread you out here and I will let these guards use you. They will use you over and over again, until your body is so defiled that even your own people will know nothing but disgust for you. Is this what you want?"

The false gentleness in his tone built the fear inside her. He was going to do it. She knew he was. She had known all along that he would take this step. What better way to torture a woman? When the electrical clamps to her nipples and clitoris hadn't worked, he had gotten more inventive. His men hadn't raped her, but the painful device he used had.

She couldn't bear more pain.

"Such a beautiful woman." He sighed.

Saudi. The accent was Saudi. She couldn't see him, her eyes were so swollen now she doubted she could see daylight if she was in it. But the accent, the voice.

"Nassar," she whispered, dazed, sobbing. "*You* betrayed us, Nassar?"

And it only supported the fact that the man she suspected of betraying the Army was a traitor. Her husband. Nassar was his friend. His contact. And so, obviously, his coconspirator.

Silence filled the void for long moments. Nassar Mallah. She remembered him now. He was a contract agent for the CIA and one of their most trusted moles. Handsome, charming, his black eyes always twinkled with humor and a smile always curved his lips. She had never guessed, never known he was a traitor.

"Ah, Greta." He stroked her cheek again, but she had distracted him. He was no longer stroking the abused flesh between her thighs, no longer threatening to open her again, to destroy her with a helplessness she couldn't accept.

"Why?" Shudders were working through her, and she knew she was finally going into shock.

Or perhaps they had meant to kill her slowly like this.

"Kill her." She felt him rise to his feet. "Use her however you please first, but when you leave this cell, she is to be dead."

"No. Nassar," she cried out his name weakly. "We trusted you. We trusted you."

"No, *you* trusted me. Fool that you were." She heard the shrug in his voice. "Enjoy your last minutes, Greta. I doubt they will spend much time enjoying your broken body. But, with these four, you never know."

The cell door clanged shut. Her fingers tightened around the makeshift knife she had managed to sharpen against the stones earlier. It was gripped in her hand, tucked along her wrist and hidden beneath her body as they dragged her from the pallet.

Reality was, she was going to die here and she knew it.

Pop. She heard the sound, but it didn't make sense. She heard someone grunt, heard something fall.

Several more of the hollow, wet pops and more shuffling.

She knew that sound. Bullets. She couldn't see, but she knew the guards were dead. Frantically, she scrabbled at the floor, found one of them, and raced to tear his shirt off his torso. Buttons. God she hated buttons. She worked them loose with stiff, swollen fingers as she heard shouts, screams, and grunts outside the cell door.

The shirt came free, and she dragged it off his body before shoving her arms into it and wrapping it around her. There wasn't a chance she could rebutton it. Pants. She needed pants.

She was frantic. She worked fast, struggling, panting, trying to ignore the pain searing her body as she worked boots and pants off the guard.

5

She belted the pants on, feeling their length and filth around her. But they covered her. She would have to do without shoes.

Gun. She had the gun in her hand, and she couldn't fucking see. She was crying, her tears burning the cuts on her face, burning her eyes as she crept to the cell door.

It swung open, sunlight piercing her eyes for too long, shadows enveloping her as she brought the gun up while trying to strike out with the small wooden stake she had managed to hone.

"Chill!" The voice was American, harsh as strong hands gripped her wrists, tore the gun and the stake from her hands and moved quickly behind her. "Extraction in progress," he hissed.

Backup. He was reporting in. Extraction. SEALs? Were they SEALs?

"You got me, Faisal?"

Hands were roving over her quickly.

"SEALs?" She gasped out.

"I only wish," he snarled in her ear, his voice deep, like aged whiskey and soothing to her shattered senses. "Try one lone fucking sniper and a teenage kid with more guts than good sense. Can you run?"

His arm was around her, holding her against him. He was warm and protective. Was he protective or did she just need to convince herself that he was? Did she need this to survive the events of the past twenty-four hours?

"I can't see." And she wanted to see him. Wanted her senses in order, her thoughts clinical, as sharp as they had been yesterday.

"I'll lead, you run?" The suggestion was almost a croon, his voice almost tempting.

"I'll run."

He had her on her feet. Her bare feet. But she would be okay.

She would run, anything to escape this cell, the hands touching her body, the voice at her ear, sinking into her head.

"Small cell here." He rushed her into the heat and blinding light. "I think we got them all, but I'm not betting on it. We have bogeys heading in a few miles out and tight quarters to hide in."

He was talking to her as he ran. Ran hard and fast, holding her against his side and taking most of her weight as she forced herself to keep up with him.

"Nassar?" she questioned roughly. She hoped the bastard was dead.

"Rode out in the only gun jeep," he informed her. "Gave us our chance."

Nassar got away. But she had the information, had what she needed to fry his and her husband's asses, and she would do just that.

"I need a radio," she gasped. "I have to report in before he gets away."

"Fuck that." Hard, scathing, the voice was nonetheless comforting. It was American. Southern drawl, Kentucky if she wasn't mistaken. "Look, little girl. I'm on a short leash here and ammo is tight. I'm a Marine sniper with no backup or comm until closer to extraction, or until the extraction team comes searching for me. I wouldn't even be here if your friend Faisal hadn't sent out a Mayday on shortwave and connected with my only comm. We gotta boogie and boogie hard, or both our asses are grass. Those bad boys back there are sure to make fine lawn mowers, too."

They were running uphill. He was barking commands. Gathering his guns, his pack. Getting ready to run again.

"Where are we?" She was fighting to breathe, to keep up.

"Bum-fucked nowhere." He was running full out and wasn't

7

close to being winded. "I have a hole a mile out. You're gonna have to hang on for the ride, sugar, 'cause we don't get there, we're all dead. And dead and me don't get along."

"She live? She live?" Young, Iraqi, the boy's voice was frantic as the man paused for just a second. She knew the voice. Faisal was one of her informants. The young boy's courage was incredible.

"She lives, now boogie your ass, boy."

"Boogie my ass, Natchie," the boy claimed. "Boogie boogie."

"Damned kid." But there was affection in his voice. That affection, that sense of protectiveness that seemed to surround her, dug into her, made her chest ache from more than the run.

How long had it been since she had felt protected? Had she ever? But she did now. With this stranger's arm tight around her waist, half pulling her, half carrying her. Rescuing her. And Chaya had never been rescued in her life.

They were running full tilt. She couldn't see, her feet were bleeding, and her bruised ribs were in agony. But she was free. Reality was, she was free, and with just a little tiny miracle, she could stay free. But she knew those arms wouldn't always be there. That strength wouldn't always surround her, and she spared just a moment to regret that.

Natches rushed the mile to the hole he had made the night before after Faisal's shortwave coded message had hit his radio. He'd made the holes, prepared them, and then went after the girl the boy had seen hauled into the dump of a terrorist camp. A small enough camp, out of the way, populated by barely a dozen hard-eyed, fanatic bastards and one little American blonde.

Hell, who had been dumb enough to lose her? She was an agent, he could tell from the automatic stamina pushing her. She didn't have the strength to crawl on her own, but her legs were moving and she was fighting to help him as much as she could.

Faisal was easily staying at his side, his dark face creased with worry at the sound of gunfire behind them. They were out of sight as they rounded the low, rolling hill, and the hole was just ahead, covered deep with stripped trees and wrapped with dead brush. A natural part of the landscape.

"Get in the hole." He lifted the first cover and pushed Faisal into it with the supplies he would need in a smaller pack.

He threw himself and the girl into the second hole and jerked the secured covering over them as the sound of a helicopter began to hum from the direction of the terrorist base.

Of course, there had to be a fucking helicopter, he thought as he lifted himself enough to stare through the natural break he had created to see if they were followed. Fuck, he didn't need this.

The hole was deep enough to sit in, the upper natural covering strong enough to hold a tank, maybe. They were secure as long as the bastards didn't have dogs. It wasn't very long, wasn't very wide, but it was the best he could do on short notice.

"Do you have extraction coming soon?" Chaya rasped.

He glanced back at her and winced. She was curled against the dirt wall, eyes swollen closed, her lips dry and cracked. She looked vulnerable, but the woman had a spine of steel.

"I have a tracker on me. They'll find me when they get in close enough. When I wasn't at the first extraction point, they'll have followed the beacon I have on me."

Her lips twisted mockingly. "Are you sure? Collateral damage is the motto these days, you know."

Fuck wasn't that the truth. "Every good redneck knows you

always have a plan B," he assured her. His team was all the plan A or B that he needed. Most snipers worked alone, but on this mission, he was numero uno and he knew it. They needed him too damned bad to allow him to become damaged.

She breathed out wearily as he pulled a canteen from his pack and uncapped it. "Here. Drink slow." He lifted the water to her lips, staring at her face as she sipped.

"I have some salve and bandages for your eyes," he said. "Bastards always go for the eyes first, don't they?"

She gave a small, bitter laugh. "At least second."

He pulled out the medical kit, smoothed the salve over her eyes, then secured bandages over them. She had the face of an angel, he thought. Fine bones, delicate cheekbones, pretty sensual lips, he bet. Right now they were bloody and swollen.

"Old lady at home makes that salve," he told her. "Bastards caught me last year, just about tore my eyeballs out before I escaped. When I went home on leave, she made the salve and made me promise to keep it with me."

"Kentucky," she whispered as the helicopter swept overhead.

"Lake Cumberland." He gently touched the scratches on her face with the salve.

She was a slender woman. Dirt caked her hair and smeared her face, but he bet she was a beauty before Nassar and his men got hold of her.

"You're New England." He nodded at her accent. "Damn pretty area. Damned pretty girls."

Her smile was tired. "There's one less now."

He sincerely doubted that. "Did they rape you?"

He was surprised at the fury that threatened to drown his common sense. Of course they raped her. They were known for it.

She shook her head and grimaced mockingly. "*They* didn't."

"*Who* did?" He smeared the salve over her swollen lips as he caught the emphasis.

"Nassar has some interesting toys." She grimaced. "But he was tired of using them. His little buddies were going to do the deed when he left. Thanks for the timing by the way."

Natches sat back on his haunches and listened carefully for noise outside. There were no caves in this area. The next hill over had several. The area he had chosen was no more than a flat, uninteresting gorge. Nothing but some scrappy foliage and dead brush. The perfect place for a hole. They would check the area, but they would be more eager to hit the caves a mile away.

"Faisal, your goat herder friend," he explained softly. "He saw Nassar bring you in. He's also got a handy-dandy military shortwave and an American Army sergeant for a buddy who taught him a little bit of code. That code caught me on my way back. I sidetracked to rescue you. All the guys at home are gonna be slapping my back for this one. I might even get a street named after me."

Her smile was slower. Dazed. She was slipping away from him and he couldn't allow that. "Faisal's a good kid," she whispered, her head nodding to the side.

"Wake up there, girl."

"Chaya. My name is Chaya." Her voice was soft, sweet. He liked her voice.

Damned pretty name for a damned pretty woman. He touched her cheek again.

"Talk to me, Chay. Tell me where you're hurt. I need to fix as much as I can just in case we have to run."

"Feet. Bruised ribs, possible concussion. No internal bleeding, no broken bones."

She was drifting away from him.

Natches leaned in and touched her lips with his. Her head jerked back as she gasped. But her hands reached out for him, her fingers—slender, fragile fingers—clenching his wrists, tightening, as though she were afraid to let go of him, before she did just that. Slowly. Hesitantly.

"There, awake now?" He moved to her feet, pulling one into his lap as he dragged the medical kit closer.

"Why did you do that?" She sounded shocked, but awake, aware.

"My kisses are potent," he bragged shamelessly, desperate to keep her grounded and aware. "They wake all the girls up."

He used a penlight to check her feet carefully, always listening, always tracking the sound of the helicopter overhead and the vehicles now moving through the ravines.

He peeked over the edge of the hole but couldn't see anything moving near enough to be deemed a threat.

He smoothed the salve over her feet, then pulled his shirt and T-shirt off. He tore the T-shirt into strips, padded her feet, then wrapped them with stretch gauze.

"All the girls like your kisses, do they?" She still sounded awake.

"They beg for my kisses." It was nothing less than the truth, but as he stared at this woman, so strong, so determined, he wondered at the women he had known before. Would any of them have found the strength to make it this far? And he knew they wouldn't have. But this one, this one would never join in the Mackay games as the others had.

"Conceited." Her smile was tired, and worry lashed at him.

She was sheet white, pain and shock setting in now that she was still and no longer enfolded in complete terror. He couldn't risk shock. Not yet.

He dug in the med pack again and pulled free the potent pain pills he carried. "Take this." He pushed it into her mouth and lifted the canteen to her lips again.

She sipped and then leaned her head back against the dirt wall behind her.

Silence filled the hole for long moments. Her breathing was short and erratic, and every few seconds she would flinch or grimace just enough that he caught the wary movements in her expressions.

He wanted to hold her. She was almost broken, maybe not physically, but mentally at the least. She had endured this far, he had to get her just a little further.

"The trucks are getting closer." There was weariness in her voice, but no fear yet.

"They'll search for a while. I'm good at this. Don't worry."

He checked on Faisal's hole. It was silent. Faisal knew how to hide; it wasn't his first time, probably wouldn't be his last. He had everything he needed to stay secure as long as no one identified the hiding place Natches had made.

"How did they get you?" he finally asked her when she said nothing else.

"Dragged me out of my car outside Baghdad, threw me in a van, beat the shit out of me, and played with some torture." She shrugged, but he heard the echo of horror in her voice.

"What do you have that they want?"

She was an American woman and she had enough strength to strip a dead man and get his clothes on in the time it took him to pop a few heads and get to her location. She was an agent; he knew that from the comment she had made about needing to let someone know about Nassar. That was going to take a few hours at least.

"I don't have anything anyone wants," she said tiredly. "I'm a relief worker. I was working in Baghdad."

"Don't pull no shit with me, sugar."

"Then don't pull none with me. You know how it goes." She copied his accent exactly. "I have to get out of here."

Yeah, he knew how it went. She couldn't disclose and he shouldn't be asking, but he was a nosy bastard and that was the truth.

"Won't be long now. I've already missed my bus," he stated. "When I'm not at extraction, they'll send a team out for me. I'm important, you know."

"Obviously more important than I am." She sighed. "Can I take a nap?"

"No naps." The helicopter was getting closer. He hoped Faisal had his deflecting blanket over his head. "Come here; we gotta hunker down."

Fear flashed across her face for just a second as he unfolded the light, silver-backed blanket and pulled it over their heads, tucking it in carefully around them. So much as a foot sticking out from beneath it would allow any heat-seeking equipment to pick them up.

He had no idea what that helicopter was packing, and he wasn't taking any chances.

He was wrapped around her like a possessive lover now, and he could feel her fear as easily as he could feel the heat building beneath the blanket.

"You know, if I was back home, the ladies would be purring at being here with me," he pointed out to her as he smiled against her head. "They like my hard body. They think I'm sexy."

A nervous laugh parted her lips as he rested his cheek against her hair.

"I can't see if you're sexy," she reminded him, and he hated that quiver in her voice.

"Oh, you're missin' out." He sighed pitifully, his voice whisper soft. "I'm damned fine, Chay. Green eyes and a nice tan. I got hard abs. Black hair. The women drool over me."

He smiled, listened carefully, and was thankful to feel a small measure of the fear ease from her. He didn't consider himself particularly handsome, but he knew what the ladies said. He had to distract her though, and this was all that mattered.

"Conceited, too." Her hands were clenched tight around his lower arms, broken nails digging into his flesh.

"Hell yeah, I am. I'm spoiled as hell."

"So what are you doing here?"

"Playing? Escaping the marriage market?" He held her closer as the sound of the helicopter hovering overhead had her shuddering against him. The camouflaged top of the blanket, added to the dead brush secured to the narrow timbers above them, would hide them from sight. He had a moment to worry about Faisal, then pushed it away. If they were caught, they were probably dead anyway, despite the extraction team that he knew would be barreling its way to him.

He had pictures, layouts, troop movements, and hidden terrorist bases. He'd been out in bum-fucked nowhere for six weeks now after completing the primary mission he had been sent on to aid in the extraction of another captured agent.

That agent had been rescued. So why hadn't a team been sent out for this one?

"They're getting closer." Her voice was a breath of terror.

"No worries, baby. By nightfall, we're going to be safe and

sound and celebrating with some homemade shine I'm saving just for the end of this mission. I'll get you drunk and seduce you."

"Seduce me?"

"Oh yeah." He held her closer. "I'll lay you down and kiss every bruise, then lick all the hurt away. I'll lave those pretty, tender nipples, and when I go lower, you'll forget all about the pain."

"Ego." She was shuddering in his arms at the sound of the vehicles moving into the ravine.

"Truth." He kissed the top of her head. "When I'm finished, this will all seem like a very bad dream. Distant and gone away. It will be just me and you, sweetheart. Sweaty and hot and doing things that might make both of us blush."

"I bet you don't blush." She buried her face in his chest at the sound of voices shouting in Arabic.

"I bet you could make me blush." He kissed the top of her head and smiled, triumph singing through him at the feel of the light vibration of the radio at his thigh. "You gonna make me blush tonight, sugar? I just got signal." He took her hand and laid it against the radio. "Five minutes and hell is gonna sweep through here. Five hours and I'm going to make you blush."

"You can't." He could have sworn he heard tears in her voice.

"Making you blush would be my sole aim in life," he murmured. "I promise, baby, I can do it."

"I'm married."

PROLOGUE II

Lake Cumberland, Kentucky

August, Four Years Later

Chaya Greta Dane found the tracking device that had been left beneath Dawg Mackay's vehicle on the side of a dirt road so deep in the Kentucky mountains that she knew she would play hell finding her way out.

She blew out a hard breath and shook her head. The Mackays weren't stupid, but sometimes her boss liked to pretend they were, and that was a very big mistake, especially in light of the fact that Cranston really wasn't a fool.

She stared around the area before brushing back her dark blond hair and resigning herself to the inevitable.

Dawg Mackay had led her on a merry chase, and he had known exactly what he was doing. Through twisting hollows, up steep mountain roads that barely passed as trails, and into the thick forests that surrounded Lake Cumberland like a protective lover.

She would find her way out, eventually, but there was no doubt she was stuck for the night. Her satellite phone wasn't cooperating for some reason, the cell phone had no reception, and night was coming on.

She straightened from the crouch where she had found the locator another agent had placed beneath the Mackay vehicle, propped her hands on her hips, and stared around the thick forest surrounding her.

It would have been enjoyable if she'd been prepared. Simple things like enough water to get her through the night, a sleeping bag maybe. She did have her weapon. And her thoughts. Too many thoughts the longer she stayed in Somerset—the longer she was around Natches Mackay and all the memories she tried to push behind her.

She shook her head and reached inside her back pocket for the habit she had picked up again in the past few months, only to find the cigarette pack she had stuck there earlier empty. Great.

Shaking her head, she wadded up the pack and tossed it into the back of the borrowed jeep her boss had had waiting for her just outside of Somerset, after she had reported the direction Dawg and his lover, Crista Jansen, had been heading in.

Crista Jansen looked too damned much like the woman brokering a missile sale between hijackers and terrorists to suit the Department of Homeland Security. It had been her job to follow Crista, to keep an eye on her and whoever she met with.

Knowing Dawg Mackay, Crista Jansen was meeting with nothing less than every inch of that Kentucky native's hard body. Dawg wasn't a traitor. He wanted those missiles as much as they did, and it was apparent he believed his woman was innocent.

But, hell, everyone thought the person they loved was innocent.

Human nature had a tendency to overlook the truth whenever it wanted to. She had learned that lesson herself, the hard way.

Always the hard way. And look at what she had lost. Sometimes Chaya wondered if she hadn't lost her soul in a desert so bleak it sucked the spirit out of a person.

She snorted at that thought as she kicked at a clump of grass and leaned against her car, determined to enjoy just a few minutes of being unreachable by her boss, Timothy Cranston. No doubt he was frantically calling both the cell and sat phones. And here she stood, breathing in the fresh mountain air, feeling the peace of the place wrap around her, sink inside her.

Beseeching her to relax. To remember. To remember one night. One man. Urging her to close her eyes and to remember his touch. A touch filled with tears and her sobs, but also with his gentleness, with the warmth of his kisses, the heat of his possession. A night she only remembered in her dreams.

Her lips kicked up in a grin at the thought. Yeah, relax and drop her guard. Hadn't she done that before? And hadn't she paid for it? Hadn't she lost everything she loved in life because she had trusted the wrong person? And here she was, a part of her wishing, regretting things she knew she had no right to regret.

Strong arms that didn't hold her through the night. A voice like aged whiskey that didn't rasp her name with heated passion at his release. Hands, calloused and possessive. And she regretted, because that illusion was the most dangerous one she could ever reach out for.

A second later an unexpected sound had her jerking her weapon from the holster at the small of her back and taking aim at the front of the car.

She knew who it was. She took the precaution of waiting,

watching, but the sound of the jeep rolling up the mountain was unmistakable. Powerful, a hard, male throb of power that her piece-of-crap borrowed jeep didn't have.

At least he was driving up in front of her rather than slipping through the trees and taking aim. He could have taken her out before she knew what hit her. And he would. No matter how well he knew her, no matter the short history they had shared so long ago, he would put a bullet between her eyes as fast as he would an enemy combatant if he felt she was a threat.

She held the Glock comfortably, confidently, as the wicked black vehicle pulled over the rise. If a jeep could strut, it strutted up the mountain and caused her to grit her teeth. Cranston could make her crazy running her in circles, but he couldn't give her a vehicle decent enough to make those circles in.

Tall tires, gleaming paint job, and a black pipe bumper. A winch at the front, the top pulled back, the man behind the wheel staring back at her from behind dark glasses, hiding those incredible green eyes.

But nothing could hide his somber expression as he jumped from the driver's seat, the engine still idling, throbbing. Like the rumble of a monstrous cat.

This was the dream, and the illusion. And somehow she had known he would be here. Here, in the mountains that bred him, as strong, as secure, as dangerously primitive as the man himself. As dangerous as the regrets that whispered through her as she watched him.

Chaya licked her lips slowly, staring back at him, trying not to notice the smooth, corded grace of his body. The way his jeans hung low on his hips and drew attention to his thighs. The way his gray T-shirt snugged over taut abs. The aura of power and male grace that seemed to ooze from the pores of his heavily tanned skin.

The wind ruffled through his overly long black hair, whipping it across his forehead and along the nape of his neck. Those thick, tempting strands had her hands itching to touch them, her fingers curling into fists to restrain the need.

Hell, she needed that cigarette bad now. She'd been working with him for months, and she still couldn't dampen the sickening nerves, the pain each time he came near her. The need. Oh God, the need wrapped around her until sometimes she wondered if it would eventually drive her insane. The need to touch. Just one more time, just one touch, one kiss, one more night to hide within his arms.

Instead, she tucked her weapon back into its holster and shoved her hands into the pockets of her jeans as she watched him. The way he moved. The intensity in his forest green eyes, the knowledge in his expression. There was always that knowledge, the words that whispered just below the surface, the memories that never really went away. The hunger that never really receded.

Natches moved lazily to the front of the jeep and leaned against the heavy bumper. He stared at her, unsmiling, as he crossed one booted foot over the other and eased the dark glasses from his face.

Piercing green eyes tore into her senses, scrambled her brain and had her heart throbbing like a schoolgirl's. Summer's heat rushed around her then, stroking over her body and reminding her, always reminding her, of things she shouldn't let herself remember.

"Busted." He lifted his brows mockingly. "Want to tell me why you're following my cousin and his woman?"

Her lips parted as she fought to drag in more breath. He could do that. Make her breathless. Make her want. With only a look, he made her feel like a virgin on the verge of her first kiss. And that was very dangerous. He was dangerous. In more ways than one.

"You're not answering me, Chaya." He was one of the few people who dared to call her by her given name rather than the name she used in the agency. Greta. It was nice and plain and unassuming. But he had to call her Chaya instead. He had to remind her of who she had once wanted to be rather than who she was.

She licked her lips again, fighting for her composure.

"You'll have to ask Cranston." She was not taking the blame for this. "His orders. I just live to obey them." That was nothing less than the truth in the past few years. He controlled her. For now.

Natches shook his head, straightened, and moved closer. Standing her ground wasn't easy. She wanted to run. She wanted to run to him, touch him, stroke all that hard, dark flesh, and let the intensity of these dangerous desires free.

She wasn't married anymore, she reminded herself. She had been reminding herself of that for years.

She watched him, wary, suspecting the danger that lurked beneath that easy smile. *Suspected* nothing, she *knew* it lurked there. She knew she was facing a man who at one time had been a cold, hard killer. He had been taken into sniper training within six months of his enlistment with the Marines and within a year was ranked as one of their most proficient assassins.

And now he was retired. Bum shoulder. He liked to grin when claiming the injury that pulled him out of the Marines. She doubted a single cell on his body was "bum."

"You know, Chaya . . ."

"My name is Greta," she grated out. "Use it, Natches." She had to find some kind of defense against him. The name Greta reminded her, kept the memories of the one mistake that had shaped her uppermost in her mind.

"Chaya." His lips caressed the words as he drew closer, within a breath of her, forcing her to stare up at him. "Darlin'. Cranston's gonna get you in a shitload of trouble. You know this, right?"

Oh God, if she didn't know it before, she was finding out now. She had thought working with Cranston would make her life easier, that the team that worked stateside only would ease her slowly away from the horror of the past and allow her to step out of the world that had begun to smother her.

"Take it up with Cranston." She forced the words from her throat as his hand curled around the side of her neck and the dark, sexual light in his wicked eyes began to gleam with intent.

That touch, just like that, the implied power and gentleness of that hold, had her knees weakening. She was a trained agent; she wasn't supposed to let emotion or lust cloud her judgment. But right now it was clouding her entire mind.

His fingers flexed against her neck, the power and strength in his arm echoing along her nerve endings. Pleasure corrupted her normally logical thought processes and eroded the control she had fought for over the years.

Suddenly, she was in the dark, fighting to breathe through the agony of a hell she couldn't accept, holding on to only one thing. Holding on to Natches's touch.

She couldn't let herself hold on to that memory.

Chaya didn't bother to struggle. She could see the desire already burning in his eyes, and she knew she didn't have a chance against him if those luscious lips actually touched hers. She would be lost in him, and she couldn't afford to ever lose herself again.

"Don't kiss me, Natches. Don't do that to me. Please."

He froze, those fingers contracting on her flesh, stroking cells that hadn't known a man's touch in so very long.

He had no idea how hard it was to turn away, to walk away. How she ached at night, tossing and turning in her bed, the thought of the promise in those cat's eyes of his burning through her soul. She wanted him with a strength that terrified her.

"Give me one reason why I shouldn't," he said, his voice low as those fingers stroked against her flesh. "You're not married anymore, sweetheart."

His gaze wasn't mocking now; it was somber, intense. The memories flashed in his eyes as well, and she couldn't bear it. It connected them, made it so much harder for her to break away, to hold herself steady as she fought through the never-ending abyss of emotions that threatened to swamp her.

"Because I can't handle you, and we both know it. Have mercy, Natches. Don't you have enough women in your little stable? You really don't need me."

And there was no way she would survive it. He was wild, intense, the most wickedly alluring man she had ever met in her life. And he wasn't the man for her. She wanted him until she ached with a force that tore at her soul, and she couldn't allow herself to have him. This man, the one who fired her soul, who made her dream when she had no right to dream.

"That's not a good enough reason."

She gasped as his lips covered hers. Sensation exploded through her body; pleasure rippled and waved over her nerve endings and began to burn along her flesh. This kiss, this man, he was like nectar, like a drug she couldn't get out of her system.

She gasped harder as her weapon dropped to the ground and

she felt Natches's hands tugging at her shirt, baring her, allowing the warmth of the sun-filled air to touch her flesh.

She told herself the perspiration was from the heat of the day, but she knew better. It was from his kiss.

Oh God. His kiss. She flattened her hands against his chest to push him away, but he wasn't budging. His hands stroked up her back, beneath her shirt, then around, the pads of his fingers at the tender swells of her breasts, covered by nothing more than lace.

Chaya struggled with the war waging within her now. Her body, eager, desperate, it knew this man's touch, knew his possession. Her heart, her head, was screaming out in warning.

And her body was winning.

"Ah, Chay." He nipped at her lips. She loved that sexy little sting and lifted closer, begging for more. "There you go, baby. Show me how you can burn again."

She breathed in sharply as his hands slid to her hips, gripping them and lifting her until she was sitting on the hood of the jeep, then lying back, his big body pressing her down as her hands tugged at his shirt.

She should be pushing him away, not baring that gorgeous body.

But that was what she was doing. Baring all that hard, delicious muscle. Feeling the rasp of crisp chest hairs against her palms, the dampness of his sweat beneath.

She twisted under him, feeling his knee press between her thighs, and saw stars explode behind her closed lashes as he pressed against the sensitive flesh between her thighs.

"Hell yeah." He groaned against her lips as he worked her jeans loose. "Burn for me, Chaya. Just a little bit. Burn for me wild and sweet, sweetheart, just like you do in my dreams."

His voice was rough, tight with arousal, and she knew it

could become guttural. That his drawl could slur his words and make him sound drunk with passion. She wanted that sound. She wanted him drunk on *her*.

"Natches!" She cried his name as his hand pushed beneath her open jeans and his fingers found her. Found the slick, too-thick layer of juices that prepared her for him, that betrayed her need.

That need was killing her.

She twisted, arched to him as his lips slid down her neck to her breasts. His teeth rasped the tender tip of a nipple as his free hand pulled the cup of her bra beneath the swollen mound.

Then his mouth was covering it, his lips closing on it, sucking it inside with tight, hard pressure that sent sensation ripping to her womb.

Long, broad fingers speared inside her vagina, drawing another cry from her. Flesh unused to any touch but her own since he had taken her so long ago. Too long.

She came instantly. The stretching heat, the feel of his mouth sucking her nipple, his tongue lashing her, it was too much. She exploded in a prism of light and color, his name on her lips and in her heart.

Oh God, she was never going to be free of him. And in this moment, exploding around his fingers, she wondered if she ever wanted to be.

She struggled to open her eyes, then lost her breath as she watched him. He pulled his fingers free of her, lifted them, and tasted her. Right there, beneath the sun, the breeze whipping around them, he opened his lips and sucked the taste of her from his fingers.

"Natches." She could barely do more than breathe his name

when his face suddenly stilled, his head lifting, like an animal scenting danger.

"Son of a bitch Cranston." He was jerking her bra in place and pulling her shirt down when she caught the sound of a helicopter coming closer.

Pulling back from her, Natches let her fix her jeans, his green eyes filled with mocking amusement as the helicopter flew around the sheltering trees and came over the clearing.

It couldn't land, but she knew who it was. The Department of Homeland Security had found her. They had nearly seen more than she could have safely gotten away with.

Natches drew farther back from her, his expression hardening. "Come on. I'll lead you back to the main road. Then you can call Cranston and tell him to meet with me. I've had enough of this crap. It ends now."

What was going to end now she wasn't certain, but she was more than ready to get the hell out of there, away from him. Let Cranston deal with him, because she knew, as sure as she was standing there she knew, there wasn't a chance in hell that she could handle him.

ONE

Somerset, Kentucky

October, One Year Later

Natches Mackay sat silently in the jeep and watched as Chaya Dane hauled her luggage into the hotel she had reserved in town. The Suites were just that. A nice hotel that offered a variety of live-in suites with a bedroom, a small living room, and a kitchenette for those required to be in town for an extended stay.

Chaya was registered for a two-week stay but the luggage she brought wouldn't have kept one woman for four days. A single large suitcase, an overnight bag, and a laptop case. She was definitely traveling light.

Eyes shaded behind the dark lenses of his sunglasses, he rubbed the short growth of beard at the side of his jaw and considered this new development.

It had been a year since she had been in town. A year since he had pulled the trigger and buried a bullet in his first cousin's head.

And seeing her again brought the memories he tried to suppress back in vivid detail.

Johnny Grace had been a disgrace. He had masterminded the hijacking of a missile shipment as well as the sale of the weapons, and attempted to place the blame on a young woman who his other cousin Dawg Mackay was in love with. To add insult to injury, he had then attempted to kill her when he found out Dawg was onto him.

Saving Crista hadn't been easy, and Natches had known, as he drove to the rendezvous point where Johnny Grace was meeting his lover and coconspirator, that Johnny wouldn't leave there alive. It was a promise Natches had made to himself. Rowdy and Dawg were family, like no one else was. If it hadn't been for them and Rowdy's father, Ray, Natches wouldn't have survived the turmoil of his own life when he was younger.

People who knew the Mackays knew you didn't strike out at one of them. All of them came running if you did. And Rowdy's and Dawg's wives, Kelly and Crista, were strictly hands-off. It was hands-off or Natches would go hunting.

Johnny should have known better. He should have known Natches would be waiting with a bullet for him. But the little fucker had been convinced he could pull it off without anyone being the wiser.

His death had ended the investigation. The missiles had been recovered, the prospective buyers had been arrested, and all was supposed to be right in this little part of the world. Not that Natches slept any easier at night, but he had found a measure of peace. That peace had been hard-won over the past five years, and he had been enjoying the hell out of it.

Until last year.

He watched as Chaya disappeared into the hotel. Chaya was the pet agent of Timothy Cranston, the special agent in charge of investigations. She was his gopher and shit wrestler, and as much as it grated on Natches to see her following the snide little man's orders, he had still considered her rather intelligent. Smart enough that he had tried to stay the hell away from her.

Maybe she wasn't as smart as he had thought. Because she was back here, and he'd be damned if any of his sources had warned him of an operation going down here.

What that operation was, either no one knew, or no one was telling him.

He rubbed at his lower lip and stared at the hotel entrance she had disappeared into. She hadn't looked happy to be back—she'd looked worn, tired, as though she had slept about as much as he had in the past year. Which amounted to less than nothing. And she looked damned good enough to eat. Unfortunately, she wasn't much into being a snack for him.

So why was Miss Dane currently taking up residence in his fair town again? It had to be under orders, because he'd warned her, she wasn't safe here, least of all from him. If she wanted to keep to that cold, lonely bed of hers then she should have found another town to sleep in.

He was brought out of his contemplation when his cousin Rowdy pulled his pickup in beside the jeep. On the other side, Dawg pulled in, his black dual cab taking up space and rumbling like the powerful machine it was.

He glanced to each side, taking in his cousins as they moved from the vehicles. The wind shifted through Dawg's black hair, which wasn't near as long as he used to wear it, but Rowdy's hair, an identical black, was longer.

Married life was keeping them decent in too damned many ways. Dawg had a decent haircut, and Rowdy let his grow out. Dawg was broader than the other cousin, a few years older. They were both just as damned powerful and irritating as they ever were.

And irritating they could be. Married and shackled and tied so damned tight to their wives that if a man just breathed in those women's directions, their hackles rose. But they still came when he called, and the thought of that tugged at something inside him. One of those bits of emotion that he fought to keep buried and hidden.

As they came up beside his jeep, Natches opened the door and stepped out slowly, his gaze still centered on the building. He'd called the little girl on duty at the front desk before he arrived to make certain Miss Dane was given the proper room.

One that looked right out on the parking lot. He wanted her to see him, wanted her to know she was being watched.

"What's brewin', Natches?" Dawg leaned against Rowdy's gray pickup, his arms crossing over his broad chest.

Natches lifted a brow as he took in the pressed jeans and white shirt his cousin was wearing. It was a damned far cry from the holey, scruffy appearance his cousin had before he picked back up with Crista Ann Jansen last year.

"Snazzy-looking duds there, cuz." Natches grinned. "Crista iron those for you herself with her own little hands?"

Dawg scowled back at him, but his light green eyes, nearly a celadon in color, flared with impatient arousal at the mention of his wife.

"Dry cleaners," Dawg finally growled. "And I don't think you called us here to discuss my laundry."

"Watch him, Natches." Rowdy grinned, his dark green eyes, sea green, crinkling at the corners with mirth. "Dawg's been a hair upset over the laundry. Crista put her foot down over the wrinkled, hole-ridden T-shirts he likes wearing to the store. She won't let him play the disinterested owner anymore."

Dawg grunted as Natches smirked absently and glanced back toward the hotel.

"That call you made earlier sounded kind of important, dumb ass." Dawg sighed as he addressed Natches again. "What the hell is going on?"

Natches turned back to him, glaring at his cousin for the nickname that was becoming more frequent.

"You keep calling me 'dumb ass,' and I'm going to split your head open for you."

Dawg grunted and it was his turn to smirk. "I think it suits you. You go moving out of your houseboat, for solitude over that damned garage, and start working like a man who's grown some principles, and I start worrying about you."

Natches's nostrils flared as anger began to churn inside him. Damn Dawg. He didn't need his damned advice or his snide-assed comments, which pretty much described the reason why his cousin was calling him names. Because he refused to listen to either.

"Cranston's running another op in town," he told the other two men before he let that anger take hold. The rest of the accusation he ignored completely.

He didn't need to get pissed right now. He'd spent a lot of years trapping that emotion so deep inside him that it didn't burn in his gut anymore. Keeping it there was important. Keeping it there kept breathing certain and Natches's conscience clear.

"What the hell does that fat little fucker want?" Dawg straightened and glanced toward the hotel with obvious animosity. "Is he in there?"

"No. Not yet. Miss Chaya Greta Dane is there right now, and if my guess is right, she's watching us right now from room three oh four. Do you think maybe she's figured out we're onto her?"

"How did you find out?" Rowdy was watching Natches.

Natches hated it when Rowdy watched him like that. Like he knew something, or saw something Natches didn't want seen.

"Anonymous tip." Natches grimaced. "And that ain't no joke. A call to my cell phone an hour ago—untraceable so far—letting me know she had hit the county line and was here for DHS. If Cranston's lost more missiles, boys, I might have to kill him."

He was joking. Kind of.

"We haven't heard anything." Dawg rubbed at his clean-shaven jaw as he glanced toward the window of Chaya's room.

She liked to go by the name Greta, but hell if that name suited her. With her multihued blond hair and exquisite features, she was as exotic as a tropical flower. *Chaya* suited her. The name rolled off the tongue, and in the darkest nights, as he jacked off to the image of her in his head, the name sounded like a prayer as he spilled his release into his hand.

"I've not heard anything from my contacts either," Rowdy murmured. "Not even a whisper that a DHS agent was coming to town."

Which meant Cranston was keeping whatever he was up to very close to his chest. And that was a very bad thing. When that rabid little bastard kept his mouth shut, then things were about to get ugly.

The thought of that had him glancing toward the hotel again. Chaya was a hell of an agent, but her heart wasn't in it. Natches had seen that the year before. She hadn't wanted to be in Somerset, and she hadn't wanted to play Cranston's games.

"She was supposed to have resigned," he murmured, his eyes narrowing against the bright autumn sunlight overhead. "Turned the papers in just after the op here was what I heard."

He was unaware of the curious looks his cousins gave him. Rowdy glanced at Dawg questioningly, but all his cousin had in reply was a brief shrug.

Natches never cared enough about anyone except his cousins, their wives, his sister, and Rowdy's father, Ray, to check up on them over anything. He often claimed when it came to people, he wouldn't stop the train from wrecking, because it was too damned amusing to sit back and watch the cars piling up.

He hadn't been nearly so amused by the role Cranston had forced Miss Dane into though. He had placed her in danger, and that had pissed Natches off. Just as Cranston had placed all their asses in the fire.

"What do you need from us?" Rowdy turned back to his younger cousin, his chest tightening as it always did whenever he stared at the other man too long.

Natches was almost cold now. It had been coming for a while, but sometimes he feared that cold had taken full hold of him, and chilled him clear to his soul.

Natches seemed to shrug at the question, as though he either didn't care, or wasn't certain what he needed.

"Doesn't little Lucy Moore work here?" Dawg asked then. "She works registration, doesn't she?"

Natches nodded at the question. Lucy was a third cousin on his mother's side, a sweet little girl, but sometimes she was a little too smart for her own good. She had put Chaya in the room he wanted her in, but she had been curious as to why he wanted her there.

"Then just wait till she leaves and slip into her room. Check

35

her shit out and see if she's as anal as she used to be with her notes," Dawg suggested.

Natches glared at him. "She's not stupid, Dawg. Those notes, if she has them, will be locked tight in that laptop and none of us are hackers."

"Slip in and seduce the information out of her." Dawg grinned at that one. "You're good at that shit. Get her to talk, then send her ass home."

It was an idea, except he knew something they didn't know. Chaya didn't have a home.

"What the hell is up with this, Natches?" Rowdy questioned him then. "You knew her before she came here; don't deny it. Now she's back with no clear reason why. Maybe she's back to see you."

Natches shook his head slowly. No, she wasn't back to see him. He came with memories, and Natches knew exactly how that worked. Those memories were too painful, and they were rife with too much emotion for Natches or Chaya to willingly touch them with a ten-foot pole.

"She's not here for me," he finally said, wondering at the regret that pricked at him. "This is an op, boys. Anonymous call, pretty agent, and no agency gossip. Cranston's trying to pull something over on us and I want to know what the hell it is."

Chaya stared through the filmy curtains at the three men gathered in the parking lot. There weren't a lot of cars parked out there, and it was as plain as the dark glasses on Natches's face that they were there because of her.

For a moment, just a moment, she could hear screams in her head. Desperate, clawing sounds that ricocheted inside her, shredded her hard-won composure and had her swinging away from the sight of Natches to pace through her bedroom.

It wasn't just her own screams she heard in her head. The feel of flames licking at her, the horror and stench of death poured into her senses and left her shaking.

She had to swallow tight, clench her fists and force herself away from the memories just as she had to force herself not to return to that window and stare at the men who occasionally glanced up at her room.

They already knew she was here. So much for the element of surprise where Natches was concerned. She had hoped to surprise him with her appearance, hopefully throw him off balance just a little bit.

She snorted at that before pacing back to the window, drawn, despite her best efforts, to the sight of him.

Natches Mackay. He was almost a legend in the Marines. He had been inducted into sniper training right out of boot camp. Within four years he had a kill ratio that made her flinch at the thought of it. Then, in a trick of fate or, as Timothy liked to say, a trick of Natches, a stray bullet had slammed into his shoulder, taking him out of the game.

For years it was rumored Natches had never regained the ability to handle a sniper rifle again. Last year, they had learned differently. Natches was just as silent, and just as deadly, as he had ever been.

She flinched as his head turned and he stared back at her. Surely he couldn't see her behind the filmy curtains, but he knew she was there. He knew which room she was in, and he knew once she saw him out there, she wouldn't be able to look away.

"Put your head down! Close your fucking eyes, Chaya. Ah God. Sweet mercy! Don't look, baby. Don't look."

She closed her eyes. The feel of him lying on her, holding her down despite her struggles, her screams, still brought her awake at night.

Very few people in the world knew that she and Natches had a history. She prayed that only she and Natches knew, because if Timothy had managed to find out exactly what happened before she came to DHS, then he would never let her go. And he would have the edge he needed to pull Natches into Homeland Security rather than merely using the Mackay cousins as contract agents whenever he could manage to trick them into it.

She opened her eyes and stared out the window again, those dark glasses shielding his eyes, his too-long black hair pulled back at the nape of his neck, the savagery of his features more pronounced than it had been the year before.

He always looked like a dark avenging angel to her. But now, he looked like a savage warrior. She knew if he pulled those glasses off the forest green eyes would be piercing, dark, and filled with knowledge and anger.

So much anger. And she couldn't blame him. Not in the least.

"You've done it this time, Chaya," she murmured into the silence of the room.

And she had. She had allowed her boss to blackmail her into another mission that threw her directly in Natches's path. Big mistake. Very big mistake.

Rowdy strode into the upstairs office of Mackay Lumber and Building Supplies and glared at Dawg as his cousin pulled a beer from the fridge and threw himself in the big leather chair behind the desk.

"Someone needs to let me in on the secret," he snapped as he slammed the door closed. "What the hell is going on? Or has gone on?"

Dawg slouched back in the chair and tipped the beer to his lips thoughtfully. A long drink later he sat the bottle on the desk and stared back at Rowdy.

"Now see, I was hoping you would have the answers to those questions." He wiped his hand over his jaw before shaking his head in obvious confusion. "He was actin' stranger than hell with her last year. Every time he got around her he was pokin' at her or watching her. Don't you think she's a little plain for him?"

Rowdy moved to one of the comfortable leather chairs across from the desk and lowered himself into it as he considered Dawg's question.

"She has pretty hair." He finally shrugged, his expression creasing into male contemplation.

"She's homely," Dawg grunted.

Rowdy snorted at that. "We've been saying that about every woman we've come across since Kelly and Crista got their hooks in us. Admit it, Dawg; we're prejudiced."

Dawg glared. "I know a pretty woman when I see one. Just because you're blind as a bat doesn't mean I am."

Rowdy shook his head. "She looks okay, I guess. Can't tell much with those loose clothes and the way she scrapes her hair back from her face."

"She smokes." Dawg tapped the desk with his fingers, his expression worried.

"You're nitpicking. What's the real problem, Dawg?" Rowdy leaned forward, watching his cousin carefully. "It's not like you to nitpick."

Dawg's lips tightened, then pursed thoughtfully.

"Natches brought a woman out of the Iraqi desert with him on that last six-week mission he took. You know he was always goin' off on a hit and taking his good ole easy time loping back to extraction so he could spy a little on the enemy?"

Rowdy nodded.

"Word got around. Natches managed to hook up with an Army Intelligence agent. Female. Beaten, tortured. He pulled her out and the extraction team picked them both up. After that, no one's talkin'. Something happened after that, Rowdy. Something that made Natches darker than ever."

"Female agent, beaten and tortured." Rowdy frowned. "She didn't have time to break his heart, Dawg. A lot of shit happened to all of us in the Marines. That wasn't a pleasant place to be."

Dawg shook his head. "No. Something bad happened out there that Natches doesn't talk about, and I think she was there. Natches knew her the minute we met the team Cranston brought in last year. That night he went on a drunk like I ain't seen since he busted up his daddy's restaurant for him."

Rowdy leaned back in his chair and grimaced at that information. He hadn't been a part of that mission. His damned cousins seemed to think he needed a vacation after dealing with the serial killer who had tried to kill his wife.

But Dawg was right, something had changed in Natches last year, something that had bothered both of them for a year now.

"Is he in love with her?" Rowdy mused.

It was damned hard to imagine Natches in love with any one woman. He seemed to like them all equally. But there had been something different about how he acted last year outside the spa in town.

40

Dawg and Rowdy had met with Natches there, while Kelly and Crista went in for their woman stuff. They hadn't felt secure enough to leave the women unguarded. And Greta Dane—no, Chaya, Natches had told them her name was really Chaya—had been there following Dawg and Crista.

Natches hadn't been able to stay away from her and neither of them acted just normal around each other.

"She's on an op," Dawg muttered. "I can feel it. Something's getting ready to go down and she's going to pull him into it."

"Hell." They didn't need that. Rowdy knew Natches. His cousin could be as impulsive as hell, and he rarely thought to cover his own damned ass until it was too late.

Rowdy pushed himself to his feet and paced the interior of the office. He knew the operation that had played out the year before and it still kept him awake at night.

"What was left untied?" He turned to Dawg. "The operation last year, the money Johnny got as a down payment on the missiles, was it found?"

"Not hardly," Dawg grunted. "Cranston was pulling his hair out by the roots when it didn't show up."

Timothy Cranston, that rabid little bastard of an agent in charge. He should be shot with his own gun. Rowdy had had the extreme displeasure of meeting him several times. He still didn't like him.

"Who else would have helped Johnny, Dawg?" Rowdy asked then, his voice heavy, his chest still tightening, even after all this time.

Johnny had been their cousin, and he had used them all. He would have killed them all if he could have. He had definitely planned to kill Dawg's wife, Crista. Him and his lover, Jim Bedsford.

"They picked up the team Johnny used to steal the missiles," Dawg said. "Johnny and Bedsford are dead, and only they knew where the million in down payment was hidden. Hell, what's left to find?"

"We've missed something," Rowdy suggested then.

"What the hell could we have missed?" Dawg cursed. "His agent is back and Natches gets an anonymous call informing him of that fact? Doesn't make sense, Rowdy. If the girl came back to get hot and sweaty with Natches, why the call?"

Rowdy frowned at that. If it hadn't been for the phone call, he'd have assumed that getting hot and sweaty was exactly what was on Miss Dane's mind. But why would someone call and warn him?

Rowdy felt the hairs at the back of his neck lift in warning, and he rubbed at them in irritation.

"Yeah, that's my answer, too," Dawg admitted. "My neck is tingling like hell. Something's getting ready to go down."

"And Agent Dane is putting Natches right square in the middle of it," Rowdy realized. "So we cover him?"

"And cause him to shoot us?" Dawg snarled in disbelieving amazement. "You know how much he likes shadows, Rowdy. We try to cover him and he'll try to kick our asses."

That left one last option. "I have some contacts I can call on." Rowdy was pulling the names up in his head as he spoke. "I'll see what I can find out."

Dawg nodded. "I'll do the same on my end. Call some of the old agents from last year's op and see what they have to say."

"Someone has to watch out for Natches," Rowdy insisted. "At least check up on him."

Dawg stared at him askance. "Fine, you do it. You've had Kelly longer than I've been with Crista. I kind of like my body in working order right now."

"You and me both."

Dawg breathed out roughly. "Flip for it or take turns?"

Rowdy dropped back in the chair. "I guess take turns." He was imagining the pain once Natches caught them. He was hell in a fight, and he would definitely fight.

Dawg slunk down farther in his chair. "I should kill Cranston."

Rowdy grunted. "Give Natches time; he'll do it for you."

And that was what they were both afraid of.

TWO

The next morning Chaya met with the team that had been pulled in to work the investigation Cranston had managed to get operational status for.

The six men were older, late thirties to early forties, and would blend in well. Their various covers worked for the area and would provide rationale for their seeming nosiness.

That would work in her favor, Chaya thought as she headed back to her room after the first, early morning meeting. They would gather bits and pieces of the gossip drifting around about the events of last year, and then Cranston could begin a list of persons of interest and the questions Chaya would ask.

They were working in the blind though, and she knew it. The problem was they had been working in the blind for five years. It had to end here. She just couldn't do this much longer. The reason she was back this time was Cranston's bribes. Her resignation was still awaiting the stamp of approval.

Gritting her teeth at the thought of Cranston dragging his feet on her resignation, she swiped her key card through the security pad and waited for the light to flicker to green before pushing the door open and stepping through.

She allowed the door to close slowly behind her. She shrugged her jacket from her shoulders, unclipped the holstered weapon she carried just behind her hip and smoothed her free hand down the side of her skirt. She wished she had worn jeans.

She dropped the jacket and weapon on the table, just inside the small suite, then turned and moved for the bedroom. The door was open, and when she stepped inside, she felt her heart catch in her throat.

Natches.

She swallowed tightly as she caught sight of him, sprawled out in the easy chair by the window, long jean-clad legs stretched out before him as his hand lifted.

She felt the flush that suffused her features as she saw the heavy, latex vibrator in his hand. The molded penis was her toy of choice, especially when visions of this man drove her crazy with need.

She hadn't managed to get over him, no matter how hard she tried.

Swallowing tightly she watched as he tilted the erotic toy toward his face and inhaled slowly.

She swore her knees nearly went out from beneath her, and arousal, sharp and hot, shot through her core.

"You amaze me," he said then, reaching out to lay the toy on her pillow. That wasn't where he had gotten it from. "You bring a

45

toy to do a man's job, knowing the man is more than willing to provide the service. Where does that make sense, Chay?"

She braced one hand on her hip, the other on the doorframe and stared back at him, forcing her features to bland interest even though she knew she was eating him with her eyes.

"Considering the fact that the man offering comes with strings, I decided it was the safer option."

He would always demand more from a woman than was comfortable. More than Chaya had been able to consider in the past years.

He chuckled at that, his forest green eyes roving over her, taking in the skirt, the silk shell she had worn beneath her blazer, and the pumps on her feet.

Maybe she should have worn stockings rather than panty hose? She had a feeling he knew exactly what she had on beneath her skirt.

"Everything in life comes with strings, darlin'." He shrugged and looked entirely too comfortable in that chair.

Shaking her head, Chaya stalked across the room, not thinking—she never thought when it came to Natches—to jerk the incriminating dildo from her pillow.

"Oh, you didn't do that." He laughed. It was the only warning she had before he was behind her, one arm going around her waist, the other catching her wrist and the toy as he rolled her to her back.

Her little screech didn't even slow him down. His legs trapped hers as he came over her, and he ignored her hands as she pushed at his hard stomach.

She could have made him let her go. She knew how. But God, she couldn't consider it. Besides the fact he would find a way to block her, she had no doubt in her mind that he would come up with a way to make certain she regretted it.

"These games are beneath you, Natches," she snapped, wishing she didn't sound so breathless.

"No, the games aren't, but you are." His brows arched, a smile curved his lips and humor flashed with suspicion in his gaze. A gaze turning hot with arousal as she glimpsed the thick wedge at the front of his jeans.

"Let me go, Natches."

He lifted the dildo and stared down at her. "How do you use it?"

Her flush became hotter. "Duh. Figure it out."

He leaned closer, his lips turning into a wicked smile now. "Do you suck it first? Do you taste yourself on it and remember how much I loved going down on you and tasting all that hot cream?"

That hot cream as he called it was flooding her vagina, saturating her panties. Was there anything more wicked than this man? Anything that tempted her past her pain more than he did?

"You're insane," she whispered, weak now. She could feel the weakness flooding her, the need. The need that had forced her to use that toy just that morning.

"When you suck it, do you think of me?"

She fought to breathe as he brushed the head of the toy over her cheek.

"Let me watch you use it."

Shock rounded her eyes, had her fighting to swallow.

"Are you crazy?"

"Oh yeah. Because the minute it sinks past those pretty pink lips I'm going to remember the feel of your mouth on my dick. I might come in my jeans. I don't think I've ever done that."

Her heart was going to beat out of her chest. Her breasts were swollen and sensitive now, the nipples pressing hard into her bra and the thin material of the top.

"Come on; let me see." He smiled, so wicked, so erotic, as he brushed it against her lips. "Let me see and remember, Chay. Just for a minute."

She knew better. She had known better than to return to Somerset. The minute she did, she knew exactly what Natches was going to do: He would destroy her with her own desires.

Her lips parted.

A tight, erotic grimace contorted his lips as he stared down at her, at the toy within touching distance of her lips, and sparks of anger filled his gaze.

The next second it was his tongue filling her mouth. His lips covering hers. She didn't know what he did with the toy; she didn't care. He was kissing her again. He was possessing her lips, eating at them, and she was eating back.

He always tasted so good, so dark and male. Her arms wrapped around his neck, her fingers spearing into his hair as she felt him jerking her skirt over her thighs, his fingers pressing her legs apart.

He was going to take her. She could feel it. She wasn't going to escape this time. Last year he had been kind, even for him, and let her go. This time, he wasn't letting her go.

"Natches." She breathed his name out in protest as he tore his lips from hers, pressed kisses along her neck, moved to the heaving mounds of her breasts.

Her nipples ached for him. For his mouth, his tongue.

"I should spank you," he growled. "Damn you, Chay. You knew better than to come back here. I know you did."

Yes, she had, and she'd had no choice but to return. But she would have anyway. She knew she would have, because the fight to stay away from him had been too hard. It had been more than she could bear.

One more assignment. Just this last operation and then—they would have time then. Not now.

She shook her head as she arched to him. Now wasn't the time. She couldn't divide her attention like this. She would end up getting killed.

His mouth buried between her breasts, his tongue licking, stroking as she moaned his name. She needed. Just one more taste of him, then she would be strong.

"Damn you." Suddenly, his head jerked up. "Why are you here, Chay?"

She shook her head. She wasn't drawing him in to this. It wasn't happening.

"Just questions," she panted. "Follow-up. I have to follow up."

She was going to have to do some heavy talking if he ever found out where those questions would lead.

"Liar." The accusation was soft, wickedly knowing. "You can't lie to me, Chay."

He pressed her legs apart with his and the toy; he still had that damned toy. He stroked it over the damp cotton that shielded her from him.

"Let's play a game," he whispered. "I ask a question, you tell the truth, and I give you something you'll really like."

"Kiss me, Natches."

As he had once bragged, his kisses were potent.

He leaned forward, brushed his lips against hers.

"Scared?" he asked softly, his eyes knowing.

"Let me get drunk on you," she urged. "Just kiss me."

"Just kiss you?" The head of the toy pressed more firmly against her hungry core. "But, Chay, you're so wet and so wild beneath me. Let's play my little game first."

She arched and cried out as he pulled back.

"First question." He licked over the top of a breast revealed by the material he nudged lower with his chin. "Did DHS send you here?"

Okay, that one was easy.

"Yes," she answered carefully.

A soft approving murmur against the curve of her breast and he was nudging the cup of her bra lower to lick at her nipple. Heat sizzled in her veins and sent her hips thrusting, grinding against the toy he held pressed to her panties.

"Good girl," he murmured. "Am I involved?"

Was he? She didn't think he was. He shouldn't be. She could be honest there.

"No." She lifted her hips again, wanting more. Damn him, she was honest. Reward time here.

He nipped at her nipple and nearly sent her into orgasm.

"Why are you here?"

Her lips parted to answer, to spill her guts just for another taste of the pleasure he could give her.

"Follow-up." She moaned.

"Hmm, Chay, my little liar." He pulled the toy back. "Come on, baby; fess up."

Her eyes opened as she stared back at him, aching, hurting for him.

"Follow-up," she repeated, the tormented whisper dragged from her throat. "It's the only reason I'm here." And it was partially the truth. Enough of the truth, and all he needed to stay safe.

He knelt above her. She watched hungrily as, tossing the toy aside, he loosened his belt, unsnapped his jeans, then lowered the zipper slowly. She licked her lips, her hands poised to help him, to catch the heavy length of his erection when it was free. To taste it. To fill her mouth with it.

"Why are you here, Chay?" She barely missed the hardening of his voice.

"Follow-up." She felt dazed, off balance, impatient. Like an addict anticipating a fix.

And just that fast he rolled away from her, moved to his feet, and was fixing his jeans, his expression still, silent with anger.

Damn. There went the fix. Her body was screaming out in protest, reminding her how mean she was being to it. How long had it been now since she had known his possession? Five years, two months, three days, and how many hours, she thought morosely.

"I guess that means I don't get any more rewards." She sighed as she adjusted her skirt and top. She didn't bother to roll from the bed. "Lock the door behind you if you don't mind. I may need some privacy after you leave."

He glared at her. The next thing she knew, the thin cord was jerked from the base of the dildo and as she watched in horror, he tore it in half.

"Oh my God. Natches, you didn't do that."

"If you need privacy, then by God you can make do with your fingers. That's what you've reduced me to." He tossed the pieces to the floor. "When you're ready to tell me the fucking truth, you know where to find me."

With that, he stalked out of the room. She stared at the floor in disbelief then at the door as the echo of the main door slamming penetrated her mind.

He broke her toy and left?

She was going to kill him.

THREE

Somerset and Lake Cumberland appealed to Chaya in a way that had surprised her. Arriving ahead of the Homeland Security team, in advance preparation more than a year ago, she had been taken aback by the friendliness of the citizens and the relaxed, peaceful atmosphere of the mountains surrounding the town.

There was serenity here. Not that there wasn't crime, or criminals, of course. The theft and attempted sale of the missiles last year was proof enough. No, it was something else. There was a quiet, easygoing feel to the area, and she had loved it.

She had missed it since the team had left last year. She had missed the community, and she had missed Natches. Unfortunately, she had missed Natches more than anything else.

And Timothy had known Natches was her weakness. That was

the problem with having a boss as manipulating and calculating as Timothy Cranston. He knew the agents under him to their back teeth. Their strengths and their weaknesses. And he didn't have a problem using both to his advantage.

Hell, she was supposed to be out of this. Right now, she should have been apartment hunting or something. She should have been getting her head straight, because it was something she hadn't managed to do in five years.

She had managed to quit smoking again. It was a nasty habit, and breaking it hadn't been easy. Timothy alone was an excuse to smoke. She bet half of his agents had picked up the habit only after having been assigned to his team.

This operation had obsessed Cranston though, worse than Chaya had ever seen him obsessed. Those missiles in the wrong hands would have been disastrous. And knowing that it had been Americans behind the hijacking and attempted sale had enraged Cranston. Finding out it had a connection to a much older investigation had made him rabid. They were so close he claimed, so close to finding the bastards he spent every waking moment of his life chasing.

He had pulled every string he could find and had broken more than one rule in that investigation last year. One of those strings was pulling in two ex-Marines onto the team. Locals known for their wild reputations and their ability to gather and filter local gossip. Dawg and Natches Mackay. And there had been the added benefit for Timothy of finally finding Natches Mackay's "weakness" as he called it.

And that one she had to roll her eyes at. She was anything but his weakness. Natches wanted her. He would spend the night in her bed in a heartbeat and she knew it. She could have him. On his terms and by his rules. And that would mean dragging him into an investigation he had no business being a part of. That, she couldn't find it within herself to do.

As she pulled her rental car into the parking lot of the local diner that the Mackay men were known to frequent, Chaya checked her weapon and breathed out a sigh of frustration.

She hated this. Hated the deception and the need for it. And even more, she hated being under Natches's radar once again. Especially after he broke her toy. And here she was on assignment. It wasn't as though she could just go out and buy a new one.

She checked her rearview mirror and there he was. That wicked black jeep pulling into the back entrance and stopping, the man behind the wheel watching her from behind dark glasses.

He hadn't approached her since he had stomped from her hotel room days before. But he had been following her since she left the hotel that morning. He had hung back, stayed distant just as he had the year before. He just watched, and just made her as nervous as hell.

Parking the sedan, Chaya gathered her purse and the heavy file she'd brought with her before stepping out into the crisp autumn air.

She could feel his eyes on her back as she moved to the entrance of the diner. Intense, blazing. The feminine core of her had been reawakened by that look over a year ago, and now, after knowing his touch again, it didn't seem inclined to go back to sleep.

She pushed her way into the diner and stood for a moment, getting her bearings as all eyes turned to her. Suspicious, curious, amused. She latched onto the amused gaze of Sheriff Ezekiel Mayes before striding across the large room.

His hawklike eyes followed her progress through the room as

he rose slowly to his feet. The dun-colored sheriff's uniform showed off a body in peak condition for a man of thirty-six years. Dark brown hair was military short and emphasized the strong planes and angles of his masculine face.

"Agent Dane." He nodded as she took her seat and laid the heavy file on the table in front of her, then he returned to his seat.

"Thank you for agreeing to meet with me, Sheriff." She tried out her best business smile, but at the narrowing of his eyes, she assumed it hadn't gone off quite as planned. "I know it was short notice."

"I wouldn't expect anything less." He picked up his coffee and took a drink before setting the cup on the table and motioning to the waitress as she moved by. "Becca, we'll need more coffee over here."

"Gotcha, Zeke." The waitress gave Chaya a quick, suspicious look before moving away.

"Have you had lunch yet?" he asked Chaya then.

"I'm fine. I just have some questions I needed to ask and a few things I'd like to go over with you before we head out to begin these interviews."

Why Timothy had arranged for this sheriff to tag along with her she wasn't certain. Ezekiel Mayes was nobody's fool. He'd spent five years as a homicide detective in Los Angeles before returning to his hometown and running for sheriff. He was suspicious by nature, perceptive, and when he had learned an operation had been conducted without his knowledge by the DHS last year, he had been in D.C. screaming in the faces of men with enough power to scald Cranston's ass.

Mayes had some small amount of pull there, Cranston had learned, and he knew exactly how to wield it. Proof was in the fact that she was working with him now.

Oh what a tangled web we weave, when first we practice to deceive. The quote whispered through Chaya's mind, and not for the first time. Cranston was playing a very dangerous game here, and Sheriff Mayes was but one of the potential enemies that he could make.

"Coffee, Zeke." Becca, the waitress, set the cup down before turning to Chaya. "You need anything else?"

"No, thank you." She shook her head, wishing she could find a way to still the nerves in her stomach as she lifted the coffee to her lips.

Becca nodded and moved off, but the sheriff's gaze never left Chaya.

"Cranston's sunk to a new low." Mayes leaned back in his chair and regarded her with sharp golden brown eyes.

"Cranston's always finding new lows." Chaya shrugged. "What has he managed to do this time?"

"He sent a pretty little girl to do a man's job." He grunted in disgust. "The Mackays are none too happy with DHS right now, and neither is the local law enforcement around here. You don't pull an op like you did last year and not inform the locals without stepping on some toes."

"We weren't required to inform anyone of our operation here. We were required to reacquire those missiles, Sheriff, not make nice with the local law enforcement. And my gender has nothing to do with my ability to conduct this end of the investigation."

He grunted at that. "Yeah, two years in military intelligence and five with DHS. You have a hell of a record under your belt, don't you?"

She did, and it was one she was proud of, sometimes, she assured herself. When she needed something to find a source of pride in, then it worked.

"I'm not a green agent, Sheriff." She leaned back in her own chair and stared back at him. "Nor am I out of my element here. You have enough pull that you were able to make certain you were contacted and included in any further investigations. I'm fine with that. But you don't have the power to give me orders or to direct these interviews. Are we clear?"

His gaze flared with anger for a moment, then the amusement was back. "Just your little lackey, huh?" he murmured, glancing over his shoulder at the sound of the bell over the door tinkling merrily to announce another customer.

Chaya sighed. It was Natches. She could feel him now.

"Shall we get down to business?" She picked up the list of interviewees that she had chosen to visit that afternoon. "Here's the short list of people I need to see today. I assume we can have this completed before too late tonight."

Mayes took the list and studied it with a frown. "This isn't the full list."

"I'm not required to give you the full list," she told him, feeling Natches moving in closer, hearing him as a chair scraped across the floor just behind her.

The sheriff's lips twitched as he continued to study her.

"You like to live dangerously, don't you, little girl?"

She barely contained her flinch. She had heard those words before, and the hell she had lived through afterward still haunted her nightmares.

"I live as I must." She shrugged. "Another of those details that I'm not required to discuss with you. Now, as you are the first on my list to be interviewed, shall we get started?"

There was a snort of a laugh behind her. The sound had her hackles rising and a curl of anger prickling inside.

Before Mayes could answer, she turned slowly in her chair and looked back at Natches. He was no more than four feet away from her, staring at her from behind those dark glasses.

"Your presence really isn't required at this time," she told him quietly. "Your turn will come."

She refused to let him intimidate her. If he managed to throw her off balance now, then she was lost. She would never be able to complete her assignment as needed.

He didn't smile; he didn't speak. He just stared at her until she turned her back on him again and shuffled through the papers in her files for the information she had tagged regarding the sheriff.

"You've been sheriff for how long now?"

"Almost six years." Mayes was definitely amused now. "They voted me back in for some reason. Personally, I think folks around here consider me a bit of an easy mark, don't you think?"

That was definitely a jibe at the man behind her. Chaya was well aware of the fact that the sheriff and the Mackays had gone head-to-head several times last year over Dawg Mackay's activities.

"I wouldn't know the reasons why." She smiled tightly. "Johnny Grace was a popular citizen in town though. You had known him for a while?"

Mayes nodded slowly. "I'd known him all his life, Agent Dane. I only spent eight years away from home, not a lifetime. Johnny and his parents are well-known to most people in Somerset and the surrounding towns."

"Yet you had no suspicion he could have been involved in the hijacking of the missiles?"

"Those missiles were taken in another county, close to an Army base." His voice was clipped now. "I had my eyes open for them, but there were those who neglected to inform me that they could be in my county." And that was a jibe at Chaya and DHS.

He was professional enough that his animosity didn't show, but she could feel it.

"Sheriff, I'm not your enemy, nor was I the head agent in that investigation. You're snapping at the wrong agent here," she assured him. "I want to complete this and head home as quickly as you want me out of your county."

Mayes tilted his head to the side. "Now, what would make you think I want you out of my county? Unlike most people, Agent Dane, I enjoy a good comedy every now and then. And this situation appears to at least have an element of amusement within it."

The bell tinkled at the door again. When Chaya lifted her head to glance at the mirror placed next to the register behind Sheriff Mayes, she felt like cursing.

The Mackays were amassing. The tall, broad forms of Dawg and Rowdy Mackay were reflected in the glass as they moved across the room. They all but swaggered. Dressed in jeans and light T-shirts, Dawg wore a denim jacket, Rowdy wore a leather jacket. Both were suspicious and more than a little intimidating as they joined Natches at his table.

When her eyes met Sheriff Mayes's again, the amusement in them had thickened.

"What about known associates of Grace's?" she asked him then, lowering her voice further. "Did you have any reason to suspect them after the operation completed last year?"

This was the wrong damned place for these questions. She knew it, and she could see the knowledge of it in Mayes's eyes. She had tried to warn Timothy, several times, this man was no one's fool. Timothy had arranged this meeting here specifically to allow Mackay involvement.

The sheriff leaned closer. Bracing his arms on the table, he stared back at her warningly.

"Are you sure you want to finish this here, Agent Dane?" he asked her, his voice official, cool.

"This is as good a place as any, Sheriff. If you could answer the question please."

"I'd have reason to suspect half the county then," he told her. "If you want to discuss specific suspects though, we're going to do it elsewhere."

That was good enough. That was the best answer she would get right here and now—that Mayes did suspect various parts of the Grace and/or Mackay family. She had spent most of her life learning how to read people, and despite the chill in the sheriff's face, she could read that much in his eyes.

"At the time of the operation were you aware that Natches and James Mackay were involved in the operation?"

Sheriff Mayes snorted at that question. "If there's trouble to be found, then James Dawg Mackay and his two cousins are always bound to be close by." He flicked a mocking look behind her shoulder. "They're trouble like that. You'd do well to remember it."

"But you didn't answer the question," she reminded him softly.

"I suspected they were in up to their necks in something, I just didn't know what." He shrugged easily. "Remember? No one informed me anything was going on."

"But you knew enough to begin your own investigation and to contact several members of the FBI as well as a contact you made within DHS and the Department of Justice?"

She handed him the memos that had made it into Timothy's

hands. The sheriff's phone records clearly revealed the calls that were made, but not which agents took those calls.

His lips tipped knowingly. "I'm a suspicious bastard; what can I say?"

"And who did you speak to at that time?"

He smiled at that. "Names elude me, Miss Dane. I just asked to speak to an agent, and they plugged me into someone."

Chaya stared back at him suspiciously. He wasn't even bothering to disguise the fact that he was lying to her.

"And what did they tell you?"

"They told me to mind my own business in my own little corner of the world," he continued to lie. "What were they supposed to tell me?"

Chaya held back her own grin though she inclined her head in acknowledgment. Truth be told, she didn't want to know his contacts and she didn't give a damn. Timothy was dying to get his little hooks into them though.

Behind her, silence reigned.

"One last question, Sheriff. Can I trust you?" she asked, allowing her own suspicions to enter her voice now. He was a friend of the Mackays; the people of Somerset were his people. She needed to know, to watch his eyes, hear his voice, to determine how far she was going to trust him.

His eyes narrowed on her again before he leaned forward carefully. "Agent Dane, I'm a duly sworn officer of the law, and this is my home. You can trust me to cover your back. You can trust me to make damned sure any suspicions you have are held in confidence. I might not like what you are or what your team did here last year, but I don't have to like you to do my job. Are we clear on that?"

"And should *friends* of yours question you regarding the interviews we're about to make? Will your loyalties then be torn? Because I have to ask you to step aside if they will be. I can bring in another agent to provide backup."

He frowned, his jaw clenching. He knew the out she was offering him, and it was one Cranston hadn't approved. There was no reason to drive a wedge between this man and the Mackays. It was his choice. And she would leave it up to him.

"You're insulting me," he bit out. "And pissing me off at the same time. I just told you my loyalty is to the law. Period."

"Excellent." She closed the file and flashed him a cool smile. "Shall we go then? I'd like to start with the first name below yours on that list if you don't mind."

His lips tightened, but he jerked his hat from the side of the table and slammed it on his head before rising to his feet.

Chaya gathered her file together, looped the strap of her purse over her shoulder then turned to face three sets of Mackay eyes on her.

Light green, emerald green, and behind dark glasses she knew were the deepest, darkest forest green eyes she had ever seen. They mesmerized, sank into the soul and left their impression forever after.

"It was good to see you boys again." She smiled tightly. "Maybe next time we'll have a chance to chat for a while."

Dawg and Rowdy ducked their heads, but Natches's expression never shifted, his eyes never left hers.

"Greta, you don't want to be here," Dawg finally muttered as his head lifted, his expression concerned. "Let this go. Make Cranston send someone else to do his dirty work."

"But, Dawg, you know how convincing he can be," she

reminded him mockingly. "I think you and I both know I'm rather stuck here. And I do have a job to do. Good day."

She nodded to them, then moved past the sheriff, who had stood back, watching the confrontation. Natches's eyes still followed her, silent, aware.

Did the memories bring him awake at night in a cold sweat? she wondered. Did he even let himself remember?

She tried not to remember, but she did. Too often . . . Remembering was a weakness, because each time she allowed herself to remember hell, then she was also reminded of ecstasy. And she wondered if hell wasn't safer.

"You want to tell us what's doin', bro?" Dawg stared across the table at Natches as he sipped at the coffee he'd finally ordered.

"Nothin's doin'," he replied, flicking his cousin a mocking look.

"Take the glasses off, Natches," Rowdy finally bit out.

And he didn't dare. He'd been out of the game too long. His eyes showed what he knew his face didn't, and when it came to Chaya, they showed even more.

There were secrets he kept, secrets he was determined to keep. And Chaya was one of them.

"I have you, Chay. Hold on, baby. Just hold on. I have you."

He almost flinched at the memory. The smell of gunfire, of violence and blood, filled his head, and the sounds of her screams. Screams so horrifying, so filled with rage and pain that he hadn't known how to live with them in his head.

"I need to roll." He pushed the coffee cup back and dug into his jeans for a few dollars to pay the bill.

He didn't have time to fuck around here. Chaya and Zeke were on the move, and Natches was very curious as to the names on that list she had shown the sheriff.

He was very damned curious as to why she was here to begin with. He had the official line. He had the rumors and he had the suppositions his contacts had come up with. None of those satisfied him. None of those reasons kept his hackles from rising every time he thought about it, or every time he saw Chaya.

He tossed the money on the table and started to rise.

"I don't want to make a mess of this diner, cuz," Dawg said then. "And if we fight, you know there's gonna be a mess. Sit your ass down here and tell us what the hell is going on. Let us help you, Natches."

He stared back at Dawg, then Rowdy. He could see the concern in their eyes, the worry that he was riding that line again. He had ridden that line a lot in the past. The one that separated common sense from pure, bloody violence.

What the hell was wrong with him? He couldn't make sense of it. He hadn't made sense of it in seven years and it still didn't make sense. When Chaya was anywhere near, he didn't know himself. He didn't know who he was and he didn't understand the needs that tore through him, nor did he understand the extreme possessiveness.

In one hot afternoon in the Iraqi desert while he waited for the calvary to ride in and listened to the enemy get closer, he had found something he hadn't expected to find.

There, buried in a hole, he had held a woman, and somehow that woman had slipped inside his soul.

How did that happen? In such a short time, how did one woman change everything a man knew about himself?

"I'm married." She had whispered the words, and they had been filled with pain, with a knowledge he couldn't have guessed at, at the time.

And what had shocked him clear to the bottom of his soul was that it hadn't mattered. As he held her, he'd known that marriage wasn't going to stand in his way. She was his, and that feeling had seared his soul.

And he had found a core of possessiveness that he hadn't imagined lived inside him. That possessiveness had shocked him clear to the center of his being, and still had the power to throw him off balance.

"Natches." Rowdy's voice was warning. "Don't walk out that fucking door."

Natches shook his head and followed the woman he couldn't stay away from. He had to follow her. He had to know what the hell she was doing and how much danger it was going to place her in.

"It's okay, I have you, baby."

He held her as she sobbed. Broken, horrific cries that ripped at his guts and flayed his soul as he carried her through hell. The smell of blood and death and broken dreams surrounded them, and all he could do was hold her.

As he left the diner he didn't feel the late autumn air, he felt the heat of an Iraqi summer, the sun blazing down on Baghdad as fire blazed at their backs. He didn't hear the traffic around him, or Dawg's voice behind him. He heard her screams. He heard her pleas as she begged him, pleaded with him to let her die, too.

"Natches, enough of this shit!" Dawg and Rowdy caught him as he neared his jeep, gripping his arm and swinging him around.

"Damn it, what the hell is going on with you? You're starting to worry us, man."

They were defensive, ducking instinctively, knowing his habit of swinging first and asking questions later. But Natches didn't swing.

He knew these two men. Knew them almost as well as he knew himself, and he knew they wouldn't let it go.

Shaking his head he pulled the glasses from his face and stared back at them. And he knew what they saw. Both men stepped back, staring back at him in surprise. He saw those eyes in the mirror every morning since Chaya's return last year, and he saw his inability to control the need riding him more every day.

"My fight," he told them both. "There's no room for all of us here. I guess I finally grew up, huh?"

It was a reminder that as Dawg and Rowdy had matured, as their hearts became involved with their women, rather than just their cocks, their possessive instincts had kicked in. No one touched what they claimed themselves. They didn't share their women anymore, not even with each other.

And they didn't need to be involved in this. He knew Dawg and Rowdy, and he knew that knowing the truth would do nothing but worry them more.

They thought they knew Natches. That was the mistake most people made. They thought they knew him, understood him. They thought they could predict him, and they had found out they were wrong.

He turned away from his cousins, ignoring the worried looks they gave each other, and jumped into the jeep. Chaya's rental car was still sitting here; that meant they were in Zeke's official SUV. That wouldn't be hard to find.

Chaya would never be hard for him to find, no matter where she was or how she tried to hide. He had proven that to her. And now he was paying the price.

He had let her leave a year ago. He wasn't willing to do that this time around. He'd find out what the hell she was doing here. Then, he'd find Chaya.

He pulled from the parking lot in a squeal of tires and a grinding of gears before shooting out into the alley and heading for the main road. He didn't know the names on that list she had given Zeke, but he'd find out tonight what was going on there. Until then, he'd shadow her and see if he couldn't figure out what the hell was going on.

Because he knew she wasn't supposed to be here. She wasn't supposed to be with Homeland Security and she wasn't supposed to be in Kentucky.

So why was Chaya Greta Dane doing exactly what she wasn't supposed to be doing in a place she wasn't supposed to be?

And why the hell did he let himself care?

FOUR

Ezekiel Mayes was leaning against his car as Agent Dane pulled from the restaurant parking lot, and he waited. He had just dropped her back at her car, and knew he wouldn't have to wait long; he was just curious who would show up.

He wasn't left in suspense, and he had to hide his smile as the black jeep pulled in behind his SUV and Natches stepped out of the vehicle.

Those damnable glasses covered his eyes. The black lenses were a shield between Natches and the world, Zeke often thought. And damned if he could blame the other man. Natches hadn't exactly skated through life. Some years, Zeke knew, he'd hung on by his fingernails alone as his father tried to destroy him.

Last year, Zeke feared, had been a breaking point for Natches.

The day he had taken a bead on his first cousin Johnny Grace and pulled the trigger.

Natches had been one of the finest snipers the Marines had possessed. Often working alone, without the benefit of a spotter, completing his missions, then hanging around to gather intel. Four years in the Marines and he had nearly been a legend by the time an enemy sniper had taken his shoulder out.

If that was what happened. Zeke sometimes wondered. Natches wasn't a man one could slip up on, even from a distance. He had instincts like the sheriff had never known in another man. Instincts honed in the Kentucky mountains and in his father's home.

An ex-Marine himself, Dayle Mackay was one hard-bitten son of a bitch. If ever a man deserved a bullet, then it was Dayle.

"Figured you'd show up eventually." Zeke sighed when Natches didn't speak. "I wasn't able to get any info, if that's what you want to know."

"Why is she here?"

"Follow-up is what I was told." Zeke shrugged; he didn't believe that one either. "They're still missing the million. I guess the government has to line their coffers somewhere, huh?"

He tipped his hat back and stared up at the setting sun as Natches stood still and silent. What the hell was he thinking behind those glasses? Reading Natches Mackay was like trying to read ancient script. Pretty much impossible.

"Who is she questioning tomorrow?"

Zeke shook his head. "Hell if I know. Said she'd give me the names when we meet up in the morning. I couldn't get shit out of her."

She was as closemouthed as Natches was, and almost as wary. But where the man was stone-cold and silent, Zeke had seen nervousness in the agent. She had known from second to second exactly where Natches was behind them, when he would round a curve, or where he would park. That little girl had been so attuned to the killer shadowing them that Zeke had been amazed.

"Would you tell me if you had?" Natches asked him then, his big body shifting dangerously as he pinned Zeke with that shielded gaze.

"In this case, yeah, I'd tell you." He nodded. "Because I want an end to this as well, Natches. What went down last year has ripped through this town like a plague. Homegrown fucking terrorists? God help us all. People are scared to trust their neighbors here now. And that bothers me. That bothers me real bad."

Pulaski County was his home, his county, his watch and his responsibility. It was one he took seriously, and until last year, he had thought he was doing a damned fine job at keeping out the worst of the evil the world had to offer.

Terrorists. Son of a bitch. It was bad enough when the bastards were foreign, almost fucking conceivable. But homegrown? A man you'd known all your life?

He and Johnny Grace hadn't been friends, but if anyone had asked him if the boy could kill, he would have given an emphatic no. And he would have been wrong. If anyone had told him Johnny had been conspiring to steal and sell missiles that would be used against his own nation, Zeke would have denied it to the last line.

Johnny had been strange. He'd been a little off in left field sometimes, but Zeke had never imagined what his smile hid.

"She's after more than the money." Zeke breathed out heavily at that thought. "There's something more important here than that."

"Like?"

"Like hell if I fucking know," Zeke cursed. "You Mackays tell me what the fuck is going on after it's done the hell over with." He flicked Natches a glowering look. "If you had been honest with me from the beginning, we wouldn't be standing here now, would we, damn it?"

"That or we'd be standing over your grave." Natches shrugged. "We were almost standing over Dawg's and Crista's. I didn't like that, Zeke."

The understatement was almost laughable. When Johnny Grace had taken Dawg's lover and tried to kill her, he had signed his death warrant with Natches.

There was nothing Natches cared for outside Rowdy, Dawg, and Rowdy's dad, Ray Mackay. Unless it was his sister, Janey. Zeke had never figured out for sure if he gave a shit about the girl or not, but he knew he'd hate to test that boundary. Natches might act like she didn't exist, but Zeke was betting the other man kept very close tabs on the girl.

"What are you going to do here, Natches?" he finally asked. "Don't get between me and the law, man. I'd hate to have to butt heads with you. But I will."

Natches's lips quirked humorously. "I'll stay out of your law, and you stay out of my way. Other than that, I don't know what the hell to tell you."

Frustration gnawed at Zeke then. He really didn't need this. Natches was, Zeke often thought, the most dangerous man he knew. He wasn't given to strong temperament, he didn't hold grudges. But Zeke had a feeling that spilling blood didn't bother him overmuch either.

"We don't need another killing like last summer, Natches," he warned him. "You didn't have to kill Johnny. You could have wounded him and left enough to question. Then we wouldn't have these folks running around now."

Natches didn't stiffen. There was nothing in his demeanor to indicate a change in mood. But the air around them seemed to crackle with tension and rage.

"Killing him was better than sex." Natches's smile was cold enough, hard enough, that Zeke wondered if he should feel an edge of fear. There was something completely unaffected in that smile.

"Better than sex with Agent Dane?" Zeke had a feeling he had just taken his life in his hands with that question.

Natches stared back at him, his expression closed. Tight. For a moment, Zeke thought he would speak, thought something would finally pass by that tightly shielded expression of his. Instead, Natches turned away, jumped back into the jeep, and shoved it into gear before pulling away with careful restraint.

Zeke slowly let out his breath, unaware that he had been holding it after asking that last question. And he had no idea which way the answer would have gone.

"You didn't have to kill Johnny. You could have wounded him and left enough to question."

Zeke's accusation didn't sit well with Natches, no more than his response had. That killing Johnny had been better than sex. Hell, killing that little bastard had set up a sickness in his gut that he couldn't seem to get rid of. Not regret. There was no regret. It was Johnny or Crista, and Crista had been innocent. No, it was something else, something Natches hadn't known since he had taken a bead on Nassar Mallah, the traitor that had kidnapped

Chaya in Iraq, and blew his damned head off. It was a knowledge that he was truly becoming a killer.

Didn't matter the why of it, didn't matter that it was monsters he was killing. What made him sick to his soul was that he no longer felt regret. He hadn't regretted Nassar, and he hadn't felt any regret over killing family.

He was afraid he was turning into the same sick bastard his father was, and that terrified him. It terrified him almost as much as the knowledge that through the day, something had shifted inside him where Chaya was concerned.

He wasn't letting her walk away again. Not without having her. Not without fucking this hunger in his gut out of his system so he could survive the next time she decided to run out on him.

It was time to do something about her.

Natches drove through the darkened streets of Somerset, made a left onto the interstate and headed to the hotel Chaya was checked into.

Tonight, he wouldn't be staring into her darkened window, wondering why the hell she was there. Tonight, he would find out exactly why she was there, and what she wanted in Somerset. He could guess until hell froze over, but if Timothy Cranston was heading this little operation that was obviously being conducted in his town, then God only knew exactly what was going on.

At least it had nothing more to do with the Mackays. Or not his end of the Mackays. He'd held back the past week, watched, gathered his own information. Had he learned this operation targeted his family, then he wouldn't have hesitated to snatch Chaya and make damned sure Cranston understood it wasn't happening.

Rowdy, Dawg, Kelly, Crista, his uncle Ray, and his sister. They were his family, and he'd not allow pain to touch them any more than it already had. The information he had attained so far assured him the Mackays weren't targeted. Anyone else was fair game, and he was willing to help.

And he couldn't stay away from her much longer. He'd never been able to stay away from her for long.

As he drove toward the hotel the memory of her rescue whispered through his mind. She'd been hurt, abused, and terrorized, and married. And when she had learned her husband had been the reason for her capture and torture, she had cried in Natches's arms, while in the hospital in which she had been recovering. And she had begged him to help her.

He forced those memories back. He hadn't cared that she was married even before they learned her husband was a traitor. She was his; it was simple. Then he had learned it wasn't that simple.

She'd walked away from him. Disappeared as though she had never existed, and for years he hadn't known where she was or how to find her. Until she'd arrived in Somerset on the operation to locate the missiles.

And what the fuck had she done when that mission was over? Run. She had run from him again without looking back, without acknowledging a damned thing that had happened in that fucking desert.

And he had let her go.

He pulled into the hotel parking lot and spotted her immediately where she stood, propped against the trunk of the rented sedan.

Her arms were crossed over the light blazer. She wore another silky top beneath it. Those short little thin-strapped tops were making him crazy. Jeans hugged her legs; the top of them rose barely to her hip bones, where the top she wore beneath the dark blazer barely met the band. And she wore boots. It was one of the first things he noticed last year; she wore leather boots. He surely did like a woman who wore boots. And boots on Chaya looked damned good.

He pulled up beside her, then he reached over and unlatched the door before swinging it open.

"Get in." He didn't ask. He'd gone too far to ask. He could feel the dominance, the possessiveness rising inside him, fighting against the restraint he was attempting to maintain.

She slid warily into the jeep and closed the door behind her before hastily locking her seat belt.

"Where are we going?" Her voice was soft, just a bit nervous, reminding him of that hidden hole and the darkness and the intimacy that had wrapped around them.

"Someplace where we can talk."

Where they could talk. Chaya stared out the windshield as Natches drove, his command of the vehicle confident, but obviously restrained. She could feel the fine thread of tension moving through him, the obvious control he was exerting over it.

And she knew what he was like when that control slipped. When the restrained man became the dominant lover. When he became a force she couldn't deny.

"What do we need to talk about, Natches?" she finally asked as he turned onto the main road and headed in the opposite direction of the marina.

"We're not going to the boat?" The *Nauti Dreams* had been his home last year.

"Winter's coming on." His voice was as frosty as that season. "I moved out to the apartment over the garage last year anyway. Damned lake is getting too busy."

There was leashed anger in his voice, a temper she didn't want to chance right now. She had heard of his dangerous temper, the cold, lashing rage he could project, but she had never experienced it herself.

Chaya couldn't imagine where she had found the courage tonight to actually get into the jeep with him. At one time she was known to have nerves of steel. Now she could feel the wariness moving through her. Not fear, but something female, something that recognized Natches as perhaps more man than she could handle.

Sometimes, Chaya reasoned, a woman just knew when she had too much man on her hands. Too much lust, too much strength, too much hunger. And all that described Natches only too well.

"You've been watching me," she finally stated. "Why?"

He removed the glasses from his eyes slowly. How he managed to drive wearing the dark shades she hadn't figured out. But when he looked at her, it happened again. The same thing that happened every time she stared into the perfect forest green of his eyes.

The breath seemed to rush from her lungs, nerve endings heated, and between her thighs she felt a flood of liquid warmth she couldn't control.

"You shouldn't have come back," he finally said as he turned and took a side road that led to his garage. "You should have resigned from DHS like I heard you had and gotten the hell away from Cranston."

"What does that have to do with you watching me here? You knew there would be further questioning conducted in Somerset, Natches. Did you think it was really over? It won't be for Timothy until he finds the money and Johnny's coconspirator."

"You're so certain he had one?" He shook his head at that. "Johnny didn't share that easily, Chaya."

77

"Unlike the Nauti Boys," she murmured.

She knew the rumors that the cousins shared their lovers and wondered at that, because Rowdy and Dawg seemed more than possessive over their women.

"Long ago and far away," he muttered.

There was something in his voice that had her gaze sharpening on him. An ache of loss, of regret. Something that assured her he was right. Whatever sharing may have gone on in the past, it was over now. Her question, though, was how much he regretted it.

Silence descended then. Chaya watched as the darkened scenery sped by and they drew closer to the garage and the apartment over it.

"Here we are." He pulled in behind the garage and parked the jeep beneath the wooden steps that led up to the second floor.

The light on the overhead porch threw a glimmer of golden rays below to add to the subtle landscaping lights behind the shrubs that grew close to the building beneath the porch.

Chaya moved from the jeep and watched warily as he waited for her at the front of the vehicle.

"Have you had dinner?" he asked, placing his hand at the small of her back and giving her a firm push to the steps.

"Sheriff Mayes and I ate after the last interview," she told him, feeling his hand tense at her back.

She swung her head around to try to see him in the dim light. She could have sworn he growled something not quite complimentary where the sheriff was concerned.

"Keep going, Chay." He crowded her, pushing her up the stairs, his larger, broader body making her feel too feminine, too weak.

She was a trained agent, or she was supposed to be, but every time she was around Natches the agent became overwhelmed by the woman.

He was her weakness; she had figured that out at a time when she hadn't needed to know it. And the certainty of it had only grown.

She stepped onto the landing and stood aside as he unlocked the door, stepped in, and looked around before turning back to her.

"Come on in."

Her heart nearly strangled her as it raced in her chest and jumped to her throat. She stepped inside, staring around the starkly masculine area as she felt her palms dampen.

Here, she was in his territory, completely surrounded by Natches. She stepped farther into the room, then paused at the mantel over the gas fireplace. A smile tipped her lips. There was a picture of Faisal, the young goatherd who had managed to contact Natches on a shortwave radio channel to inform him that a female agent was being held and tortured in the desert.

He was her savior as well that day. Faisal had covered Natches while he pulled her out of that dark, hellish cell. She knew the extraction team that had picked them up had made certain Faisal made it back to his goats.

"I talked to him a few months ago," he told her. "He said you were still sending messages and money."

She nodded slowly. She couldn't protect him; all she could do was try to make things easier.

"He makes a monthly trip past one of the bases in the area. I make certain he has something waiting for him there."

She could feel him behind her as he asked, "Do you ever talk to him?"

Chaya lowered her head and shook it. "No. I don't contact him personally."

She couldn't. She'd tried several times, had actually gone so far as to purchase the phone cards and send him her number. She knew he had his own cell phone now. One he was very proud of.

She turned back to him. "Do you talk to him often?"

He nodded, the movement sharp. "His family was killed just before your rescue. I've been trying to make arrangements to get him over here. I haven't had much success yet."

Yes, she knew that, just as Cranston did. It was one of the promises versus threats he had made to force her into this operation. Cranston would make certain Faisal would be given his entrance into America, if this operation completed to his satisfaction.

She felt a chill race over her head at the thought, then down her spine. Then it sort of went over her body as she forced herself to move away from Natches. Once Natches knew who DHS had targeted, he was liable to kill her and Cranston.

"What do you want from me, Natches? You know I can't give you this mission or Timothy's suspects; so what's left?" She stared around the large living room with its heavily cushioned furniture and male accoutrements.

There were pictures of Natches and his cousins Dawg and Rowdy. A few that were taken while he was in the Marines with buddies. There was a picture of Natches with Faisal.

A table had been set up at the side of the room with a jigsaw puzzle. Hell, she didn't know people still did those.

There were some oil lamps on a table and a heavy lamp on the end table next to the couch. The kitchen and living room were separated by a bar. There was no dining room, but the kitchen was large enough for the heavy oak table that was set to the side of the room.

She assumed the doorway off the living room went to a bedroom, but she wasn't checking that one out.

And as she stared around, she realized Natches hadn't answered her.

She turned back to him, watching nervously as he strode past her and moved into the kitchen, his expression stark, furious. This was it and she knew it. Natches wasn't going to let her avoid the past any longer.

"I'd have followed any other agent," he finally growled, pulling out a beer from the fridge and unscrewing the top with a quick jerk of his hand.

Broad, long fingered. Those hands could make a woman think of heaven even as hell moved in around them. And she knew they could make a woman fly, steal her senses and her thoughts with their touch.

Would he ever want to touch her with those hands after Timothy's operation finished here in Somerset?

"I didn't think I'd see you back here," he said, staring back at her with a hint of sensuality, a hint of anger.

"Cranston has a way of convincing agents to do his dirty work for him." She shrugged with a mocking smile. "Come on, Natches, you know how it works. The follow-up was important. He wants that money and he wants to make certain no one else is involved here. That's all."

"Are you investigating my family?" Short and to the point. And here was where things were about to get sticky. Because she couldn't lie to Natches. He had saved her, not just once but twice, and then he had held her and let her fly while she found her sanity once again.

"As far as Cranston is concerned, everyone is suspect," she reminded him dryly. "You're all on my list to question."

"Why did he send you?" He lifted the bottle to his lips and drank, his gaze never leaving hers, the dark green depths dragging her in and leaving her breathless.

She was an agent, fully trained to ignore sexual need or even fear during a mission. But she couldn't ignore Natches. He made her weak, made her need, and he made her fear herself.

"Because it amused him?" She lifted her shoulders as though she didn't know and didn't care. "He was pissed over my attempted resignation and decided to play with me. Cranston's good for games like that."

"Cranston's good at games, period." Natches finished his beer, then tossed the bottle in the trash as Chaya watched him closely now.

He ran a hand over his face before staring back at her.

"Do you have any idea how much I missed you?" he said, his voice soft. "How much I ached for you last year?"

Chaya backed up a step, her movement jerky as she tried to look everywhere but at Natches. She didn't want to talk about last year; she didn't want to talk about five years ago. She wanted this over with. She wanted to run and hide, to bury her head in the sand and pretend this mission and this man could be ignored.

"That wouldn't have been very wise then, and it wouldn't be now," she answered, her throat tightening as she watched him, as she watched his expression flicker with primitive lust.

He wasn't going to just let her go this time, and she knew it.

82

He was going to force her to face everything she didn't want to face, and she didn't know if she could do it.

Chaya shook her head at the look. "Don't, Natches."

She couldn't handle his touch, not now, when this entire mission hinged on betraying him. She wasn't cold-blooded enough; she wasn't the agent Timothy thought she could be.

"Don't." He shook his head wearily before running his fingers through his thick hair and staring back at her with an expression of torment. "How long is it going to lie between us like a double-edged sword, Chaya? When are you going to forgive me?"

No. Oh God, she couldn't deal with this. Her throat tightened and closed with pain and fear as she saw the determination in his eyes.

"I don't want to talk about that." She gave her head a hard jerk. "We can argue over this operation or Cranston or anything else. But not that." She had to fight her tears, her sobs. She had to fight the memories that wanted to return in a rush of agony.

"Damn you." He was across the room before she could avoid him. His hands gripped her arms as he jerked her against him, and she felt the heat of him, felt the weakness that threatened to flood her as she dragged in a hard, gasping breath.

"Five years." He moved, forcing her to back up as she stared up at him in shock. "Five fucking years, Chay. How much longer do we have to suffer for something that neither of us caused?"

"No." Her cry sounded too close to hysteria. "Stop, Natches. I can't discuss this. I won't."

"She was a beautiful little girl. I saw her pictures later." His voice was agonized, tormented.

Chaya heard the pain-filled moan that left her throat. Even when she was being tortured, she hadn't made a sound like that.

"He stole her." He groaned the accusation as she felt his forehead press against hers. "She was safe with your sister, wasn't she, Chay? If he had just left her there."

"Don't do this."

"She looked like you. She had your smile and your hair. Your innocence."

"Stop it!" She screamed the words at him, tearing from his embrace as she pressed her fist against her stomach and swallowed back the sickness rising in her throat. "You didn't know her. You didn't raise her, and you didn't love her. And it's none of your damned business."

Beth. Sweet Beth.

"She was three years old, and your husband had her flown to Iraq. While you were being tortured, she was landing at the airport in a military transport believing she would see her mommy again."

Her heart felt as though it were shattering in her chest now, and she didn't want to collapse from the pain of it. She had lost everything in that damned desert. She didn't want to remember it, and she didn't want to think about it or talk about it. Especially not with the man who had been there to witness it, who had held her back, who had covered her with his own body to protect her while her child died.

"Why?" She turned on him, tears she swore she wouldn't shed escaping now. "Why are you doing this to me? Do you think I don't know what happened?"

Her voice was rasping. She sounded nothing like herself. She sounded like the demented creature she had been the day she lost Beth.

"Army Intelligence didn't know he had your child." His expression looked as agonized as hers felt. "They didn't give the orders to

84

bomb that hotel, did they, Chay? Someone else did. Something fucked up like it always fucks up, and your baby was killed."

She shook her head. Her body shook. Tremors raced through her as she stared at the ceiling. But she didn't see the ceiling; she saw the missiles, ribbons of steam flowing behind them, the hiss of flight, the fiery destruction with impact.

"I know who killed her," she whispered. She had always known.

Her husband. Beth's father. He had killed their child just as surely as he had ordered his wife's torture and death. But she knew even more than that. She knew there had been others, those who knew what her husband had done, and they had struck out. They had killed her child when there had been a chance of saving her.

She lowered her eyes back to Natches and saw the pain, his eyes so dark with so many emotions. Grief and sorrow and need.

"You hold her between us as though it were my fault," he said then, his voice graveled, accusing. "As though I ordered the attack or I arranged her death, Chay."

Chaya swallowed tightly and turned away from him again. She didn't know which way to turn, which way to run. She wanted to run. She wanted to escape the shared memories, and she wanted to escape her own loss.

Natches had been with her when they had learned where Beth and Chaya's husband, Craig, were staying. The suspected head-quarters of a terrorist cell. He had raced after her when she went to rescue her child. He had thrown her to the street, held her down, and tried to shield her eyes as missiles slammed into the building.

"I held you when you identified her. I held you then, and I held you through the night. Did you think I wouldn't hold you longer, Chay, if you had given me the chance?"

FIVE

Craig Cornwell had been a major in Army Intelligence and a traitor. He had been selling secrets to Iraqi terrorists, and when he'd known he would be identified for it, he had arranged for his daughter to be brought to Iraq, believing he could hold her for Chaya's cooperation in helping him escape.

He couldn't have known the cell he was tied to had already been targeted and that their headquarters would be taken out so violently.

Natches stared into her face now, paper white, her golden hazel and brown eyes dark with the memories that tore at him as well. And he wanted to howl out in rage, in agony. Because he felt the need to wipe the horror from her. To tear aside that wall she had placed between them.

"I don't blame you." She tried to tear herself from his hold again. "I never blamed you for her death."

"You blamed me for saving you instead," he snapped, fury rising inside him at the thought of losing her like that. "Is that what you wanted for me, Chaya? For us? To have it all end that way?"

And despite his anger, he could only touch her with tenderness. He lifted his free hand, brushed back the hair that fell over her forehead, and he ached.

"There was no us."

She only infuriated him with that statement, because he knew better. He'd always known better. From the moment he'd torn into that fucking cell and seen her struggling to drag that dead guard's clothes on, her eyes swollen shut, lips bloodied, and courage shining in her face, he'd known there was going to be an "us." It was just a matter of time.

And later, buried in that hole, waiting on extraction, he shouldn't have been attracted to her. She had been in shock. She had been hurt and fighting so valiantly to stay conscious. And in such a short time, she had dug her way inside him. Into a place he hadn't realized existed within the killer he had been shaping himself into.

He'd breathed in her pain when she'd realized her husband had betrayed her to the enemy, that he had betrayed his country and their marriage. And he had soaked in her pain the night she'd lost her child. He'd stroked her trembling body as she'd begged him to hold back the horror of what she had seen. He had taken her, amid both their tears, and the next morning, when he'd awoken, she had been gone.

He released her now, grimacing, feeling his flesh tighten over his muscles, as though something within him stretched danger-ously, confined by his own skin and growing impatient.

"I guess there wasn't, because you were gone the next morn-ing," he bit out.

"And you were gone that night when I returned," she snapped back, anger trembling in her voice, anger and something else. A finely threaded emotion that had his gaze sharpening on her pale face. "You didn't come back."

Natches stared back at her, his eyes narrowing. Had she come looking for him when he had believed she was gone?

"I was called in that afternoon for a mission. It was a quick strike; I was flown directly to my drop-off. I returned three days later, and you had left Baghdad," he told her.

He remembered his rage. He had torn apart his quarters with it, and then he had torn apart the hotel room they had shared. The MPs sent after him hadn't fared very well either.

As he stared at her now, he remembered all the reasons why he had gone insane over losing her. The lush lips, the stubborn angle of her chin. The way she knew how to smile, the feel of her coming alive against him. He had known all that before the day she had lost little Beth. He'd known it because he had spent two weeks haunting that damned hospital, teasing a kiss out of her, a laugh. Knowing she was married, knowing she was bound to a traitor.

And she had known. She had known, and like a flower opening to the sun, she had slowly begun opening for him.

She shook her head now, her eyes, that deep golden gaze locked with his, the color shifting, shadowed with so much pain. "Timothy said he checked. He was there that morning I went in to finalize custody of Beth's remains."

She crossed her arms over her breasts as though she were hugging the pain inside herself when all he wanted to do was wipe it from her. "He wanted me to leave immediately to take Beth home, then join DHS. I wanted to talk to you first." She shrugged stiffly. "You were gone. He said he checked to see if you were on a mission and you weren't."

Lying bastard. Natches grunted at that. "DHS ordered the mission. They had a line on Nassar Mallah. I went out after him. When I finished and returned, you were gone."

Chaya bit her lip as she moved across the room and lifted herself heavily onto one of the stools that sat at the counter. She looked tired; she looked hopeless. And that look tore at his heart.

"Sounds like Timothy." Her voice was nearly toneless. "But it didn't matter, not really. I couldn't function then, Natches. Not for either of us."

God he wanted to hold her now. What the hell was it about this woman? She was inside him, and five years of fighting it hadn't managed to push her out of his soul.

Was it love? Hell if it felt like anything he had seen out of Dawg and Rowdy. He didn't feel gentle. He felt like he wanted to devour her from head to toe. He wanted to roll around in oil with her. He wanted to lift her to that counter and spend hours eating the tastiest flesh he'd ever found between a woman's thighs.

She was hurting, enmeshed in memories that he knew had to be ripping her guts to shreds. The sight of it made him crazy. He would do anything, say anything, to ease her pain, but by God she wasn't hiding from him anymore.

She held that past between them like a spiked shield, and he'd had enough of it. Five years. He'd let her torment him through endless, aching nights. He'd suffered every nightmare he knew she suffered, and his pain for her sliced through his soul with each memory.

"You've had long enough to begin functioning then." He had to force himself to stand back from her, to not touch her.

She looked lost, lost and lonely, almost as broken as she had looked the day they told her her husband was the traitor who revealed her to the terrorists who had kidnapped her.

He watched as her shoulders straightened then, her chin lifted. He didn't know what the hell she had in her mind now, but he knew exactly what she intended to do, and he'd be damned if he would let her.

She was not walking out on him again. Not like this. This was the closest he'd managed to get to her since the night her daughter had died. And then, it had been comfort, not need, not hunger. She had needed someone to hold on to. Someone to take her away from reality while she found a way to handle the coming grief.

He'd given her that. He wasn't willing to be that someone to her again though. He wasn't a warm body to hold back the pain, and damn her to hell, he was sick and damned tired of being relegated to her past. A part of a memory she desperately wanted to forget.

"I would have divorced him for one night with you." And all the need, the hunger, the driving, aching desperation he felt himself was echoed in her voice.

Her declaration surprised him though. And he could tell by the tone of her voice that it filled her with guilt.

She turned to him then, her gaze haunted. "Using the excuse that our marriage had been lost before then doesn't help. I took vows, and I meant them. But I was going to leave him, even before I knew he had betrayed me. I was going to leave him, Natches, and I made that decision because of you."

He could feel the "but" coming, and he knew it was going to

piss him off. He could feel it in the tension gathering in the air around them.

"He was a bastard," he snarled before she could say anything more. "You knew it, even if you didn't have proof of it."

He had known it. Any man who allowed his wife to face danger alone deserved to lose her to another man. Women were precious. Women who loved, who honored their vows, were more precious than the finest gems. And Chaya would have honored those vows until the ink dried on the divorce papers. He knew it. And sometimes he wondered if he hadn't hated that part of her.

"That doesn't excuse it," she said, staring at him from where she sat, her expression somber, her gaze flickering with guilt. "I wanted your kiss, Natches. I wanted you; I wanted your touch and your voice whispering all those naughty little secrets you used to whisper to me when I was in the hospital. I wanted it. I was married, and I ached for it. And I paid for it."

It took a moment, one long, disbelieving moment, for that comment to soak into his head and light the spark of his normally rational temper.

"Son of a bitch." He stared back at her in complete amazement. "I'll be a son of a bitch. You've let that bastard steal your soul even from the fucking grave." His voice rose as he spoke. "Is that how you're blaming yourself now, Chay? That Beth was taken from you because you wanted me?"

Anger poured from him as he watched her flinch, saw the truth in her eyes. Stubborn pride lined every curve of her body. She actually believed what she was saying. Believed every word of it.

"I don't expect you to understand," she whispered, her voice hoarse.

"I understand this, by God. If you were my wife, Chaya—my woman—you'd never, fucking never, be on a mission without me. You'd never face danger alone, and you'd never know a night that I wasn't in your damned bed. How long had that bastard been out of your bed?"

"That's not the point." Her voice trembled. He could see the fear in her eyes now, a fear that made no damned sense because she had to know he would never, never harm her. But damn her to hell, he was so furious with her that he wanted to slam his fist into a wall to relieve the rage burning inside him.

"The fact that he was fucking every trainee he could get his hands on didn't matter either, I guess," he sneered, furious, consumed by that fury as he realized the ways she had made herself pay for her daughter's death. And her hunger for him. "The fact that he managed to get your baby on a plane to Iraq without your knowledge because he was fucking your sister before the two of you left didn't matter either, did it?"

Her face only tightened further. Her eyes raged though. He saw her eyes; he saw the banked fury, the agony that she tried to dim, tried to hide.

"Did it matter, Chaya?" He strode to her, his fist slamming into the top of the bar as she flinched from the sound of his voice and the crack of his flesh against the Formica. Hell, he cracked it again, and he didn't even give a damn. "Answer me, damn you!"

"That was no excuse," she screamed back, shuddering from head to toe, everything he needed to hear, everything he wanted to know, in her voice now. She wanted. Just as he did, she ached and she hungered for what was between them, and she was too damned scared to take it. "That didn't give me the right—"

"No, it gave *me* the right."

Before he could stop himself, and God knew he didn't want to stop himself, he jerked her into his arms and slammed his lips down on hers.

He wanted to be gentle. She deserved it. She deserved sweet, liquid kisses. She deserved gentleness and warmth, and all he had was hunger, lust, and heat.

All he had was the need to taste the passion without the grief. The woman without the pain of loss.

And he had her. He felt the first resistance, shock and surprise. Her hands pressed against his shoulders, then her fingers curled. A second later, she made that whispery, whimpering little sound of surrender that he had only ever heard from her lips.

They parted beneath his kiss, opened to the stroke of his tongue, and a second later, a firestorm of need rocked through his body.

She kissed like a wanton, like a woman whose need for pleasure had grown to the same torturous depths his own had grown to. Satin-soft lips slanted beneath his; her tongue met his, licked and consumed and had him strung as tight as a banjo string within seconds.

It wasn't enough. The kiss was only the tip of the iceberg. He needed so much more from her. He needed more than he had known in that fucking desert, more than he had fantasized of over the years. He needed her rocking in his arms, lifting to his thrusts.

He groaned into the kiss, lifted her closer, felt the soft swell of her stomach cushioning the hard-on raging beneath his jeans, and knew he couldn't live without tasting more of her.

She was like a drug in his system, impossible to get rid of. And there were times he wondered if he didn't embrace this particular addiction. Her lips moving beneath his, her moans filling his head.

He fought back a growl as she tore her lips from his. He needed more.

"I need more of you." Her lips were on his neck, biting, sucking, kissing, as her hands lowered to his belt. "I need to taste you, Natches. Taste you all over."

"Ah, hell." Her fingers were lowering the zipper, parting the material, and shoving it aside to release the fully engorged, throbbing length of his cock.

As he watched, she went to her knees. How many times had he dreamed of this? Dreamed of her taking him like this.

"Damn you." He flinched in agonizing pleasure as her lips parted and took him.

She was too hungry for preliminaries, and that only made him hotter. The head of his cock disappeared into her eager little mouth and immediately set flame to wildfire.

It flashed through his body, drew his balls tight, then had them knotting with ecstasy as her nimble little fingers began to caress and play with them.

And she sucked. She sucked his cock into her mouth, nearly to her throat, and drew on it, milked it until he was growling with pleasure. Her free hand wrapped around the shaft, stroked, tightened on it, and drove him crazy.

His hands were in her hair, his hips moving, fucking her mouth, and he loved it.

"Is this how you used that little toy, Chay?" The thought of that damned dildo infuriated him. "Did you think of this, baby? Of me inside your mouth, fucking those sweet lips?"

He had been dying to do just that, and she had filled her mouth with something else? Damn her. Not again. Never again.

She moaned around his cock head, and he nearly came from

the pleasure of it. Sensation rippled through the shaft, into his balls, and up his spine. Holding on wasn't going to happen for long. He could feel the cum boiling in his balls, knew he wasn't going to be able to hold back.

"Damn you. Suck it, baby. Show me how you sucked that damned toy and thought of me."

His teeth clenched as she moaned again, her mouth tightening, her tongue stroking and licking and drawing him so damned tight he felt as though he were going to break.

He was going to come. Ah, hell. Close. So damned close.

A second later he jerked back, fury pulsing, raging through him. Chaya fell back with a cry as he pushed her to the side and jerked the gun from the top of the couch where he had placed it and cursed furiously.

The door had crashed open, Dawg and Rowdy rolling into the apartment like pure vengeance itself as Natches stared back at them in unholy fury.

"What the fuck are you two doing?" He barely had time to pull his finger back from the trigger as the men rose from the floor, their own weapons lowering.

Sometimes some information just took a minute to process. His head was still filled with the sweet scent and the heated feel of Chaya's mouth.

And rather than searching for her own weapon, what the hell was she doing? Laughing. He glanced at her in disbelief. She lay on the carpet behind him, their bodies sheltered by the couch, which faced the door, and she laughed.

Her lips were red, her face flushed, and she was laughing with such damned amusement it made his back teeth clench.

And pure fury was burning in his brain, demanding he take

action now. That he kick them out of his apartment with his foot up their asses for daring, even daring, to interrupt his pleasure.

The bastards were shadowing him.

There was no other explanation for their presence or the lock that had been torn free of the door. He only barely remembered hearing and ignoring their knock. He hadn't cared enough to answer the damned door because his head had been ready to explode with ecstasy.

He slowly fixed his pants and tightened his belt. He laid the gun on the counter cautiously, watching as Chaya stared at him in something akin to wary surprise as she climbed to her feet, her eyes still bright with her laughter. He was glad someone was amused.

"Natches." She laid her hand on his arm, her voice shaking as she obviously fought back more of those feminine, joyous giggles. "It's just Dawg and Rowdy."

She was staring at him now in rather the same way he would eye a rabid animal. And she had good cause to watch him just that carefully.

He turned back to his cousins, her hand still on him, and he was loath to break that contact. It was the only reason he wasn't charging them now. The only reason any of them were still standing rather than busting the walls of his apartment with their heads.

"You broke my door," he said carefully, staring at the two men as they watched him just as carefully.

Dawg sniffed, blushed to the roots of his black hair, cleared his throat, then glanced at the door and the lock that had ripped from the wall. "Yeah. Well. We were just coming up for a beer. Thought you could use some company and thought we heard fighting. Right, Rowdy?" He nudged Rowdy.

Dawg was obviously lying through his teeth, and Natches knew it. He turned to Rowdy then, forcing his fingers not to curl into fists as Chaya kept her hold on his arm.

Her grip had actually tightened in response to the flexing of the muscles beneath her hand.

"Right, Rowdy?" Dawg hissed again. Under other circumstances it might have been comical. Dawg was bigger, heavier, and his fist was a damned sight harder than Natches's. Sometimes. But it was obvious he didn't want to return to his wife bruised.

Natches turned to Rowdy.

And Rowdy grinned, because he knew. Natches saw in his eyes the knowledge that Chaya held him back, that Chaya could always hold him back.

"Nah, we were freezing our butts off outside because we thought Agent Dane might have a little more up her sleeve than a few questions." Rowdy's grin was cocky, which only pissed Natches off further.

Dawg winced. "Dumb ass," he muttered to Rowdy.

"Thanks for the vote of confidence, guys," Chaya laughed, and Natches felt her move.

"If you try leaving this apartment, then I'm kicking their asses the minute you walk out the door," he warned her.

She paused, and when he glanced at her, he could see the caution in her eyes again. "There are two of them, Natches."

"And I have pure mad on my side. Want to take bets who will win?" He made damned sure she saw nothing but determination in his gaze.

"Looks like you're going to have to head to the *Dreams* tonight anyway." Dawg cleared his throat, and it might have placated

Natches, seeing a hint of nerves in his cousin, if the amusement hadn't been so bright in his green eyes. Dawg was clearly enjoying the fact that he had interrupted something here.

"I need to get back to my hotel." Chaya stepped back, and Natches let her.

He was careful to keep his expression bland as he glanced at her. She might try to run, but she wasn't going far. Hell, she was going to finish what she started before the damned interruption, and he was going to make sure of it.

"We'll, umm, fix the door." Dawg smiled, clearly enjoying the fact that, for the moment, Natches was leashed. "You go ahead and take Miss Dane back to her hotel, Natch. We'll have that beer at the boat."

"If I see you on my boat tonight, I'm going to shoot you, Dawg," Natches warned him, and he was afraid he just might be serious. "You can try the beer tomorrow afternoon, not a moment before."

Natches moved too fast for Chaya to avoid him this time, his fingers curling around her upper arm before pulling her with him to the door. "And make sure you nail the door tight. Some bastard walks in and steals my beer, and I'll kill you for sure."

"Natches, I'm not going to that damned boat," Chaya protested as they neared the door. "I have a job to do. You're taking me back to my hotel. Period."

"Sure I am," he agreed.

She almost paused, would have if he hadn't tugged her after him. "You are?"

Had he agreed too easily? He almost smirked.

"Sure I am. Sometime. I'm sure you'll need more clothes in a few days." He hardened his voice, firmed his grip, and ignored her curse.

She could bitch until hell froze over, but they weren't finished. Talking, fucking, he'd take either one he could get, or both, but tonight, he wasn't letting her go.

Dawg rubbed at the back of his neck as he heard Natches's jeep drive off, and he turned to Rowdy slowly. His cousin had a thoughtful expression on his face.

Rowdy was a thinker. He always had been. He rarely jumped into anything impulsively, unlike his two cousins. He always weighed the evidence, the pros and the cons, and sometimes he could be damned scary in his predictions.

"You could have backed me there, cuz," he finally sighed when Rowdy stayed silent.

When his cousin turned to him, it was with a smirk that almost had Dawg bursting out in laughter.

"Why bother?" Rowdy grinned. "She has a chain around his neck thicker than a junkyard dog's. He wasn't about to jump into a fight. That boy doesn't want a bruised body right now either, Dawg. We both know that one well."

Damned if they didn't.

Dawg remembered a time when a good fight and a good drunk was almost as good as sex. Now, since Crista, a fight, with the bruises, busted ribs, and/or swollen lips, was something he avoided at all costs. He liked the feel of Crista's hands on his body, demanding and wild as she moved against him. The thought of losing so much as an ounce of that pleasure to pain was intolerable.

Evidently, Natches was already considering that fact. Dawg chuckled at that thought as he moved to help Rowdy with the door.

"She's still not pretty," he told his cousin. "But at least I didn't smell the smoke."

Rowdy grunted. "Smoke wouldn't have mattered to Natches, Dawg," he pointed out.

And that was the damned truth. Even last year, when she was lighting up every time Natches came around her, their cousin hadn't been able to stay away.

"She's still not pretty," he said again.

"What's your problem with her looks?" Rowdy paused as they propped the door up and Dawg went in search of a hammer and nails. "He won't have to use a bag for her head. Hell, Dawg, I don't care what she looks like. Natches isn't ice anymore. He was scaring the shit out of me with that cold attitude of his. We're not far from losing him forever, if you haven't noticed."

And Dawg had noticed. Natches had been drawing further and further away over the years. He pulled the hammer and nails from the kitchen drawer and moved back to the door.

Her looks shouldn't bother him, and Dawg knew it. Crista had just torn into his butt the night before over a similar comment.

"It's not just her looks," he finally admitted.

"Then what is it?"

"It's her eyes. Look at her eyes, man. They're dead inside. That woman isn't even alive, and you can see it in her face. Her expression and her eyes. She'll destroy Natches."

Rowdy was quiet for long moments then. The sounds of the hammer striking wood and the four-inch nails sinking into the frame were the only comment Dawg received.

Finally, the door was secure, and Rowdy was just staring at it.

"She's not dead inside," he finally said, his voice soft.

"Same as." Dawg shrugged. "You didn't work with her last year. She's cold inside, man. She can get nervous as hell, she can get scared, and she did a fine laugh tonight, but there ain't no love in her for anyone."

Rowdy shook his head at that. "There's too much emotion." He looked at Dawg then. "Just like Natches. And she's determined to hide it. You can't see past that need we both have to keep protecting our little cousin, Dawg. Sometimes I think we forget he's all grown-up now."

"And just as alone as he ever was," Dawg growled.

Rowdy shook his head. "Not anymore."

SIX

He didn't take her back to the hotel, just as he'd told Chaya he wouldn't. She didn't remember Natches being *this* damned stubborn. Not that he couldn't give the proverbial mule a run for its money. But practically kidnapping her wasn't something he had done before.

"Why bring me here, Natches?" she asked him as they stepped into the comfortable living area of the boat, and she stared around in interest.

"Because we're not finished." He closed the door, locked it, and reset the security system.

She felt her heart race at the sound of the muted little beep from the security console. Somehow the boat seemed much more intimate than the apartment had. It wasn't just that the space was less open and smaller; it was as though a part of Natches himself was infused within the interior.

Dark browns and desert tones made up the color scheme of the furniture. The carpet was a creamy white. Small dark maroon pillows rested at the arms of the couch, and a rug of the same color was laid at the door. Heavy desert brown shades covered the windows, and the splash of golden light that fell from the table lamps softened the room.

The kitchen was separated by a combination table and bar. Laminate flooring stretched to the curved metal staircase at the far end of the kitchen and beyond, to what Chaya assumed were the bedrooms.

She turned back to Natches when he didn't explain further, and watched him warily. He reminded her of a caged beast straining against his restraints. It was there in the wild glitter of his dark green eyes, in the taut planes and angles of his face.

"Why the hell did Cranston have to send you here?" he finally asked, the guttural tone of his voice causing her to flinch.

"That was my question as well." She shrugged, watching him carefully as he strode past her to the refrigerator in the kitchen. "His answer was that I was his best bet. He didn't tell me what the bet was though."

"Driving me bat-shit crazy?" he asked as he twisted the cap off a beer and tipped it to his lips.

Watching him drink from the longneck bottle was sexier than it should have been.

"Probably." She finally admitted there was a chance that that was exactly why Timothy had sent her rather than another agent. "He wasn't pleased with you or Dawg last year. And he does enjoy his petty little revenge games."

Actually, he normally had a solid reason for those games, they were just irritating as hell.

But the real conversation she and Natches were having was beneath the actual words, thrumming with tension.

Chaya couldn't forget. Anytime she was near Natches, every time she was within touching distance, the memories and the pain returned. And the need. The same need that had his erection buried between her lips earlier. The need to touch and be touched was stronger than the pain.

It had been five years. Losing Beth had nearly driven her crazy, but the years had helped her to sew closed the ragged wound that loss had left. She still cried sometimes; she still ached most of the time. But she had learned to go on. Beth was gone; there was no way to bring her back.

But Chaya had always known that Natches was still alive. And the guilt she felt at the thought of going to him had always held her back.

While Natches had been teasing her in that hospital, seducing her, making her laugh, her daughter had been in danger. While she had made plans for a future that didn't include her traitorous husband, her daughter had perhaps been crying for her mother. And while she had been laughing with Natches, someone had been planning to bomb the building Craig had taken their child to.

Hunger, guilt, anger, and need vied inside her now just as they had for the past five years. They twisted inside her, making it impossible to see past what she had lost long enough to decide what she was running away from. And now she had no choice but to face it.

Whoever that faceless organization was that had managed to authenticate a strike code on that hotel in Iraq, it had to be stopped. It was too dangerous, its influence becoming too corrupt. There were moles in Army Intelligence, and Cranston had traced them to the op here.

"I'm going to kill Cranston when this is over." Natches set the beer bottle down on the bar, his heavy-lidded gaze moving over her again.

That look made her sizzle. Chaya could feel all the nerve endings in her body coming alive. That look could make women across the world weak in the knees. He could bottle it and make billions.

"Good luck." She shoved her hands in the pockets of her jeans to keep them from shaking. To keep herself from shaking.

"Take your clothes off."

Chaya blinked back at him, certain she hadn't heard what she knew she had heard.

"Do you think it's just that easy?" She shook her head and wished it was. "Sorry, Natches, I'm not here to be your toy. I'm here to do a job."

"So you can do both now." He grabbed his beer and finished it before tossing it in the trash can in the corner. "You can be Agent Greta Dane during the day and my toy at night. I promise you won't be in the least neglected, Chaya."

Oh, she just bet she wouldn't be. And when the time came that Timothy decided to let them all in on the little game he was playing, what then? Would she be cast aside as all his other playthings had been?

"You have plenty of other toys, Natches; you don't need me." She wanted to sound flippant, uncaring, but she could feel the ache building inside her.

Five years. It had been five years since he had taken her. She had been so filled with pain then that she hadn't been able to appreciate the pleasure that had torn through her.

But she remembered it. She remembered his tears mixing with hers as he kissed her, just as she remembered how easily he had coaxed more than one explosive orgasm from her.

She watched him uneasily. He wasn't just going to take no for an answer, and she didn't know if she had the strength to hold back if he touched her again.

And he was going to touch her. She pulled her hands slowly from her jeans pockets as he advanced on her, his expression predatory.

"Natches." She whispered his name in warning.

"There's the door; run, little rabbit," he suggested, his voice wicked as he nodded to the door that led to escape. "Go ahead. Or do you have the courage to actually take me on without excuses?"

Her fingers curled against her palm as he challenged her. The chance to touch him again, to feel whatever it was she had felt that night that she hadn't been able to forget. She hadn't been able to touch another man after that.

"That so isn't going to work," she retorted and wished her voice sounded stronger, wished it had more conviction.

She could feel herself preparing for him despite the protest. Her breasts were sensitive and swollen, the nipples throbbing. And between her thighs, she could feel herself dampening, her clit engorging.

She wanted. She ached. She had been aching this past week with a strength that had forced her to masturbate several times. And it hadn't been enough. It was never enough when she thought of Natches.

"You want me." He was too close now, standing in front of her, forcing her to look up at him.

He was so wicked. A rogue. She had called him that once, and he had laughed and winked as he agreed with her.

"Does just wanting make it all right?" she whispered, catching his wrists as his hands settled on her hips. "Wanting isn't always enough, Natches."

"It'll be enough for tonight." There was no plea in his words, just pure demand. "I'm not asking for forever, Chaya. I wouldn't dare."

And before she could question the angry tone of those last words, he was kissing her. His lips covered hers, his tongue pushed between them, and he was taking what he wanted. There was no question of giving it to him, because he didn't ask for a damned thing.

This wasn't the teasing seducer she had known five years before. This was a conqueror. This was a man who refused to ask. He knew what he wanted, and God help her, he seemed to know exactly what she needed, too.

Chaya felt the world tilt around her; she could have sworn the ground shook. Whatever it was, it was Natches holding her, his lips on hers, his muttered, hungry moan vibrating against her lips as his mouth slanted across them and his tongue tempted and teased hers into an excited, erotic duel.

It was fire and lightning, this kiss. It was being awakened from a lifetime of nightmares and finally given light. It was like being reborn.

Chaya heard herself cry out, felt her arms latching around his neck, her body arching to him, needing more. More contact. More touch. Oh God, she couldn't get enough of him, and the need would destroy her. This need rocked her to her very core, to the center of that lonely, almost broken, spirit that had sent her running before. Because she couldn't face losing anyone else. She couldn't face losing Natches, too.

She trembled as she felt his hands caressing her, running along her back, pushing beneath her top and touching bare flesh. He moved against her, pressing his thigh between hers, rocking her against him.

She felt the delicate, sensitive flesh between her thighs flame. Wicked, greedy wildfire swept through her, and nothing mattered but more. More of his kiss. If she didn't get more of his kiss, she would lose her mind from the need. More of his touch. She wanted to be naked in his arms. Naked and shuddering and surrounded by Natches. Surrounding him. Burning as she only burned in her dreams.

"There, Chay." He pulled her closer, one hand on her butt, forcing her to ride the hard muscle of his thigh as she ground herself against him. "See how good it is, baby? Remember how hot it is?"

Oh yes, she remembered. She remembered begging him for more, screaming for more. The memories were hazy because the pain had been overwhelming that night. But she remembered enough to know why she had ached in the darkness of the night after she'd left Iraq. She remembered enough to know that, once he took her, she was never going to be the same again.

No more sleepwalking. She had existed the past five years, forcing herself through each day, refusing to acknowledge that a part of her, that hidden, feminine core of her, was right here. In Natches's arms.

"Natches, let me breathe. Let me think," she gasped as his lips slid from hers—lazy, confident—and nibbled at her jawline. Her nerve endings rose up in a crescendo of pleasure.

"No thinking allowed." The rasp of his day-old beard sent shards of the most incredible pleasure washing through her body. "Now, let's get these damned clothes off."

It was sexy. It was erotic. It was the most gentle act of sexual intensity that she could have imagined. He pulled her arms from around his neck, then, staring down at her, his forest green eyes darkening to moss, his palms touching her flesh along the way, he slid her blazer from her shoulders and over her arms.

Chaya stared up at him, unable to break the contact, the connection. He had done that before, she remembered. Stared at her, watched her eyes as he undressed her.

"This isn't a good idea." She tried to protest, but it sounded more like an invitation. It was an invitation. Everyone knew Natches did anything anyone else considered a bad idea. And the more erotic, the more wicked, that bad idea was, the faster he was there.

"Who needs good ideas? Come here, baby. Let me see those pretty breasts just one more time. Lift your arms for me." He pulled the hem of her shirt up and over her head, off her arms. It dropped to the floor as a hungry growl left his lips and long, thick lashes feathered over his eyes.

When he looked at her like that, she melted. Then she felt his hands at the belt of her jeans.

She was naked from the waist up, or practically naked, because the bra she wore didn't hide much from view.

"Natches, I don't think I can stand through this."

And she didn't. Her knees were weakening. She could feel her legs turning to mush, right along with her objections. This was

Natches. Wicked, erotic Natches. His kisses were a flame that burned to the icy core of her. His touch was an inferno, warming her from the inside out.

And she needed to be warm. Just for a little while. She needed to be warmed by him, just one more time.

As his lips moved over her neck, her arms found strength. As his hands pushed beneath the waist of her jeans, she struggled against him, pushing at his arms.

"Easy, Chay."

"Not easy." She nipped at his neck, clearly surprising him as she tugged at his T-shirt. She wanted him bare as well. She wanted to feel him against her, bare flesh to bare flesh. She needed it.

He whipped the shirt from his body and tossed it aside as her hands went to his belt. Shaking, uncertain, her fingers pulled and tugged at it.

"There you go, Chay. Get naughty for me."

She tore at the metal button, then eased the zipper over the hard, throbbing length of his cock. She moved it down slowly, working it over the stiff ridge as a hard growl passed his lips.

He wanted her naughty? She wasn't naughty; she was starving for him. Five years of pent-up hunger blazed through her, erupting from a well of need that she'd had no idea existed within her.

Those distant memories from five years before didn't compare to this. The feel of his body, so large and broad, hard and muscular, bending to her, almost protectively. His lips on her neck, teeth rasping. His hands working her jeans over her hips as hunger seemed to permeate the air.

Chaya could feel perspiration gathering on her body, the heat building inside them, flowing around them, as she pushed at his jeans, frantic to get to the heated flesh of his cock.

"There you go, sweetheart; burn for me," he growled as his hands slid around to her rear, clenched, then lifted.

He raised her along his body, dragging her from her goal as a protesting cry fell from her lips. A second later, she felt the cool top of the low counter, heard a chair falling to the floor as he kicked it out of the way, and then Natches was kissing her again.

She couldn't get enough of his kisses, or his touches. She couldn't kiss back enough, couldn't touch enough. She was consumed, inside and out, by a need so fiery she didn't have a hope of controlling it.

"Here, get these off." He pulled away from her, despite her attempts to draw him back and the mewling sound that fell from her lips.

His hair was tangled, mussed from her fingers and framing his roguish face. Dark eroticism sharpened his features, his eyes. His bare chest was sheened with sweat, the hair prickling her fingers as she ran her hands down it.

She ached for him now. Ached with a power that had her arching as she fought to breathe, as he pulled the boots from her feet and tugged her jeans down her legs.

She was naked but for the bra and panties. Scraps of material that did nothing to shield her from his eyes. And he was looking. His gaze went over her slowly as his hands smoothed up her legs, her inner thighs, parting them as he centered on the wet core of her body.

"You still shave?" He ran the backs of his fingers over the damp cotton that shielded the swollen folds of her sex.

Chaya swallowed tightly. "Wax."

Pleasure and anticipation tightened his features, and the look caused her womb to clench in response. He was aroused, dangerously aroused. She could see it in his face, feel it in his body.

"Five years." His voice was guttural. "I've dreamed about that one night, Chay, for five fucking years. Tormented by it. Driven fucking crazy by it."

Her lips parted at the intensity behind the words. To be wanted like that. She had never been wanted so desperately by a man as Natches wanted her. And only once—five years before—had she felt this kind of desire for a man.

Five years. Too long. Too many memories, too many dreams and fantasies to fuel this hunger.

"I—I ached. Every day." The words came from her, unbidden, the strain from the attempt to hold them back causing a sob to pass her throat. "Natches—you're going to destroy me."

His fingers hooked in the band of her panties, and he drew them slowly over her hips with the soft command "Lift."

She arched her hips, watching his eyes, his face, watching the hunger grow in him and feeling it grow in her.

He dropped the scrap of material to the floor, a grimace contorting his features as he forced his gaze from the glistening flesh between her thighs and stared back at her.

Chaya felt caught, trapped, and it terrified her. The power this man held over her. How was she supposed to fight this? Control this?

"Now for this." His fingers moved to the front clasp of her bra.

Chaya's breath caught in her throat as he flicked the tiny clasp open, then peeled the cups back from her breasts and pushed the straps over her shoulders. Her fingers dug into the countertop as she leaned back at the urging of his hands against her shoulders.

"So pretty." His hands framed the swollen mounds, his fingers dark against her lighter flesh as he lifted them, caressed them.

Calloused fingertips stroked over the hardened nipples. Her womb convulsed, and she felt the damp warmth of her juices spilling from her.

"Natches." She arched to him, distant memories of him bending to her, taking her nipple in his mouth, flashing through her mind a second before his actions followed her memories.

And the reality was better. She arched and cried out at the feel of his mouth, hot and hungry, devouring her nipple. His tongue lashed at it, rasped over it as he suckled, sending exquisite sparks of pure sensation exploding through her system.

"Oh God, Natches." Her head fell back as she felt her arms weakening.

As though he knew, sensed her inability to hold herself up to him, one arm curved around her back, tightened, and allowed her hands to lift from the counter as he lowered her, her arms curling around his shoulders, her nails digging into his flesh.

His mouth was so hot, his tongue like a brand burning across her nipple. First one, then the other. He sucked at the hard points greedily as she became lost in a vortex of pleasure she knew she could never escape.

"Ah, yes, that's my Chay." He ran his tongue in the valley between her breasts.

She shivered at the caress, her thighs tightening on his, her hips undulating at the subtle pressure of his cock head against the slick folds of her sex.

She needed him there. She needed him to take her. Hard. Fast. Deep.

"I missed this," he crooned as his lips began to kiss a path down her stomach. "Missed touching you, feeling you against me."

Her back arched as a tremulous cry tore from her.

"Do you remember it, Chay? So hot it burned us alive? So much pleasure we thought we were dying."

She remembered it. She remembered all of it. Like an inferno blast that she had convinced herself was no more than her need to escape her pain. It had been so much more though. Because it was hotter this time, the ache deeper. It was Natches. His touch was like an addiction, and the need only grew the longer the separation. There was no going cold turkey. No escaping the effect of it.

"Ahh, so sweet." His tongue licked over the top of the mound between her thighs. So close to her clit. So close she could feel the heat of it, anticipate the wild ecstasy it could bring her.

When it came, it shattered her. Because it was even brighter, hotter, than she remembered, the pleasure swirled through her fear and dissipated it. The need for control evaporated. She was lost in the pleasure, and there was no other place to be. No other place she ever wanted to be.

His tongue slid around her clit, and he groaned against it.

"So sweet, Chay. You taste like summer."

Her hands speared into his hair, the thick, silken strands twining around her fingers as she fought to pull him back to her.

And he chuckled against her flesh, a dark, greedy sound. His tongue licked slow and easy through the narrow slit so rich with awakened sensations. Nerve endings came fully alert, too close to the surface of her skin, reveling in his touch again.

She called out his name, her voice hoarse with need, begging him to take her. His hands pushed her thighs farther apart, his head dipped, and his tongue filled her. Ecstasy nearly shattered inside her. So close. She was so close.

"Please." She moaned, feeling her release, so close, almost there. Oh God, she needed to come. She needed that wild explosion tearing through her, the release she had only known one other time, had only known with Natches.

"Are you mine, Chaya?" His voice was a dark, seductive croon, pulling her in as he licked again, drawing her taste to him, stroking her into an abyss of sensation and pleasure.

She would give him anything for this. Be anything he wanted as long as she had this.

"Yours." She was barely aware of the word tearing from her lips. "Always yours, Natches. Oh God, I've always been yours."

He paused, a short moment of stillness that her breath caught, then his lips surrounded her clit, drew it into the suckling heat of his mouth, to the licking tip of his tongue, and he pushed her over that edge.

She felt the explosion rip through her, drawing her up, arching her against him as a throttled scream left her lips and she dissolved into him.

She melted. For a moment, just for a moment, she felt herself sinking into the very pores of his flesh, and understood that this was where she belonged. This was the addiction that was Natches. To belong to him so deeply that she was a part of him.

And it lasted for an endless moment. Then he was lifting his head, pushing her legs apart, and before the final wave of release washed through her, he began working the hard length of his erection inside her.

"Look at me, damn you."

Chaya's eyes jerked open at the command. Dazed, almost unfocused, she stared up at the dark vision of every woman's sexual fantasy come to life.

Black hair framing savage features, green eyes almost glowing in his sun-darkened face, nostrils flared in desperate hunger as his lips drew back from his teeth.

Raw erotic pleasure tore through her at the sight. This man, this sexual intensity, centered on her. On plain Chaya Dane, and God only knew Natches was more man than she had any hope of controlling.

And there was no need to control him now. Pleasure swamped control. There was no thought of control, only sensation—the feel of him working his cock inside her, the thick crest parting tender tissue as perspiration began to form on his shoulders and chest and run in small rivulets along the center of his body.

"Look at me, Chay." His voice was deep, hoarse. "Let me see you, baby. Let me see if I'm making you feel good. Does it feel good, Chay?"

Feel good? He was destroying her with pleasure. Her lips parted to tell him, but all she could do was moan his name and stare back at him. And feel him. Feel him stretching her, burning her. She was locked in a grip of ecstasy—it thrummed through her veins, heated her blood and tormented her nerve endings.

"Look at me, Chay." His voice hardened when she would have closed her eyes.

Forcing them open, she stared back at him. His jaw was clenched, sweat dripped along his forehead and down his face. His shoulders bunched, and she felt his thighs tighten as he pulled his erection back, then worked it into her farther, deeper, taking her until she was trying not to scream, until she was burning around him, and with a strangled groan, he buried himself full length inside her.

Hard hands clenched on her hips as he penetrated her fully, and some dark emotion in his eyes flared.

"Has there been anyone else?" She watched him speak, heard the words and tried to make sense of them.

"What?"

"Other men. Has another man taken what's mine, damn it?" Pure male dominance flashed in his expression, in his eyes.

Another man? She shook her head; she couldn't bear another man's touch. Didn't want it. Never, ever thought of it.

She shook her head again. "No one. No one but you . . ." She wanted to tell him she only wanted him, only needed him, but as the words tried to slip past her lips, he moved.

As though the admission broke the last of his own control, he was moving inside her, plunging, fucking her with fast, furious strokes that threw her almost instantly into orgasm.

It was like that with Natches. So wild there was no hope of holding on. So hot there wasn't a chance of not burning alive.

She arched and cried out his name. Her eyes closed, her neck lifted, and she felt him tighten, heard his hoarse exclamation before she felt him spill inside her. Heated, fierce jets of semen spurted into the quaking depths of her vagina and pushed her into another, destructive release, and to an edge of fear. Just the tiniest spark of concern because she knew there was something she should have remembered, something she should fear in this pleasure. A pleasure that left her sated, filled, and somehow, she knew, irrevocably bound to Natches in a way she never had been before.

SEVEN

Natches wasn't certain what brought him awake just after daybreak. The sun wasn't shining through the windows yet, and there was a light chill to the air.

At the end of October, it could get cold on the water. His bed was warm though, and he was drowsy and seeking the touch of Chaya's body when it hit him.

She wasn't in the bed.

He listened carefully and couldn't hear her moving on the house-boat or in the shower. Irritation washed through him instantly, as well as a healthy dose of anger.

He sat up in the bed, his eyes narrowed against the gloom that filled the large bedroom as he glanced at the clock.

It was barely seven, too damned early to be up and moving around unless he had actually intended to be at the garage that day. Which he hadn't. He'd intended to spend the day happily rolling around the bed with Chaya.

As he moved to flip the blanket back, he saw the paper on her pillow and picked it up before reading it silently.

Am meeting Sheriff Mayes this morning. I have work to do. Will call you this evening.

She would call him this evening?

He crumpled the note slowly in his hand, and for just a second, only a second, a grim sort of humor touched his mind. How many times had he either written or stated that sentiment, never to return?

Oh, if she thought for a single damned minute she was getting away that easily, then he'd just have to show her different. He'd let her go twice. *Third time's a charm, sweetheart,* he thought furiously. This time, she was stuck, and he'd make certain she understood that. Clear to her soul. No matter what it took.

Stomping from the bed, he headed for the shower. If he knew Zeke Mayes, and he did, then sweet little Chaya's day wasn't going to begin until after ten. Zeke had his rounds to make, his paperwork to do, and then he headed to the diner for breakfast around nine thirty or ten. Plenty of time for Natches to get ready and reach Chaya's hotel. He'd drag her back to the houseboat and show her exactly how this relationship was going to work from here on out.

He paused as he stood beneath the shower spray. Relationship. Hell, he'd never had a relationship. Until now. Until Chaya. He'd never kept a woman around long, never wanted to, but he was starting to suspect he wanted to keep Chaya forever.

He finished his shower, dressed, and was downstairs in the living room pulling on his boots when a fist landed in imperative demand against the door.

His head jerked up, then he lowered and shook it in resignation. He knew that knock.

Pushing to his feet, he stalked to the door, pulled the shade back, and glared at Dawg as he slid the door open.

"Isn't Crista draggin' your ass to the lumber store?" he smirked. Dawg's wife kept him on a very short leash. Dry cleaned and pressed clothes that looked presentable rather than day-old and holey. A decent haircut. But the scowl on his older cousin's face hadn't changed by much.

"Crista's not feeling well this morning." Dawg shrugged as he stepped into the boat. "Where are you headed off to this early? I thought you took Fridays off from the garage now."

Natches watched curiously as Dawg prowled the living room and the kitchen.

"When did you start checking up on me?" Natches leaned against the wall and crossed his arms over his chest as he watched Dawg.

"When you came back from Iraq and started actin' brick dumb." Dawg grunted as he turned to face him. "You know, I always wondered what the hell made you so much harder while you were gone. What did she do to you? Screw around on you? And you're heading right back into trouble with her?"

Natches stood still. "You don't want to go there, Dawg," he told him carefully. "Chaya's not the reason for however the hell I was acting or whatever I may have done. I didn't poke my nose into your hijinks with Crista, so I'd suggest you stay out of my relationship with Chaya."

"Relationship?" Dawg narrowed his eyes on him. "You've never had a relationship in your life, Natches. Are you sure you know what the hell you're doing here?"

Natches uncrossed his arms enough to scratch at his jaw and remember the fact that he had forgotten to shave. Again. But his cousin's attitude was bothering him more than the growth of beard on his cheek. Dawg had been acting strange ever since he had learned Chaya was back in town.

"Did you know what the hell you were doing with Crista?" he finally asked. "Come on, Dawg; you blackmailed her into sleeping with you. Did I give you grief over it?"

Dawg grimaced at that. He stood there in his jeans, shit-kicker boots, and that perfectly pressed long-sleeved shirt of his and glared at Natches again.

"Why is Agent Dane back here anyway?"

Natches shrugged. "Tying up loose ends is what I hear. What do you hear?"

"I hear Cranston's running another op," he snapped. "And Agent Dane is smack in the middle of it. Did she let you in on that little piece of information?"

"We didn't exactly get around to discussing it," Natches informed him. "First you and Rowdy broke down the door to my nice warm apartment, and once I got back here, I wasn't exactly in the mood to fight with her. What the fuck is your problem anyway? You're acting like a worried father. I didn't exactly stay out past curfew." He smirked at the thought. "Man, Crista is so domesticating you that it isn't even funny."

And damned if a flash of pride didn't hit Dawg's expression, rather than anger at what he would have once termed an insult.

"Look," Natches breathed out in irritation. "I know you and Rowdy have been following me around like a spy after secrets. You can stop now, okay? I'm a big boy. I do real good on my own."

"Until Agent Dane hit your life?" Dawg snapped. "I've been doing some checking. Before that bullet took out your shoulder, Natch, you were self-destructing like hell. Taking every mean-assed suicide assignment you could find. Why? And why the hell did it come around just months after you rescued some blond agent from a hellhole in the Iraqi desert? Tell me that agent wasn't the same one messing your head up now."

Natches was quiet for long, silent seconds. He stared at his cousin, promising himself he wasn't going to lose his temper. If he lost his temper, then he'd miss Chaya. And on top of that, he and Dawg would end up whipping on each other with enough force to leave both of them bruised and limping for days. Nope. Wasn't going to happen.

"Lock up when you leave." He turned and walked out the door before stepping from the small deck onto the floating walk.

He heard Dawg curse behind him, and he ignored it. His cousin was fishing, and Natches wasn't biting. It was Dawg's favorite means of getting answers from Natches, and it used to work. Piss him off and get him fighting. He didn't give a damn what he said to Dawg or Rowdy then. He would just spill his guts right there in the middle of a fight.

Natches grinned at the thought. Hell, those were the days. Before the Marines, when they were young and wild and filled with too much damned ego. Long ago and far away. More than eight damned years ago.

As he dug his keys out of his pocket and moved from the docks to the parking lot, he glanced back down the marina, flashed

Dawg a smile, and lifted his hand in farewell. His cousin was standing there with his hands propped on his hips, and even from where he stood, Natches could see the scowl on his face.

Dawg had never liked Chaya, and Natches knew why. His older cousin had spent too many years trying to protect his younger cousins. Seeing Chaya again last year had ripped Natches's guts out. It had torn into him knowing she wasn't ready to push past all that pain inside her yet, knowing it wasn't time to claim her. And unfortunately, Dawg had witnessed Natches's struggle; he just hadn't been positive who the woman was.

Sometimes it concerned Natches, the way he knew things about Chaya. Knew when to push her, when to just hold her. It was in her eyes, those needs she had, swirling in the golden depths. And the harder she fought it, the more she needed.

Last night, she had been like a firecracker ready to explode before he had even touched her. Those pretty golden brown eyes had been frosty, her expression closed, every line in her body straining to hold distance between them. Because what she felt scared her, scared her all the way to the bottom of her soul, and she knew it.

He unlocked his jeep and pushed the key in the ignition as he considered that, and the implications of it. Maybe Dawg had reason to worry, because Natches had a feeling he was only just beginning to realize how far over his head he was with Chaya. He was very much afraid that he just might love her.

Dawg watched Natches drive away and shook his head before jumping the short distance between Natches's deck and his own. And Crista was waiting for him, standing in the door, watching him curiously as he cast another scowl back at Natches.

"Well, you're still in one piece anyway." She looked up and down his body, her eyes twinkling in her still-pale face.

"You should be lying back down." He let his gaze sweep over her now, his heart softening in his chest even as his cock hardened in his jeans. Damn what this woman could do to him.

"I'm feeling a little bit better." She shrugged, looking away from him before turning and moving back into the houseboat.

"It's too cool outside for you to be standing in the doorway like that." He closed the door before frowning.

Maybe it was time to move out to the house. It was almost finished. He could push the contractors and get the carpet laid sooner than the spring date they had quoted him. A little extra money and they'd come out sooner. It hadn't been too cold last year, but still cold enough that she had insisted on wearing too many clothes. And the walkway had gotten icy a few times. He didn't want to risk her falling into the water.

He made a mental note to call the contractors later that morning, deciding he didn't want to spend another winter on the water. Summer and fall would work if they decided the house didn't suit them to live in year-round.

"I'll be fine, Dawg."

He grunted at that as he moved to the refrigerator. "You ready for breakfast yet?"

She was silent; he turned back to her, and he swore she was more pale than she had been moments before.

"I think I need to go lie back down." She headed for the stairs.

"I think you need to see the doctor." Something snapped inside him then. Fear. Dawg had rarely known fear, but he had never seen Crista sick either. "Call him this morning, Crista."

"I'll be fine." She shook her head as she headed up the stairs, her voice strained.

"Like hell," he muttered, moving behind her and catching up with her as she was pulling the blankets over herself.

Sitting next to her, he touched her forehead. She felt clammy, but she wasn't running a fever. She was pale though, and that worried him.

"It's just a bug." She sighed. "Everyone's sick at the store, Dawg. Just because you can't catch a virus doesn't mean the rest of us can't."

She sounded jealous, and he had to grin. "We'll get you nice and healthy before no time," he promised her. "Just living with me will rub all those good healthy genes off on you."

She snorted at that. "Go away and let me sleep. And you need to check the deliveries this afternoon. Don't forget that."

He frowned. "I'll have Layla's husband check them. I'm staying here with you."

"Hmm." She looked up at him, her gaze sharpening for a moment. "Why are you so upset over that woman staying the night with Natches?"

She didn't sound jealous; she sounded concerned. The question had him rubbing at the back of his neck in irritation.

"She's up to something. That's Timothy Cranston's little pet, Agent Greta Dane. I don't like it."

"Is that all?"

"She's too damned plain," he muttered, knowing she wouldn't understand any more than Rowdy did.

Her lips quirked in amusement. "You're not the one sleeping with her; so why should you care?"

He glared at the dark carpeting on the floor before lifting his gaze back to her. "I don't know. It bothers me."

"She's actually a very pretty girl," Crista told him. "It's not her looks that bother you."

A frown snapped between his brows. "I know a pretty woman when I see one."

And she smiled at that. A smile he didn't quite understand. It was patient and amused and made him grit his teeth.

"You know, it's mothers who are supposed to protest the girl's looks, not fatherly cousins."

Her comment had him staring at her in disbelief.

"You're crazy."

And she shook her head. "You have to let them go sometime, Dawg. Natches is all grown-up now. Let him try his wings a little bit. It might not be as bad as you think." She was on the verge of laughing at him.

"You obviously have a very strange virus," he grunted, put out that she was laughing at him, that she just didn't understand what he didn't understand himself. "Go to sleep."

She didn't protest. She just yawned a little and pulled the blankets closer to her chin. "It's cold in here."

Yeah, maybe it was time to move to the house. He was definitely calling those contractors. Then he was going to make another call and find out just what the hell Agent Dane was doing back in town.

Chaya made sure she spent no more time in her hotel room than she had to. She was betting Natches was a very early riser. She showered, dressed, dried her hair, and pulled it back into a ponytail, and within an hour she was out of there. And not a moment too soon. When she pulled her rented sedan onto the interstate, she swore that she saw Natches's jeep headed toward the hotel.

She glanced at her watch and breathed out roughly. She had an hour to kill before meeting the sheriff at the diner. That was going to be a long hour, considering the fact she had to make certain to avoid running into Natches.

And who the hell was she kidding? An hour later, she pulled into the diner and stared at the wicked black jeep sitting beside the sheriff's cruiser, and clenched the steering wheel of her car.

He was in there, waiting on her. She had run out on him this morning, terrified of what had happened the night before, leaving only a note. At least she had left a note this time, she assured herself. She had told him she would call him this evening, hadn't she?

She jerked her case from the seat beside her and pulled herself out of the car. She forced her chin up, stared around the parking lot, and glimpsed both Rowdy's and Dawg's vehicles as well. Didn't any of those damned Mackay men work? Surely they had something better to do than to harass her this morning?

Evidently they didn't.

As she entered the diner, she flicked a look at the table beside the one Sheriff Mayes was sitting at, and restrained the urge to grimace. Three Mackay men sipping coffee. Rowdy looked amused, Dawg looked pissed, and oh boy, Natches looked ready to hit the damned roof.

Sheriff Mayes, that bastard, didn't even bother to hide his laugh as she walked in.

She moved through the diner, thankful there were very few customers, and stopped in front of Natches. "Are you following me today as well?"

He tipped the glasses he wore lower on his nose and glanced up at her from over the dark lenses. She almost flinched at the anger burning in the forest green depths. He was livid.

"I'm going with you," he stated. "As soon as you tell Mayes over there that's the deal."

Shit. That wasn't the deal. That was expressly—with an unqualified no—forbidden.

"I can't do that, Natches." She forced herself not to show her own nervousness, or a reaction. She couldn't, not here. He would take any weakness and run with it.

"You don't want to do it like this, Chaya," he warned her then, and she could feel her stomach tightening in dread.

"I don't have a choice." She refused to glance at the other two men for their reactions. "This is my job, Natches, and you're no longer a part of that team."

And then he smiled. She could feel her throat going dry, and she swore she could feel her stomach drop with pure female terror. This was one full-grown, pissed-off alpha male, and she was going to pay. She could feel it clear to her bones.

Not painfully. Not in bruises, in blood, or in insults. But, oh boy, was he going to get her for this one.

"Well, Natches, I guess she's not as easy as we all thought she was." Dawg leaned back in his chair and shot her a tight smile. "Natches seemed to think you could see reason, Agent Dane. He even said you were smarter than to say no to him."

She turned her gaze to him, keeping it cool, detached.

"Oh, I see reason quite well, Mr. Mackay," she assured him. "And if I had my preferences, then his company would be welcome. Unfortunately, Special Agent Cranston made his wishes clear before I arrived. And in this case, that prevails."

Natches muttered something uncomplimentary about Cranston that she highly agreed with.

Dawg shook his head, his smile jeering now. "Loyalty, Agent Dane? Where's your loyalty? To your own butt or to those who can watch your back?"

"Enough, Dawg." Natches's voice was hard with warning.

"Let her answer the question, Natches." Dawg held her gaze. "I'd like to hear her answer."

"I'll tell you what." Her smile was benign, emotionless. He didn't like her. He'd never liked her, and she didn't give a damn. "Why don't you go? Then you can share that federal prison with me when Cranston finds out about it. I hear big, tall guys like yourself are really popular there. You're cute, James Mackay. They like cute rednecks with attitude there. Consider them a challenge, you know."

Rowdy snorted, and she could have sworn Sheriff Mayes was choking behind her.

Dawg's eyes narrowed. "You're playing in the big league here, little girl. You don't want to keep this up."

"I said enough, damn it!"

Even Chaya flinched as Natches's hand hit the table and he came halfway out of his chair. She stared at him, shocked, surprised as he and Dawg both seemed to hover over the table, almost nose to nose.

"Watch it, kid," Dawg snarled. "I still remember how to wipe the floor with you."

"And I still remember how to lock both your asses up in the county jail." Sheriff Mayes, his voice hard, commanding, stood by the table now. "Come on, Agent Dane, before you cause these two to fight like the hellions they used to be rather than the grown men I thought they were."

Chaya stared at Natches, amazed, disbelieving as he straightened, his body tense, his expression furious.

"If you get in a fight, I'm not going to be happy with you," she stated coolly.

"About as happy as I am with you right now?" he snapped.

"Try even less so." She lifted her chin a notch and reined in her anger as she turned to Dawg. "And if you don't back down, I'll have a talk with your wife. I have a feeling she's more inclined to act decent than you are at the moment. I wonder how she would feel if she were to find out about this little fiasco this morning?"

"Don't you threaten me with my wife." He glared back at her, but some of the heat seemed to leave his voice.

"Then don't push me, either of you. Because I could get sick of dealing with thick-skulled rednecks really fast. Unlike you, Dawg, I don't bite and snarl; I get to the heart of the problem and the solution. When you're willing to tell me what your problem is, then we'll talk. Until then, stop sniping at Natches, or I'll talk to Crista at first opportunity. Good day, gentlemen."

She turned on her heel, ignoring their surprised looks before joining the sheriff at the door and leaving the diner. And here she had hoped the most she had to deal with was a pissed-off Natches. Now she had a pissed-off Natches, a mad Dawg, and a laughing Rowdy. Her day couldn't get worse.

Dawg sat back down in his chair and scowled at the door while Natches slowly took those damned glasses off and glared at him.

"Son of a bitch, I'm going to kick your ass," Natches cursed.

Dawg sneered back at him. "Yeah right. Go right ahead. You think I didn't see your balls shrink when she gave you that cold little look? You ain't kickin' no one's ass today."

He was pissed. Pure pissed. Son of a bitch, she threatened to tell Crista on him? Like he was a little boy acting bad, and she was threatening to tell Mommy? How the hell old did that mouthy little agent think he was anyway? And he really wanted to beat Natches's ass, too. Snarky little upstart. He never could take advice worth a damn.

"What the hell is your problem?" Natches dug a few bills out of his pocket and slapped them on the table for the coffee. At least he was paying this morning instead of mooching off the rest of them. "Why can't you get the hell off her case?"

"Because she's lying to you," he snarled back, keeping his voice low, anger egging him on. "I don't know what the hell she did to you in Iraq, and I'm getting to where I don't give a damn. But right now, she's lying to you, and those lies could get you killed. And she's fucking plain."

Natches snapped back, blinked, and stared at Dawg as though he didn't know him. He glanced at Rowdy, but Rowdy seemed pretty interested in something he had found on the ceiling and refused to look over. Natches shook his head, as though befuddled.

Watching Natches, Dawg knew he was acting like a damned bastard, and he couldn't help it. Hell, he knew a lie when he saw it, and this whole setup Dane was involved in was a lie.

"Look, Natches, man," he breathed out roughly. "You're getting in over your head. She's up to something; I can fucking feel it.

131

Like an itch at the back of my neck every time I see her. She's trouble, and she's going to get your ass killed."

That was the problem. That gunsight between the eyes thing. Sometimes, Dawg swore he could feel someone with a gunsight between Natches's eyes, taking aim, getting ready to fire. And it was worrying the hell out of him.

"Rowdy, take him home to Crista," Natches said, his voice hard, and that was a bad thing. Natches might shoot him himself now. "Tell her he needs help fast. Before I kill him and make her a widow. Understand me?"

"Sure, I'll get right on that." Rowdy nodded slowly, pulling his gaze from the ceiling to stare at both of them. "While I'm doing that, why don't one of you mosey over across the street and ask Aunt Nadine why the hell she's been watching us all so close through the window from that shop?"

They turned. Across the street, in the wide shop window, stood Nadine, hatred flashing in her expression before she turned and stalked away.

"Shit," Natches cursed. Just what he needed, the damned Mouth of the South running her vicious mouth now.

Dawg muttered something Natches was sure he didn't want to understand, and Rowdy stood slowly to his feet.

"Dawg's right about one thing," he said. "There's trouble here, and it's starting to circle around your Agent Dane. But he's wrong about something, too."

"Yeah? What?" Natches snapped.

"She's not plain. She's actually kinda pretty. Dawg just can't see past Crista. Or his own daddy complex."

With that, he walked away from the table and out of the diner.

Natches sat back down slowly. He still wanted to kick Dawg's ass. He stared back at his cousin and scowled.

Dawg glanced out the window, to his coffee cup, then sighed. "Do you really think she's gonna tell Crista about this?"

And he'd be damned, but Dawg was worried.

EIGHT

"Hello, Mr. Winston. Thank you for agreeing to talk to me." Chaya sat down on a worn, faded couch inside the single-story weathered house on the outskirts of Somerset.

Clayton Winston was a widower, and his son was a traitor. His son, Christopher Winston, had been arrested along with the Swedish mercenary and his merry band of men during the raid on the warehouse containing the stolen missiles.

Mr. Winston was stooped, his face lined with grief and pain. Rheumatoid arthritis had a cruel grip on his joints, and heart disease was draining him fast.

Sheriff Mayes stood on the other side of the room, watching Winston silently, his expression compassionate, somber.

"I didn't raise Chris to be a traitor," the old man sniffed. "He's still my son, but he wasn't right to do that."

He rubbed his grizzled cheek with a shaking hand before taking a handkerchief from his pants pocket and wiping his eyes. Those pale blue eyes were swimming with tears.

"I'd offer you some coffee or something," he told her. "But the cold makes it harder to move in here."

"I'll get the coffee, Clay." Mayes headed for the Spartan kitchen.

"Good man, Sheriff Mayes." Clayton nodded. "Better than his daddy. His daddy was always more concerned with getting elected again than he was with doing what was right. Zeke knows that, too. He makes up for it."

"Don't be talking about me, Clay," Zeke called from the kitchen. "I'll tell Miss Willa on you."

Clayton's smile was sad. "I like to brag on the boy. He's a good boy."

"Sheriff Mayes is a very kind man." Chaya nodded, her heart aching for the man sitting across from her.

Clayton Winston had served two tours in Vietnam. He had a medal for bravery and a file filled with commendations. Chaya's heart broke for him as she thought of the son that had turned his back on the life his father had believed in.

"You wanna talk about Christopher, I guess." His voice roughened. "How's he doin'? They moved him to that place in D.C. where they said I could come visit if I wanted, but I wasn't able to go see him. And he can't take calls." He hunched his shoulders as despair flickered in his gaze.

Chaya's lips parted to answer him when a knock sounded on the door.

"I got it, Clay." Zeke moved from the kitchen, casting Chaya an impatient look as he moved to the door.

"Hey there, Zeke. Fancy seeing you here." Natches pushed

past him and moved into the room. "And Agent Dane. You're looking nice today."

Chaya rose slowly to her feet. "Natches, you're not supposed to be here."

She had to speak between clenched teeth. She couldn't believe he had barged into this interview.

"That's my fault." Clayton's shaking hands reached out to Natches as Natches knelt beside his worn recliner. "I called him when gossip came around you was askin' questions. I asked him to be here."

Chaya's lips thinned. Sitting back down slowly, she glared at Natches. "You didn't mention that to me," she stated, her voice clipped.

"We didn't get a chance to discuss it. You left." The accusation in his voice had her breathing in deeply.

"Natches can stay if that's your choice." She turned back to the old man, watching how he held on to Natches's hand with his gnarled fingers.

"Another good boy with a lousy sire." Clayton's voice trembled. "I used to sneak him sweets when ole Dayle wasn't lookin'."

Chaya watched Natches's face, his eyes. This old man meant something to him, and there were few known people that Natches cared for.

"Natches, get in here and help me with the coffee," Zeke snapped.

"I'll be in the other room, Clay." Natches rose to his feet, staring down at the grizzled, gentle giant who watched him fondly. "I'll hear every word. Okay?"

Clayton nodded as Natches threw Chaya a hard, warning look and moved back into the other room.

"Do you think I'm going to accuse you of anything, Mr. Winston?" she asked him softly. "That's not why I'm here."

His lower lip trembled for the briefest second before he seemed to suck it back in and his shoulders squared.

"Christopher's my boy. What he became, it's on my shoulders, Agent Dane. I realize that. But—" He lowered his head and shook it. "Sometimes I don't think as clear as I used to. I asked Natches if he minded being here to make sure, if I was arrested, that my cat was taken care of."

The cat was curled along the back of the couch and blinked at her lazily. The cat looked as old as Clayton Winston, and as tired.

"I'm not here to arrest you, Mr. Winston, for no reason," Chaya told him gently. "I'm not here to accuse you of anything, because what your son did was his choice. You chose to defend your country, sir. Your son made other choices. I'm trying to find out why he made those choices and who else may have influenced him there. That's all."

From the corner of her eye, she watched as Zeke walked out with two cups. He sat Chaya's coffee cup on the table in front of her. The other, a closed thermal cup, he put in Clayton's hand.

"It's just good and warm, Clay. I put ice in it, just like you like."

Clayton nodded, and Chaya's throat tightened with emotion. She couldn't remember an interview she had ever done that was quite like this one. Natches and Zeke were as protective over this old man as a mother with a child.

"Clayton, I told you Miss Dane would take good care of you," Natches told him from the doorway.

"He did." Clayton nodded. "But I feel better, Natches, with you and Zeke here. If she has to arrest me, then old Hisser here might go hungry; we can't have that." He reached up and stroked the cat's tail as it curled over his shoulder, and Chaya wanted to cry.

"Mr. Winston, I just have a few questions. If you prefer not to answer them, or if Mr. Mackay feels it's not in your best interests to answer them, then I want you to know now that there will be no repercussions. I'm not here to see you hurt further. I merely need to clarify some things and make certain I didn't leave any loose strings."

Clayton nodded to that as he lifted his cup, both hands wrapped around it, and sipped from it.

This man, so patriotic and kind, was facing what had to be his greatest nightmare. The questions Cranston had given her weren't recriminating or accusatory. They were simple—asking about Christopher's friends, if he was part of a hunting group, or if his friends were military. She asked him about his son's teen years, his friendships then. Strangely, he and Johnny Grace hadn't been friends. Yet he had ended up involved with Grace in the theft of those missiles.

"Christopher was always preaching about America and politics and how all this nation lives for is money." Clayton shook his head wearily. "Said we needed a revolution to wake the people up. That boy, he never understood." A tear tracked down his cheek as he stared back at her. "I lost friends and a brother in Vietnam. I was willing to give my life to provide this great nation for him, Agent Dane. Many, many great men shed their blood for my boy, and I never realized how little he appreciated that sacrifice. I raised him wrong. I should be in that cell." His chin wobbled. "Locked away like that, and I can't even hear his voice, see if anything of my boy remains." Another tear fell as Natches moved forward and took the thermal cup before Clayton dropped it. "I didn't teach him right," he whispered. "And I'm sorry about that."

Chaya had to blink back her own tears. Ignoring Natches and Zeke, she reached out, covered the old man's hand, and waited until he could focus on her.

"Mr. Winston, your sacrifices and the sacrifices of your friends ensured his choice. What he did with that choice is on his shoulders, sir, not on yours."

"You believe that?" he whispered.

"I believe that with all my heart. You, sir, are, and have been, one of our nation's greatest assets."

"You're not going to arrest me?" he asked then.

"Not in a million years," she whispered. "But I am going to arrange that phone call for you. I promise you that. I'll make sure you get to talk to your son."

It wasn't for the son, who she'd just as soon see flayed alive. It was for the father. The soldier who had saved countless others, who had given all but his life for the freedom his son had never cherished.

Clayton blinked and his eyes filled with tears again. "I'd like that," he whispered. "Just for a minute. To hear my boy's voice."

She nodded to that and rose, making another promise to herself. When this was over, if he could make the trip, if he wanted the trip, she would make certain he got to see his son. And she would make damned sure that son showed him the respect this man deserved.

"She's a good girl, just like you said, Natches." Winston looked up at Natches, a shaky smile crossing his lips. "Don't you let this one get away. She's tough enough to put up with you."

"That she is, Clay." He gripped the other man's shoulder gently as he stared back at her, and she didn't want to feel the warmth that bloomed through her at that look. "That she is."

Chaya straightened and nodded, heading for the door.

"Agent Dane."

She turned back to Clayton as Natches moved aside behind her. "Yes, sir."

He frowned, his rheumy eyes thoughtful as he rubbed at his whiskered chin. "I just thought—Christopher, he wasn't friends with Johnny a'tall. Or that Bedsford fella. But he mentioned some friends once, called 'em by something. Called 'em his compatriots, said they were starting their own club or some such stuff. Freedom boys or something. I don't remember right off."

"If you remember, could you contact me? Just let the sheriff know, and I'll come right over."

He nodded to that. "I'll think on it. See what I remember."

"Good-bye, Mr. Winston."

"And you'll remember to get that phone call for me?" His voice was filled with hope. "Just for a minute. Just so I can hear his voice one more time."

She was going to cry. Oh God, don't let her cry here, in front of this proud old man.

"Department of Homeland Security will be contacting you to-morrow, Mr. Winston. I promise."

He nodded again, reached for his coffee cup, and brought it to his shaking lips. She wanted to howl at the unfairness of it, and she couldn't. All she could do was walk out the door and move to the sheriff's car.

"I'm going to stick around and make sure Clay gets dinner."

Natches caught her arm and pulled her to a stop. "I'll see you tonight."

She shook her head. "Not tonight."

"Like hell. Tonight, Chay, and that's final. I didn't know Miss Willa wasn't coming over here every evening to take care of Clay's dinner, and I have to fix that now. But you can bet on the fact you will be seeing me this evening."

She pulled away from him and followed Zeke to his car, getting in and slamming the door behind her as she continued to fight her tears. She would rather interrogate a roomful of terrorists than ever have to face that old man with so much as one more question regarding his son.

She was losing it. There was a time when she could have questioned him and pushed back her sympathy, her compassion. It was what she had been trained to do. She was an interrogation specialist. She knew how to do her job without worrying about the consequences.

At least, she used to know how.

"One more to go," Zeke said as he got in the car and looked over at her. "I believe it's the widowed mother of another of those boys."

She nodded. A man who had paid his mother's bills, bought her food, and took care of her, and now his mother was suffering.

Her fingers curled into a fist, and fury spiked hard and hot inside her.

"No. We're finished for the day."

Zeke paused as he slid the car into gear. "It won't be any easier tomorrow, Agent Dane. Trust me, I can tell you that one for a fact."

She stared out the window, ignoring her own reflection, afraid of what she might see. She knew tomorrow wouldn't be any easier.

"I've interrogated dozens of terrorists. I've interrogated suspects' families. I've been a bitch and remembered what I was fighting for, for years now." She was twenty-eight years old. She had come into Army Intelligence right after boot camp and worked her way up. She knew what she was doing, she knew how to do it, and she couldn't stand the thought of one more parent forced to face the choices his child had made.

"Yeah, I hear you're real good at your job," he murmured.

"Am I?" she whispered, refusing to look at him as he pulled out of the driveway.

The yard around the Winston house was overgrown. Clayton Winston's only son used to keep it mowed and trimmed. The trees needed trimming, and there was no one to do that now.

"You know, you didn't make the choices those boys made any more than Clay did," Zeke told her as they headed away from the house. "It's our job to stop them, your job to make sure we stop all of them. It might hurt like hell; it might cut us up until nothing helps but a shot of whiskey and a tear or two. But we do what we have to do."

"For as long as we can stand to do it," she said softly. "Take me back to my car, Sheriff. I told you; I'm finished for the day."

She returned to her hotel and ordered a bottle of wine. She showered and changed into a robe and curled up on the couch, where she put in a call to Cranston. Two hours later, suffering the effects of a furious, heated argument over the phone call she had promised Clayton Winston, she'd arranged it. At noon the next day, he would have ten minutes with his son.

The bastard. Christopher didn't deserve to hear his father's voice. Didn't deserve to know that the man who had lost a brother and countless friends in the service of his country still loved him.

It would bring Christopher Winston more comfort than it would bring his father, but even a small amount of comfort was reason enough.

And what of the widow? she asked herself. What was she going to promise her? What about the wife and two small children of another man they had taken? A man with a promising career, who had laid it all on the line to betray his country.

She pushed her fingers through her hair and fought the scream welling in her throat. What about those children who had lost their daddy and didn't understand why? The wife whose eyes were haunted in the surveillance pictures, who hid in her home and tried to ignore the gossip swirling in this small town?

She rose to her feet and paced to the window. She stared out at the darkness falling over the mountains, the lights of the city around her, and she could feel the tears inside her.

When had she ever cared before? The men they had arrested had made their own decisions, yet she was beating herself up over the fact that she had to question their families.

It wasn't those men facing the consequences of what they had done to their families, staring into their haunted eyes. It was her. Her and the people who had loved them.

As she stood there, she heard the door to the suite open. Through the reflection in the glass, she watched as Natches entered the room, and she had to clench her teeth to hold back a sob.

His expression was somber as he crossed the room, his gaze dark, concerned.

She expected him to castigate her for questioning Clayton Winston. For making his pain worse. Instead, she was shocked as he came to her and turned her against his chest.

"It's okay to cry, Chay," he whispered at her ear. "Clayton wouldn't think less of you for it. And neither would I."

She shook her head, but she felt the tears building in her chest. Crying didn't help. It wouldn't bring back Clayton Winston's pride in his son, and it wouldn't ease the pain of a widowed mother or a family damaged by betrayal.

This beautiful town. These people that she had somehow let into her heart right along with Natches were tearing her apart.

"He deserved better," she whispered, holding on to Natches, desperate to find some way now to control the emotions she didn't know how to handle. "This is why I hate you," she cried out. "I get around you, and I start feeling. I start laughing over two nitwits who broke into your apartment because they thought I was going to somehow hurt you. I cry over old men who deserved better but are a whole lot better off knowing the truth. And I start aching for things I never needed before. I hate you for this."

She was shaking in his arms, felt them tighten around her as she dug her nails into his back and held on for dear life.

"You love me, Chay," he whispered against her hair, his voice quiet and deep. Secure. Damn him, he was always so secure, always so confident, and at this moment she felt as though she was struggling just to hold on to reality.

"You make me feel too much," she whispered. "Make it stop, Natches."

Make the pain go away.

She shook her head against his chest and jerked away from him.

"I didn't mean that." She had done that to him once before, asked him to take away the pain. She had never forgotten the way he had looked at her. The regret in his eyes, the sorrow. Because it wasn't him she was asking for; it was solace.

"Chay, come back here." He pulled her back to him, one hand holding her head to his chest as his arm wrapped around her. "Do you think I mind being your shield against the world, or the pain?" He tipped her head back, forced her to look at him, and her vision blurred with tears. "Sweetheart, my shoulders are broad enough for your tears, your fists, or those sharp little teeth. However you need to hold on to me. I'm here."

"What about you?" Her voice shook now, almost as badly as Clayton Winston's had trembled earlier. "Always a shield and never shielded, Natches?"

He chuckled at that, his gaze gentle. "Is that what you think?" He touched her cheek, ran his thumb over her lips. "That I have no shield? Don't you know, Chay? You've been my shield since the day I met you, whether you were here or not. The memory of your laughter, your tears, the memory of your touch and your kiss. You changed me, Chay, and I think it's only fair that I'm changing you as well."

Changing her, and that change was destroying her. Before he could say anything more, before the tears welling inside her could fall, she reached up, grabbed his head, and fought for his kiss.

She needed this. She needed to feel him burning inside her, just one more time, because she could feel parts of herself unraveling that she didn't know how to handle.

She was being attacked by emotions she had promised herself since she was a girl she would never feel. All her life, she had maintained distance, but distance wasn't possible with Natches.

He lifted her off her feet as his lips controlled the kiss despite her battle to lead it. He chuckled at her attempts to nip his lips, and nipped hers in turn. He slanted his lips over hers, pushed his tongue inside, and lit a fire in her that she knew would burn her to ashes.

She was tearing at his clothes as he laid her on the bed and stripped her of her robe. She couldn't get him undressed fast enough.

She fought him as he wrestled her to the bed, his lips and tongue burning over one nipple, then the other. He sucked one into his mouth, lashed at it with heated licks of his tongue, and filled her with passion.

She had never known passion until Natches. She had never known this heat, this fire that became a void of loneliness and loss when she walked away from him.

How had she ever walked away?

She twisted beneath him, gasping, crying his name.

"I need . . ." She arched as his teeth raked the hardened peak, and he growled against it. "I need you, Natches."

"I'm right here, Chay." His voice was deep, rough. It grated across her senses and made the pleasure deeper, hotter. Because she knew he felt it. Knew he was as lost in it as she was.

"Now." Her head tossed against the mattress as he held her in place, his lips sipping at her flesh, his tongue licking it. "Don't make me wait."

His hand cupped between her thighs, heated, calloused flesh meeting swollen, wet folds.

She arched and cried out as two fingers thrust inside her, throwing her higher, deeper into the maelstrom overtaking her.

And she let it have her. She let him have her. She arched, pulling at his shoulders, feeling him come to her. Thick and hard, his erection worked inside her, stretching her, easing her, building sensation and emotion into a kaleidoscope of color and pleasure.

When he was buried to the hilt, his breath rasping, his expression twisted in lines of hunger, she felt his desperation to meld with her inside her very pores.

"Hold on to me, sweetheart." He shifted and knelt in front of her, gripping her hips and pulling her to him until her rear rested on his thighs, his cock buried full length inside her.

Her hands grabbed his wrists as his smile, strained with need, seared into her brain.

"You hold on tight now," he crooned. "I'm going to make you scream."

He braced his hands beside her on the bed as her legs curled around his hips. And he began to move. Hard, driving thrusts that buried his flesh inside of her. Again. Again. Sending lightning crashing across her nerve endings, fire building in her womb.

She held on and, as he promised, she screamed. She exploded around him, her back bending, her hands gripping his wrists, and heard his cry echoing around her. Heated warmth filled her as he began to ejaculate, deep, fierce throbs of his release sending her arching into more pleasure.

He destroyed her. And he remade her. And when the final tremors eased, he pulled her into his arms as a tear fell from her eye. Just one tear, she told herself. She could afford to shed just one.

And that one tear seemed to last forever.

NINE

Rebuilding her defenses against Natches wasn't going to work. He bullied her into returning to the houseboat for dinner with him, then he made certain she was too exhausted to return to her hotel that night.

She fell asleep in his arms, drained emotionally and physically, and knowing that if she wasn't very careful, Natches Mackay could destroy her.

The next morning, as she had the morning before, she slipped out of his bed and off the boat. Her cab was waiting at the marina office, and as she opened the back door and glanced behind her, she saw him. Standing on the top deck of the *Nauti Dreams*, fog whispering around him, his chest bare. She wondered for a second why she bothered to try to run. And why it was so damned hard to face him after the wild loving he gave her.

It was a problem that followed her through the day, just as Natches followed her from one interview to another.

The first two interviews didn't matter. They were surface tests, no more. Former friends of Johnny Grace who had already been cleared in the investigation. But she had to make it look good. Timothy had an idea of who was of major concern, and as the day progressed, Chaya became more nervous over that particular interview.

Because Natches was following them in his black jeep, watching her, always there.

As they pulled into the driveway of Nadine Grace's home at about three o'clock that afternoon, Chaya felt like drying her sweating palms on her jeans before getting out of the car.

"You sure about this?" Sheriff Mayes stared at the house, his expression concerned, before glancing at her. "Johnny was her son. The only person in this town she really liked. She's not going to be polite."

Oh, there was someone else in town Nadine had liked, and the thought of it sickened Chaya.

"I'm not here to win a popularity contest, Sheriff," she told him as she gripped her briefcase and opened the car door. "I'm just here to get answers."

"And rile the Mackay cousins up?" he asked as he exited the vehicle. "I ain't seen those two as pissed off at each other as they were yesterday morning in years. I'll end up having to lock them up tonight if they get into a public brawl."

She flicked him a disagreeable look. "They're not going to fight."

"And how do you know this? They nearly tore up that diner about two years ago or so. I had them in a cell for a weekend, and trust me, that's not pleasant."

She rolled her eyes. "To start with, Dawg's not going to risk making his wife that angry. And Natches wasn't nearly mad enough to fight yet. Dawg won't push him that far either."

Mayes shot her a disbelieving look but didn't say anything more as the front door jerked open.

"Zeke. That's a Mackay whore, and I don't want her on my property." Nadine Grace's pretty face was twisted in fury, her green eyes blazing with rage. "Get her out of here."

Slender, still attractive at fifty, and filled with anger, the other woman glared daggers at Chaya.

"I wish I could, Mrs. Grace." Zeke sighed, glancing at Chaya as she stared back at the other woman coolly.

"Mrs. Grace, I'm Agent Greta Dane, Department of Homeland Security." She pulled her badge folder from her jacket and flashed the ID at the other woman. "Mackay whore isn't my title today. Catch me tonight though, and you might hit it right."

Nadine's nostrils flared as though picking up a disgusting scent. "Get off my property."

"Sheriff," Chaya said to Mayes. "Please have Mrs. Grace detained and brought to your office. We'll change this from an interview to an interrogation. I'll call the main office and apprise them of the situation." She didn't take her eyes off Nadine Grace.

"Now, Agent Dane, we don't want to do that." He sighed.

"Of course we do." She smiled tightly. "If she doesn't want to cooperate, then I don't have to be nice. Do I?"

The other woman was nearly shaking with rage now. Her gaze was spitting fury, her face pale with it.

"Nadine, just a few minutes of your time, and then we can leave," Sheriff Mayes assured her. "Agent Dane has a few questions. That's all."

The woman was going to crack her jaw, she was clenching it so hard.

"You have ten minutes." She turned away from the door, her dark blue dress swishing about her legs as she stalked into the house.

Chaya stepped inside, instantly shivering at the stark white walls and furniture. The place looked like an ice cave, there was so much white.

"Take your damned shoes off," Nadine snapped, glaring at them from the living room as she took a seat on the white sofa.

Chaya glanced at the sheriff before putting her briefcase down and tugging off her boots. Mayes followed suit, but clearly didn't like it.

She padded into the living room and took the chair facing Nadine as she pulled a recorder from her case and laid it on her knee. Nadine spared a look at the small device, her lips curling into a sneer.

Chaya turned it on, stated the date and time.

"For the record, you're Nadine Mackay Grace, mother to Johnny Grace," she stated, then stared back at Nadine.

"I am," she snapped.

"Mrs. Grace, were you aware, at the time, that your son, Johnathon Ralph Grace, was involved in terrorist activities?"

Nadine's eyes narrowed. "He was not. Johnny wasn't involved in anything of the sort."

"There's clear evidence that he not only masterminded the theft of several government missiles and guidance chips, but he also murdered the driver transporting those missiles. He contracted and brokered the sale of those missiles. He shot and killed Jim Bedsford, his lover and partner, and attempted to kill Crista

Jansen. Were you aware of those activities before or during the time they were taking place?"

Nadine was breathing roughly, her fists clenched on her knees, her face splotching with a furious flush. She wasn't nearly as pretty now as she had been when they had entered the house.

"I don't have to answer these ridiculous questions," she snarled.

"We can answer them here, or we can answer them under more formal settings," Chaya told the other woman. "If you would like to contact your lawyer, we can Mirandize you and take you into the sheriff's office for interrogation. Why waste time, Mrs. Grace?"

"My son did none of that," Nadine retorted, her voice harsh. "Those cousins of his, they did it all and they framed him. Those bastards made it look like he did it so they could kill him."

And Nadine knew better. She was lying through her teeth. Chaya stared back at her silently, her eyes holding the other woman's for long seconds before Nadine looked away and pretended to blink back tears.

What was she lying about though?

"Mrs. Grace, were you aware of the theft of those missiles at any time before your son was killed?"

"No." She shook with fury as she answered the question, but once again, she couldn't hold Chaya's gaze. She turned to the sheriff. "Isn't this enough yet?"

Chaya ignored Mayes and continued to stare at Nadine until the other woman glanced back at her.

"Did Johnny tell you where the money he gained on deposit of those missiles was hidden?"

"No." Like an animal, Nadine's lips curled back from her teeth and her eyes glittered with malicious glee.

"Who would he have told?"

"No one. He didn't do it."

"You're saying the Mackay cousins framed him?"

"That's exactly what happened." Nadine's teeth snapped together.

"Why would they do that, Mrs. Grace?"

"They always hated Johnny. He was always smarter; he always did what was right. They hated him for it."

"Was James Dawg Mackay aware Johnny was also the biological son of his father, your brother Chandler Mackay?"

"That's a *lie*." Nadine nearly screamed the word, hatred burning hard and bright in her eyes.

Chaya watched her carefully now. "Mrs. Grace, we have a recorded statement of your son bragging about those crimes. Just as he admitted to being the son of Chandler Mackay, your deceased brother. DNA testing from blood collected after his death and compared to James Mackay's, proves this to be the case. Are you stating, for the record, that your son was not conceived in an incestuous relationship between yourself and your deceased brother, Chandler Mackay?"

This was the part Chaya hated. The part she had argued and fought Cranston over for days before leaving for Somerset.

Nadine was silent. She drew in a hard, deep breath.

"I want to call my lawyer now," she stated.

Chaya flipped off the recorder and placed it back in her briefcase before standing. Sheriff Mayes followed suit, his expression granite hard as he glanced at Nadine Grace, then to Chaya.

"You do that, Mrs. Grace," Chaya told her softly. "And when you do, perhaps you had better warn him to advise you on your rights should you lie under oath. Because the next time we question you, you will be under oath."

"There won't be a next time," Nadine spat back at her.

Chaya smiled and walked back to the front door, where she put her boots back on before straightening and staring back at the other woman.

"There will be a next time, Mrs. Grace. I'd contact that lawyer if I were you. You're going to need him."

She didn't give the other woman time to protest but stepped out of the house and moved toward the sheriff's cruiser. Natches was still sitting on the other side of the street, staring at her, his expression hard but thoughtful as she and the sheriff got back into the cruiser.

"Would you like to tell me what the hell was going on in there?" Sheriff Mayes asked her carefully, coldly. "No matter what he did, Agent Dane, she was still his mother. And you showed no respect for that."

No, she hadn't, and it didn't sit well with her, but she knew Timothy's suspicions and she knew the evidence he had amassed so far. At this point, she couldn't afford to worry about respect.

"Sometimes, Sheriff, we all have to do things we don't particularly like, as you reminded me yesterday," she finally answered, glancing at him as he reversed out of the driveway and passed Natches's jeep. "Have you ever had to arrest a friend? Did the fact that he was your friend sway you from your sworn duty to arrest him?"

He spared her a brief, flinty glance. "No, it did not."

"The fact that she's a mother can't sway me from mine, and there's a difference between her and Clayton Winston," she informed him. "Johnny Grace killed an innocent soldier, stole those missiles and their guidance chips, and negotiated a rather low price for them. The money is missing, and pertinent information regarding the whole deal is missing. He had another partner. Nadine Grace was lying for her son; Clayton Winston didn't. And I want to know what she was lying about."

"And you think it was his mother helping him?" He clearly didn't think it was, but then neither did she.

"What I think doesn't matter. I have a clear set of questions for each person I'm interviewing. Those recordings will be transferred to DHS, where they will be gone over by the experts there and determinations made as to who will be pulled into formal interrogation. DHS won't let this go."

Sheriff Mayes wasn't stupid. He wasn't letting it go either, but he clearly wasn't saying anything more.

"Who's next on your little list then?" he finally asked.

"Wenden Frakes," she answered.

"Shit," he breathed out. "Johnny's uncle."

"Ralph Grace's half brother." She nodded.

"Just what I need," he growled as he made another turn and hit the interstate. "Wenden Frakes pissed off. That's just gonna round out my day."

Wenden Frakes wasn't pissed off. And he didn't end up pissed off. He was feeding cattle when they arrived and agreed to talk to them after a careful silence.

His answers were cautiously worded, his expression disagreeable, but he didn't give them any trouble. Didn't like that little bastard Johnny, he declared. Everyone knew he was Chandler Mackay's kid because everyone knew Nadine Grace was doing the nasty with her brothers. Not just one brother, he stated, but both Chandler and Dayle Mackay.

When they left the Frakes farm, the sheriff heaved a hard sigh. "We're going to the Mackay Marina, aren't we?"

Chaya almost felt sick inside. "I don't have a choice, Sheriff."

Sheriff Mayes shook his head. "I sure hope you know what you're doing."

She didn't. She only knew the list, the questions, and the vague sense of disquiet slowly stealing over her. Timothy had plotted out each person to question and the order of the interviews. He knew something; he was pushing someone, and she just couldn't figure out whom. She knew she was growing more and more concerned though. And by the look Natches had flashed them as they passed him, he was growing angrier with each visit they made today.

As the sheriff turned into the Mackay Marina, Chaya drew in a slow, control-restoring breath. Natches had guessed where they were headed, too, because there was Rowdy Mackay at the front of the marina office, his wife standing beside him.

They watched as she and the sheriff stepped from the car and Natches drew the jeep into the parking space beside them. Chaya paused. She had no intention of fighting him over this one.

"What are you doing, Chaya?" His voice was harder now, suspicious.

"My job." Turning to him, she tried to push past the ache in her chest as she saw the suspicion in his eyes. "They're just questions, Natches. That's all. I swear."

"Why?"

"Clarifications. Making certain DHS has everything. Timothy isn't targeting Ray Mackay; I can promise you that much."

"Who is he targeting?" Ice formed in his tone.

She shook her head, aware of the sheriff watching them in interest. "I don't know. All I have are the questions. That's all."

156

He didn't say anything for a long moment. His arms crossed over his chest as he glanced to the marina, then back to her. "Just questions? Or accusations?"

"Questions, Natches. And the questions aren't in the least accusatory."

He glanced to the marina office again, and she followed his gaze. Ray Mackay stepped outside, his broad form powerful, his gaze piercing, and his expression confident. Everything about him the same as she remembered from the year before. This was the man who had practically raised Natches, the man who had sheltered him through what had obviously been a hell of a childhood.

"He's a good man," she said softly, turning back to the angry man watching her. "I would never take that from him. And I wouldn't let Cranston do it either—not without warning you first. Not without fighting him every breath of the way."

He finally nodded, his arms uncrossing before his fingers curved around her arm and he walked her to the marina.

"You young fools." As they reached him on the stoop, Ray shook his head before smiling back at Chaya. "Nadine's done called everyone in the county, spitting out poison. I figured you'd be here sometime today."

"Hello, Mr. Mackay." She extended her hand in greeting, pleased when he took it in a firm grip. "I just have a few questions if I may. Alone, please."

"Not a chance in hell," Rowdy objected.

"Son, I don't need you watching my back." Ray glared back at his son with fatherly reproof. "Put your back down, and keep Natches and the sheriff here company. Me and Miss Dane here will just have a little chat in the office."

"Damn it, Dad—"

"And don't curse in front of the women. I taught you better than that." Ray glared back at him before turning to Chaya and inviting her into the marina office. "Come on in, Agent Dane. These boys can stand out here in the sun and let off some steam while we talk. It's the best thing for them."

She liked him. She had liked him the year before, the few times she had seen him. He was protective of his son and his nephews. He had protected them as well as he could when they were children, and he continued to do so after they were grown.

Ray Mackay, for all intents and purposes, didn't have just one son, he had three.

"Right back here." He opened the office door as his wife stood by worriedly. "Maria just made fresh coffee. Would you like some?"

"No thank you." She felt like slime as she took the seat he offered her and waited as he closed the door and moved behind his desk.

Then he was staring back at her with too-perceptive blue eyes and a concerned expression. "You're sure making a mess of my boys." He sighed. "I heard Dawg and Natches almost came to blows at the diner yesterday. And Natches is fit to be tied right now."

Chaya nodded. "I know. It couldn't be helped."

Ray Mackay was what Chaya had always thought a father should be. At fifty-nine, he was trim, his hair black and silver, his face weathered. And kind. He had a kind face, and that just made her feel worse.

She pulled the recording device from her briefcase hesitantly.

"I need to record this," she told him.

He nodded in agreement.

She turned the machine on, stated the date and time, and looked up at him. "Your name is Raymond Douglas Mackay. You were Johnny Grace's uncle. Brother to his mother as well as to Chandler Mackay."

"I am." He nodded.

She swallowed tightly. "Were you at any time aware of Johnny Grace's illegal activities here in Somerset or outside the county?" She watched his eyes, and he didn't turn from her, didn't flinch.

"No, ma'am, I didn't know Johnny was capable of such activities."

She nodded to that.

"Mr. Mackay, as stated by Johnny Grace, he's the half brother to his cousin James Mackay. A product of the incestuous relationship between his mother and her brother Chandler Mackay. Did you know this?"

"I suspected a time or two," he said softly. "My brothers and sister weren't my concern after I left my mother's home, Agent Dane. I lived my life, and I stayed out of theirs."

She nodded again.

"Would his mother be capable of aiding him in those illegal activities?" she asked him.

"His mother would have aided the devil himself if it meant destroying Dawg. If it meant destroying any of those boys outside there. She hated them. Even more than Dawg's and Natches's fathers hated them."

"Was she also sleeping with her brother Dayle Mackay? Would he have aided her and/or her son in those activities?"

Ray stared back at her silently for long moments. "I'd like to say no," he finally said.

"But?"

"But I learned with Johnny that nothing is impossible. Honestly, I wouldn't know, Agent Dane. Dayle's ex-Marine, always seemed damned patriotic to me. He preaches about it, argues politics, and votes in every election. Hates foreigners, and my first thought would be he'd never betray his country. But after Johnny . . ." He shook his head. "What the hell do I know?"

"There's a million dollars in cash missing, and connections Johnny or Jim Bedsford couldn't have had aided in the near sale of those missiles, Mr. Mackay. Who would have helped him?"

Ray scratched his cheek as he thought, then finally shook his head. "I just don't know. Things like this don't happen around here, Agent Dane. Somerset is a quiet little town, and this whole thing . . ." He shook his head again. "It's spooked a lot of folks. Hell, I think it spooked me."

"Wenden Frakes, Ralph Grace's half brother, says Johnny spent a lot of time on the lake last summer. Did he use any of the boats off your marina?"

"Not one of my mine." He shook his head firmly. "I didn't let Johnny Grace rent out my boats for no reason. He had a tendency to tear them up. Those boats are hard to replace. Besides, Dayle had a boat he kept out at his cabin farther up the lake. Johnny used it some, I think."

She nodded again and flipped off the recorder. She had what she needed here.

"Thank you, Mr. Mackay," she said when he stared back at her in surprise. "I know the questions weren't comfortable, and I apologize for that. They weren't questions I chose; I want you to know that."

Ray leaned back in his chair then and watched her with the

narrow-eyed intent of a man who knew people and, sometimes, knew them too well.

"Dawg says you're cold," he stated then, surprising her. "That you're just using Natches for whatever DHS has going on here. Is that true?"

Chaya slid the recorder back in her case before lifting her eyes to Ray. She let him hold her gaze, just as he had allowed her to hold his. "Natches is my weakness, Mr. Mackay," she finally admitted. "And he doesn't take no for an answer sometimes."

"That doesn't answer my question," he said, his voice gentle as he smiled back at her. "Are you using my nephew, Agent Dane?"

"No, Mr. Mackay. I'm trying to protect your nephew."

And to that, he nodded slowly. "And I believe you. Now I think you have some bridges to repair outside. Rowdy's got a slow burn. He doesn't do mad easy, but he's getting close to mad. Dawg is ready to fight. And Natches will stand between them and you, but I'd hate to see that happen. Fix it, if you don't mind."

"And I'm supposed to do that how?"

"By being honest, Miss Dane. As honest as you can be. Those three boys ain't no one's dummies, no matter what that Cranston fellow wants to think. And after today, they're going to block you unless you're smart enough to work with them."

"And if that threatens Natches?" she asked softly.

"Then now's the time to warn him." He rose from his seat and watched her with that fatherly look that demanded action. The right action. "Let him help you, Miss Dane. You'd be amazed how easy he can be to get along with then."

And he was right. She couldn't tell them the truth, because even she didn't know the whole truth. But she could tell them enough to perhaps get them to back down. Because they had to back down, just for a little while longer.

He stared at the caller ID on the phone before answering it, his jaw clenching in anger.

"Yes?"

"They were here." Nadine's voice was shaking with fury. "We have to do something now."

His lips thinned. "Settle down. Now's not the time to do anything, peanut. We sit back and let her ask her questions. She can't hurt us."

"She knows something," Nadine hissed. "I could tell. And she'll get what she needs. If she finds out, she'll fry us."

"If you don't calm down, you'll fry us. You don't know anything, remember that. Johnny was a good boy and you're his mother. Period."

"They recorded Johnny bragging about belonging to Chandler. They did DNA tests. That bastard Dawg gave them blood and they matched it. They know it's the truth. If they keep digging, they'll find the connection."

Now that piece of information was worrisome. He hadn't expected that. He'd managed to keep that information buried for too many years, he didn't like it coming out now. Didn't it just figure that Johnny had to brag? As though it were something to brag over.

"The connection is hidden, peanut. Take one of your pills and calm down. As soon as I can I'll be there and we'll talk. We'll figure this out. Until then, remember, they can't get anything unless you tell them." He hoped.

"Do something," she whispered. "You have to do something

before they question anyone else. They've already been to Wenden's and Ray's. If they keep digging, they could dig up something else."

If Johnny had revealed the truth about Chandler, God only knew what else he had let out. He grimaced at the thought of that. Hell, he had thought Johnny was smarter than that. He hated being wrong.

"I'll be there as soon as I can," he promised her again. "If they show up again, don't answer the door. Pretend you aren't home. I'll check into things and I'll have something when I get there."

He heard her breathing, heard the little sigh of relief.

"Will you stay the night this time?" she asked then, that little whisper of hope bringing a smile to his lips.

"I'll try to arrange it. I'll call you when I'm coming. Promise you'll stay calm, peanut."

"I promise. Until you get here."

"Until I get there."

He disconnected the phone, tapped his finger against it thoughtfully and began to make plans. It was sooner than he liked, but it was time to start cleaning things up.

TEN

Natches caught her as she came out of the marina office. His fingers latched around her arm and before she could do more than breathe a protest he began dragging her toward the *Nauti Dreams*.

He had no idea what the hell was going on here, but he was getting ready to find out. She wanted to question the rest of the damned town, that was fine and dandy by him, but when she started questioning family, then he expected answers.

And when she started dealing with that rattler Nadine, then he sure as hell expected those answers to be forthcoming.

"I don't like being dragged around like a child, Natches," she told him as he pulled her onto the deck of the boat and unlocked the door.

He pulled her into the houseboat, slammed the sliding door closed behind him, then stalked to the kitchen for a beer.

All shit aside, he'd seen a new side of Chaya today. For the first time, this morning, he'd seen the agent. Steel eyed, her demeanor cold, she refused to back down. And rather than turning him off as it should have, it had made him hard. Because he knew the woman underneath, liquid hot and burning for him alone. Dawg called her plain, and he'd wanted to smash his cousin's face in for the comment despite the fact that he knew, had seen, the metamorphosis she somehow managed to undergo.

The agent, with her hair slicked back into a ponytail, her eyes cold and hard, her expression emotionless, blended into the background for most people. Not plain, but easily passed by for some reason. Natches had always seen the woman beneath that look though, because he knew her, in all her expressions, in many of her moods, and he knew there was nothing plain about her.

She was complex, complicated, and sometimes too damned sharp to suit him. And she was good at hiding. Hiding herself as well as her secrets.

He turned back to her after downing half the bottle of beer he'd pulled from the refrigerator, remaining silent as he watched her.

Dressed in jeans because she knew they made folks more comfortable and a light sweater beneath a dark blazer. And those boots. Those boots made her legs look longer, made them sexier. The gray sweater brought the soft golden highlights in her eyes free, and softened her delicate face.

And when she crossed her arms over her breasts and glared back at him, his cock throbbed in anticipation.

"The Mackays are going to have to keep their noses out of

this," she snapped. "You and Dawg following me around town all day, then showing up here. What the hell did you think I was going to do anyway? For God's sake, Natches, you know how an investigation works. There are questions afterward, loose ends to tie up and, considering there's a million dollars missing and possible co-conspirators, facts to find. You don't just drop a case like this."

He didn't say anything. He finished the beer, tossed it in the trash and narrowed his eyes on her once again.

And it infuriated her. He could see the mad rising in her eyes. The distant expression he referred to as her "agent face" began to peel away. A light flush worked over her cheeks, her lips lost that thin, cool little line and the lower curve became almost lush, definitely sensual.

Here came his Chaya, the woman.

"Timothy's playing a very neat little game," he said then. "I can see it in every move you're making and I know you can, too. He gave you orders I'm not to accompany you on these interviews? Have you asked yourself why?"

"Probably because you're too damned nosy and you don't know how to stand down," she muttered.

He almost grinned at the accusation.

"Because he knows he's going to be poking in my business," he informed her. "Whatever the hell he has going on here is going to piss me off and he doesn't want me to know about it until he has no other choice."

"This does not concern Ray Mackay, Natches," she told him again, and he saw the truth in her, felt it. "Are you going to go off the deep end when I question Dawg? Rowdy? What about Crista Mackay? Are the Mackay cousins going to close rank against me then?"

He paused and stared back at her. Is that what she really expected? That he would side with his cousins, with anyone, against her? Hell, he had risked his damned hide for her in Iraq, not just once but twice. Did she think he would do any less for her here?

"I have a job to do, Natches. I don't have the option you chose last year of telling Timothy Cranston to get fucked. And to be honest, this time, I don't want that option. I want to know who the hell thought they could get away with murdering that kid that drove the transport vehicle. I want to know how Johnny Grace got away with nearly killing Dawg's woman. And I want to know why the hell this little town is suddenly a beehive of terrorist activity."

His brows almost arched at that statement. The last year, he and Dawg had admittedly been concentrating on their own lives. Had they somehow managed to miss something going on that they should have seen?

"I haven't seen many terrorists this week, Chay," he finally stated, tilting his head and watching her curiously. "Is there something here that I should know?"

She inhaled slowly. "Last year you had nearly a dozen terrorists near or around Somerset. The Swede that laid that down payment on those missiles wasn't a happy little camper after his arrest, and he has friends. Friends who most likely are sitting right here just waiting to see who they should target to get that money back. A million dollars is a hell of a lot of money, Natches, even in today's economy."

His brow arched. "That was one of your flimsier excuses," he told her. "Try again."

Chaya stared back at him, recognizing the slow, lazy drawl as it passed his lips. It wasn't what he said, it was how he said it. It was the dangerous throb of suspicion just beneath the careless tone, the warning that he wasn't buying whatever she was selling. And she had warned Timothy he wouldn't. No matter the truth of it, Natches knew there was more going on. Somehow, the list of names she had interviewed today, in that little group, she had managed to tip Natches off, and it wasn't just her questioning of Ray Mackay.

"Someone in Somerset was helping Johnny," she told him. "Someone who had more contacts than Jim Bedsford could have managed. Bedsford was a front, Natches, nothing more. Someone else was pulling the strings."

He leaned against the low counter, crossed his arms over his chest and stared back at her with those frighteningly observant eyes of his. Sometimes, she swore he could see clear down to her soul with those dark green eyes.

"What's your proof?"

"Bedsford's contacts couldn't have gotten him and the Swede together last year for that missile deal. That group doesn't deal with penny-ante thieves. They're too slick for that no matter how impressive the merchandise. Someone else brokered that deal, someone from Somerset. Someone Timothy's been chasing for years. That's all I know."

"The deal in Iraq?" he asked her then. "The one Craig was involved in? Does it tie in?" The illegal transfer of arms and information to terrorists, and the unsanctioned attack on the hotel, the explosion that killed her daughter.

She flinched at the question and forced back the more personal aspects between herself and Natches now. There were things they had to deal with, later. Right now, she had to deal with this, and she hated it.

168

"It ties in," she told him. "It also ties in to several other thefts the public is unaware of, that were made too close to Somerset. Those thefts go back further than Iraq and the threads of suspicion lead right back to Somerset."

"So you're here to do what? Avenge Beth?" He shook his head wearily as he pushed his fingers through his hair and stared back at her. She could see the memories in his eyes, too. The loss. The pain.

"I'm here to ask the right questions and see if I can't force them into making a move. Timothy has other agents watching persons of interest." She held her hand up as he started to speak. "I have no idea who they're watching. I'm here to ask the questions; they're here to see who moves after I ask those questions. This isn't about Beth, Natches. It's about stopping it."

"So he's put your ass in the line of fire and he's hoping to catch whoever puts you in their sights?" he bit out. "Son of a bitch, Chay. He's working you. He's using your baby and your pain, and he's working you."

She didn't like to think of it that way, but she inclined her head in agreement, because there was always the risk of that. Timothy was definitely capable of it.

"He's hoping to catch whoever he's watching through the questions he's sending me to ask. He's spent years investigating this, Natches. He's not going to stop now." She sighed.

"And you think he didn't expect me to get involved?" He threw her a disbelieving look as he paced to the other side of the room and turned back to face her, his hands propped on his hips, his expression forbidding.

"I was told to keep you as far away from this as possible. He knew you wouldn't stay away from me, but he was hoping you would stay out of the rest of it."

"And here I thought you were more intelligent than that. Hell, I thought Timothy was," he growled. "Do you believe that bullshit, Chaya?"

"No. But I'm asking you to do it anyway," she told him. She didn't want him involved in this. She wanted him as far away from Timothy Cranston's games as possible. She knew how Timothy worked. He lied and he connived and manipulated everyone to get what he wanted, the way he wanted it. She didn't want Natches pulled into the webs Timothy created.

"All I have to do is ask the questions," she repeated. "The danger is limited, Natches, and he's watching whoever he suspects."

"He suspects someone he knows I'll try to protect, or he wouldn't have sent you." He snorted. "And that one, I have to admit, has me as confused as hell. Because Timothy knows me, too, and he knows there's few people here that I'd protect."

"No one you would protect could be involved," she argued. "Rowdy, Dawg, Ray, or their wives? For God's sake, I know for a fact they aren't under suspicion. Do you think I didn't do my own damned homework? Do you think I would let him try to crucify someone I believe is innocent?"

"Timothy wouldn't try to crucify someone who's innocent." Natches shook his head as he stared at her from across the room.

He looked dangerous, too controlled, too suspicious.

"Timothy's a lot of things," he continued, "but he doesn't do witch hunts. Whoever he suspects, you can bet they're guilty, he just needs the proof of it. And he'll sacrifice anyone or anything for that proof, Chaya. Even you."

He had already sacrificed her, and she knew it. He couldn't have guessed that Natches would give a damn about her if his cousins turned against her. And it appeared that was exactly what was happening.

And perhaps Natches wasn't standing by her. He was angry, she knew that. Suspicious.

She turned away from him and moved to the sliding doors, staring beyond them to the nearly deserted boathouses. Summer was over. There were very few year-round residents here. And she didn't blame them. It was colder than hell on the water.

"Dawg, Rowdy, and Ray aren't under suspicion. Neither is Crista. I have Timothy's word on it," she told him quietly. "According to him, he doesn't want you involved in this because you draw too much notice and you're too temperamental where the Mackays are concerned. The questions he has me asking involve family, connections between Chandler Mackay, Nadine, and Johnny Grace. I record the answers and send the recordings via FTP back to him."

She didn't know what Timothy was looking for, and she was beginning to wonder if it even mattered. Timothy knew who he was after by now. The questions had begun changing, taking a new direction, leading her straight into the heart of too many family secrets. At this point, he was merely playing a delicate little game designed to catch his quarry faster.

"I want to see the names and the questions before you leave each morning."

She swung around. "I have direct orders that you're not to see anything." And she followed orders. The agency had been her life for the past five years. It had held her together when nothing else could have.

He smiled.

Chaya felt her stomach tighten as he moved across the room. Clothes did not hide the shift or power of the muscle lurking beneath them, nor did it hide the sheer arrogance of the male animal she was now facing.

"I said, I will see the names and the questions before you leave my bed each morning," he growled, his eyes darkening, his expression forbidding, and for the first time in ten years, Chaya faced a force that had her swallowing back her nerves.

"Or what?"

"Oh, Chay, sweetheart," he crooned. "Now we just don't wanna go there, do we? We wanna wake up in that big bed of mine, nice and warm every morning, and work this out together. Because, if we're not working this out together, then we're going to be fighting. Yelling. At odds. Out of sorts. And if we're out of sorts, then bad things might start happening. I might follow you into these places where you're questioning folks. I might make things rather hard."

She stared back at him in confusion. "Why? I swear, your family is not involved in this."

"Something more important than family is involved here," he said then.

"What?" She threw her hands up in disbelief, amazed that Natches could find anything more important than family. From what she had seen since coming to Somerset, he wouldn't just die for them, he killed for them. "What could be more important to you than your cousins or your uncle?"

"You."

She blinked up at him, and she swore she felt the very air around them become thicker, still, heavy with tension.

"You don't mean that." She shook her head slowly. He had to be lying to her. He loved his family, he was loyal to them, loyal enough that he would lie to her.

It broke her heart, but she accepted it. She had no other choice.

"You don't have to lie to me," she whispered, moving around him as she put her hand to her brow and eased her palm over the perspiration forming there. "I know you have priorities."

"I'm glad you do. And I thought you knew, Chay, I don't bother to lie to anyone. Wastes too much of my damned time."

She held her hand up while keeping her back turned to him. She couldn't handle this. If he needed this bad enough to lie to her, then fine. He could have it. It wasn't enough to tip Timothy off, and she knew Natches was going to do whatever the hell he wanted to do anyway.

"You can see the list and the questions," she whispered, picking up her briefcase before turning to face him. "I'll meet you at the hotel in the morning."

A sharp laugh left his throat. "Bullshit. You're not leaving me. Not again, Chaya. I'll tie you to the damned bed at night."

"And I'm not going to stand here and let you lie to me to protect your family." Something was building in her, shimmering like a bloodred cloud in front of her vision as she watched his eyes go from dark to light, watched moss green go brilliant green, like a forest in spring.

"You actually believe I'd lie to you like that?" He glowered back at her. "Baby, I don't have to lie to you to get that list, those questions, or anything else I need out of you. All I have to do is get you beneath me."

And it snapped in her head then. Chaya felt herself almost sway in shock. He hadn't used a condom last night or the night before. He had been bare, his semen spurting inside her, sending her crashing into another wave of release even as a part of her mind had whispered the warning. Each time, and her emotions had been in such disarray that she had ignored the implications.

She wasn't protected.

"Not without a condom you won't be." Her head snapped up, her vision clearing as fear surged through her. "And not without the truth between us."

"What the hell do you mean by that?"

"The truth? It's a fairly easy concept . . ."

"I mean the condom." His hand sliced through the air. "I'm safe, Chay, and you know it just as well as I do. I may have played some games in my life, but I always protected myself."

"This isn't about STDs," she snapped. "I'm not protected, Natches. I went off the agency-sanctioned shots last year when I thought I was resigning and didn't have time to restart them. You need condoms. I can't believe you didn't use one last night."

Natches stared back at her. From her eyes, to her stomach. Back to her eyes and her stomach again as he swallowed tightly.

She wasn't protected? He'd filled her more than once with his release the night before, pumping into her, crying her name, feeling her so sleek and hot, milking it from him.

Use a condom now? The first time he'd taken her, there'd been nothing between them either, and he remembered that last mission, wondering about the agency protection she used. Wishing she didn't. Wishing he could fill her with his baby, to give back to her everything she had lost.

He blinked now, feeling the sweat that gathered on his back, the sense of hunger that suddenly raged through his body. He'd rationalized those thoughts as insanity years before. Her grief had marked him in a way he hadn't expected, couldn't have been prepared for, he had told himself.

But now it wasn't grief. He was staring at her belly, seeing her growing round with his child, and the hunger for it grew.

"Are you okay?" Her eyes narrowed on him as he jerked his gaze back to hers. "I'm safe right now, Natches, but that doesn't last long. Get the condoms. And stop lying to me. We'll get along much better that way."

"No." He shook his head slowly, barely able to believe that word had slipped past his lips. They were numb, his throat was tight, thick with so many emotions he didn't know how to make sense of them.

"Why?" She had a death grip on that briefcase and one on his soul. Hell, even he hadn't known the grip she had on him until now. "Is the truth so damned hard?"

"The truth is easy." He had to fight to hold himself back, to keep from latching onto her, to keep from devouring her. "I meant, no condoms."

Chaya went silent. Even her thoughts seemed to stop in shock as she stared back at Natches. He couldn't have said that. He didn't just say that.

"I see." She wet her lips. Had he changed his mind that quickly? Was she misunderstanding something important in this conversation? "If you don't want to have sex with me, I can understand . . ."

"I want to lay you down and lick every inch of your body. I want to bring you over me and watch you ride me. I want to fuck you so many ways, so many times, that neither of us can find the energy to crawl from the floor let alone the bed. Oh, baby, wanting you is like a sickness with me, and it never fucking goes away."

"Oh." Her heart was racing. Each word out of his mouth had her skin sensitizing, her clit swelling. "Then what do you mean, no condom?"

He stalked to her then. Slowly. His expression was more savage than she could ever remember seeing it, his eyes bright, his lashes lowered over them. He looked dark. Dangerous. And something in that look terrified her.

"I mean, if you don't want my baby, then you better get your ass to a clinic and take care of the birth control yourself." His hand flattened on her stomach as she stared back at him in a shock so deep, so overwhelming, she wondered how she was standing upright. "Because I'm betting I have the fastest, slickest little soldiers in the state of Kentucky. Just a breath of a chance, sweetheart, and you're pregnant." His expression, his eyes, grew taut with possessiveness. Possessiveness and lust. "And I could very much get into making damned certain they have every chance."

Chaya felt herself swaying. She could feel the blood draining from her face, even as it began to thunder in her ears.

She could feel Natches's hand on her belly, his eyes boring into her soul, as though will alone, and nothing more, could make her conceive.

And it didn't make sense. She couldn't understand this. He couldn't be serious.

"Why?" She forced the word past numb lips. Why would he want to tie himself to her like that?

"Ah, Chay," he whispered, his expression gentling, just a bit, just enough to force her to trap a sob in her chest rather than give rise to the cry that seemed to echo through her soul. "Sweetheart. Don't you know I'd give everything I possess to hold you to me? And the thought of giving you my child, of watching that pretty belly grow large with my baby, makes my dick so damned hard I wonder if it's going to push straight past the zipper of my jeans."

She felt the briefcase drop from her fingers as she stared back at him, searching his eyes, searching for the lie. There had to be a lie there. But lying didn't make sense. She knew Natches. Knew he would never, ever risk a child of his so cavalierly. He was so damned protective over family that even Cranston feared him. He would kill for them. He had proven it.

"Chay." He breathed her name against her lips, and she felt herself weaken. Her knees. Her soul. Something inside her, something she needed for protection, to hold back the dreams and the loss and the years she had run, even from herself, began to crack. "Let me have you like that. Just us. Just the chance that we could dream together like that."

ELEVEN

Natches could feel himself shaking inside, a need, a hunger he couldn't control, didn't want to control, rising inside him.

Chaya. Just her name invoked the power to make his knees weak, to make him hard, to make him want to believe in miracles and to reach for them.

The boy inside him that had once screamed out in the darkened forest, howling in fury at the loneliness, the pain that melded through his body, howled out now in hope.

Because Chaya was here. For such a brief moment in time in a foreign desert, in a hostile land, Natches had known peace. One night, so far away that it felt like a dream, he had held her in his arms and knew she belonged to him. No matter what happened, no matter where life took either of them, he had found the one person that was his alone.

Chaya.

He stared into her eyes. Honey eyes. Eyes that drew him in and promised him life, promised him joy. He could find joy with her. He found joy with her.

"You're not serious," she murmured, her voice as dazed as he felt lowering his hand once more to her stomach. There, his child could be growing even now. Sheltered in the warmth of her body, growing strong and sure.

Sweet God—the prayer slipped into his mind unbidden—*let my child rest there*. Within the woman who held his soul.

"I'd die for you," he said softly. "I'd kill for you, Chay. And I'd go to my knees for you."

He had never willingly gone to his knees for anyone, man or woman, no matter how many times his father had tried to force him there.

She blinked back at him. Those clear golden eyes of hers flickering with dreams that she fought to keep buried, with hope that he knew she tried to hide.

She was his hope, but he knew, to the bottom of his soul he knew, he was hers as well.

"Natches." She shook her head, her lips parted, fully, lush now with the arousal he knew was moving through her.

It made her wet, just as it made him hard, the thought of coming together, bare, unprotected, spilling into each other to create something new. Something innocent.

It shouldn't have been that way. He knew that. Hell, the last thing he needed to think about with his childhood was a kid. But a baby with Chaya? Something to bind her to him forever, just as he would be bound to her.

Family was his salvation. His uncle Ray, his cousins, they were all the family he'd had. He'd never had his own. Until now, he hadn't wanted his own.

"You want me like that, Chay, don't you?" He lifted her shirt, flattened his hand against the bare skin of her stomach and watched her eyes.

It was Chaya's eyes that held her secrets. There, they flickered in those honeyed depths, the soft golden brown color warming him no matter her mood.

"Bare, Chay." His jaw clenched at the hunger. "I want to pump inside you and feel you reaching for me. Milking me. That sweet hot body taking my seed and nourishing it."

Her face flushed instantly, hot, as her eyes flickered with fear and with dreams.

"I want to watch your stomach grow round with my baby. I want to lay my head against it, feel our child move within you."

She trembled, shuddered, and her eyes darkened as they always did when she began to surrender to him.

He wanted that surrender.

Before his knees gave out on him he swept her up in his arms, ignoring her little cry of protest and he carried her through the boathouse to the stairs. Up the rounded staircase, to the bedroom, to the big bed that awaited them, the sun-drenched warmth that welcomed them.

"We can't just decide to make a baby." She was breathing hard, rough as he set her on her feet and pushed her blazer over her shoulders.

"Of course we can," he crooned, knowing, as he had always

known, how much she loved that sound. When his voice roughened, deepened. She shivered in response to it. A sound he had never known how to make, had never given another woman.

"It's completely irresponsible," she protested, but it was a moan, filled with surrender as his hands stroked down her arms then gripped the hem of her shirt.

"It's every dream I've ever had," he told her as he tore the shirt from her body and cupped those pretty breasts as they filled the lace of her bra. "I want to watch you nurse our child here." He kissed the full mounds as they spilled over the cups of her bra. "Chay, you know you want it, don't you, baby? Bound to me? You won't be able to just walk away anymore. Think of it, sweetheart. No more reasons to run, and every reason to lie in my arms night after night."

It was her nightmare and he knew it. He used it shamelessly, because he also knew it was her weakness. His Chay. So tough, so determined to never lose again, to never hurt as she had hurt before. To never risk having what she cherished most taken from her.

She had run from him, because she couldn't face losing him. He'd figured that out about her. Knew it about her. Just as she surely knew he wouldn't allow her to run any longer if she ever returned to Somerset.

The running was over.

"Natches, this isn't a good idea." She was thinking. He could feel her thinking.

His lips moved to hers. He sipped at her lips as a breathless moan passed them. He stroked them with his tongue as he nearly tore his shirt from his own body. He caught that lush lower curve between his lips and laved it, nipped at it, and watched her lashes flutter over eyes gone dark with hunger.

No thinking right now, he decided. That sharp little mind of hers needed to rest; it needed to be stroked and loved, tempted and teased. And he was just the man to do it.

He loosened her belt, aware of the weight of her weapon at her hip, and almost grinned at the thought of it. His woman was a tough little warrior. She would walk by his side. She wouldn't put up with his moods, and she'd tell him like it was. Always. The thought of it turned him on even more. She was a fitting mate for the darkness inside him, because she lightened it.

He released her jeans, slid the zipper down, and, as he released her lips, slid his palm beneath her panties to the sweet, rich flesh beyond.

So hot it almost burned. Swollen, slick with her sweet juices. His mouth watered at the thought of tasting her again. Of burying his tongue inside her, and lapping at her like hot, delicate candy. Like nectar. Like life itself.

"There, baby, let me have you," he urged as she shook, trembled, her nails digging into his shoulders as he held her to him. "Remember how good it is? How hot?"

He worked her jeans and panties over her hips, careful to keep in contact with the wet folds between her thighs, his finger caressing, his palm grinding against her clit.

And she was burning for him. Her hips shifted, moving against his hand, grinding her clit against his hand as he eased her to the bed.

Her cry of protest flamed through him as he moved his hand, but the taste of her exploded against his tongue as he pressed a kiss against the swollen little nubbin of her clit.

As he kissed, licked her gently, he worked her boots from her feet and finished undressing her. When she was soft and hot and naked, stretched across his bed and immersed in her arousal, he paused long enough to jerk his boots off and finish undressing himself. When he turned back to her, his sensual little kitten was on her knees, gold eyes glittering with hunger now, her features flushed, desire raging in her eyes.

This was the woman he dreamed of. The woman who had taken him to heaven that night so long ago.

His head went back as she came over him, her lips on his, her hands sliding over his damp shoulders, nails raking as he ran his hands up her back and prepared to hold on for the ride.

He remembered Chaya, wild and hungry, too long ago. He had ached for that woman, needed her as he'd needed nothing else, tempted and teased her, and here she was. The balm to the wounds that had festered inside his soul.

Chaya felt Natches ease back on the bed for her, felt his hard, muscular body laid out for her, hers for the taking, and it was like coming home. Like being in the cold and then sinking in front of a fire that filled the soul.

Natches's fire filled her soul. And he offered it to her willingly. A sacrifice to the unbearable hunger raging inside her now, untamed, breaking free of the fear that had housed it for so many years.

Oh God, how had she stayed away from him? Five years. She had been without him for five years and each day had been an eternity of need and loss that she hadn't realized, until now.

"God, Chay," he growled, a deep, rough sound that stroked her senses as his hands stroked her back. "There you go, baby. Come to me."

She nipped at his lips, caressed them, and let him devour her.

He didn't let her control the kiss; he never would, she knew. He was powerful, dominant, but he gave his body freely, and tonight she intended to take. And take.

She trembled at the thought of taking all of him. Of giving all of herself. And she knew that was exactly what she was doing, giving herself.

Lifting her head she stared down at him, at those wild green eyes, the way his thick black hair fanned out from his savage face. The way the muscles flexed in his shoulders and arms, the perspiration that trailed down his neck. And she had to taste it.

She lapped at it with her tongue, filled her senses with the taste of him, and gloried in the sound of that rough male groan.

"I missed you." The whimpering sob shocked her as it fell from her lips, pressed to his flesh. "Oh God, Natches. I needed you. I needed you until I burned. Until I thought I'd die without seeing you, hearing you."

His hands flattened on her back, held her closer.

"I was right here, baby."

Right here. In his bed, waiting for her.

Sleek and hard and hungry.

Her lips slid from his neck to his chest, feathered over hard male nipples before her teeth raked first one then the other. He jerked beneath her, and she thrilled at the evidence of his pleasure.

Another thing he gave her freely, his pleasure. She didn't have to worry about how to please him, because every touch she had ever given him, he had urged her on, relishing it.

"Ah, Chay, sweet baby." His hands slid to her sides, to the curve of her breasts, and the backs of his fingers caressed them with subtle heat.

He wasn't stingy with his touches or his words.

Chaya luxuriated in the generosity. His heat, the friction of his hair-roughened male chest against her swollen nipples. The feel of his muscles tightening, his breath rasping in his lungs as her lips slid lower.

She took quick, heated kisses down the center of his body, moving with slow, delicate greed to the thick, steel-hard shaft that reached up his lower stomach, eager for her touch.

Natches shifted, his hands pulling at her hips as her head went lower. And she remembered that. Remembered how she had taken him in that humid little room in Iraq. The night her tears had mixed with her release, and they had drunk from each other.

She tasted the head of his cock, her tongue licking over it, curling around the engorged crest as the shaft jerked in response.

Natches lifted her leg as she slid into position, pulling her hips over his face and blowing a heated breath against the wet folds of her sex.

A whimper fell from her lips, because she knew what was coming and she couldn't wait. She lowered herself to him, feeling his tongue slide through liquid heat and tender tissue to burrow inside her vagina. Her lips opened over the head of his cock, her hands stroked the heavily veined shaft and Chaya let herself be taken, even as she took.

She worked her pussy on the thrusting tongue tormenting her with wicked pleasure. And with her mouth, she tormented in turn, crying out with delight, with need that bordered on pain.

His hands stroked over her rear, between the full curves, and teased the delicate flesh there as he worked his tongue through the slit of her pussy, circled her clit, and rubbed at it erotically. Stealing her mind.

She couldn't allow him to steal her mind. Not yet. She needed

185

to stroke him, touch him. She needed to pour the past five years of loss and loneliness into every touch. Then she needed to take him as she had dreamed of taking him. Riding them both into ecstasy.

Before he could stop her, not that he tried hard, she swung away, lifting herself from his lips despite his growl of displeasure and her own aching regret.

She couldn't touch him as she wanted to if he stole her strength as she was doing so. When Natches touched her, she melted. Tonight, she wanted him to melt.

And Natches was melting. He stared down his body, strung tight with the most incredible pleasure. Pleasure that went beyond pleasure and bordered on agony of sensations. Chaya knelt above him, straddling one hard leg, rubbing the slick heat of her pussy against it as she worked her mouth on his cock head.

Sucking and licking, moaning in pleasure as her honey gold eyes darkened further and glittered with the needs rising inside her.

God he loved this. Seeing her like this. The agent disappeared beneath the woman's demands as those demands took over.

She sucked greedily at his cock head. Her hands stroked the shaft of his erection and his balls as they drew up tight at their base.

He was in an agony of sensation now. Her hands were silken heat, her nails rasping, her mouth. . . . Sweet heaven, her mouth was like ecstatic fire licking over his flesh as her heated, wet pussy rubbed against his leg.

She was pleasuring him as she pleasured herself. Taking him and twining deeper into his soul as she did so.

Chaya lost herself in each touch, in each taste of Natches's hard body. As though she had been born for this, to belong to him.

Drawing back she licked the hard crest one last time before allowing her tongue to taste the thick, silken shaft. Heated iron met her lips, silken heat stretched tight. Heavy veins throbbed with anticipation just beneath the flesh, and with each lick, she swore his cock grew harder, pulsed harder.

"You're killing me." His voice was graveled, thick and rasping as she kissed the base then licked the tightly drawn sac below.

He flinched, jerked, and moaned hard and low.

Chaya clenched her legs around the hard thigh rubbing against her pussy and knew she was drowning in this pleasure. She was sinking into a sensual storm and had no idea how to save herself. She didn't want to save herself. She wanted to ride the waves. She wanted them cresting over her, surrounding her, swamping her.

She lifted her head and dragged herself over him, embracing his muscular hips with her thighs and lowering herself onto the rigid, heated flesh rising to her.

"There, Chay. That's it, sweetheart; take me. All of me, Chay. It's all yours."

She stared into the narrowed bands of green as he watched her, his expression twisted into lines of savage lust and determination.

She couldn't keep from sobbing at the pleasure. The feel of him penetrating her slowly, taking her as his hands moved up her back, down her arms, then his hard fingers linked with hers.

"Take me, Chay," he demanded. "This ride is all yours, baby."

He was barely buried inside her, his cock throbbing, eager to take her.

"Ride me, Chay, like we've both dreamed."

She straightened, flung her head back at the incredible pleasure racing through her, and she took him. Slow and easy, then with quick, shallow strokes. Her hips twisted, rose and lowered and she lost that final piece of herself.

Nothing mattered but the pleasure. Nothing mattered but the

sensation of flying within his embrace, knowing he was there to catch her if she fell, that he would hold her if she faltered, and he would give her the reins when she needed them.

She needed them now.

Holding on to his hands she took him to the hilt, feeling all that wild heat and hardness penetrating her, stretching her, a burn that was pleasure and pain, and she gloried in it.

She twisted against him, and she rode him as he lifted beneath her, driving his erection deeper and harder inside her. Perspiration gathered between them. It rolled down her shoulders, ran in rivulets down his chest. Slick and heated they clashed together, twisting and thrusting, strokes that speared straight to her soul as the driving rhythm grew, deepened, heated until she was exploding, flaming out of control and screaming out his name.

Deep wracking shudders jerked her body tight as her womb spasmed, her vagina convulsing, milking around him as his hard, throttled shout was followed by the deep, heated spurts of his seed inside her.

Chaya's eyes jerked open, met his and locked. She felt his cock jerk inside her, felt each pulse of his release, and felt her body heat and shudder further at the feel of it. That final hard orgasm rippled through her as his gaze held hers, as his soul wrapped around her. Forcing her to see, to know, nothing in life could be as good as right here, in his arms.

As the final, desperate tremors washed through her, she sank slowly against his chest, just fighting to breathe, to make sense of the woman she became when Natches touched her. Because it wasn't the woman she had known before she met him five years ago.

It was as though he had opened something inside her during

that time in a cramped little hole in the desert. He had rescued her. He had protected her. And as danger swirled around her he had teased her and made her want to fight at a time when it felt as though the fight had been sucked out of her.

And that was how he made her feel now. Like fighting. Like tearing down the obstacles she knew stretched between them, and she knew it could be done so easily.

She could betray Natches, or she could betray the rules she had lived her life by. And at this moment, she knew the choice she was going to make. No matter what tomorrow would bring, she chose Natches. The naughty dream that haunted her, the man who owned her soul.

I love you. She mouthed the words against his chest because she couldn't bring herself to say them yet. As sanity began to whisper through her mind once again, that one shred of fear remained. She had only told one person in her life that she loved them, and that tiny vision of purity was gone now, jerked from her so brutally that she had feared she wouldn't survive it.

That edge of fear still held its grip on her, strangling her with the words that wouldn't whisper past her lips and bringing tears to her eyes as she held on to Natches tighter.

"I love you, too, Chaya," he said, his voice rough. "It's okay, baby, because I love you, too."

TWELVE

Somewhere in the darkness of night, she had to have lost her ever-loving mind. And finding it again didn't appear to be an assignment Natches was going to allow her.

"Look, you have the information, the interview files, and the recordings," she told him the next morning as the first rays of the sun began to peek over the tops of the mountains. "I need to return to my hotel room—"

"And check out," he interrupted her, his voice controlled, mild, as he went through the files she had transferred to his laptop. "You'll move into the apartment with me. Dawg and Rowdy should have the door fixed by now."

She inhaled deeply. "That's not going to work right now, Natches."

He lifted his head slowly. It was a curiously dangerous movement the way he did it. The calculated restraint in it had her holding back the shiver that would have worked up her spine.

"Why? Because you won't have a chance to rebuild all those nifty little defenses you keep between us?" he asked, his mocking smile grating on her temper.

"Because I won't have the investigation compromised any more than it has been already," she told him. "I'm sharing information with you despite direct orders to the contrary. Do you have any idea how many years Cranston could put me behind bars for that?"

He merely grunted at that and turned back to the file.

"I'm meeting Mayes in just a few hours. I need clean clothes, and I have my own notes to put together as soon as Cranston sends the new list of interviewees this morning. I can't do that with you breathing over my shoulder."

"You might as well give it up now," he murmured. "You're not driving back to that hotel alone and you're not staying there alone. You don't want to stay at the apartment, that's fine. I'll stay at the hotel."

He said it absently, his eyes narrowed on the laptop screen, as though simply because it was his decision then it was a foregone conclusion that it was happening.

"Natches, you seem to be forgetting something here," she told him coldly. "This is my investigation and my job. I don't need your help doing it."

"So you keep tellin' me." That smooth southern drawl deepened, causing her to wince. This wasn't the sexy, lazy drawl. This was the cool, velvet drawl of a man who had no intentions of backing down.

"Do I poke my nose into your garage?" she finally snapped. "Do I tell you how to fix cars or how to deal with customers?"

He lifted his head and stared back at her. "Not yet."

That shut her up and she hated it. Turning her back on him she propped one hand on her hip as she nibbled at her thumbnail and glared at the covered window.

Despite Cranston's orders to keep the Mackay cousins out of the investigation, she would have cheerfully told him to shove it if she thought the investigation would proceed better with Natches involved. Unfortunately, she had a feeling she knew exactly where it was headed, and she didn't need Natches there for that.

She had read his file so many times she had nightmares about the childhood he had endured. His father was ex-Marine and a sorry bastard. Dayle Mackay was a bully, heavily muscled; he had nearly beaten a young Natches to death more than once. Natches's back still held the scars of the most brutal beating that he had taken, at the age of twenty. The night his father had disowned him, he had beaten Natches to the floor then ripped his back to shreds with a lash. All because Natches had refused to allow his father to strike his sister, Janey Mackay.

"You'll only complicate matters for me at the moment, Natches. As well as bring Cranston out of the woodwork." She turned back to him as he lifted his head once again and stared back at her. His forest green eyes were mocking, his smile knowing.

"It's not happening, Chay." He closed the files out before leaning back against the couch and watching her with hooded eyes now. "From this moment on, just call me your shadow. Because doing this alone isn't going to happen."

"I have the sheriff with me. Most of the people I'm talking to seem to share a dislike for you, Natches. It wouldn't be conducive to my investigation if you're there."

He just smiled. A patient, questioning smile as though he were trying to figure out exactly why she was still arguing with him.

She propped her hands on her hips and glared back at him. "Okay, let's try it this way. You are not accompanying me on those interviews. Period."

"It makes me hard when you get mean, Chay," he drawled. "Come over here and sit on my lap while we discuss it." He patted his knee invitingly and she wanted to kick herself for almost moving toward him.

"You're just being an ass now, Natches. Stop it and let me do my job. I can be amazingly adept at that when I don't have to deal with men who think they can do everything better than I can." She smiled with false sweetness.

"It's hard to watch your back when you're concerned with watching where you're going." He shrugged. "I watch backs real good. Ask the Marines, they loved me."

Of course they had, he had been a suicide mission waiting to happen for over four years and probably would have taken another tour if a sniper hadn't taken out his shoulder.

There was talk that Natches had arranged the hit, that he knew it was coming and managed to deflect the damage. Chaya knew better. Natches didn't play games. Oh, he may well have known the danger was there and that the shot would be taken. His instincts were so well honed that he had probably felt it coming and, yes, deflected the damage. But it wasn't arranged. Natches was too honest for that, too in-your-face to ever play those games.

"I don't need you to watch my back here," she told him. "That's the sheriff's job. You have no place in this assignment, and you don't need to be involved."

And he just smiled. Again.

"Damn it, Natches. You're not even a contract agent on this assignment. I am not letting you butt your nose into it."

"Are you ready to go pick your stuff up at the hotel this morning? You can pack while you're waiting on Cranston's e-mail to come through."

He was as immovable as the mountains surrounding them. Stubbornness defined his expression and the cool green of his eyes, and had her gritting her teeth to hold back her anger and her desperation.

Was it too much to ask for just a few hours to think? To clear her head enough to make sense of what she had done the night before? Was that too much to ask for? Evidently it was as far as he was concerned.

"You are not returning to the hotel with me. I know how to pack on my own." There was no getting out of moving in with him, and she knew it. But at the moment, that was as far as she was willing to go. "You can give me that redneck pride and stubborn look until hell freezes over, but I'm a fairly competent agent, Natches. Until Cranston begins sending names that might actually trip some tempers in your fair little county, I'm doing this by the book. Period. And my book says I follow orders. And those orders say no Mackay cousins involved. Period."

Frustration flickered in his eyes—and an edge of anger—as he rose from the couch, standing to his full, impressive six feet two inches. And he glared at her. Natches's glaring was sexy as hell, but it was also damned intimidating.

"You don't know this town or these people," he argued again. "You don't know which questions will trip tempers, and from the looks of the previous questions, tempers were more than likely tripped further than what you believe. This isn't the city, Chay. It's Kentucky."

"You make it sound like another planet." She rolled her eyes at his tone. "They're still people, Natches."

"Are they?" he growled. "One of the good ole boys you questioned can shoot a deer from over a half mile out and his hunting rifle is sighted for even farther distances. How much easier would it be to take out one lone little agent?"

"And now you stop bullets, too?" She widened her eyes in mock surprise. "Why, Natches. Why didn't you tell me sooner that you were freakin' Superman?"

She watched him grind his teeth, the bunching of his jaw muscles, the flattening of his lips. Yeah, it was sexy as hell, but pretty damned intimidating.

"I was a Marine assassin," he snarled. "Do you think I won't feel those sights on you before some stupid bastard takes the shot? I know what it feels like, Chay, and you don't want me going hunting if something happens to you, because the first son of a bitch I'd look up would be Timothy Cranston."

Chaya almost took a step back at the banked anger in Natches's eyes. She wanted to tell him yes more than anything. But if she gave in to him now, then she may as well turn the entire investigation over to him because she would completely lose control.

"And do you think I don't know when I have gunsights leveled on me, Natches? Do I really look that fucking green? That I'm not aware of when I'm pushing too many damned buttons?"

"International fucking terrorists are not damned pissed-off rednecks," he almost yelled. "No rules here, Chay. No warning. No instinct, unless you're one of them."

She held on to her own temper by a fingernail.

"My strength in these interviews is the fact that you aren't with me, and though you've been shadowing me, you're far enough away that most people are more amused than concerned. You'll hamper my ability to get the answers I need, Natches, and that will only hinder the investigation."

"And you think people aren't going to know you're living with me?" He crossed his arms over his chest and glowered back at her.

"Where I sleep isn't as big an issue as you sitting there terrifying everyone I question or having you chauffeur me from place to place. If we change the process at this point, we hamper it."

"And what the bloody hell does that have to do with me returning to the hotel with you this morning?" His voice rose slightly, just enough to assure her that his patience was reaching its limit.

"Because I need a few minutes to think if you don't fucking mind," she yelled back at him. "Excuse me, Natches, but you have my brain in so many damned pieces it resembles a puzzle right now."

"He does have that habit." Dawg stepped in as he slid the sliding glass door open and stared at Chaya, who fought to pull her anger back and adopt the cool, unaffected appearance she gave everyone but Natches.

And evidently, she was failing, because he was staring at her as though he didn't know her. His eyes narrowed, his celadon green eyes, so light they were almost colorless, watching her curiously.

"What the hell do you want?" Natches growled at his cousin. "You know, Dawg, this nosy attitude of yours is really starting to piss me off."

"When hasn't it?" Dawg finally shrugged. "I just thought I should let you know that I have a call coming in about a half hour on that project we were working on. I need you there."

Natches glared at his cousin. The project was this damned assignment Chaya was on, and it was obvious Dawg was hesitant about including her in on it.

"Yeah, I'm sure he has information now regarding your little project," she snorted knowingly as she stomped across the room and pushed her laptop back into the case before collecting the keys to her sedan, which the sheriff had had delivered to the marina the evening before.

As if she didn't know what the hell they were talking about. She wasn't a moron, and she didn't enjoy being treated like one.

From the look on Natches's face, he was still intent on following her though.

"Don't turn this into a battle, Natches," she told him fiercely. "Not yet. Not now. Being your lover is a far cry from being your lapdog. I don't heel worth crap, and you should know that right up front."

"Like I didn't figure that shit out in Iraq." Throttled male irritation spiked his voice and almost had her grinning.

Dawg didn't bother to hide his smile.

"Damn, son," he drawled at Natches. "I think you're losing this battle. Do you need any pointers? Advice?"

"So says the man who blackmailed his lover." Chaya rolled her eyes. "Really, Dawg, I don't think Natches needs any advice from you. It could end up getting him arrested."

Dawg scowled as he turned to Natches. "Not like you to tell tales, cousin."

"He didn't tell the tale. I believe it's become something of a local legend. I've heard about it from several sources, Dawg. Small-town secrets and all that." She smiled grimly.

"Go home, Dawg." Natches hadn't taken his eyes off her nor had his face lost the edge of irritation burning into anger.

Dawg grinned. "But this is more fun. Crista's sick again this morning. That virus is kicking her ass for some reason, and she ran me off."

"Then go to work." Natches and Chaya snapped the order back at him simultaneously, causing him to chuckle.

"Sorry, kids, but this project is kind of important right now and I've been working long and hard on it." He turned to Natches. "You know where I'm at when you two get this ironed out. Try not to take all day though, because Crista's getting put out over my absence from the store. Like she can't run it better than I do anyway—when she isn't sick." He shook his shaggy head as he turned to the door, slid it back open and stepped outside.

When it snapped closed again, Chaya pushed her fingers through her hair and stared back at Natches, aware that if she gave in to him now then she may as well turn every ounce of independence she possessed over to him.

It wasn't that he was controlling, there was a difference between protective and controlling, she was finding. Her first husband, Craig, had been controlling. Natches was protective.

"I'll follow you back to the hotel." He grimaced, adding, "Then head back here. I'll meet up with you at the diner."

"No, Natches. I don't need a bodyguard."

"What's wrong with having a damned partner? Hell, Chaya, I'm not asking for anything you can't give me here."

She had never had a partner though. She had worked independently within a team, but she had never had a partner.

She shoved her hands into the pockets of her jeans and breathed out roughly. "You can follow me back to the hotel if you need to, but not to the room. I need to take care of checking out, and I have an early meeting scheduled in one of the other rooms with the other agents working the case. I'll be lucky to make it to the diner on time this morning."

She rubbed at her neck as she stared back at him, watching his expression settle a bit, though not by much. He still wasn't comfortable with this.

"I'm not used to a partner either, Natches. I'm used to working alone—you know that. But I'm trying. I really am."

And she was, but she needed this morning to get a grip on herself and what was changing in her life. He was changing things inside her that she had never imagined she would allow.

"You're too damned independent sometimes, Chaya." He stalked across the room and pulled her into his arms. One broad hand cupped the back of her head, his head lowered, and his lips covered hers.

Instantly, heat rose within her. Her breath caught and the passion that raged through her with each touch began to burn across her system.

"That's why." He pulled back, his gaze so intent, so filled with emotion that she felt her chest clench at the sight of it. "Because I've never known what you make me feel, Chay. And losing it would destroy me."

Those words haunted her that morning. She parked at the hotel, feeling his eyes on her as she entered and got the paperwork started for her checkout.

She moved from there straight to the meeting in one of the other agents' rooms, thanking God there were donuts and coffee because she had refused the breakfast Natches had offered her. Her nerves had been strung too tight, her senses too off balance to eat that early.

As the meeting wound up and she saved her notes to her laptop, she was looking forward to finally getting to her room. She would have an hour, maybe, to shower and get her thoughts in order before checking for Cranston's e-mail and making her notes for the interviews.

That hour didn't help though. As she stored her luggage in the rented car and stared back at the hotel, she felt the old fears rising inside her again. The same fears that had kept her from staying the year before. The ones that had kept her chasing danger rather than making a trip to Somerset long before any missiles had been hijacked.

That fear of loss.

As she slid into the car, she thought about living versus losing, and realized that if she didn't manage to lose Natches, then it would be the first time she had managed not to lose someone she loved.

She had lost her parents in her teens. Not to violence or to death, but to sheer disinterest. Her socialite mother and career-intensive father had no idea what to do with the little girl that always needed a hug or a kiss.

Her sister—she had thought she'd managed to maintain that relationship, before she found out Craig had been sleeping with her. The woman she would have trusted above anyone, the one she trusted her child with, had been sleeping with her husband.

Not that there had been a relationship between her and Craig for years. After Beth's birth, Craig had drifted away, and Chaya had slowly realized she didn't even miss him. When she had been called out on that last assignment in Iraq, she had already informed her superiors that she wouldn't be remaining after the assignment finished. She was resigning to stay home with her daughter. Beth was only three, and she needed her mother.

She forced back a muted sob at the thought of her little girl, her laughing eyes, her rounded, pretty face. Beth had been her life. And within a few short hours after her rescue, Natches had become her heart.

That betrayal was the one she had fought to forgive herself for. While her daughter was in danger, Chaya had been flirting with another man. Natches had sat in her hospital room, teased her with kisses, brought her flowers. He had slipped candy to her and he had made her laugh. And during that two weeks when she had been unable to contact her sister, Beth had been in Iraq with Craig.

She had been falling in love, and Beth had been in danger.

She hated herself for it. She had screamed out so many times in the darkness of the night, sobbing, begging for a forgiveness she couldn't give herself.

And now what was she doing? She laid her hand against her stomach and tried to fight the panic building inside her. Was she risking the life of another child?

She shook her head. She couldn't do this. First thing this evening she was stopping at a drugstore and picking up the condoms herself. It was her choice, Natches had warned her. If she wanted them, then she would have to remember them. She would have to remember them because she didn't know if she could face the consequences.

But a child. She had always wanted to be a mother. To make a secure, happy home filled with laughter and love, the very things she had never seemed to find until she had found Natches. Or he had found her.

And he wanted a child with her. The playboy of Somerset, the wildest, the most wicked of the Nauti Boys, and he wanted to keep her. He wanted to laugh with her, and he wanted to raise babies with her.

It was inconceivable.

Shaking her head, she started the car, then looked up in surprise as the sheriff's cruiser, followed by Natches's jeep, blocked her in.

Frowning, she opened the door and started out of the car.

"Get your case." Natches jumped from the jeep and in two short strides was pulling her away from the car before reaching in and grabbing her briefcase. The door slammed behind her as Sheriff Mayes went to the ground, rolled onto his back and wedged himself beneath it.

"Move." Natches was dragging her away from the sedan.

"What the hell is going on here?" Jerking her arm out of his grip she looked from him to where Sheriff Mayes's long legs stuck out beneath her vehicle.

Her gaze jerked up once again as three other vehicles pulled in. Dawg, Rowdy, and Ray Mackay jumped from their pickups and moved quickly to the car.

"Have you checked under the hood yet, Zeke?" Dawg called out.

"Get your asses out of here. I have an explosives squad on the way. Don't you touch that car."

Male voices were filling the area as hotel employees and a few guests began to move from the building.

The sheriff rolled out and jumped to his feet. "It's here," he snarled. "Get the hell away from the car. Now!"

Chaya started in shock as Natches all but lifted her off her feet and pushed her into the jeep, forcing her to crawl over the console as he moved in behind her. With a jerk and a squeal of tires, the jeep raced a safe distance from the car, then with a hard twist of his wrist, Natches turned it in a quick half spin to face the vehicle as Chaya stared at him in complete disbelief.

"What the hell is going on here?"

Natches turned to her, dangerous. Here was danger. Forest green eyes were the color of moss, savage planes and angles marked his expression, and rage flickered in his gaze.

"You lost an agent this morning," he bit out, his voice dangerously soft.

Chaya stared back at him in mute shock.

"What are you talking about? They were all at the meeting just an hour ago. I left them there."

"Kyle Denton made it about three miles out of town before his car exploded. It took out a nice chunk of the interstate and the back end of the eighteen-wheeler he was driving behind. There's nothing left of him but fucking pieces. The minute Mayes learned it was Denton, he called me and we rushed here. Now tell me Chaya, who the *fuck* is Cranston after here?"

Chaya felt her face go numb with grief and shock. She had just spoken to Kyle. He had told her about his engagement, to his third wife. He was barely forty. He had laughed about her showing up late and the news that she was moving into the boat with Natches. Accusing her of going above and beyond the call of duty.

He had a daughter in high school. She had worked with him for years. He was going to retire after this assignment. Go into private security, he had told her once. Plenty of money and none of the hassles. A man made it to forty, and he wanted a chance to enjoy just a few years danger free.

And he was gone.

"There is a bomb under your car that was not there this morning," he told her then. "Dawg and Rowdy checked that car before we went out to it. I checked it before you got into it; do you remember that, Chay?"

She nodded slowly staring back at him as she tried to think, to figure out where and how and why.

"Someone planted that bomb after you arrived here. Are you still safe, Chay? Did you check that motherfucking car before you got in it?"

She licked her lips slowly. "I ran the transmitter over it. I always do that. I did it this morning. I used the mirror in my bag to look beneath it."

"But it was hidden," he snarled. "Do you realize that? A pro put that bomb in there, sweetheart. Tell me, Chay; do you realize that?"

His voice was rising, his hands tightening on her shoulders until she was afraid he might start shaking her.

"Natches, I am neither a moron nor a candidate for suicide," she informed him coolly. "I didn't find the bomb, which means it was well hidden and expertly placed. And someone has already taken out one of the other agents, so this assignment is severely in danger." She pulled her cell phone from her bag, flipped it open, pressed the secured speed dial and waited while he glared at her.

"Cranston," Timothy barked into the phone.

"We just lost Denton to a car bomb. We're compromised."

"Are you with Mackay?"

"Natches, yes." She stared back at Natches.

"Keep your ass there. I already have calls out to the other agents to park their vehicles immediately and contact the sheriff for pickup. I just received word myself. I'm on my way."

He disconnected and Chaya slowly flipped the phone closed.

"Who is he after?" Natches snarled again.

"Military intelligence and DHS have tracked the persons responsible for the hijacking and theft of military weapons, including those missiles, across the nation to a paramilitary group. Freedom's League. Five years ago, Freedom's League was hijacking and stealing weapons in Iraq as well. Their members are military and ex-military. They steal the weapons by hijacking them one at a time here and there, or in large shipments. Some they sell, evidently to fund other missions they undertake.

"It was Freedom's League members I was investigating when I was captured by Nassar in Iraq. It was those same members that executed a false order for those missiles to be launched on the hotel Craig and Beth were staying in when he was trying to escape. They've managed to infiltrate the military to a degree that DHS is now desperate, and Timothy is rabid to capture one of their generals.

"The League is located in the eastern, southern, and western states, and their leaders are well trained and well organized."

"I didn't ask you what. I asked you who," he snarled back, so furious she flinched.

"I don't know who," she screamed back at him, her fists striking his chest to get away from him, to escape the ragged pain she could see in his eyes, that she could feel in her heart. "If I knew who, I would have killed him myself, and Cranston knows it."

She jerked around, staring out the windshield, watching as the other Mackays, the sheriff, and several deputies worked to tape off the area and roll other vehicles away from her rental car.

"All I know is that one of the head members of the League has been tracked here, through the operation with the missiles. The

Swede attempting to buy the missiles finally made a deal with the government. In exchange for a lighter sentence, he gave them the information he had on this one buy. The League was involved and he was contacted by someone he trusted and had dealt with in the past. He wasn't originally contacted by Johnny Grace. He didn't know his name, didn't have a description, all he had was the fact that his contact had been in the military, and he was based here in Somerset, working within the League to gather the funds and the arms to launch a future revolution in America."

She watched as Dawg and Rowdy rolled another car out of the way. The agents who were still at the hotel were now marking their vehicles, but it looked like four were out.

"You're in danger, Chay," he told her, his voice throbbing with his anger. "They obviously know why you're here and who you're after."

She shook her head. "That's not possible. I don't know who. I don't think Timothy knows. He makes his list night by night, his questions as well, based on the answers I pull in from each interview. You know how this works," she repeated. "It's not an easy process, and this link is the only one Timothy has managed to find in five years. If we can manage to identify one of the head members and take him alive, then we can bust the organization."

"Until they re-form?"

"But even that takes time." She turned back to him, staring into his tormented eyes, seeing the same fears that plagued her. The fear of loss. "Sometimes, even a lifetime, Natches. We fight one battle at a time, as long as we can fight, then we turn the rest to the new generation and pray they're as diligent. What more can we do?"

THIRTEEN

Four of the six agents' vehicles had been wired, Chaya's among them. Three of the four, including Denton, were assigned to watch the subjects after interview. It was obvious someone was getting spooked, and Chaya couldn't figure out how.

"The only questions we asked that could have possibly tripped anyone's radar were the ones involving the Mackay family," Chaya told the sheriff and Natches that afternoon as she sat in the back of the cruiser, headed for the last name on that morning's list.

Timothy Cranston had called and ordered the interviews for that day be completed. Natches hadn't been pleased, and Chaya knew he was only biding his time. She could feel the temper rising inside him as they drove toward one of the more popular nightclubs—or bars, as Natches called them—in town.

The sheriff pulled into the parking lot, and from the corner of her eye, she caught his grimace as he glanced toward the Harleys parked close to the building.

"Biker bar?" she asked him.

"We could only get so lucky." He shook his head as Natches moved from the front of the car and opened the back door for her.

"Ever been in a honky-tonk, sweetheart?" Natches asked her then.

Chaya stared around the parking lot and shook her head. "What's wrong with honky-tonks?"

"The question is: What's not wrong with them?" The sheriff sighed as he jammed his hat down on his head, his expression intimidating. "Who's on the damned list for this place anyway?"

She pulled the small notebook from her pocket and glanced at the name. It was cute. "Rogue Walker."

She nearly bounced into Natches's back as he came to a hard stop, turned, and stared over her head at the sheriff. Swinging around, Chaya got a glimpse of complete male horror a second before it was gone.

"It's a cute name," she announced.

"Lord have mercy on us," Sheriff Mayes muttered before Natches gripped her arm and led her to the door.

"Try not to piss her off," he suggested.

Chaya would have grinned at the suggestion if her nerves weren't still rattled over Denton's death and the bombs they had found in the vehicles the agents drove. Someone was definitely trying to send a message. That person didn't like the questions and was going to put a stop to them.

"The file Cranston sent stated that Ms. Walker—"

"Don't call her miz nothin'," Natches interrupted. "Call her Rogue. Period. Don't comment on her clothes, her hair, or her motorcycle, and no matter what you do, don't even hint at mentioning her past employment."

Chaya stopped and stared up at him with a frown. "She was a schoolteacher; what's so bad about that?"

"Lord help us if you ask about it," he muttered. "Let's get this the hell over with. If fists start flying, get back to the cruiser. We'll be right behind you."

Oh yeah, she just bet he would be. He was probably praying for a fight to get rid of some of that testosterone.

Shaking her head, she followed him into the bar and picked out the subject immediately.

Dressed in black pants, boots, and a snug vest, Ms. Rogue Walker was tipping a beer to her lips and glancing to the door in boredom.

Long golden red hair cascaded down her back in thick ringlets; pale creamy flesh was accentuated by the black attire and gave her an almost feyish appearance. She was slender but curvy. Full breasts pressed against the front of the vest, and deep, pretty violet eyes widened before a sharp, disinterested mask descended over her face and she turned away.

Interesting. Chaya looked back at Natches. "A former conquest?"

"Even I wasn't that damned brave," he growled. "Now get this over with so we can leave."

"Fine, get a beer, park your butt at the bar with the sheriff, and leave me alone."

He grabbed hold of her arm, keeping her from turning away as his head lowered, his eyes darkening in irritation. "Not gonna happen."

"Better happen." She smiled tightly. "Or else? I can do 'or else' really well, Natches, and I can make it stick. This is the wrong place to decide to take over, and it's definitely the wrong place for a public quarrel." She jerked her arm out of his hold and tried to tamp down the adrenaline still racing through her. It made her cranky and it made it more difficult for her to hold on to the patience she knew she needed right now. "I'll just be a few minutes. You can see me perfectly fine while having a beer."

"And when I get you home we're going to have a talk about this 'do it your way' crap," he said, scowling. "First thing."

"Fine." She nodded. "First thing. I'll be ready for you. Are we doing it naked or clothed?"

Before he could do more than narrow his eyes on her, she turned and moved down the bar to where Rogue Walker was watching the confrontation with interest now.

"I wondered when you would get to me," she said as Chaya stepped to her.

Her voice was beautiful. Chaya cocked her head to the side and stared at the petite woman. She was a few inches shorter than Chaya's five feet seven inches, and much smaller boned.

"Do you sing?" Chaya asked her as she lifted herself onto one of the barstools and turned to face the other girl.

"In the shower," she said suggestively, running her eyes over Chaya. "Want to hear me?"

Strange, Rogue Walker's file hadn't said anything about an alternate lifestyle. Or a lover of any type.

"Natches gets jealous." She sighed mockingly.

Rogue rolled her eyes. "As many games as that man played before he left for the Marines, he has no right to jealousy."

"Does any man?" Chaya countered.

Rogue laughed, a soft, amused sound. "No, they don't, Agent

Dane. But I'm sure that's not why you came here to talk to me. I assume this has something to do with that little bastard Johnny Grace?"

Chaya pulled the digital recorder from her jacket pocket and laid it on the bar. "I need to record this," she told the other woman.

Rogue shrugged. "I sound like crap on it, but whatever." She lifted the beer to her lips and sipped as Chaya set the recorder and stated the date, time, and subject.

"For the record, your name is . . ."

Rogue stopped her by laying her hand over the recorder and staring at her hard. "I imagine you know my full name?"

"I do."

"State it and we're going to fight. My name is Rogue Walker, period. Understood?"

Chaya inclined her head. "Understood."

"And don't state my age, please." Her smile was all teeth. "If you don't mind."

Chaya didn't know the game this girl was playing, and she didn't care. When Rogue lifted her hand, Chaya continued, as requested, and received Rogue's affirmation that she was aware she was being recorded.

"For the record," Rogue drawled mockingly. "I thought Johnny Grace was a teeny-tiny little maggot that needed to be blown away, so you're looking to the wrong person if you think I was helping him."

"Who would have helped him?" Chaya kept her voice low enough to keep those around from listening.

Rogue shrugged. "His uncle Dayle. He's a son of a bitch, but I'm sure Natches told you that. He wouldn't have helped kill soldiers or steal weapons though. Dayle Mackay likes to knock the women around, and he likes to run his mouth about politics, but he wouldn't sell missiles to terrorists unless he had them rigged to blow them to hell and back."

"What about Johnny's mother?"

Rogue sneered maliciously. "The only thing that bitch knows how to do is fuck her brother. Johnny got drunk one night right before he died and decided I should know that. Dayle tells her what to do, and she does it. She doesn't make many moves without Dayle's permission."

"But Johnny did?"

Rogue stared across the bar as she tipped the beer to her lips and narrowed her eyes thoughtfully. Finally she set the bottle back on the bar and shook her head.

"I would have said no, but it appears he did." She shrugged again.

"Why would you have said that?" Chaya asked.

Rogue pursed her lips. "Johnny was a weaselly little thing. He craved male attention and approval. I wouldn't have thought he would have done that, simply because his uncle Dayle would have been disappointed in him. And he couldn't have borne that. It was bad enough when Dayle found out he was gay."

"What happened when his uncle found out he was gay?"

Rogue tapped a fingernail against the bar, frowning down at the movement for long moments. "Johnny didn't walk for weeks," she finally said. "I kind of felt sorry for him, went to the house to check on him." She shook her head on a bitter laugh. "Dayle had beat him from head to toe. Johnny was in a dress, stockings, and a wig. Said it was his punishment." Disgust marked her expression. "Damn, sometimes I wonder why I don't just go ahead and move back to Boston. You know better than to get involved with people there."

Chaya glanced around the bar. There weren't many customers, but those who were there seemed to keep an eye on Rogue. And Chaya.

"Did Johnny spend much time in bars?" she asked the other woman then.

Rogue shook her head. "Not really. Johnny was the home-and-hearth type. I guess that's why it surprised a lot of us when we found out what he'd done. He didn't seem the type."

"And you don't care that you're telling me all this?" Chaya injected. "Getting people around here to talk hasn't been easy. Yet you're more than willing."

Rogue smiled. A wicked upturn of Cupid's bow lips, and eyes filled with cynical amusement. "Lady, this county holds no love for me, or me for it." Bitterness flashed in her eyes. "The only difference between me and the fine upstanding citizens of this town is that I tell the truth as I see it. Let's see. Example. I bet a half dozen spiteful little bitches are going to tell you, if they haven't already, how hard they partied with Natches the weekend before you lit back into town." She smiled gleefully. "I can tell you Natches hasn't snacked on any homegrown offerings since he came back from the Marines. Now, the good sheriff over there? Widowed at a young age, he sampled the fine pleasures of one Janice Lowell just last week. And from what I hear, he's a real go-getter. An all-nighter." She leaned over and waved at the sheriff over her shoulder.

Chaya glanced back and was surprised to see Sheriff Mayes watching the other woman with narrow-eyed disapproval.

"He does the whole good-cop routine so well." Rogue sighed elaborately.

"What else can you tell me?" Chaya asked her then.

"I can tell you a lot of women want to claw your eyes out. Weekend gossip is so much fun. And I can tell you that one of your agents—" She paused and shook her head, the brittle amusement dropping for a second. "Hell of a way to go. I heard he was killed this morning and several others almost went up in flames as well. What do you want me to tell you, Agent Dane?" The mocking, devil-may-care grin was back.

"Who was pulling Johnny's strings? Even better, who set the bombs?"

"If I knew, I'd be barbeque, too." Rogue grimaced. "All I hear is a little gossip here and there." She shook her head, the tiny bells at her ears chiming softly. "The Mackay family is damned weird though. Ray, he's a good guy, so are Dawg, Rowdy, and Natches. I didn't know Chandler before he died, thank God, but I know he and Dayle were having one major fight the night Chandler and his wife were killed. And I know Nadine Mackay Grace and Dayle like to get the nasty on a little too often." Her smile was all teeth; her eyes were bitter and much too cynical. "If I had known anything more, trust me, one of the Mackay cousins would have known, because there's nothing in this world I would have loved better than bringing down Nadine Grace."

"Why?" Sometimes that was the most important question a person could ask.

Rogue picked at the label on the bottle of beer, then reached over and turned the recorder off.

"Interview over," she said softly.

Chaya picked up the recorder, transferred it back to her pocket, and watched Rogue expectantly. "Just between us girls then," she told her. "What did Nadine do to you?"

Rogue glanced at where Natches and the sheriff sat, then turned her eyes back to Chaya. Somehow she wasn't surprised to see the hollow pain reflected within them.

"She helped create me," Rogue said then, her voice low and haunting. "One of these days, I'll get to remind her of that. Create a monster, and it can come back and bite you in the ass. Isn't that true, Agent Dane?"

Chaya nodded slowly. "That's very true, Rogue. Very true."

"Natches, you're making a mistake here," Zeke muttered as they watched the two women. They couldn't hear the words, but a look told a thousand tales. "You need to pull her out of this."

Rogue, the one woman who men in three counties feared on a daily basis, almost blushed, and she softened. She looked younger; her gaze twinkled in humor. Then her expression shifted again, sorrow, and then bitterness. Natches swore that in the years he had known her, which hadn't been many, he'd rarely seen anything but hard, mocking amusement in her eyes.

As he watched Chaya though, his chest clenched. He'd been ready to tie her to his bed and force her out of this. Make her swear she would duck and hide until this was over and let him deal with the mess Cranston was creating.

But as he watched her, he remembered crashing into that filthy little dirt cell in Iraq. The smell of blood and death had filled the cramped area, but there had been Chaya, crouched, a gun in her hand, dressed in her tormentor's uniform.

Her eyes had been so swollen there had been no way she could have seen out of them. Her feet had been ragged, though he hadn't known that at the time. She had been so bruised and mauled, he'd seen his own life flash before his eyes. Because he couldn't have left her, and there hadn't been a chance he could've carried her out of there.

But she had run. There had been no tears, only strength. No excuses, no recriminations. She had fought to live and fought to fight, and it was those qualities that had first stolen his heart.

And he thought he could take that from her now?

"That's not my job," he finally murmured.

"It's your job to protect her, damn it," Zeke cursed.

And to that, Natches nodded. "It's my job to watch her back while she does her job. You don't change what you love, Zeke, or you never loved it to begin with."

He had fallen in love with the agent. Strong, independent, fiercely determined. Take those things away from her, and she wasn't Chaya. She wouldn't be his heart or his soul, and that he couldn't allow.

Natches escorted Chaya back to his houseboat after the interview, the tension burning hot and heavy through them.

"The boat has been checked thoroughly," he told her as they walked along the floating docks toward it. "Alex hit town a few hours ago. He and his team went over it from top to bottom while we were on our way in."

Alex Jansen was Special Forces and worked closely with Cranston. Chaya had worked with him several times. He was also Crista Mackay's brother.

It was already dark and growing bitterly cold for the season. The wind off the water felt like ice and cut through Chaya's thick jacket like the sharpest blade.

She felt cold from the inside out. As though icicles were growing in the pit of her stomach and freezing her with fear.

What the hell was going on in this beautiful little county? A place where young men were punished in such horrible ways for their sexual preferences, where young women, like twenty-four-year-old Rogue, were more cynical than women twice their ages. And agents, good men, family men, were being targeted to die in an inferno.

"Alex and his team are at Dawg's right now." Natches's voice was low, restrained. "We'll wait till later to meet with them. After you've had a chance to rest and eat. You haven't eaten today, Chay."

Was that concern in his voice? God, she didn't want to hear the gentleness in his voice when she knew he was furious. Probably furious with her. She was furious with herself. She hadn't taken the proper precautions. Somehow, she had missed something during the interviews she had conducted. An expression, a flash of maliciousness, a lie. There were always signs. Always. It was always there, in the eyes, in the small shifts of the face, and she had missed it. And because she had, Kyle was dead.

Cranston had arrived in town as she left the bar. The text message had flashed on her phone, warning her that he would meet with her the next morning. On Natches's houseboat. She hadn't told Natches yet.

"Come on, baby." His voice was a breath of warmth against her ear as he unlocked the door and they stepped into the heated interior.

After locking the door behind them, he slid her jacket from her shoulders and unclipped her weapon from her side.

"You need a shoulder harness for this." He laid the holstered gun on the jacket at the end of the couch.

Chaya stared at the gun for long moments. She hated it. She hated carrying it, she hated being tied to it, and she hated the life she had led for the last five years. God, the last ten years. The only part of her life that had seemed worthwhile was the time with Beth. And with Natches.

She shook her head. "They aren't comfortable."

She wanted to turn to him, she wanted to beg him to hold her, to take away the pain, and she couldn't. She was the agent, this was the life she had chosen. What right did she have to burden him with her regrets now? He would only feel as though he should fix it, somehow drag her from it, and now she couldn't let it go.

"Chay." His arms came around her as she felt her throat tightening with emotion. "I have you."

His head rested against hers, and his warmth surrounded her.

"I need a shower." She pulled away from him. "Do you want to order dinner? I could probably fix something when I get finished."

"How domestic." He let her go, though his tone grated on her nerves, that hint of knowledge, patience, and just a tinge of condescending male. "I do know how to cook, Chay," he told her a second later as he breathed out roughly. "I've been doing it for a while now."

"Since your father threw you out of your home." She turned on him, feeling it burn in her now, that icy rage. Nearly everyone she had spoke to knew about it, mentioned it, seemed to wallow in the dirty gossip and nasty stories they thought they knew.

"It was never my home," he said simply. "It was a place to crash for a night or two."

He said that so simply, as though it didn't even matter.

"The scars on your back? He beat you senseless . . ."

"Yeah, well, he managed it that time." His grin was smug if tinged with bitterness. "He has a few scars on his back now though. What the hell is this, Chay? I was barely twenty years old. We got into a fight over my sister and ended up fistfighting. He had the bigger fists at the time. Too bad, so sad. I survived it." He shook his head and stared at her in confusion. "If you want to crucify Dayle Mackay, I'll be the first in line to help you, but that's not what this is all about."

No, it wasn't. It was about the fact that he had every intention of jerking her out of that bar. That he had informed her, quite bluntly, that they would be discussing it when they returned here.

Well, she was ready to discuss it now.

"You haven't yelled at me yet, and I'm sick of waiting on it." Her hands were shaking with nerves, with reaction. "Go ahead and do it and get it over with. I should have come straight back here this morning, right? I should just let you take care of all the pesky little details of my job and of protecting me. Go ahead. Say it." She waved her hand back at him as she felt the tears trying to fill her eyes. "Get it off your chest."

She was yelling. She was irrational. She had never been irrational in her life but as Natches stared back at her with that expression of patient male understanding, she wanted to scream. Men didn't understand. They didn't feel the same things, they didn't hurt the same way. They didn't fear the same things. And she knew damned good and well he hadn't understood anything when they entered that bar.

"So. Let me get this straight." He crossed his arms over his chest and tilted his head, watching her curiously. "I should be chewing on your ass for doing your job? Despite the fact that it just impressed the fucking hell out me. Kind of like it did in that damned desert. Now, suddenly, I'm supposed to change everything about you that made me so crazy about you to begin with?"

"You didn't want me to go," she snapped back. "You were ready to tie me up and drag me back here."

He infuriated her as he nodded slowly. "Yes, I was. Until I remembered this is who you are. You couldn't walk away now even if I demanded it. No more than I could. I don't want to change that part of you, Chay."

She pushed her fingers through her hair and turned her back on him.

"Why aren't you angry with me?" She turned back to him a second later. "I could be carrying your child and I went out there anyway. I finished those interviews knowing someone wanted me dead."

"And I made sure you did what you had to do, while I watched your back," he said simply. "Chay, I don't want a lapdog. If I wanted a woman willing to say yes to everything I wanted I could have had it two hundred times over by now. I want you."

"Why?" She clenched her fists at her side as that anger poured through her. "Why do you want me?"

"Hell, do I have to have a damned reason?" he fired back. "For God's sake, Chay, because you know how to stand up to me? Because you know how to live? You know how to love."

"I don't."

He stopped. "You don't what?"

"I don't know how to love, Natches." She felt the tremors shaking through her body then. Deep, hard shudders, the ice building, tightening inside her until she wondered if she could ever be warm again.

He smiled then. That slow, wicked smile that sent a flame

shooting through the ice and a ragged tremor of response ripping through her senses.

"Well, I guess that's why you need me then."

"Why?" She did need him. She needed him until she couldn't breathe without the thought of him. And she still couldn't fathom how to deal with it.

"To show you how to recognize all that love burning within you," he answered.

He moved to her, stalking across the room until she had to look up to hold his gaze, to stay connected to the only security she had found in all the years she had lived.

"Where?" She needed to know where it was, how to open it, and how to set it free.

"Ah, Chay," he whispered, framing her face, his lips brushing against hers. "It's all just right here, baby. Burning inside you. All you've got to do is let it burn."

FOURTEEN

Natches wanted to kill. As God was his witness, the moment those shattered honey gold eyes locked with his after they entered the houseboat, he wanted to kill.

He wanted to make her dead husband, Craig, die again. He wanted to make Nassar Mallah suffer. He wanted to beat Cranston to a bloody pulp and he wanted to rip whoever had dared to kill Denton, limb from limb.

He wanted their blood to wash over his hands, but even more, he wanted to ease the haunting pain from Chaya's eyes.

"Look at you," he said, keeping his voice low and gentle. "Running on nothing but coffee and a few donuts. Shaking in my arms and staring at me so fiercely. I bet if your eyes hadn't been swollen shut when I rescued you, I would have seen that same will to fight in them then."

"Don't do this." She shook her head. "I'm not what you see. I'm not that strong."

He flashed her a wicked smile, because he knew better. A smile as smug and confident as any self-appointed sensualist had ever given a woman. And it succeeded in bringing a flush to her face, a glitter of anger to her eyes.

"You think you know everything." She pushed at his chest, as though he was actually going to let her go now. "Let me go."

He laughed at that. "Baby, I watched your back and let you fight. I took you into the baddest honky-tonk in three counties and sat at the bar like the good little boy I was told to be. This is my territory now. I don't have to be a good boy here."

"As if you've ever been a good boy," she snorted and tried to twist in his arms.

Natches chuckled at that. "I've always been a good boy with you, Chay. I let you run every time you wanted to run, remember?"

"You're not letting me run now," she snapped. "And all I want to run to is the damned shower."

He held her easily, letting her twist, letting that sleek little body stroke and rub against his. His cock was rock hard, it had been ever since he had watched her in that damned bar.

He'd wanted to wrap her in his arms and rock her, and at the same time he wanted to fuck her until she knew to the bottom of her soul exactly who she belonged to.

"Yeah, but I'm tired of being a good boy today." He grinned and dipped his head, stealing a kiss before she could do more than gasp in protest.

As she struggled, he managed to wrestle her shirt off her. She had changed clothes at the hotel, but he realized her luggage was likely up in smoke somewhere. The bomb squad had set several of those suckers off just to match the debris with the dead agent's car.

The thought of how close she had come to going up in flames as well had his hands trembling as he held her hips against him and took another kiss. A deeper kiss.

Hell, if he didn't forget the bone-chilling fear he felt when he realized her car was rigged to blow, then he might disintegrate from the inside out.

"Natches." Her voice was more a breathy moan now. "You have to stop this. I have to think."

"No thinking allowed here."

He let her struggle, let her twist until she turned and met the edge of the bar that separated the living room and kitchen. And then he pressed her shoulders down.

He wasn't going to go for slow and easy tonight. Slow and easy would come later. Right now, he was burning alive for her.

He loosened her jeans and dragged them over that very shapely ass. The prettiest ass in fifty states he swore as he hurriedly released his own jeans and freed the tormented length of his erection.

Fucking her was ecstasy, and he couldn't do without it much longer.

"What are you doing?" Breathless, hot, her voice washed over him. She wasn't protesting, she was losing herself in it, just as he always lost himself in her.

"We're trying to make a little Natches, remember?" He tucked the head of his cock against the swollen, saturated folds of her pussy before pressing into her.

Damn. It was like pressing into a living flame. Natches groaned, feeling sweat coat his flesh as she burned him alive. He worked his cock farther inside her, feeling her tighten around him, feeling the delicate muscles of her vagina milking and caressing his sensitive flesh.

Nothing was this good. There was no pleasure on earth that could ever be as good as taking Chaya like this. When she reached back for him, her short, neat little nails digging into his thigh, he gave her more. Slow, easy strokes that buried him inside her a little at a time. Gave him a chance to relish every ripple of response around the ultrasensitive head of his cock.

"Damn you, Natches," she cursed him even as she tugged at his thigh, trying to force him deeper.

Her voice was thick, a feminine little growl of demand that had him grinning with the pleasure of it.

"What? You want me to stop?" He stopped. Buried halfway inside her, his cock head throbbing, dying for more.

"You're insane," she cried out.

"Hmm. Good thing one of us is sane then." He leaned forward and laid a row of kisses between her shoulder blades. "Our kid needs at least one sane parent. You be the sane one." He pressed in farther.

He felt the wash of her juices and had to grit his teeth to hold back his release. His balls had drawn tight against the base of his shaft, electric sparks of sensation racing from them with the need to come.

"Oh God, Natches, we can't keep keeping doing this." She was breathing hard now, panting little breaths that assured him that she was as far gone to the pleasure as he was.

"Doing what?" Sweat trickled along his temple as she burned him clear to his soul.

"Talking babies."

His hips shifted and he drove another inch inside her, quick and hard, and gritted his teeth as she arched, a hungry little moan begging him for more.

"The thought of giving you babies makes me harder," he panted. Hell, the thought of her breathing made him harder. He stayed hard between each release at just the hope of having more of her.

"Everything makes you harder," she gasped, and he had to laugh.

"Everything about *you* makes me harder." He drew back, the head of his cock poised just inside her liquid heat before he forged inside again.

A throttled, feminine wail filled the air as he took her again. Pushing deep inside her, pausing and drawing back, only to push inside her again. Impaling her with slow strokes, then one fast hard thrust that pinned her to the table and had her trying to scream his name.

"Did you get those condoms today?" He could barely think, let alone talk. But it was the love play she needed tonight. That, and the slow realization that it was going to happen. She was going to belong to him. All of her.

"Damn you," she cursed, but there was no anger, an edge of laughter, maybe.

"Oh, man, that's too bad, Chay." His hands clenched on her hips as he drew back.

"Natches, don't you dare stop," she cried out, panic filling her voice. "Oh God, please, don't stop."

There wasn't a chance.

He thrust inside her to the hilt, snarled at the pleasure that bordered pain as he forced himself to stop, to hold deep inside her. To feel her.

She was close to orgasm. Her pussy was clenching around his shaft, stroking the sensitive head, rippling over him like a thousand hungry little fingers caressing him at once.

"You feel so good." He leaned into her, kissed the shell of her ear then drew the lobe between his teeth to worry it erotically. "So tight and hot around me. I could stay inside you forever, feeling you come for me, over and over again, Chay."

He could feel the perspiration coating both their bodies now. Her nails were digging into his thigh, a sharp little pain to keep him centered amid the pleasure.

"Are you ready for me, Chay? I'm going to take you hard. I'm going to take you so hard and deep you'll think you're dying. Then, before the last tremor is gone, I'm going to take you again. Over and over again, until you feel all that love burning and heating inside you. You hear me, sweetheart? We're going to find all that love."

She cried out his name. The sound of her voice, dazed and thick with the pleasure he was giving her, was almost, just almost, enough to send him over the edge right then. He had to clench his teeth, had to fight to hold back his release. But he knew holding back wasn't going to happen for long.

Gripping her hips firmly, he began to move. He started slow and easy, but slow and easy wasn't what either of them needed. She needed to burn through her pain and he needed to guide her through the heat. He needed to feel her come apart around him, shattering with the ecstasy as she shattered with hers.

Within seconds, the thrusts built. He was slamming against her, burying his cock inside her with blinding, furious strokes as she begged for more. For harder. Harder, stronger, until he heard her wail fill his head and felt her pussy, like a fist tightening on his cock, milking it, pulling his release from him, tearing through him with fire and lightning.

"Ah hell!" He barely recognized his own voice. "Chay. Ah God, baby, yes, take it. Take all of me."

He poured himself into her as he felt the contractions of her pussy spill her release around him. Deep, violent spurts of semen tore from the head of his cock, the racing pleasure tearing through his body as he thrust against her, buried himself deeper, and felt stars exploding in his head as she cried out his name.

He collapsed over her, his knees weak, and damn if he wasn't starting to feel as exhausted as she had looked earlier.

The contractions flexing around his cock were easing, and as he kissed her shoulder, he smiled.

"You know what, sweetheart?" he drawled.

"Hmm." She was boneless beneath him, sated, relaxing.

"You know you are *so* pregnant now, don't you?" Pride flared deep and strong inside him, and he swore he was growing hard again. "See? I told you, the thought of making babies with you just makes me harder."

No sooner had Chaya showered and eaten the impromptu meal Natches had waiting for her than his family converged on them. Rowdy and his wife, Kelly; Dawg and his wife, Crista; and their uncle Ray and his wife, Maria. And Crista's brother, Alex Jansen.

Chaya knew Alex Jansen fairly well—he was better known as Timothy Cranston's muscle, though Chaya doubted the Mackays knew that. And from the warning look he had thrown her, he didn't want it known, either.

Oh, how tangled this little web was becoming. She knew Alex could report back to Timothy and cause her more trouble than she wanted to face, but she also knew the man's incredible loyalty to his little sister, Crista.

Which way would Alex's loyalty swing in this one though?

As the men converged on the beers Natches had stacked in an ice-filled cooler and the women came bearing snacks, sandwiches, and chips, Chaya got a look into the relationships between the Mackays, their wives, and the uncle that had more or less raised all of them.

Ray Mackay was the complete opposite of his brothers or sister. He loved his son and his nephews, he was incredibly protective over all of them, and the loyalty and warmth seemed to extend around Alex as well. And maybe even Chaya herself.

He had hugged her as he walked in, patted her shoulder, and told her not to worry, the Mackays were going to take care of everything.

She'd wanted to grin at the proclamation, but she had a feeling he was entirely too serious.

Now, as she sat back and watched the men going through the printed reports Natches had taken from her laptop, she had a moment to worry about involving any of them. If something were to happen to even one of them, it would affect the whole family. And it wouldn't just affect them; it would devastate them.

"The subjects you questioned were all ex-military members." Rowdy cast her a narrow-eyed look from across the wide table as he laid down the file he had been going through. He flipped two files toward her. "Hollister Mcgrew."

Chaya stared at the picture clipped to the corner of the file. Hollister Mcgrew's pitted face, framed by limp brown hair and sporting a bullish look, stared back at her. He and Johnny had been reported to have been friends in high school, and later had run and drunk together in many of the local bars before Hollister signed up for the Army.

He wasn't gay, actually considered himself quite the ladies' man, despite his rotting front teeth and sour breath. His honorable discharge from the Army had been medical. Hollister hadn't handled the Army well.

"George Mack." Rowdy tossed out another file.

Pole skinny with straight, thinning brown hair and dirt brown eyes. For a few years, he and Johnny had been best friends, until George had joined the Navy. As with Hollister, George lasted only the first tour before receiving discharge, though his had been less than honorable. He'd nearly ended up in Leavenworth.

There were others. Many of them were rumored to be involved in drugs, grand theft, or burglary. The few who weren't ex-military, such as Rogue Walker, a former friend of Johnny's, were persons of interest who may or may not have had information tying Johnny to other persons of interest.

"Johnny was the one who admitted to masterminding the whole deal," she pointed out, playing devil's advocate.

"None of them had the brains or connections to have helped Johnny put everything together, nor could they have kept their dirty little paws off a million in cash," Alex stated. "They are the pawns. Who's the king?"

That was a good question. Chaya pushed her fingers through her hair in frustration. That one she hadn't figured out yet.

"They have ties to others as well," she stated. "The mayor and chief of police. George Mack is Mayor Sunders's second cousin. Hollister worked for Sunders as a handyman for several weeks.

The same pattern follows for everyone I've questioned. I received three to five names each day as well as their most likely locations or residences. And the questions."

"The questions aren't that hard," Dawg snorted. "And it's damned easy to lie."

"And sometimes, it's damned easy to see that lie." She shrugged. "I've been trained to see the lies. I'm an interrogation specialist, Dawg. This is what I do well."

She had been lied to quite a bit during the questioning, and the knowledge of that had gone into the notes she sent to Cranston each evening. The same notes everyone here now held.

"There's no one here Johnny would have trusted," Ray told them all as he looked through the files. "He was a strange boy, but trust wasn't something he gave easily."

"Trust was something he traded with," Natches said, his voice curiously bland. "Johnny only trusted his mother and Dayle. And we know Nadine would lie out of her ass if it got her something she wanted. Dayle's no better."

That was his father, but there wasn't so much as a hint of emotion in his voice.

"Cranston's arriving here in the morning," she told them. "I received his message before we returned to the boat. I'm hoping he'll have more answers."

"I'd suggest he come bearing answers." Natches's more dangerous drawl was back now. If Timothy didn't have answers, then he was going to have to deal with more than one pissed-off Mackay.

"Several of these boys were military, too," Alex noticed. "The team we captured after Johnny's death was all ex-military. Penny-ante troublemakers, none of them did well there, but thought they were Rambo once they came home.

"The group we're after, Freedom's League, uses such men to help steal the weapons they've targeted. But the League has never attempted to sell something so powerful to terrorists before.

"The few times they managed to steal weapons of any strength, DHS was there to stop the sales. Smaller caches the agents allowed to slip by as they worked to identify and capture those heading the militia group.

"If the League was involved, then it would have been a hit. They would have taken out the Swede and his group, and they would have used men better able to pull the operation off," Alex stated.

And Crista agreed with that—to a point.

"Except the Swedish broker has, according to evidence he turned over, worked with the contact in this area before. The missiles went cheap. Two million?" She scoffed. "Give me a break, they could have gotten twenty million for them. And that was the intention. The broker was only buying the rights to transport and arrange auction on the missiles. And that was what Johnny didn't know. He thought the missile sale was a done deal."

"Which means someone was pulling the strings somewhere else," Natches mused, sitting back in his chair and staring at the papers on the table before lifting his eyes to Chaya.

She saw the bitterness now, the anger.

"Each step we take points in that direction," she agreed.

"Fucking Somerset, Kentucky, a hotbed of illegal militia sales and homegrown terrorism." A cynical laugh passed his lips. "Son of a bitch, boys." He looked to his cousins. "Have we been sleeping or what?"

Chaya shook her head, aching for him. This was his home, and she knew his love for the mountains, the lake, and even in some part, the people.

"Somerset is only one of many small towns," she told him. "The guerilla militias can grow and thrive in such areas, because of their family and community ties. They know who to target, who they can trust and who they can blackmail. Most of them are harmless. Good ole boys plotting to defend God and country against aggressors. They have ties to military personnel, gain a few weapons here and there, and it makes them feel safer. Doesn't make it legal, but they feel safer. Then, every now and then, you get something like FL. And they twist it, pull in those once harmless groups, and suddenly they have an army with ties all across America. If we could capture the person or persons pulling the strings here in Somerset, then there's a chance we could take the entire network down."

"And you think asking a few dipshits some sticky questions is going to do this?" Dawg flipped his hand over the files in disgust. "I didn't see a damned thing in there about Freedom's League or a network of homegrown terrorists."

"You didn't read her file," Natches told him quietly, his gaze still locked with hers. "I did."

Chaya pressed her lips and dropped her eyes. She had asked the questions she knew could come back on Natches and his father. How loyal was he to his father? He claimed he wasn't, but family ties often had strong undercurrents. And Natches wasn't always as easy to read as he pretended to be. In some areas, his secrets went far deeper than most people could imagine.

"The questions Cranston is sending to me now are becoming more specific. Centered on Johnny, his friendships, and his ties. And there are certain threads that bind each one. Johnny's parentage." She watched Dawg's jaw bunch. "His loyalties. His friends. Who he associated with the most, because within those groups, we'll find the contact we need."

"Not in that group of names you won't," Rowdy snorted. "I've gone over these files, Agent Dane. There's nothing here to identify any kind of leader of a homegrown militia network. These people are misfits. They can't decide where to use the bathroom next and you expect me to believe they're part of some growing grassroots terrorist group?"

"I'm more inclined to believe they're the pawns of such a group," she snapped back. "I've worked this case for five years, Rowdy. I know the signs. And they're all here."

"Who in Somerset could organize and lead something like this?" Dawg looked to the others then his eyes flashed with anger as he leaned toward her. "Fucking Mackays. Me, Rowdy, Natches, we could do it," he snarled. "Is Cranston after our asses now?"

She shook her head.

"Bullshit." His hand slapped the table. "There's no one in this county with more expertise in military, paramilitary, or plain dirt-assed killing than the three of us."

A sniper assassin, an explosives assassin, and Rowdy, one of the Marines' finest commanders. They'd all left the military early. For Dawg and Natches, after one tour, both with medical discharges. Rowdy had taken two tours and signed out. No sooner had they returned than the League had begun growing within the area.

"I investigated that option myself," she told them, staring back at Dawg coolly. "You don't have the ties nor do you personally have the temperament needed for such work."

He almost gaped back at her, rising halfway from his chair as Natches stood fully to his feet.

"Don't tell me I don't have the temper for it, little girl," he snarled. "That piddling-assed little car bomb that took out your agent looks like a firecracker compared to what I'm capable of."

"Back off, Dawg," Natches warned him.

"Leave him alone, Natches. I can handle it." She smiled back at Dawg tightly as his wife came up behind him, her eyes sparkling in anger as she glared at Chaya.

" 'That piddling-assed car bomb,' as you call it," she bit out, "had a signature. We've tracked it before."

"I don't leave fucking signatures," he snarled.

"Exactly. You don't. And that alone is your signature," she told him. "Don't play dumb, Dawg, just because you don't like me." Chaya came to her feet, her hand gripping Natches's wrist. "You, Rowdy, Ray, your wives, and your closest friends were investigated first. Thoroughly. I headed that investigation. I know how thorough it was, because I knew none of you were evil. Snarky, damned mean when you need to be, and so damned arrogant you make a woman's back teeth clench. But you're not traitors, and you're not terrorists. And I proved it."

"She's right." Alex spoke up, drawing their gazes. He was leaning back in his chair, his gray eyes lit with amusement. "You'd make lousy terrorists, and you made lousy soldiers. I believe that's why the Marines let you all go so easy, because you don't follow orders worth shit." He leaned forward and smiled placidly. "But they think I do. And Chaya knows her stuff. She's not the only one who's been working this case. Now, if we're all through playing these little power games, maybe we can get back to work here and figure out who the hell Timothy is chasing. Just in case he hasn't figured it out himself."

Natches stared back at Dawg, furious, bordering enraged, but the rage wasn't directed at his cousin. It was building inside him, threatening to burn out of control, because of his own suspicions. No, his own certainties.

He let Chaya pull him back to the chair and ignored her worried looks as the work continued. Finally, she moved away from them as Alex filled them in on the Freedom's League and their ties. It was information she already knew in abundance. She knew it, because that damned organization had killed her daughter.

He watched as she moved to the living room, sitting outside the group of women. Finally, Maria drew her forward, her smile kind. Maria was the kindest damned woman Natches had ever known until his cousins began falling in love. They had chosen women with those same qualities.

Finally, Chaya and Crista were talking. Natches watched them, noticed Dawg watching them, and caught his cousin's eye. They were going to have to talk about this, and soon. He couldn't figure out Dawg's problem with Chaya, and he was beginning to not even care what the problem was. It was going to stop.

Finally, as the hour grew later, they stood and stretched, shook their heads and admitted they would have to wait on Timothy. Natches stayed silent, watchful.

Chaya was exhausted and he led her to bed, tucked her against him, and waited for her to go to sleep. While he thought. And all the thinking in the world wasn't helping him to make sense of the knowledge brewing in his gut, or the anger tormenting his mind.

Thinking was only making it worse.

FIFTEEN

Natches left Chaya, exhausted, sleeping peacefully in the bed he'd dreamed of her sleeping in.

When he'd returned from Iraq, he had thrown the bed he'd partied in for so many years right into the lake. He'd come in at night, taken one look at it, and something inside him had shattered.

The man who had slept in that bed wasn't the same man who had returned to it. The man who had returned belonged to someone now and was no longer the man that bed represented.

Before he left, he'd been the bastard everyone thought he was and had been on a fast track to self-destruction. It was why he joined sniper training; it was why he worked without a spotter; it was why he had become one of their most proficient killers. Because life didn't matter to him—not his, and not those he was sent to kill.

To the man he had been, happiness was something others felt.

All he had felt then was the rage, the bitterness, the knowledge he was tainted by the blood of an incestuous, child-beating son of a bitch. And the fear that somehow, part of Dayle Mackay lived inside him. And then, he had seen true strength. He had seen a woman who should have been weeping in horror, in fear, and she had stood strong. She had lifted her chin defiantly and she had kept fighting.

And in those two weeks of recovery, she had let him hold her when she cried, when she learned the husband she thought she could trust had betrayed her and his country. He had teased her into laughter days later, and stolen a kiss. He had watched her eyes sparkle and his soul had claimed her.

And she had changed him. In that short time, she had erased the man he had been, and shown him the man he wanted to be. A man who was worthy of a woman that strong.

He stood on the deck now, leaning against the rail and staring into the dark water stretching out behind the boat, and realized that he had grown up long before his cousins had realized it. Maybe it had begun before Chaya, but he just knew it had cemented with Chaya.

He had bitched about the sharing that didn't continue after they came home, but only because to not bitch was to reveal too much. And he didn't want to explain Chaya. He didn't want to relive in words what he couldn't forget in his memories. And he couldn't betray Chaya by taking another woman.

He'd let others think he had. Hell, he even watched Dawg take a few, but he hadn't been tempted to join in. He hadn't wanted to be tempted to join in. Chaya had been so firmly entrenched in his head and in his heart, that no other woman came close to the memory of her.

She loved him silently, as though she was afraid that to love him any other way would break her.

And his heart broke. As wild, as vicious, as his life had been at one time, it was nothing compared to the loss Chaya had suffered in the space of a few seconds. The death of her child, the knowledge that the father of that child had betrayed them both.

He breathed out heavily, tightening as he felt the boat rock, felt a presence behind him.

He knew who it was. He knew Dawg wouldn't be asleep any more than he was tonight. Not with the events that were beginning to reveal themselves and the knowledge of the danger surrounding all of them.

He stood still, staring out into the water until a longneck beer was thrust in front of his face. His lips quirked as he took the bottle and glanced at the man who leaned against the rail beside him.

Dawg. They nicknamed him that for a reason. He never let things go. He chewed and chewed on a problem, worried it and fought with it until that problem either evaporated or bowed before him. He was as stubborn as the damned wind.

Natches took a long drink of the beer and waited.

"You changed," Dawg finally said quietly. "Others didn't see it like I did when you came home. You played a good game of pretending you were fucking the girls, of being as wild and woolly as you always were, but you weren't."

Natches stared at the bottle as he shook his head. "No," he finally admitted. "I wasn't."

"You had no intention of sharing Kelly with Rowdy even if it had been what he wanted, did you?" Dawg grunted. Rowdy would have killed both of them if they had touched Kelly.

"Neither did you unless Rowdy really still needed it." Natches brought the beer to his lips thoughtfully. "Your game was just as good."

Dawg sighed, the sound rough, worried. "I don't have a daddy complex," he finally growled. "What I've got is a complex against games. Cranston's games and Agent Dane's, especially after what I learned tonight. She almost destroyed you once . . ."

"She lost her daughter in a missile attack against enemy headquarters in Iraq five years ago. That was the false order initiated by the League. I suspect to keep their own activities secret. Beth was three. Her father was military intelligence and slipped her into the country after he deserted to the other side."

Silence filled the void as Natches held the beer loosely between his palms. "It was two weeks after I rescued her from the terrorists who had taken her while she was on assignment. Terrorists her husband betrayed her to. Nassar Mallah raped her with a baton, Dawg. He beat her face until her eyes were swollen shut. He kicked her and beat her until I wondered how she was still standing when I broke into that fucking dirt cell. But there she was. She'd torn the clothes off the guard after I took his head off; barefoot and in shock, she was ready to run."

Dawg breathed out a vicious curse. A sound rife with the horror Natches described, the images blooming between them, steeped in blood.

"We hid in a hole I'd made, and I activated the beeper for extraction. My team was waiting not far out, and I knew it, but too far to wait on them to rescue her. I bandaged her feet there, I covered her eyes, and in that dark little hole, I gave her my soul." He lifted the beer to his lips and finished it before turning to stare at the cousin that was more a brother, who was almost a father to him. "Cut her again, and we're finished. As friends, as family. Do you hear me,

Dawg? That woman owns me, and she always will. You cut her again, and we're finished."

Dawg stared at Natches. Between them a lifetime of memories and trials, tears and brawling male adventures stretched. He'd have sworn years ago that nothing could come between him and his cousins. But as he stared at Natches, the youngest of the cousins and the one most scarred inside, he saw something he'd never imagined he'd see.

He was used to seeing Natches as the battered kid he was always helping to rescue from Dayle Mackay's brutal fists. Then as the wild, too charming, troublemaking hellion he grew up to be. Then they went into the Marines.

And he guessed they really had grown up. Except Dawg hadn't wanted to see it in Natches. He hadn't wanted to see the horrors his cousin had survived when they were separated. And now, he saw it. But he saw something more. There was a core of pure hard steel inside him. That steel had pulled the trigger and killed another cousin to save Dawg's heart. That steel faced him now, and damned if Dawg would have blamed him if Natches had already decided to cut him out of his life.

Natches had given him and Rowdy a loyalty that, Dawg didn't realize until this moment, he hadn't given his cousin in return.

"Fuck." He sighed, wiping a hand over his face. "I didn't mean to cut her, Natches. Son of a bitch, if I didn't want to hate her though. And I was wrong."

Natches continued to stare out on the water, and it broke Dawg up inside, seeing the pain on his cousin's face. Hell, he'd have killed anyone else if they so much as thought to cut that little agent as he had. The Mackay cousins stuck together, it was that simple.

"I'd have never let anyone else do it," he admitted, and it

wasn't easy. "We might fuss a little between us, Natches, but you know that."

Natches nodded then. "It's the only reason we're talking now, Dawg. It's the only reason my fist hasn't gone down your throat and my boat is still here. Because I know that."

Dawg almost felt a spurt of fear. How had he let his enmity, his fear for his cousin almost bring them to that point? *Fucking dumb redneck,* he thought to himself. That was how. Sometimes, he was still the dumb redneck he had been when he was young.

"She's not plain," he finally grated out. "But she's tough. And whatever she's dragging you into scares the shit out of me because you're not sharing it with us. And I know you, Natches. I know you know what's going on. You're protecting her from us when you don't need to and risking yourself. And *that's* what's pissing me off about her."

He watched as Natches lowered his head, his gaze slipping to his cousin's bare back, and he still flinched. After all these years, so many years, as the moonlight washed over the scars on Natches's tough, sun-bronzed flesh, fury still spiked through him.

Natches's father had done that. That mean fucking bastard had lashed Natches until he nearly killed him. He'd broken his rib, got him down, and then beat the living hell out of him. When Dawg, Rowdy, and Ray had burst into the house, Natches had been curled in on himself, nearly unconscious, his back in ribbons, and Dayle still laying the fucking lash to him.

And Dawg had sworn that night, sworn to God, it would never happen again. That no one, fucking no one, would scar Natches like that again, physically or mentally.

And still, something had had almost as profound an effect on Natches as his father had. A woman's pain. A woman's scars.

In that second, he realized that was what pissed him off now. Once again, Natches wasn't watching his own back. He was more concerned with someone else's safety, someone Dawg didn't know and was too damned wary to trust.

"Natches, stop looking at the fucking water, man. Tell me what the hell is going on. I watched you tonight going over those files. You put something together, and you're still trying to protect the rest of us. Let us help you. We didn't take that from you when we were in trouble. Don't do it to us now."

Whatever it was, Natches had figured it out slowly, because he hadn't hit the roof, he hadn't dug out his sniper rifle, and Dawg and Rowdy hadn't heard the rage. Natches was easier to figure out when he hit a hard, fast rage. The slow ones, those were damned scary. And Natches was in a slow-building rage.

As he stared at Natches, the boat rocked again. Dawg looked up as Rowdy crossed the deck now. Their boats were close enough to jump from one to the other. Rowdy wasn't being cut out from this late-night conversation and Dawg could tell from Natches's grimace that he knew it, too.

"Beer's in the cooler," Natches said softly, finishing the one Dawg had handed him. "Get me another while you're at it."

He turned and lobbed the empty bottle into the trash can at the corner of the railing.

At least Dawg didn't have to look at those fucking scars anymore. The sight of them just pissed him off, even now, so many years later.

Rowdy got the beers and moved to them, his expression still as he handed them over.

"You two going to fight?" he asked, and his gaze narrowed on them. "I'm not up to refereeing tonight, I'll tell you."

Dawg snorted. "No, I've just been trying to convince knuckle-head here to tell me what the hell is going on with his woman and that damned Cranston. My neck is starting to itch damned bad. It's keeping me awake at night."

"Natches will tell us when he needs to." Rowdy shrugged, but Dawg heard the question in his voice as well.

"Your neck itches," Natches said then, his voice eerily quiet. "Have you felt the sights between your eyes yet? Playing with you, targeting you, just waiting, because the time isn't right yet?"

Dawg froze. His gaze slashed to Rowdy's and saw the same shock in his face that Dawg felt.

"What the fuck are you talking about?" Rowdy snarled.

Rowdy rarely cursed, Kelly just didn't like it, and he tried to clean his mouth up. For a Marine, that was some hard shit to do. And the fact that he was slipping told more of his fury than anything else could.

Natches lifted his head then and stared at the mountains around them. The grief they saw on his face then, the heavy, quiet sorrow had Dawg's guts cramping with dread. Because he knew. God help him, he was terrified he knew exactly what was getting ready to come out of his cousin's mouth.

"It's Dayle, isn't it, Natches? That's who Cranston is after; he's the one who was helping Johnny. That's why he's playing games with you, and with your agent." In a heartbeat, Dawg knew the truth.

Natches grimaced, a tight, mocking smile twisting his lips before he tilted the bottle to his lips and drank. In seconds the bottle was empty and crashing into the trash hard enough to rock the can as Dawg and Rowdy flinched.

Natches stared at the can, wishing he could free enough emotion where his father was concerned to just get mad. Just mad. Just enough to rage at the injustice of life that allowed something as rabid as Dayle Mackay to sire a child.

But he couldn't. All he could feel was that cold, hard core of knowledge inside him. The same one he had felt when he realized Johnny Grace was as dangerous as a rattler coiled to strike. His fingers itched to caress his rifle, to take out the threat, to make certain, damned certain the bastard couldn't strike at Chaya, Rowdy, or Dawg. Or, God forbid, Ray.

Dayle couldn't touch his sister, Janey, at least. She was away at college, far, far away; Natches had made damned certain of it.

"He's been playing with me," Natches commented. "Not right now, but often enough. He must have been busy this month, I haven't felt his gunsights in a while. But right after I terminated Johnny, I felt them. I felt them hard enough that I wondered if he'd finally made his mind up to do it."

"And you didn't say anything?" Rowdy growled, furious. Natches could hear the anger in his tone.

Natches shrugged. "I know how to give back. I let him feel *me* for a while." And it had amused him. Just as he knew it had amused Dayle when Natches felt those sights between his eyes. Once a sniper always a sniper, but once an assassin, a man always knew when it was turning back on him. Dayle amused Natches for the most part with his games. He didn't know how to target, didn't know any more than an experienced hunter knew. The wind positioning was never exact. He was always too far off. But he liked to pretend he could kill his son. The mess cook turned gourmet cook who thought he was a general in a revolution. It was so fucking laughable Natches still had trouble believing it.

Dayle Mackay had the temperament for what he was doing though. He'd learned enough in the Marines to know how to be hard. He'd made connections, and he'd kept those connections. And Natches had known, as he'd read those reports, as he had begun to put the pieces together along with the mental snapshots of the past few events that had tied in. Natches had known.

"How long have you known who Agent Dane is chasing, Natches?" Dawg asked.

Natches could feel his anger, too. Protective, that was Dawg. And he knew Dawg would never forget the night Natches hadn't been able to protect himself. The night he had nearly let his father beat him to death, to protect his sister. And he would have done it again. If Ray hadn't found a way to make certain Dayle was too scared to leave so much as a bruise on Janey, Natches would have let his father kill him to protect her.

Because no one in the damned county had the balls to stop it. They were terrified of Dayle Mackay. Bullying, cold, mean to the fucking bone. And a fucking gourmet chef on top of it. It was almost enough to leave a man rolling in laughter at the thought of it. Dayle Mackay could make a meal that would leave a man crying in joy at the taste. And he could beat a man to a bloody pulp with the same cold precision.

"I knew before she arrived." Natches finally shrugged. He hadn't wanted to admit it to himself. He'd refused to even consider the suspicion. But he had known. The day Johnny had died Natches had stared into his father's eyes across the town square and Dayle had known who had killed Johnny. And Natches had known, in that one instant, who had helped Johnny. Hell, helped him nothing. Johnny hadn't masterminded that little deal, Dayle Mackay had. And now Natches had to deal with it.

"Cranston has Chaya playing a smoke game, and I know it. Not enough to cause Dayle to target her, but enough, he's hoping, to make Dayle mess up just enough to rain down the wrath of Timothy Cranston on him. The wrong phone call. The wrong meeting with the wrong person. Just enough to pull him in on suspicion of terrorist activities."

Silence surrounded them. Natches didn't feel the chill of the night on his skin, he felt the chill of betrayal in his gut. And of fear. Because the one thing he hadn't considered until tonight, until that bomb had taken the other agent out, he hadn't considered the risk to Chaya.

Dayle had no problem whatsoever targeting her. Killing her would kill Natches, and figuring that out wouldn't take rocket science, especially not after the past few days.

"I'm moving the boat tomorrow," he told them then. "I'm going to dock her behind the garage for a while."

"The hell you are." Rowdy faced him, cold, hard. "We stick together, Natches. He'll expect you to separate yourself from us. We don't separate."

Natches shook his head. "Kelly and Crista . . ."

"Are just as fucking innocent in this as that woman you have in your bedroom now," Dawg snarled. "I might not like the situation, damn it, but I'll be damned if you'll pull away from us like that. There's safety in numbers, man. And right now, Dayle isn't going to take that risk here. We'd all know who did it. We know his style and his signature, he can't take that risk. You make yourself a target, and he can take you out easy."

Natches scratched at his cheek and gazed out into the night.

That was the only insurance Natches had ever had against his father's wrath. He'd rubbed Dayle's nose in it, too. He couldn't take Natches out without the whole damned town knowing it. And a part of Natches had never really believed his father would try to kill him, until recently.

Hell, he should just pack himself and Chaya up and leave. Making a life somewhere else wouldn't be that damned hard. Except there was no way in hell she would go for it. She was an agent, and she didn't break her word, she wouldn't betray DHS that way. She would resign, and that was a given once this assignment was finished, if they survived it.

"Have you discussed any of this with Chaya yet?" Rowdy asked.

Natches shook his head. He had only let himself believe it tonight. "She's sleeping."

She was curled in his bed, safe and warm for the moment, where he needed her to be always. Safe and warm, and sheltering his child under her heart.

"She's pregnant." He let the words slip past his lips.

He knew she was pregnant. He could feel it clear to his soul. The moment she told him she wasn't protected, that knowledge had slammed clear to his gut.

Silence again. Rowdy's eyes widened and Dawg's seemed to bug out.

"She's what?" Dawg wheezed. "What the hell? She's not been back here long enough, unless . . ." He let it trail off.

"It's mine." His child. Boy or girl, it didn't matter, it wouldn't matter. "She won't admit it, but I know she is, Dawg. The first time, she wasn't protected and I didn't give a damn." But now, fear sliced inside him. His baby rested inside her, barely more than an instinct, and already that child was in danger. "I haven't given a damn since."

"Damn," Rowdy breathed out roughly. "Okay, another reason why you don't go running off solo. Your ass is staying here. And so is hers."

"You're risking your lives," Natches told them both. "Kelly and Crista need you two. This is my fight."

"He wants me to kick his ass," Dawg snapped.

"No, he wants a cold bath tonight, and I might oblige him by tipping his ass over that rail and into the lake," Rowdy said with a healthy dose of disgust. "Get over yourself, Natches. Later today, we tackle Cranston. That little bastard has gone too far this time. He should have contacted us to start with."

"He did."

Dawg and Rowdy stared back at him in surprise. "When?"

"The anonymous call the night Chaya came into town. I finally recognized the voice despite his attempts to disguise it. It was Cranston. That was his warning."

"Then he needs to brush up on his social-fucking-skills." Dawg's smile was one of those nerve-racking curves that always denoted trouble. "And I'll just enlighten him on that little tidbit when we get hold of him."

Natches stared at Rowdy, then at Dawg, and shook his head. He hadn't wanted them involved, but hadn't they always been? Dayle would never be satisfied if he managed to take Natches out, because he hated his nephews with the same consuming fury that he hated his son. And his brother Ray? His hatred for Ray ran so strong and so deep that Natches had worried for years that Dayle would strike back at him.

"We meet back here in the morning, then tomorrow night,"

Rowdy told them both as he moved to the rail of the boat. "We hash this out then and figure things out. And we do this together." He stared back at Natches, his gaze hard, determined.

Natches nodded. There wasn't a chance they would let him do it alone, he knew.

He watched as his cousins, his family, jumped from his boat to Dawg's. Dawg headed inside while Rowdy made the jump to his own houseboat, his shadow barely visible even under the clear sky and nearly full moon.

He stared up at that moon, and before he headed back inside to Chaya, he whispered another prayer. This one for protection. God, don't let him lose Chaya, because he knew beyond a shadow of a doubt that he would never survive it.

Chaya smiled as she felt Natches move silently beside her in the big bed, then gave a little shiver as his cool body curled around her.

"You're cold," she murmured, not quite awake, not quite asleep, but content to drift where she was, content and peaceful.

"You gonna get me warm." His voice washed through her, just a little rough, tinged with masculine amusement.

"Hmm." She shifted against him, her legs rubbing against his hair-roughened ones as a sense of completeness began to make itself known.

She shouldn't feel comfortable. She shouldn't feel like she was home in his arms, because she hadn't known what home felt like until Natches.

"I'm really cold," he murmured, rolling her to her back as her lashes lifted and she stared into his shadowed face, glimpsed his quick smile.

She loved his smile, though she hadn't seen it nearly enough since coming to Somerset. She wanted to see it every second of her day, she realized. A smile on his lips and in his eyes.

She let her hands slide up the arms braced on each side of her body, until they curved around his neck. She was ready for his kiss when it came, and he had no right to claim being cold, he was an inferno, heated and hungry.

His kiss sank into her, his lips slanting across hers as he moved over her, sliding between her thighs and nestling the head of his erection against the slick folds of her sex.

"You feel warm now, Natches," she whispered, feeling the need beginning to grow inside her again.

As he slid inside her, thick and hard, her breath caught in her throat and her back arched, taking more of him, taking him deeper and fighting to hold him tighter. Though she was stretched so tight around him that a thought couldn't have slid between his flesh and hers.

"Downright hot now." His breathing was rough, his hands demanding, gentle, as he stroked her body, his head bending until his lips and tongue could play over her nipple.

"Yeah, you feel kinda hot," she gasped, then moaned as he suckled her deep and thrust heavily inside her. "Oh God, Natches, what are you doing to me?"

But she knew what he was doing to her. Binding her so tight to him that there was no way to escape, no way to protect herself.

"Loving you," he murmured against her nipple before kissing

it softly and turning to the other tight peak. "Can't you feel me loving you, Chay?"

She could. Thrusting, sliding so deep and warm inside her, like a dream. He was taking her like a slow, lazy dream, making every stroke memorable, every touch burning inside her heart.

"Keep loving me." She almost sobbed the plea, and she bit his shoulder as he raked his teeth over her nipple, sending sensation after sensation shooting clear to her womb. "Don't stop, Natches. Don't stop loving me."

"Not gonna happen," he groaned. "Always love you."

And she had known it, just as she had known she felt the same. She mouthed the words against his arm, felt him nip the curve of her breast, and the pleasure began to spiral. His thrusts became harder, deeper. They stroked, penetrated, and filled her with ecstasy as she flew in his arms.

Her hips lifted, her legs wrapping around his hips as she held on for the ride of her life. Each time with Natches was better than the last. Each touch, each kiss, each heated thrust inside her body bound her more tightly to him. And when she exploded, felt him explode and felt their release mingling, she knew his intentions of binding her even closer would only give them more to share. There was no way of binding her closer; he already was her soul.

Each spurt of silky release flowing into her had her crying out though. Her name on his lips, his name sobbing from hers as he finally collapsed against her and rolled to his side.

He still held her. He didn't let her go, just tucked her closer to him and let their breaths ease as drowsiness stole over her again.

"I love you." She whispered the words to herself.

Or so she thought. Natches felt his heart expand, nearly tearing from his chest at the sleepy, almost unconscious words.

I love you. Such a simple statement. Yet, those three little words embedded inside him and filled him with determination. He wasn't going to lose her. He'd kill again first, and just as with Johnny, he would never regret it.

SIXTEEN

Timothy Cranston, a.k.a. the rabid leprechaun of DHS, strode into Natches's houseboat as though he owned it. He was followed by the other five agents assigned to the Somerset case, and they looked harried, sleepless, and concerned.

Behind them strode Sheriff Mayes, and he looked ready to explode with fury. His golden brown eyes were sizzling with anger and his tall, hard body was tense with the effort at maintaining self-control.

"What happened?" Chaya stood from her seat at the table, her eyes going from Timothy to the sheriff.

"Someone tried to kill Rogue Walker last night." Zeke's voice grated with fury. "And they almost succeeded."

"Damn!" Chaya turned away, scrambling through the files laid out in front of her, looking for information. "Rogue didn't know anything. She would have told me if she did."

"Maybe she just didn't know she knew anything," Natches suggested as he propped himself against the edge of the table and sipped at the coffee cup he held.

His green eyes were like flints of ice as he watched Timothy. "Isn't that how it usually works, Timothy? It's what a person isn't aware they know that always trips them up. Or what someone suspects they know?"

"Rogue knew something," Timothy growled. "She rides with that damned group of troublemakers on a regular basis. Several of them were tied to Grace and Bedsford."

"By association only." Natches shrugged, but Chaya caught the calculated drawl in his voice. "Hell, arrest the whole town and pull them into interrogation. Everyone but everyone associates eventually here."

"This little town of yours isn't as closed off as you want to think it is, Natches," Timothy snapped. "The tourism rate is incredible. Lake Cumberland is one of the greatest draws in the area."

"So now we're looking for tourists?" Natches lifted his brow and Chaya almost winced.

He'd been cool and focused all morning, going through the files, making notes, answering her with short, brief replies.

"I hate Mackays." Timothy sighed.

"Yeah, especially when they're self-proclaimed generals of a homegrown militant group." Natches grinned tightly, then reached behind him for the files he had stacked there, and threw them to the table. "Try those boys and see if you come up with more than I did."

Chaya stared at him in shock.

"What are you saying, Natches?" Timothy stilled, the agents around him adjusting their posture, their hands in close proximity to their weapons.

Natches laughed at the moves as Sheriff Mayes angled himself to cover Natches if needed. Interesting. A man Chaya would have sworn didn't uphold loyalty over the law, yet he was silently aligning himself with Natches.

"Stop baiting him, Natches." She turned back to him, narrowing her eyes at the gleam of anger in his gaze. "We want to keep Timothy calm, remember? I'm certain his secretary wasn't able to slip his meds in his coffee this morning, so let's not tease him."

It was a running joke that his secretary needed to dose his coffee with sedatives. He was so hyper sometimes he drove the rest of them crazy.

"Look at the last file." Natches shrugged as he finished his coffee and set the cup aside. "You'll see what I mean."

Chaya hadn't seen the files. Natches had been up working before she awoke, and he had stayed distant, refusing to discuss whatever he was working on.

"You're not dealing with clumsy, drugged out hometown boys here," Natches informed them as Timothy pulled out that bottom file.

Chaya barely managed to stifle her gasp.

"You're dealing with men who have had a dream all their lives," Natches stated mockingly. "Instead of sending Chaya in and risking her neck on this fool's errand you gave her, you should have come to someone who would know."

Dayle Mackay. There were three pictures on the front of the file. Dayle Mackay, Chandler Mackay, and another man who Chaya knew was suspected to be part of Freedom's League. These were obviously the men they had needed to target.

"Chandler wasn't in the military," she said, her voice low, shocked.

"Nope, Chandler liked to play war games though. His pansy ass was too important to risk, big-shot architect that he was. But he liked to show his kid how tough and strong he was, usually with his fists, though his wife did have a measure of control over him.

"Now, good ole Dayle Mackay, there's another story."

Natches had once thought he had pushed that part of his past behind him, that he had conquered that hatred, that bitterness. Maybe he hadn't fully managed it, he thought as he watched Cranston read the file.

"Dayle didn't care who he beat up on, or how bad. And he kept his wife sedated enough that she didn't really give a shit either. He married money, confiscated the money on her parents' deaths, and let her live to watch all his glory plans move right along. General Dayle Mackay. That's what he calls himself in private. But then, he always has, so it wasn't easy to put it together at first."

He moved aside as Chaya shifted closer to him. Hell, he'd thought he could have a life with her, and now that was being tested in the worst possible way. The son of a traitor? She had been married to one traitor already; he was pretty sure she wouldn't want another in the family.

"The other files, those are the men I remember from years back who made late-night visits, sat and drank his fine wine and talked about the golden future they could create."

He had been a kid then. Those memories were always rife with pain. Natches had been a nosy kid, and sometimes he had been caught being nosy. And he'd paid for it.

"They're all right here together," Timothy exclaimed as he pulled free one of the few pictures Natches had stolen out of the house before his father had disowned him.

"That picture was stolen by accident." He grinned. "I used to steal family pictures, not that we had a lot. His wife, Linda, she tried taking them for a few years, but finally gave up. She liked being sedated better."

Natches looked at the picture. Six men. Dayle, Chandler, and the men he remembered visiting when he was younger. And one woman. Nadine Mackay Grace between the two Mackay brothers, their arms around her as they grinned for the camera.

His mother, Linda, wasn't in the picture. Just those hard-eyed men and the sister the Mackay brothers had used for their own pleasure.

Natches moved back to the coffeepot, feeling the need to slip away, to hunt. His rifle was clean and ready, ammunition prepared, his knapsack was packed. He could leave at a moment's notice and no one would have a clue where he was going. Or that the need to kill the man who sired him was eating him alive.

"Delbert Grant is your explosives expert," he told them. "He was in town a few weeks ago. He's been out of the service a hell of a long time. But his son was with him; I guess every man needs an apprentice."

Natches almost snorted at the thought.

"How do we get the evidence we need against them?" Timothy mused as he turned to his agents, and Chaya moved to Natches.

He tried to pull away from her again, to ignore her gaze.

"Don't. Please." She stared up at him, then laid her head against his chest and he wondered if his heart was going to shatter in that moment.

He couldn't stop himself from touching her, from letting his hands flatten against her back and feel her melting against him.

But he stared over her head and watched as the agents went through the files, comparing names, associations, and placing each one at specific points of operation.

They weren't incredibly wealthy men. They were plotters, planners. They were bullies and self-appointed saviors. They were the worst kind of enemy.

"This one has a boat on the lake." The sheriff tapped the file of one of the more well-to-do members of the group. "He has a group out here several times a year. They don't cause trouble, but they give you a clear feeling of trouble."

"Uncle Ray wouldn't let them dock here," Natches told them.

Timothy's head raised at the mention of Ray's name. "Where are your cousins? And Jansen? They're not around this morning."

He stroked Chaya's back as she turned in his embrace to watch Timothy. She was still relaxed against him, conforming to his harder, larger body, as though her petite frame could cushion him against any of this.

"They're around," he said softly.

Chaya tensed at the sound of his voice. Soft, almost gentle. A lazy drawl that held no warmth, no comfort.

Chaya watched as Timothy narrowed his eyes on them, taking in their position, the way Natches held her against him. It was an unmistakable picture and the special agent's gaze flickered with knowledge.

"Yeah, that's what you wanted, wasn't it, Timothy?" Natches asked, and Chaya forced herself to remain silent, to keep her eyes on Timothy. "You sent her in here stirring the pot so you could draw us out and make us do your work for you."

Timothy exhaled roughly, ran his hand over his balding head, and gave Natches a wary grin.

"I knew if anyone could do it, you boys could." He finally shrugged. "I was getting nowhere. All we had was the Somerset connection and Johnny's connection to your dad and your uncle."

"Don't," Natches snapped. "Never title those two with those names again. You call them by name; you don't relate them to me."

Cold bitter rage cut through his voice then, and Chaya felt her heart breaking. She had to blink back her tears, and watched as Timothy lowered his head and ran his hand over his face before nodding sharply.

"Yeah, you're right." The agent sighed. "They don't deserve it. You're a fine man, Natches, you and your true uncle and those cousins of yours. You're damned good people. I'm not fighting you for that. Nor am I going to argue over the stench the other two have cast on the rest of you. But we have to deal with this now." His fingers flicked to the files Natches had produced in the early hours of the morning. "We can't arrest them without proof." He looked at Chaya. "And we don't have anyone tying them close enough to Johnny Grace yet."

"You will have," Natches stated. "When you're fishing for the big bass, Cranston, you just have to have the right bait."

"And who's the right bait?" Cranston asked him warily.

"I am."

Chaya felt her heart nearly stop in her chest as fear began to drive a spike through her soul. She twisted around, ignoring his attempt to hold her in place, and stared into the hard, savage expression that had settled over Natches's face.

This wasn't the man she knew. The man who teased or laughed or even the man she had known to be angry. This wasn't anger, it wasn't even rage. It was pure icy terror packed into six feet two inches of tight, hard Marine assassin. This was the man who had killed Johnny Grace the year before, the man who left Timothy Cranston sweating in fear for months after that operation. And seeing the icy, frozen core of that man sent a tremor of wariness through her.

And he knew it. His gaze licked over her, icicles and cold fire, causing a shiver to race down her spine.

"You're the wrong bait." Chaya had to force the words past her throat. "He knows we're together; he knows I'm an agent. He won't go for it."

"Sure he will," Natches drawled, and God she hated that sound. There was nothing warm or comforting in it.

"How do you figure?" she bit out, pulling farther away from him to stare back at him angrily. "He'll know it's a trick. A trap. He'll never mess up like that."

"Keep looking in those files," he told her then. "Check out Fletcher Linkins. We were in sniper training together."

Her gaze moved to the files and then back to him. "Good ole Fletch is dead, did you know that?" He directed the question to Timothy.

Timothy nodded. "Car wreck while he was on leave about four years ago."

"He didn't wreck his car," Natches snarled. "He was killed. I went looking for him after I returned home. I wanted to know why a fellow sniper took a bead on me and tried to take my head off. He was already dead when I found him. Because he had failed the mission the Freedom's League gave him to kill me. Check his link to good ole Dayle."

Timothy shook his head. "Why target you?"

261

"Because I was helping Chay in Iraq." Natches smiled tightly. "I was investigating the orders that sent those missiles into that hotel and I was the one that took out Nassar for torturing her. They wanted me out of the way. They didn't want me tying the threads together, because then I would have known."

"And you didn't know what was going on in Iraq until Chaya came back this time," Timothy mused, nodding his head. "It makes sense."

"Dayle's involved in this up to his eyeballs. He's connected with the men in that photo, and those men are all connected in various ways to military intelligence and/or DHS. They're not wealthy, they're not powerful, but they're going to be. If they're not stopped."

Chaya wrapped her arms across her breasts and listened as Natches and Timothy discussed how to trap them. She watched Natches, and she knew he'd already decided exactly what he was going to do. He was only going through the motions here, letting Timothy get his say in. He was patient, controlled, and Timothy had no clue that Natches was already formulating his own plans.

It was the reason why the other cousins weren't here. It was why Alex wasn't here. Because they were already working their end. He'd already discussed it with them.

The knowledge of that had her jaw clenching as she stared at him, willing him to meet her eyes. When he did, she wanted to flinch. Because she could see beneath the ice, and she could finally see the pain building inside him.

Finally, Timothy and his agents were gone and Natches was locking the door behind them. He stood still as he set the security system, his gaze focused on the digital settings, glaring at them, trying to push back the need to destroy something.

He'd mastered those uncontained rages years ago. The ones that left every stick of furniture around him in slivers. The ones that left his hands bloody from ramming them into the walls.

He breathed in deeply and caught Chaya's scent. A fresh, clean smell that almost, just almost, pushed past the putrid scent of betrayal in his mind. The smell of his own blood, his own pain.

"You lied to Timothy," she whispered then.

Natches turned back and watched her. Dressed in his T-shirt and another pair of borrowed leggings. He was going to have to remind Dawg to check on her luggage, see if she had any of her own clothes left.

"Why did you lie to him, Natches?" Her voice was soft, and the sound of it tried to ease the ragged edges of his soul.

"How do you know I lied?" He crossed his arms over his chest and stared back at the woman who held his soul with such silken bonds that he knew he would never be free.

And he felt just as unworthy of those bonds now as he had in Iraq. Not that it was going to stop him from tying her to him, and better she learn what he was now, rather than later. But sometimes, in the darkest reaches of his soul, there were moments that he cringed at the thought that he was dirtying her.

"I'm a trained interrogation specialist, lover. That's what I do. Remember?" Her smile was just as hard and just as tight as his had been earlier. But that word on her lips. *Lover.* Hell, no one had ever called him "lover," even teasingly. It was such a simple word, and often used so carelessly. But it wasn't a word Natches had used, or had used for him. And it sank inside him, tried to warm him in all the places he had gone cold and hard. For years, he had existed on autopilot, a Marine, a man who knew he had no true home, no family other than the cousins and uncle who still yet belonged to others. Nothing was his alone.

Until Chaya. And here he stood trying to protect that one precious thing in his life, perhaps two, and he could tell she was going to fight him tooth and nail. Just as his cousins fought him.

He shook his head and moved into the room, staring around it, and realizing why he had moved from the houseboat to the garage apartment the year before. This wasn't a home. He hadn't wanted it to be a home.

"Natches, you're not talking to me." His head jerked around at the slightest thread of fear in her voice.

She stood across the room watching him, her arms wrapped across her breasts as she stared at him. And those pretty eyes, such a warm, sweet honey color, seemed to spill inside him.

"He was part of the reason your daughter was killed." He spoke the words slowly and watched her flinch, watched her and made her accept that betrayal. The group Dayle Mackay was a part of had found a way to authenticate a strike that had never been approved. The strike that had killed her child.

"You weren't." She swallowed tightly as he watched her battle her tears.

He had only seen her cry once, and God help him, those tears followed him in his nightmares. Wrenching sobs tore from her soul as he held her safe beneath him, forced her head to his chest and watched that hotel explode.

And that night, the first time he had loved her, the night her daughter had died, he'd had to tear his gaze away from her, turn his back on her and clench his fists to keep from going after

264

Dayle Mackay then and there. Killing him would only solve a part of the problem. Just one part out of a dozen. But he wanted to kill.

Because he remembered her screaming sobs as he dragged her back to the small hotel where he stayed sometimes. There he had held her, rocked her, loved her, and he let silent tears fall from his own eyes.

"His blood is mine." He turned back to her and shook his head as he felt the chill inside him.

"And your blood?" she whispered as she moved to him, took his hand and placed it on her stomach. "You're blood is here, Natches."

He caressed her stomach through the clothes; he couldn't help himself. Her heated flesh met his calloused hands, and as he did when he held her at night, he imagined he felt life there. Hope.

He shook his head and wanted to pull away from her, but he couldn't force himself to.

"And when this is over, you may curse the night you allowed me to come inside you." He found the strength to pull back from her, to walk away.

"You son of a bitch!" He didn't get far before her fingers gripped his wrist and she jumped in front of him. "Excuse me here? But are you daring to walk away from me?"

He dragged his fingers through his hair, a frown jerking between his brows at the anger on her face, the accusation in her eyes.

"I have things to do, Chaya."

"And of course you're not going to do the 'partner' thing you've been preaching about here and tell me what the hell they are. Right, Natches?"

He nodded slowly. "That about sums it up."

She looked as though he had slapped her. Natches stared back at her in confusion as she backed away from him, her face paling.

"So much for all my courage and strength that you so highly respect," she sneered. "I guess, once again, I'm delegated back to the weak little woman who has to be protected. Right?"

"This is my fight," he bit out.

"Because it's your blood?"

"Fucking A," he snarled.

"Well, excuse me, Mr. Mackay, but there's a damned good chance I'm carrying your blood inside me, so I think that makes it my damned fight as well."

And how the hell was he supposed to counter that argument?

"It doesn't work that way, Chay." He tried pure male dominance and decisiveness.

"Because you decree it?" Her eyes were fiery now, not just in anger, but in confrontation, in determination.

Hell, he was getting hard. He could feel his arousal stretching to life, the ice that had encased his emotions beginning to melt as she glared back at him.

"You can decree to hell and back, Natches, and it's not going to do you one damned bit of good. You dragged me into this relationship, you're the one that made damned sure my soul was so tied to yours that I couldn't breathe without feeling you, and then you did everything in your power to help create life from it. Damn you, you're not backing away now."

"Backing away was never in the cards." He lowered his head and growled the words at her. "Did I say you could leave this relationship?"

Her eyes widened and disbelief filled her face. And that made him grow harder, because the disbelief was filled with scornful amazement.

"Oh my God, you take the cake." Her hands went on her hips, and his cock just got harder still. "I can't believe your complete arrogance."

"You should, you've dealt with it before." He wasn't budging. If he told her what he had planned, then she would just stick her nose into it. Her nose was far enough on the chopping block; he wasn't going to allow it to go any farther.

"You are not doing this without me!" The words were said with such snap that his brow lifted mockingly.

"And you're not going after him with me." She'd lost enough in her life; he wasn't going to allow her to lose any more. Not her life, or their child's. And he knew that child was there, resting securely within her. He intended to make damned sure he kept that child safe. The child and his or her mother.

"I've worked this case for five years," she said furiously. "Five years, so you could come in with your lies and your damned charm and force me out of it? 'Oh, Chay, I just admire your courage and strength,'" she sneered, her face twisting in fury. "Fuck you, Natches."

"And I didn't lie." His voice rose, unintentionally, fueled by the anger and the arousal rising inside him. "Do you think I don't admire it? That I'd want to change a damned thing about you? I'm not trying to change anything, damn you, but I will protect you."

"Screw your protection."

He clenched his fists, not in rage, but to keep from touching her, to keep from jerking her to him and taking all the wild passion, driving into it until they both forgot the pain and the danger moving in on them.

"Chay, don't push me on this," he growled back. Damn her, she was tearing him apart inside. He could see the betrayal in her eyes, the hurt, and he hated it. "This isn't a fight you can be a part of."

"And it's not a fight I'll let you push me out of," she yelled back.

Turning, he watched as she stalked to the table and snapped her laptop shut. She gathered the files, stuffed them with the laptop in her case, then jerked her boots from the floor and sat on the couch.

"What the hell are you doing?" He grabbed the boot from her hand and held it out of her reach as she came off the couch, fury stamped on her flushed features. "You're not leaving here."

"The hell I'm not." When she couldn't jerk the boot out of his grasp, she pulled the case on her shoulder and moved to the door barefoot.

"You can't go outside without shoes. It's cold out there." He parked himself in front of the door as she stood before him, breasts heaving, her little fists clenched at her side as though she were actually going to use them on him.

"Better the cold outside than the cold in here." She slapped his chest. "Now get out of my way."

"Chay, you don't want to keep this up," he grated out. "Calm the hell down."

"Don't you tell me to calm down, Natches Mackay." A finger was in his face, pointing too close to his nose as he looked at it, then slowly looked up at her.

"Put that finger down, Chay." There was something about that finger in his face that made every male instinct inside him stand up in outrage.

"Make me." That finger jabbed into his chest. "Come on, tough ass. Make me. You've cheated everywhere else in this relationship, you might as well cheat here, too. What are you going to do? Tie me to the bed? Because damn you, that's the only way you'll keep me here."

SEVENTEEN

There was something about that finger in his chest and the complete and total fury transforming Chaya's expression that did it to him.

"It" being completely wiping his mind of everything but possessing her. "It" being imagining her on her knees, naked, nipples tight, hard, and red, while he fucked that sarcastic little mouth with shallow thrusts.

"It" being owning her soul because she owned his. He knew, even as he stood there mad as hell and fighting it, that there wasn't a chance in hell he could keep her if he did this alone. And that just made him madder. Just made him hornier.

"That finger is getting ready to get you in trouble," he warned her softly.

Her lips flattened, then she did something he would have never imagined. Something that had his eyes widening in shock. She lifted that cute little hand and her middle finger shot up like a flag.

She didn't have to say a word. Her expression said it all as she turned her back to him and began to move through the living room. Probably heading to the back deck door.

Oh, that was just too bad.

He jerked his boots off and let them thump to the floor as she reached the kitchen. And she kept going. His shirt came off as he moved after her, and he tossed it to the couch.

And she knew. She threw a look over her shoulder and almost managed to run a step or two. Before she made it past the table his arm hooked around her waist and he dragged her to the stairs.

And like the little hellion she was, she fought him. She kicked, she wiggled, she snarled, and he swore she bit his shoulder. But she wasn't fighting hard enough. All that heavy breathing wasn't just because she had her mad on. Hell no, she was as wet as he was hard, and he was betting his cock on that fact. Because that was the portion of his body that was going to fall off if he didn't get it inside that hot little body of hers. Fast.

He couldn't remember a time that he had been so enraged and so aroused at the same time. He could feel his muscles pumping with blood, his dick throbbing like an open wound, his balls tight with lust.

She wasn't getting by with a single bout of anything today. Double helping, he thought. He was going to have that wet, impudent little mouth, and he was going to have that slick, heated little pussy, and when he was finished . . . hell, when he was finished, he was going to figure out how to give her what she needed and keep her safe at the same time.

But he didn't have to tell her that yet. Hell no. She was spitting mad and clawing at his shoulders, cursing him even as he tossed her to the bed and stripped his jeans off.

Chaya tore off the shirt she wore, then the bra. She was certain the strap snapped at some point. As Natches stepped out of his jeans, she wiggled out of the leggings and panties and she was waiting on him.

His shoulders were scratched from her fury, and she was certain she would be reasonably sorry for that later, but right now, smug possessiveness curled her lips instead.

"I marked you," she snarled at him as he stepped toward the bed.

He smiled. A slow, lust-worthy curl of his lips that had a fist punch of reaction jerking in her stomach.

"That's okay, baby, because I'm sure I'll mark you, too, before the night's over."

She crawled to the edge of the bed and licked her lips, staring up at him from beneath her lashes and waiting. Anticipating.

"I thought of you every time I used that toy." She taunted him now and watched his eyes flare with wicked heat. "I sucked it until I could take it to my throat, and thought of you. I heard your groans in my head and I moaned around it as I touched myself."

"To your throat?" His voice was a raspy, guttural growl.

"To my throat. And I moaned." She licked her lips as she lifted one hand from the bed and let it run down her body. "And I touched myself." She touched herself now. Her fingers slid through the slick juices, circled her clit, and her lashes fluttered in pleasure.

"Did you come?" He was closer, coming closer, his hand circling the thick shaft as the engorged crest tightened and throbbed in hunger.

A small bead of pearly pre-cum dampened the tiny slit, drew her attention and her hunger.

"I came," she teased him. "I came and I moaned, and it wasn't enough. Because it wasn't you."

And she had needed him. Needed him until parts of her had felt barren and lost.

He came closer, the head of his cock almost within reach.

"You're going to take me to your throat, Chay," he warned her, his voice so rough, so deep it caused her knees to weaken, her heart to pound in her chest.

"Make me, Natches." She smiled, then her breath caught as she raked her finger over her clit, and knew he was aware of the pleasure she was bringing herself.

One hand snaked out, catching her hair, tangling in it as he held her still. Her tongue swiped over the broad head and she moaned at the rich earthly taste of the liquid bead on her tongue. Passion infused with lust. A storm, heat and lightning. It filled her senses and drenched her fingers with her response.

Then his cock was filling her mouth. Thick and iron hard, the head throbbing violently as he pushed inside her. Chaya moaned and heard his answering growl as she did what she promised. She took him to her throat, her tongue rippling beneath the underside as she relished the taste of him.

One hand gripped his shaft, stroking it fiercely, determined to rip his control from him the same as he had managed to rip hers. Damn her, she had never given anyone, man or woman, the finger. That was what he did to her. He made her crazy. He made her insane to have him, made her want to fight and love him.

And God help her, how she loved him.

"Damn you," he snarled as she lifted her lashes and stared up at him, taking him as deep as she could as she touched herself, stroked herself. "Your mouth is illegal, Chay."

She would have smiled, but she whimpered instead. Because she needed him, hungered for him. Because she wanted to taste his release, glory in it.

She sucked him harder, flicked her tongue over the head as he fucked into her mouth, and swallowed him deep.

"Hellion." He pushed the fingers of both hands into her hair, tightened and pulled, and she moaned again, knowing the sound was vibrating against his cock head and glorying in his response.

"Sweet Chay." Sweat drenched his face, his shoulders. It ran down his neck in tiny rivulets and dampened the hair that fell over his face.

He looked like a pirate. He felt like a pirate, because he had stolen her heart and her soul and she didn't want them back. She just wanted his in return.

"Sweet." He groaned, his lashes lowering, a dark flush on his cheeks as his lips appeared heavier, fuller, more sensual. "Sweet Chay. Suck it, baby. Suck it deep."

She drew him deep, moaned, licked, and felt the warning throb of his impending release. His abdomen tightened, sweat rolled down it, and a second later his head tilted back, his jaw clenched, and her name tore from his throat as he exploded.

Hot, rich, a taste of salt and man and the storm rising and he was filling her mouth with it, making her drunk on him. She took each furious blast and whimpered in loss as he pulled free of her.

"Enough." He pulled her hand free of the pulsing flesh of her pussy a second before her own loss.

Her eyes snapped open. "I was ready to come," she almost howled as he flipped her to her back.

"Yeah. I know." His grin was pure wicked male. "If you want to come, baby, all you have to do is ask nicely."

"Asshole!" She grabbed his hair as he moved between her thighs and pulled. Pulled until his lips were buried in the tormented flesh and her legs were wrapped around his shoulders.

"Oh God. Yes. Damn you, Natches." She arched, her shoulders grinding into the mattress as his tongue dove deep inside the clenching depths of her core.

And he licked. "Oh yes. I love it. Love it when you do that." Her head thrashed; her fingers dug into his hair.

He licked and lapped inside her like he was eating candy and loving every minute of it. She was dying. Right there in his arms, she was dying and she didn't know how to stop it. She didn't know how to handle the burn or the violence of her response to his touch.

She was twisting against him, mewling in need as his hand landed on her rear. The rough little caress only made her burn brighter.

"More." She twisted. She arched. "Oh God, Natches. More."

He gave her more. More of the rough caresses, the heated little smacks over her butt, and more of those delicious licks inside her. Then outside her. Then around her clit. He sucked the little bud into his mouth, and she exploded into fragments.

She screamed his name, pulsed and shattered, and before she could catch her breath, he pushed her legs apart, rose above her, and buried his cock inside her.

Full length. One hard thrust. He pushed inside her with hungry demand, her name on his lips as he began to thrust hard and fast. Stroking and fucking inside her and sending her crashing into wave after wave of fiery release.

And he didn't stop. She was burning, drenched in both their perspiration when he pulled free of her, flipped her on her stomach, and lifted her rear.

And he was pushing inside her again.

"Take all of me." He groaned, coming over her, his fingers lacing with hers as he held her beneath him. "Feel me, Chay. Feel all of me and I know I belong to you."

Her head tipped back as his teeth scraped her neck and he surged inside her again. Again. He pounded inside her until she shattered, flew, until she swore her soul left her body and merged with his as she felt the violent, harsh pulses of his semen shooting inside her.

If she wasn't pregnant yet, she knew she was now. She could feel it, that bonding, a connection she had never believed she could feel with another human being. And yet, with Natches, he had given her no choice. He had stolen her heart. Made her a part of him, and now, the fight was over for it. That didn't mean he was getting his way though.

"I love you," she whispered as he collapsed over her, his head lying against her shoulder, his eyes opening to meet hers as she turned her head to stare back at him. "With my soul, Natches Mackay, I love you."

Natches sighed heavily as he forced himself to pull from her, grimacing in pleasure at the heated friction along his cock.

Lowering himself beside her, he pulled her into his arms and pressed his lips against the top of her head.

"I love you until, sometimes, I wonder if I can breathe without you now," he told her then, staring into the sunlit expanse of the bedroom as he caressed her back with one hand.

She was still and silent against his chest, though he knew that indomitable will of hers was still firmly in place. She was the strongest person he had ever known in his life, and he wanted nothing more than to allow her to be weak.

And that was the redneck in him, he knew it was. The man who wanted to protect his woman against any and all threats. To be a partner until danger rolled around. But he had chosen a woman who refused to hide from danger.

That courage she possessed terrified him.

"Dayle Mackay is dangerous," he said softly, staring at the ceiling now, his brow creasing into a frown as he let the memories of his childhood wash over him.

He didn't do that often. The past was just that, it was the past. When he had met Chaya, seeing her courage and her will to laugh had somehow helped him to dull those memories, but nothing could eradicate them.

"Dayle wanted a carbon copy of himself in a son," he stated. "A bully without a conscience, and one he could control. He didn't have much luck with me. I was a smart-mouthed little bastard eaten up with rage. I defied him every chance I had, and I gloried in it, even when he was taking his fists to me."

That had been his relationship with the man he refused to call father.

"You're not facing him alone." Her voice was soft, sweet, it was tinged with emotion and struck a bolt of feeling inside him that had him closing his eyes against the strength of it.

"There's no other way to face him, but alone." He sighed. "That's what it's come down to here, Chay. Just me and Dayle. I've avoided him, I've put it off. Hell, I should have just killed the son of a bitch before I met you, like I wanted to. But Uncle Ray would have felt as though he failed to raise me right, and Rowdy and Dawg, well, they would have had something to say about it."

Not much. But they would have said something, Natches thought.

He should have felt an edge of sorrow, hell, he should have felt guilt over the fact that it would be that easy to kill a man. But Dayle Mackay wasn't a man—he was a monster.

Yet, he still hadn't killed him, and Natches was never certain what stopped him from doing it. Maybe because until now, Dayle had never really done anything evil, even though Natches had known he *was* evil.

And he wasn't going to kill him now. Not unless Dayle gave him no other choice.

"You can give me the silent treatment until hell freezes over." She lifted her head and stared him in the eye. "But you're not doing this alone."

He, Dawg, Rowdy, and Ray had come up with the plan while Chaya slept. Their voices quiet to keep from disturbing her, their minds made up.

Natches knew the one thing Dayle had always wanted from him. Loyalty. It came down to something that simple. From the time Natches had been small, Dayle had been enraged at his affection for Ray and the two cousins he hadn't even known until they started school together. They had been instantly drawn to each other. And Natches had begun slipping away from his own home and sneaking to Ray's.

He and Dawg had been fascinated by Ray Mackay's gentle if sometimes gruff demeanor.

"If you're with me, he'll never talk," he told her, keeping his voice firm, keeping himself strong. "You're not a part of this, Chaya. There's no way to make you a part of this."

He watched her as she laid her head on his chest, her eyes glittering with tears. And Chaya didn't cry easily. She didn't use tears to get her way; she didn't pull any of the female tricks to force a man's agreement he had seen over the years from other women.

Kelly, love her heart, she shamelessly used tears whenever she felt Rowdy was being too stubborn. Shamelessly because she and Rowdy both knew what she was doing. It wasn't a game to her so much as a way to get past Rowdy's sometimes stubborn mind-set. She was sweet and innocent, and sometimes she didn't understand the evil that existed in the world. Though he knew she would argue that sentiment.

Crista was stronger, but still, she was so completely female that Natches could only grin at the battles Dawg fought with his wife. She led the big, tough Dawg around with a crook of her finger and managed to get past even his most stubborn decisions. Like running the lumber store himself. Taking responsibility for it. Dawg was turning into a real businessman, courtesy of one little stubborn female.

Chaya, Natches knew, would never be like Kelly and Crista. Not that there was anything wrong with either woman. It was just both of them saw the world as it existed around them; they didn't know the darkness that existed beneath it. And Dawg and Rowdy would kill anyone that tried to show it to them.

Chaya was different. She knew the evil. She had lived with it. She knew the darkness, because she had spent years navigating it. And she knew him. And because of that, she was going to be hell on his nerves and he knew it.

"You better find a way to make me a part of it," she stated. "Because you're not doing it alone."

He wanted to grin at the tone of her voice.

Turning her onto her back, he stared into her eyes and laid his palm on her lower stomach.

"Do you know I swore all my life I'd never allow a woman to have my child?" His fingers caressed her belly where he knew their child lay.

"Don't use that against me, Natches. That's dirty."

He shook his head. "I'm not doing that, Chay; I'm trying to make a point here."

"You're point being that I'm risking our child if I try to help you. What about you? If anything happens to you, who is going to help me raise our baby? Who's going to teach him how to be a man?" Her eyes didn't glitter with tears now, they glittered with anger.

His lips quirked at the sight of that anger.

"If anything ever happens to me, you'll be taken care of," he told her. "Just as Kelly or Crista would be taken care of if anything happened to Rowdy or Dawg. But that wasn't my point."

"Then get to your damned point so I can tell you how much of your time you've wasted. I'm keeping track of it by the way."

He had no doubt in his mind that she was.

"My point was, Chaya, until you, I never dreamed I'd find a woman strong enough to make certain my child was protected. Even if it had to be protected against me."

Her eyes widened then, and Natches forced himself to face the fear that had followed him most of his adult life.

"They say blood will always tell," he told her. "Dayle Mackay uses his fists at the slightest provocation. He's one of those men that should have been sterilized before he had a chance to breed. To make certain that kind of mean wasn't hereditary."

"Are you crazy?" She jerked away from him then, her expression incredulous as she rolled from the bed and stared back at him furiously. "You just wasted a half hour of my time with that crap?" She was almost snarling now. "Get your ass out of the bed, get dressed, and tell me what the hell you have planned before I have to shoot you."

"You're strong enough to stand up to me, Chay. But I don't know if I'm strong enough to keep from murdering Dayle Mackay if you have to see the monster that sired me."

There, it was out. He said it. That was the end of the subject as far as he was concerned. He rolled from the bed himself and jerked his pants from the floor. When he straightened, he stared back at her, feeling that inner rage flashing through him.

"Cranston needs that son of a bitch alive," he told her. "I don't want to take away from your courage or your pride, Chaya, but this is my battle, and it's my fight. I won't have the control to keep from blowing his head off if he strikes out at you. And he will. Just to test me. Just to make sure he has what he wants, he would do it."

"Like hell," she bit out. "Natches, what could he want that would make him so stupid? He's worked with the League most of his life from what I understand. He's been damned good at what he's done. What could he want so much that would make him mess up to that extent?"

Chaya was furious. She stood her ground in front of him, glaring back at him, enraged that he would try to protect her when he needed her.

"My soul," he said bitterly. "What does any monster want, Chay, but your soul?"

"Natches . . ."

His hand went over her mouth, and when she stared into his eyes, she saw something that almost terrified her. Something more frightening than the icy rage she had seen before, something more destructive than mere fury. She saw a feral determination, animalistic, almost uncontrolled as he stared into her eyes.

"If he so much as breathes violence in your direction, so much as curls a finger to touch you, *he will die*." Natches's lips curled back from strong, clenched teeth. "If he breathes the same air you're breathing, so much as dares to step in your direction, I won't bother to think, I won't bother to try to control my rage. Is that what you want?"

She swallowed tightly, the anger draining away to be replaced by a sorrow so strong it nearly stole her breath as her hand lifted and she touched his face. "What did he do to you?" she whispered.

"He created me," he stated coldly. "Now, he's going to have deal with me. But if DHS wants him alive when we're finished, then you'll stay out of it. Otherwise, I'm not making any promises."

EIGHTEEN

With Cranston aware of what they were looking for, it didn't take long to get the files of the men in the photograph with Chandler and Dayle Mackay, or to find the connections that brought them together.

They were in the same Marine Corps unit for nearly eight years. They had stayed in touch afterward. Hunting trips. Fishing trips. Covers for their own dreams of glory as they drew in more and more recruits after they left the service but stayed involved in various military groups.

They had no true power backing them, individually, but they had gained it as a group. Here and there. Drawing in like-minded soldiers, at first, discharged soldiers, and slowly working their way up until their recruits were coming in from active service.

They had them tied in together. They connected the dots

through the day until Cranston was certain it was only a matter of time before they had those responsible for the strike order in Iraq that had killed Chaya's child. But to ensure their arrest and the complete disclosure of all their members, they needed something more to bring Dayle Mackay in.

Natches would get them more. And Chaya was terrified how he would manage that, and what it would do to his soul.

Letting go of the fight over his decision to meet with Dayle Mackay by himself wasn't easy for Chaya. But she'd seen that the more she argued with him over it, the more determined he became.

Redneck pride and stubborn will. She'd heard about it; she'd just never seen it. Not that he was a whole lot different from any other man of his kind. It just rankled more perhaps because he was hers.

And that was the part that was driving her crazy. He had charmed her, seduced her, loved his way right into her soul, and now he was shutting her out.

She looked over at him from where she sat at the table. Stretched out on the couch, one arm behind his head as he supposedly watched television.

He wasn't watching that droning news report any more than she was. He was wired, tense, waiting. Whatever Dawg and Rowdy had done that day evidently wasn't going to have immediate results.

As she watched him, her cell phone beeped imperatively at her ear.

"Dane," she answered the call, watching as Natches tensed further.

"You want to tell me what the hell your boyfriend's cousins are up to?" Cranston snarled in her ear. "They just had a rather heated, if amusing, argument in the parking lot of Mackay Lumber. It seems they've had a bit of a falling out with their cousin over a fucking picture he found."

God, what were they doing?

She lifted her eyes as Natches sat up and turned to face her. His eyes narrowed as she stared back at him.

"I don't know," she finally answered. "And he's not talking."

"Agent Dane, we don't need fuckups here," Cranston bit out. She could imagine him scowling, his face wrinkling like an irate bulldog's. "Find out what the hell is going on."

"And you expect me to do that how?" she asked him, still watching Natches, fear building inside her. "Do you have the details of the conversation?"

"Oh, something along the lines of wiping their hands of him forever because he destroyed evidence against someone. A picture. One that implicated someone they didn't name, but anyone with a brain could put it together."

She licked her lips nervously as Natches rose slowly to his feet and walked toward her. Her teeth clenched as he slipped the wireless unit from her ear and brought it to his own.

"Chaya's rather busy right now, Timothy," he said quietly. "Try again later."

He disconnected the call and tossed the unit to the table.

"Don't answer it." He pointed his finger to the ringing phone, then turned and walked into the kitchen.

And Chaya had had enough. She stood to her feet, gathered the files she was working on, and pushed them into her case. Shutting her laptop down, she pushed it into the case as well and carried it to the door.

"Walk out that door and I'll tie you to the bed." His voice never rose.

"I'm sick of that threat now." She sat down on the chair and pulled her socks on her feet before pulling her boots to her.

He pulled a beer from the fridge, opened it, and moved back to the living room, where he sat down on the couch and watched her, his green eyes intent, his expression carved from stone.

"I'm not Crista or Kelly," she told him. "I won't be pushed behind you and protected, nor play the helpless little woman. If that's what you think, then you should sit down and rethink your options. That one isn't working."

She pulled the first boot over her foot.

"He'll be calling sometime tomorrow," Natches stated. "Alex will be contacting Cranston tonight. At present, this marina, as well as the lumber store, is under surveillance by three of the men in that photo." He pointed to the picture laid out on the table. "If you walk out of here, you compromise me, is that what you want?"

She let the boot fall back to the floor.

"What have you done?" she whispered, staring back at him as she felt her chest clench with dread. She remembered the year before, the operation that had very nearly ended with Crista Jansen's death because Dawg had played games with Johnny Grace. And now, Natches was setting himself up as a target.

"Everyone knows the Nauti Boys always stick together. Nothing comes between them. Now something has; there's a division. Nadine glimpsed it that morning Dawg and I were arguing at the diner over you. Remember?"

She nodded, remembering the morning she had threatened to tell Crista on Dawg.

"They've seen us arguing more than once here lately, over you and this investigation. That worked in our favor. Now it appears that Dawg and Rowdy are arguing between them because I destroyed a picture that implicates someone in the investigation. And Dawg's letting his opinion that 'blood will tell' be known."

Chaya shook her head slowly. "What kind of blood? What does he mean, 'blood will tell'?"

"Meaning, Chaya, that evidently, when it comes right down to it, my loyalty is to the bastard that sired me rather than the family that raised me."

"And you've kept me in the dark about this for what reason?"

"Hoping I could keep you out of it?" He arched his brow mockingly. "I'm telling you, because I've decided there's no other choice. Have you considered how someone found out who your agents were and managed to plant highly professional explosives on their vehicles?"

"Cranston suspects a leak," she whispered. "He's been going over the files. So have I."

Natches shook his head. "There's no leak, sweetheart. You were all staying at the Suites. You met there, in one particular room for a meeting most every morning."

"How did you know that?"

"Because dishonorably discharged Private Michael Wheeler works there. And he's very good friends with Dayle Mackay. Look at the files on the men who have joined the ranks of the League. Most are dishonorably discharged for abuse, ignoring the chain of command, sex crimes. Those who weren't in the military are malcontents with a bitch, nothing more. Except maybe dreams of glory. Once I determined who at the hotel could have gotten in a position to watch you, it was easy to figure out. That's where Cranston made his mistake. He was afraid blood would tell, so he sent you in so he could watch me, see which way things would swing before he pulled me in."

"He was afraid you would protect Dayle Mackay."

"Just as his agents were. Just as his agents no doubt discussed in that room after you left each morning. The room could have been bugged, individual rooms could have been bugged. Who knows? But Dayle found out what was going on, and he knew Cranston was onto him; otherwise they would have never struck out at the agents."

She nodded slowly. She had argued this with Cranston, warning him to bring Natches and his cousins in on this phase of the investigation, but he had refused. Now she knew why.

"What are you doing now?" she asked.

"Letting blood tell." He shrugged. "Dayle's going to think about this. He's going go think about that picture, think about what I could know, then he's going to call me. The break he's been waiting for. A sign of loyalty to him rather than to my cousins or my uncle."

"Or your country."

"Or my country," he agreed. "We'll set up the meet. Alex will cover me; he's a hell of a sniper. Dawg and Rowdy will back me up from a safe distance, and I'll get the information DHS needs."

She shook her head. "That's not going to work. Any defense lawyer in the nation will blow you off the stand if you testify against him. With your family history, it will never work."

"It's the only chance we have," he told her.

"You go in wired . . ."

"Won't work; he'll check me for a wire, Chay. He's not incompetent, he's proved that already."

"A different sort of wire." She leaned forward intently. "A cell phone, Natches, the receiver inside it will stay activated whether the cell phone is turned on or off. It's new. Something he won't suspect. You carry it right on your belt, in clear view. He'll never know."

He stared back at her silently.

"It's not even something our agents know about. Cranston had a friend of his working on it. It works; we've tried it out several times. Reception is perfect. We could get the meeting recorded, get our evidence, and fry him and Nadine and all his friends."

"Do the agents working with you know about it?" That was the risk, Natches thought. If this was something the other agents had known of, or discussed, then Dayle could already know about it and suspect.

But Chaya shook her head quickly. "I'm telling you, only three of us know about it. Cranston, me, and the electronics expert Cranston works with on the side. He's not even agency. And I know Cranston has it with him. He's just been waiting for a chance to test it."

It could work. He narrowed his eyes, watching her silently for long moments. If it didn't work, if reception didn't go through, if the electronics failed, then what the hell. Nothing lost. Except blood. If DHS couldn't make the charges stick on Dayle, then Natches, as much as he was finding he hated the thought of it, would take care of things himself.

His home had been torn apart in the past year because of Johnny and Dayle's crimes. Once news had leaked of the activities some of their citizens had been involved in, the town had been left in a state of shock. It was time for it to end, one way or the other.

"This could work, Natches," Chaya urged him softly. "We can have the van in town before daylight if I contact Timothy now. I'll call Alex; he'll be able to get to Timothy without anyone else knowing. Everything can be ready and waiting before Dayle ever calls you."

What was there left to lose? If it worked, then he wouldn't have to face Chaya after shedding more blood. Despite what he had told Sheriff Mayes—that killing Johnny was better than sex—he admitted now it had put a mark on his soul. Not a regret, but a knowledge that he sometimes found himself shying away from.

If he killed the man who sired him, what example then was he laying for his children? Children who would grow one day to no doubt hear the tale. Some secrets you just didn't keep when everyone pretty much knew everyone else.

"Call Alex." He finally nodded. "I'll get a message to Dawg and Rowdy. They can slip over without the eyes watching ever suspecting a thing. We'll get things ready to go."

Chaya felt her heart almost explode in joy. He wasn't dismissing the idea, he was embracing it. He didn't want her involved, but he was willing to allow her to back him, and that concession, she knew, hadn't been easy for him.

Being with Natches wasn't always going to be easy, she had found that out. When he decided something, he could obviously get incredibly stubborn about it, even with her. But he could listen to reason. That was all she asked of him, to listen to reason.

"Look at your face." His lips quirked with a hint of amusement as he reached out and touched her cheek. "You'd think I just gave you diamonds."

Chaya shook her head slowly. "Something better than diamonds, Natches."

"What could be better than diamonds?"

"Your trust."

Natches stared back at her now, almost confused. Chaya's

eyes were shining, the golden brown a rich honey color, filled with warmth and some strange glow of happiness. Hell, a man would think he had just given her the crown jewels or something.

"Chay." He shook his head, letting his fingers trail down her cheek before pulling back and continuing to stare at that strange sight. "Baby, you've always had my trust."

"Not all of it, Natches." She shook her head. "Not when it came to being here for you, with you. It's something you don't even fully allow Dawg and Rowdy."

He frowned at that. "I discussed this with them. We made up the plan together."

"And then you sent them away," she told him. "You gave them just enough to satisfy them, just enough to make them feel as though they were a part of it, but you were still going in alone."

"I'm still going in alone," he warned her, making certain she understood that. "You're not going in with me, Chay."

"But I'll be there with you," she whispered. "And I'll be close. I'll know you're safe, and you're willing to allow that risk, so I can make certain you're safe."

"Hell." He rubbed at his jaw roughly. "Like you'd back down." He glowered back at her. "You'd give me a run for stubborn any day, do you think I don't know it? You just came up with a solution I wasn't aware of. I'd have figured something out before the meeting."

It wasn't that big of a deal, he kept trying to tell himself. He'd walk into the meeting, see what the hell was going on, get some information then hand Dayle Mackay over to Timothy Cranston and DHS. It was that simple. But he didn't intend to take any chances with Chaya's life.

"And let me tell you something now," she said then. "Earlier, you said he created you. Dayle Mackay didn't create you. You made yourself. That's all any of us do."

Natches shook his head at that before reaching out and dragging her from the chair to his arms.

"You're a dangerous woman," he told her as he held her against him. "And maybe you're right. Either way, I'll be the one to bring him down. Now make that call to Alex and get your plan set up. I don't want Dayle calling before you have everything ready."

He let her go and watched as she moved across the room to retrieve the wireless earpiece to her laptop.

"Just in case the cells aren't secure enough at the moment." She frowned as she sat down in front of the laptop. "I prefer not to take chances."

She sent the encrypted e-mail quickly. A short, terse request for a new cell phone and accompanying accessories. Cranston would know what she was talking about.

Within minutes, his reply came through. An affirmative and already in place. As usual, Cranston was moving ahead of everyone else, she thought with a smile as Natches read the message over her shoulder.

"Bastard," he muttered, but there was that vein of amusement again.

"What time are Dawg and Rowdy supposed to be here?" she asked as she rose to her feet and moved to him, eager, almost desperate to touch him now.

She needed him, a part of her was so hungry for him, to be held by him, that she wondered if she could bear to wait even as long as it would take to undress.

He caught her immediately, his arms, so strong and sure, wrapping around her, lifting her to him. "We have plenty of time," he promised. "God, Chay, I'd steal time if I had to for this."

He tumbled her to the couch, coming over her as his hands pushed at the cotton leggings she wore and stripped them from her.

His lips came over hers, his tongue delving deep, tangling with hers as her hands tore at his belt, at the fastening and zipper of his jeans.

It was always like this with Chaya. Wild and explosive, so searing that sometimes he wondered if he would survive it. And always desperate. As though a part of him couldn't believe she was actually here, in his arms, a part of his life.

He'd let her run from him for too many years. Trying to let her have the time and the space she needed to come to grips with everything that had happened in her life. And he wondered if that hadn't been a mistake. For both of them. The years they had lost could never be returned. But they would ensure that he cherished every moment he had with her.

As he stripped off her clothes, then tore his own off, he stilled, staring down at her, naked and aroused, her body flushed and heated as he spread her thighs and moved slowly between them.

Her breasts were swollen, her little nipples peaked and hard, reaching out to him, eager for his hungry mouth. He took first one, then the other, sucking at the sweetness of her flesh and the tight warmth of the tender peaks. He kissed the curve of her breast, then her shoulder, as he rose over her.

"I love you, Chaya," he whispered in her ear as he began to press his cock inside her.

Instant, silken heat began to enclose his sensitive cock head. Liquid fire tightened around it and sucked him inside, inch by inch until he was gritting his teeth against the pleasure consuming him as he buried himself full length inside her.

It was like living in ecstasy, the moments that he was a part of her. The way she took him, so freely, without hesitation, giving every part of herself to him whether she realized it or not.

He had always known it. Whether it was one of the kisses he stole, or now, buried so deep inside her that he didn't know where he ended and she began, he could feel her soul clasping him. Just as surely as the depths of her pussy encased him, her soul encased him as well.

Natches sheltered her beneath him, held her to him and began to move, to thrust slow and easy inside her. Each penetration dragged a hard breath from his chest and caused her to breathe in roughly. She trembled beneath him, shuddered with the pleasure he gave her. She made him feel stronger than he knew he was, more powerful than he had ever imagined he could be.

"Oh God, Natches. It's so good." Her breathless cry sent a surge of pleasure racing up his spine.

"Hold on to me, Chay." Her arms were already wrapped tight around his shoulders, her nails digging into his flesh. He carried her marks every time he took her, and he gloried in it.

His head lifted so he could watch her face as he took her. Watch the flush that washed over her expression, the perspiration that gleamed against her flesh.

Nothing in his life had ever been so beautiful as Chaya in her passion. And nothing, no one, could strip his control from him as she did.

He moved against her, harder, deeper. He groaned out at the tight clasp, the feel of her pussy tightening around him, trying to hold him inside her each time he withdrew. The feel of her pleasure mounting, the convulsive clench of silken muscles around him, her rising cries, the demand in the return thrust of her hips.

He was losing control. He could feel it. His muscles tightened as he fought to hold back just a little bit longer, to feel just a little bit more of her pleasure.

Then she melted beneath him, around him. Her hips slammed into his and her cry filled his ears, and holding on was impossible.

Her name was on his lips as he thrust inside her again, again, lost in the release rising inside him until he buried inside her one last time and felt the hard, forceful jets of his release throbbing from his cock.

Nothing had ever been this good in his life. Nothing else had ever filled him, fulfilled him, as Chaya did.

"I love you," she whispered at his ear. "God help me, Natches, I love you so much."

And those words, they completed him.

NINETEEN

Natches moved the *Nauti Dreams* from her berth beside his cousins' houseboats and pulled her into a spare slot at the other end of the marina. To preserve the illusion, he had told Chaya. His expression was still, too still and too quiet, as though he were with her in body only.

Chaya leaned against him as he maneuvered the craft from the second-floor control room. He sat back in the custom leather captain's chair, guided the huge craft into the empty slot, and watched as two of the marina's part-time workers secured her to the dock.

It was dark; clouds rolled over the moon and blocked the stars as a cold wind whipped around the glass-enclosed control room.

"When this is over, we'll find a house," he said as he stared off into the mountains surrounding them. "I think a baby needs a real house."

Chaya pressed her lips together and found the ache and the panic building inside her at his voice.

"A baby just needs a home, Natches," she told him softly. "And two parents."

What he was getting ready to do wasn't without an element of danger. Chaya had read Dayle Mackay's Marine file. He had been a mess cook with control issues. He used his fists indiscriminately, not caring who he hurt, or how he hurt them. But he was proficient with weapons, namely, a knife. His hand-to-hand skill rating was high, and from everything else she knew about him, he didn't have a conscience.

But it wasn't the thought of the physical danger that had him staring off into the distance; it was who he was going up against. What he was going against. The man who should have been his father.

"I was seven the first time he locked me in the closet," he said. The lethal throb of cold determination in his voice had her hands tightening on his shoulders from where she stood behind him.

"He kept me in there until I thought I was going to die," he said. "Almost two days. No food, no water. When he dragged me out, I was almost senseless with fear. After I managed to get cleaned up and he gave me a drink of water, I lied for him, just like he wanted me to do before he put me in that closet. And he told me, 'Loyalty, son. That's all I want from you. Just be loyal.'"

Natches couldn't even remember what his father had needed him to lie about at the time. Something inconsequential. It always was. Just something to prove his loyalty.

"And what did you want?" she asked him.

Funny, he could hear the ache in her voice for him, just that easy. As though he were that much a part of her, that he knew how much she ached as he talked.

He had never felt another person the way he felt Chaya. The way he had always felt Chaya.

"I caught Faisal's transmission the day they brought you into that camp," he said instead of answering her question. "I checked the area, desperate for a place to hide you, because I just knew I was going to pull out a mess when I went in for you. The caves were a no go. It was the first place they would have checked. There was no other cover, no other place to hide but a hole."

Chaya felt her heart clench as he caught her hand and pulled her to his lap, surrounding her with warmth when she wanted to surround him with it.

"I made that hole. I was going to shove you in it and try to find cover above you. I hate closed-in places, Chay. Dark, small places. That was always my weakness."

His cheek brushed against her hair.

"You were in that hole with me," she whispered.

And he nodded.

"I couldn't leave you in there by yourself. You were all but blind, hurt. When I killed Nassar later, Chay, I think I scared myself, because I enjoyed it. I saw you, so brave and strong, and trying so hard to fight when you should have been leaning against me, crying, doing something other than storing your strength in case you had to go down fighting. And you would have gone down fighting."

She felt his heart beat beneath her cheek and held on to him, because he had forced himself into that hole with her.

"I was losing it," she told him then. "Before you pulled me out of there. I was ready to break, Natches. And in that hole, when I heard them coming for us, I was screaming in my head until you kissed me." That kiss had pulled her back, it had saved her. "You made me strong. Because of you I was able to run. You held me up, you almost carried me. And because of you, I was able to stand the darkness in my own mind, and the fear that they were going to hurt me again. I didn't want to hurt anymore. And when I lost Beth. You kept me sane. With your touch, with your kiss, with all the wild pleasure you poured into me that night." She stared up at him, seeing his somber expression, even in the dark, her heart breaking for the man who had forced himself into that hole with her, and was now trying to face his own nightmare. Alone.

His expression was shadowed, dark, but his eyes were alive. And they brought tears to her eyes. Fierce, shockingly determined. He would do whatever he had to do to make sure Dayle Mackay never hurt anyone he loved, ever again.

"Clayton Winston called while you were in the shower earlier," he said. "He got to talk to Christopher. Then DHS called him back. They've arranged transportation through a private broker to D.C., where he can see his son in a supervised visit."

Chaya closed her eyes, thankful Cranston had followed through with that.

"Clayton's dying," he said. "Doctors don't think he'll see the year out. He needed this before he passes on."

"And what do you need, Natches?"

It felt like an epitaph, the way he was talking, as though he wouldn't return to her, and she refused to consider that.

"Come on." He lifted her from his lap and drew her through the doorway into the bedroom. There, he closed the door to the control room and locked it with a flick of his fingers.

"You didn't answer me." She turned to face him in the darkness of the room. The drapes had been drawn that morning and the room was almost pitch black now.

He turned on the low lamp by the bed and turned to face her.

"You're coming back to me," she whispered, her breath hitching. "Don't you look at me like that. You're going to be covered, and you're coming back to me."

And tears filled her eyes, because she couldn't imagine anything less.

"I'm coming back to you," he promised her. "One way or the other, I'm coming back, Chay. But how will you see me, how will our child see me if I come back with blood on my hands?"

His father's blood. She could see it in his face, his uncertainty that he could leave Dayle Mackay alive.

"Bullies are weak," she told him huskily. "You get what DHS needs and they'll break him. I swear to you, Natches, they'll break him and they'll put the rest of that group away for good. You'll win."

She knew they would. She was the interrogation specialist, but she only interrogated subjects of interest, she didn't interrogate suspects, nor did she interrogate suspected terrorists, homegrown or foreign. There was a division for that, men and women who made her worst nightmares seem like a picnic in the park.

He nodded. The confidence, the sheer knowledge in his eyes that he would do whatever it took to protect what belonged to him, humbled her. He tried to be a shield between the world and those he loved, always trying to protect them, to make certain danger never touched them. And he never expected, never asked, for the same, though he knew Dawg, Rowdy, and Ray Mackay had always been there for him. He had never asked.

"We're good to go then." He nodded before moving to her, his lips settling on hers like a promise. A gentle, forever promise, as sweet and heated as a dream.

"We're good to go." She nodded, and she pushed back the fears. She would cover the angles, she would create a bubble around him that could do nothing less than protect him from any outside forces.

But inside that bubble, Natches had to face the knowledge that he wasn't just betraying a monster. He also had to confront that last glimmer of hope, that the monster had a soul.

Monsters didn't have souls though, Natches assured himself as the meeting with his cousins and Alex Jansen drew to a close.

Not for the first time, he found himself amazed at Chaya's knowledge, and her ability to find workable solutions to the problems that were going to face them when it came to executing the plan they had conceived.

Illegal wiretapping was nothing new, and Cranston wasn't above using it to make certain a plan was coming together. A call had been made to Dayle Mackay by one of the men watching the Mackay cousins, informing him of the division between Natches and his cousins over an old picture, evidence against a citizen of Somerset in the stolen missiles case, and Natches's refusal to give the authorities pertinent information where that citizen was concerned.

And Dayle had been interested.

Natches listened to the other man's voice on the digital recording Alex had slipped in to him. The smug certainty in Dayle's voice—that, finally, blood had thickened in Natches's veins and become more substantial than water.

He turned his back on his cousins as the recording played, kept his expression calm. This wasn't a Mackay he was going after; it was just another monster. Just as it had been in the Marines. It wasn't a person. It was a target, nothing more.

"Moving the *Nauti Dreams* was also noted," Alex told them all softly and switched to the recording of another call. Natches's phone call to another marina and the arrangement of transportation for his houseboat was given as well. With each call, Dayle became more confident, more certain that his son and cousins were finally making the split he had been waiting on.

"That's my boy," Dayle mused softly, smugly. "I knew it wouldn't take long."

"What about the woman? The agent with him?" the voice on the other end questioned him. Daniel Reynolds was one of the men in the photo, one of the fanatical leaders of the future revolution.

"Women are easy to get rid of," Dayle snorted. "An accident, a few little drugs popped into her drink, and she does the bar on a Saturday night. Natches'll drop her."

"She's still an agent."

"And she doesn't have the information he has," Dayle pointed out. "No doubt, that relationship will terminate soon enough, on its own. I'll call him soon."

"Are you certain about this?" the other voice pushed determinedly. "We can't afford to mess up."

Dayle laughed at the question. "Trust me, Daniel, I know my son. I knew it was just a matter of time. The boy's a killer. He was a killer in the Marines, and he'll always be a killer. That kind of cold only adheres to its own kind. He'll come in."

"Very well," Daniel agreed. "Arrange the meeting and contact us when you've finished."

The sound of the recorder disengaging flipped a switch in his mind. Cold. Hard. Yeah, he was a killer. He turned slowly to meet his cousins' eyes.

"Chaya, do you still have those files?" He knew she did.

"They're upstairs in my case." She moved for the staircase but not before she cast him a suspicious look.

As she disappeared upstairs he looked at his family. His cousins and the man he called friend.

"This might not go as easy as she thinks it will," he told them quietly. "If anything happens to me, you take care of her and my child." He looked to Dawg and Rowdy. "Give him what Uncle Ray always gave me, and make it stick."

Dawg and Rowdy glanced at each other.

"Man, this is going to be a walk in the park," Dawg protested. "Alex has point, your woman has your wire, DHS in the van, and me and Rowdy in place. Nothing's going to happen." Dawg's gaze sharpened. "Unless you do something dumb. You gonna do somethin' dumb, Natches?"

Natches's lips quirked at the question. "Have I ever done things any other way, cousin?"

"Hell."

"He's going to do things right, or he'll find me standing beside him."

Natches jerked around, frowning at Chaya, who didn't have those files in her hand. But her hand was propped on her hip and her expression was something just this side of pissed off.

"Isn't that right, Natches?"

He inclined his head smoothly. "I'll play by the plan," he promised her.

But he knew Dayle. And he knew Dayle would never play by any kind of rules. This was it and he knew it. When he walked out of that meeting, one way or the other, it was going to be over.

And she didn't believe a word he was saying.

"Here's the cell phone." Alex pulled the phone out of his pocket and handed it across the table. "Cranston's proud as hell of this little puppy. He said not to break it; it's the only prototype they've managed to complete successfully."

Natches lifted the phone from the table, flipped it open, and checked it for anything that Dayle could use to identify it as a wire rather than a phone.

"It even makes phone calls," Chaya told him with a hard smile.

"Cranston has the van parked in town, one agent inside. As soon as he has the location point he can park it within half a mile and still receive clear reception," Alex informed them. "As far as any listening ears at the hotel could know, he's raging over Natches's refusal to join the team or to help Agent Dane complete her mission. He's making plans to pull out of Somerset once she contacts him."

"Which will be tonight," she told them. "I'll contact Cranston and inform him that he should pick me up in the morning and that I'll be returning to D.C. with him."

"That's when I assume Dayle will make his call." Natches nodded.

"I'll need to activate the cell phone to your number rather than using your own cell," Chaya told him. "We want a recording of it. Calls will transmit with no possible trace outside the half-mile limit."

"We'll be ready to move when Cranston gives the order." Alex nodded to Dawg and Rowdy. "We'll have everything in place and ready to move."

"And he'll have his own watchers," Natches warned them.

"He has six we've identified, and we'll have men covering them. We'll allow them to stay in place until the last minute before taking them out."

It was a damned good plan. Natches nodded to the three men as he curled his arms around Chaya and pulled her back against his chest, one hand against her lower stomach as he stared back at his cousins, his look intent.

They knew. Brief nods assured him they knew. If anything happened to him, then Chaya was to be protected, just as he would have protected one of their wives, one of their children.

They had made that vow long ago and far away. Three boys that should have been brothers, that had wished they were. They had become brothers. And they had made that vow, what belonged to one was the others' to protect. That simple.

Chaya felt his hand on her stomach and stared at Dawg and Rowdy fiercely. No matter what Natches wanted, he was to be protected. Their gazes flickered to her, then back to Natches, and she hoped, she prayed that the nod they gave was an affirmative to that silent demand.

The Nauti Boys were thick as thieves, it was said. Their loyalty was to each other and to family alone. That bond would protect Natches.

"We're out of here then." Alex got to his feet and looked to the back of the boat. "Damn, that water's fuckin' cold tonight."

"And Kelly and Crista have electric blankets and hot coffee waiting on us. That's the best you're going to do tonight, Alex," Dawg informed him.

"Yeah, the two of you curl up with a warm body, and I get stuck with an electric blanket," he grunted. "I always get the short end of the deal with you boys."

"Yeah, and we'll remind you of that one of these days."

They disappeared along the hallway, silence slowly descending through the houseboat. There wasn't a splash, a dip of the boat, or a slide of a door to indicate they had left.

"Come sit with me." Natches drew her to the couch, but rather than sitting, he stretched out on the cushions and drew her into his arms.

"Just sit?"

"Just let me hold you." He tucked her close, his body warm and hard, strong and secure.

"Stop making this feel like a funeral, Natches. Nothing is going to happen."

He chuckled at that, then sobered. "You know, Chay, the last time I spoke to him I was twenty. I had cracked ribs, one was broken, my mouth was full of blood, and I could have sworn I was dying. I told him, as Dawg, Rowdy, and Uncle Ray dragged me off of that floor, that the next time I spoke to him, I'd kill him."

He'd spat his blood on the bastard's shoes and made a vow, and Dayle had laughed at him. Natches had never forgotten that gloating laugh; he had heard it again tonight.

"And you're not going to kill him," she told him.

"Yeah, I am." Natches smiled as she stiffened in his arms, and at the thought of what he was going to do to Dayle. "Betraying him to DHS will be the same as death for him. It's the ultimate revenge for me. Because I'll know, every day, that he's breathing; we'll both know I beat him."

He held that inside him, though he knew clear to his gut that things weren't going to be that easy. He was a Marine. A sniper. An assassin. He'd always worked alone, without a spotter, sometimes without extraction. Because shit happened after blood was shed, and when shit happened, information came out. He'd learned to go with his gut. To know when to run and when to hang around. And when something wasn't going to go as planned.

This wasn't going to go as planned.

And if it all went to hell and back, then he wanted this night. He wanted to hold her, he wanted to talk to her.

His hand slid along her stomach once again.

"If our child is a boy, I want to teach him to play baseball," he told her softly.

She laughed at that. A soft, amused little sound that had a smile curling at his lips.

"If it's a girl, you'll be a tyrant."

A girl? A frown drew at his brows. A daughter, with her mother's hair and eyes and, God help him, Mackay blood. He shuddered. "I'll lock her up until she turns fifty."

"You will not." Her hand covered his, her fingers twining those of his other hand as it lay on her thigh.

"I promise you. Till she's fifty. That girl will be wilder than the wind and harder to control than a green mule."

She looked up at him, the dim light in the room catching the sparkle in her eyes, the love, the concern, the fears that would ride her until this was finished.

"She'll be a lady." The sound of her laughter was almost a giggle, because she knew better, just as he did.

"Wild as the wind," he argued again.

"And a boy wouldn't be?" She reached up and touched his face, and that touch, tenderness and warmth combined, was another memory he stored inside him.

"Boys are different," he told her.

She frowned, just as he knew she would. "How do you figure?"

"Boys are born to be wild."

"And girls are born to tame the wind," she said softly. "What are you doing, Natches?"

He knew what she was talking about. Why was he just holding her, just talking, just building memories?

"I'm creating my shield." He lowered his head and kissed her lips. "You're my shield, Chay, you just don't know it. Soft and sweet, born to tame the wind and to tempt my dreams. When I walk into that meeting, I want to carry this with me."

"Why?"

He was silent for long moments, wondering if there was any way to make her understand.

"So I won't kill him," he finally admitted. "Because this memory and all the others will be wrapped around me, and I'll remember what you're fighting for and how important keeping him alive really is. You're the only thing standing between him and death, Chay. Just this, and knowing he's more important to your fight than he is to mine."

"Then I'll be your shield," she whispered, turning, facing him, embracing him. "Always, Natches, I'll be your shield."

TWENTY

He didn't make love to her that night. He waited until the sun rose and carried her to the bed. There, he stripped her slowly, gently, and gazed at the woman splayed out before him.

Sweetly rounded breasts, her nipples hard and red. Her stomach was smooth, only slightly rounded. There was no sign yet that his child rested there, but he knew it did.

Sweetly curved thighs, and between them, silky bare flesh.

The hours he had spent holding her, kissing her, stroking her, had stoked the fires inside them to a burning simmer. Something Natches had never known before. It was the first time in his life he had ever spent time just holding a woman, just stroking her, just laying velvet kisses wherever he could reach.

He'd been hard for hours. He could have fucked her ten times over in the time he had taken just loving her on that couch. But he wouldn't have traded it for anything he'd known in the past. Each touch, each kiss, each little laugh, sigh, and whispered love word had bound them closer together.

She had felt it. He felt it. He knew there were silken-wrapped chains in his soul now, and they led back to her. The burn was now a flame though. Natches smiled down at her, wild, wicked hunger raging inside him.

He'd been born as wild as the wind, and like the wind, he had torn through his own life, whipping around it without direction, shearing his own dreams as he moved, until he met Chaya.

And she had been born to tame that wind inside him. Not the man, she made the man wild, made him hungry. But the rage, the burning fury that had driven him before that day in a dry, hot desert, was now tamed, held in the hands of one tender woman.

"Are you going to just stare at me all morning?" She stretched beneath his gaze, her eyes flickering to where he stroked his cock, anticipating, holding back that final moment when he would have to let her go.

"Would you let me?" He smiled, using one finger to trace a line from between her breasts to the silken, soft mound between her thighs.

"If that was what you wanted to do." She lifted her hands and let her fingers trail along the path he had made. "I didn't take you for a watcher, Natches. Though I'm sure we could adapt if that's your kink."

If that was his kink? He almost laughed; he did smile. God, he loved her. Smart mouth and all.

"What if it is my kink?" He lifted his brows curiously. Not that it was, but he could play with her. That was the joy with Chaya, she enjoyed playing. Even patched and healing in that hospital in Iraq, she had enjoyed playing with him.

"Isn't it too bad you broke my vibrator then?" She let her fingers whisper over her mound before returning, stroking along the top of the glistening slit.

Hell, he'd come in his own hand at this rate.

"You would have let me watch?" He hadn't anticipated that.

"Oh, I would have," she whispered, letting her finger dip into the folds, her hips arching as he watched. "I would have shown you how I survived five years without you. I would have let you watch, and let you hear me crying because I couldn't reach the same peak you could bring me to. Would you like to see that?"

See her cry? God no.

"I'd finish you, baby," he promised her. "I'll let you show me how you do it, then I'd show you how it's done." His wicked smile drew a light vein of laughter from her, a twinkle of the same wicked hunger to her eyes.

"Then show me how it's done." Her fingers lifted from her flesh, dewy with her juices and he couldn't help himself. He snagged her wrist and brought her fingers to his lips.

Her taste exploded against his tongue. Sweet and earthy. Nothing tasted as good as Chaya's passion. He covered the tips of her tasty fingers, licked them clean, and watched her eyes darken as he caressed the sensitive tips with his tongue.

"I'll show you exactly how it should be done," he murmured. "You should be savored."

He stretched out between her thighs, pressed them wide, and blew a breath across the dampened flesh, his gaze lifting to her as a tremor shook her body. "Savored in the most delicious ways.

With a kiss." He covered her hard little clit in a heated kiss, nudged it with his tongue, and felt it throb in anticipation.

"Just a kiss?" Her voice was hoarse with pleasure now.

"Hmm. A kiss wasn't enough?" He kissed the silken folds, drew the taste of her juices onto his tongue, and hummed in appreciation.

"Not enough." Her hands were in his hair now as she tried to press him closer.

"A taste?" He dipped his tongue inside those luscious folds, licked softly, slowly, felt the soft flutter at the entrance of her core and the echo of the clenching need building in the muscles there.

"Taste isn't enough." She writhed beneath him, her hips arching, pressing her pussy closer to his mouth as he kissed and licked and listened to her cries of pleasure building in his head.

Making love. He'd never made love before Chaya, but that was what he was doing now. Making love to her. Loving her with everything inside his soul.

"Kissing or tasting?" His own voice was ragged now. "Demanding little thing, aren't you?"

He lifted his head, smiling back at her as she watched him, lashes lowered sensually, a sheen of perspiration on her face now.

And those sweet, lush breasts. They were swollen, her nipples hard, tight, and flushed with need. He couldn't help but lift one hand, slide it over her stomach, and cup one of those sweet mounds as he went back to kissing, tasting. And licking. He licked around her clit. He laid little kisses on it, pursing his lips and drawing it inside the heat of his mouth until she unraveled beneath him, arched and cried his name in release.

Before the tremors finished sweeping through her, he jerked to his knees, lifted her legs until they lay against his chest, and began working his cock inside her.

Fuck. She was tight. So hot he had to clench his teeth, tried valiantly to think about car motors, anything, everything but the destructive, velvet grip encasing his cock.

And nothing worked. Nothing filled his mind but the scent and the feel of her. Her voice crying out his name, her hands gripping his wrists as he held on to her hips. Until he was buried fully inside her, balls deep in the sweetest, slickest haven a man's soul could ever find.

"Natches. Oh God, it's so good."

Good wasn't even a description. There was no description for this pleasure; it defied any poet's ability to voice it. He tightened, arched deeper inside her and felt the sweat running down his chest as sensation upon sensation whipped over his body, dug into his nerve endings and filled him with ecstasy.

His head lowered until he could kiss her ticklish little ankle, before she jerked, a panting little cry falling from her lips.

He glanced up at her and grinned before licking over the side of her foot. And she moaned, her foot flexing as he lifted one hand from her hip to her foot, and as he began to thrust, let his teeth bite down, just below her big toe.

Chaya screamed with the sensation. He bit her. Bit her foot and thrust inside her, once, twice, and she was coming again. Exploding into a million brilliant fragments as his hips moved harder, moved faster. He was pounding into her, his expression tightening, sweat rolling down his neck as she felt herself flying from one peak to another, then joining him as his release flowed into her.

She watched him, the way his eyes narrowed on her, became sensual and heavy a second before they closed and a shudder wracked his body.

"I can't get enough of you," he breathed out roughly as he

collapsed over her, allowing her legs to embrace his hips before sliding to the bed. "Every time, I only want you more."

Running her fingers through his hair she smiled. "Good. Because I can't get enough either."

He rolled to his back, dragging her to him until she was draped over his chest, weak and exhausted and knowing there was no time to sleep.

They lay like that, their hearts finally easing in their chests, their breathing returning to normal.

"When you leave the boat, don't look back," he told her. "Don't stop, don't pause. You're a woman walking away from something she can't deal with."

"I know how to do my job." But her voice caught on a sob. Walking away from Natches without looking back?

"I know you do. But it won't be easy, Chay. And you can't pause. You have to keep going."

She nodded against his chest.

"I have a duffel packed for you. Some clean clothes Dawg brought over in a plastic bag last night. Your other clothes. You'll take your briefcase, but only your laptop inside it. They can tell by the way you carry it, the way you move, the way it hangs from your shoulder or your hand if there's anything more in it."

She nodded again.

"When it happens, when I meet with him, you're not to come near until he's cuffed. Do you understand?"

His voice was so hard, his tone cool, but she could feel the emotions coursing beneath the surface. As able as she knew she was, she had also come to realize something. He called her his strength, but she could also become his weakness. Just as he could become hers if anyone ever wanted to hurt him to strike back at her.

"Not until he's cuffed," she agreed, praying she could keep that promise.

"Let's get you ready to go then." He lifted her from his chest and moved from the bed with her.

Standing beside it, he touched her face and gave her a hard, lingering kiss.

"When I get you back here, you're not getting out of the bed for a week."

"At least a week," she promised, standing still as he moved back and stared down at her.

"I don't like this," she finally told him. "You shouldn't be alone with him."

His smile was tinged with bitterness, but no regret. "I won't be. Remember? You're my shield."

And she had to be content with that.

"Go shower. I'll get your things together."

And then she would leave him alone. Alone to think, alone to remember, and Chaya knew it. Just as she knew there was no other way to convince the monster that Natches was alone.

Leaving him this time was breaking her heart.

TWENTY-ONE

Natches gave Chaya time to get started up the boardwalk before he stepped onto the deck of his houseboat to watch her leave.

Instantly he felt the rifle scope between his eyes, which meant, hopefully, he was drawing it away from Chaya. He smirked at the would-be assassin, daring him to take the shot, knowing none would be taken. But he was smart enough, instinctive enough to feel it.

Then he turned his gaze back to Chaya, keeping his expression carefully mocking, as though watching her walk away meant nothing to him.

It wasn't forever, he reminded himself. Hell no. After this, he was never going to watch Chaya walk away from him again, he would make damned sure of it.

Shaking his head as though amused at something, he turned and walked back into the living room and closed the door behind him.

Chaya's cell phone was tucked at his belt; it was turned on. According to her, even disabling the battery wouldn't disable the wire.

All he had to do now was wait for Dayle Mackay to learn Chaya had left and to call. And he would call. Cranston was betting against it, as was Alex. Three against two, because Dawg, Rowdy, and Natches all knew Dayle would call.

He didn't have to wait long. Two hours that he spent pacing the living room, going over the plan, trying to make certain he'd considered every angle, and the cell phone rang.

He unclipped it unhurriedly and flipped it open before bringing it to his ear.

"Yeah?" As though he didn't know who the hell it was.

"We need to talk, son." Grating, smug, Dayle's voice came over the line clearly.

Natches stayed still, his fists clenching. He took the phone from his ear and flipped it closed, disconnecting the call. He didn't want to appear too eager, did he? He had to swallow back the urge to throw up at the sheer confidence in Dayle's voice.

How could anyone deceive himself to the extent that Dayle had, believing he would ever carry the right to call Natches "son"? Even with the slight evidence Dayle had been given, how could he ever imagine Natches would have a desire to speak to him? To kill, yeah, killing him might assuage a hell of a lot of anger, but in the long run, it would only end up pissing Natches off more.

Natches liked to think he wasn't a man who fooled himself easily. He'd thought Dayle wasn't. It seemed he was wrong, because a half hour later, the phone range again.

"What the hell do you want?" was his answer.

"We need to talk," Dayle repeated, his voice throttled, anger evident in it.

"About what? Your treasonous activities? They've already caused me enough problems if you don't mind," he sneered. "If you're going to save the world, try to do it without involving me. Okay?"

Save the world his ass. He almost choked on that one. Damn, he'd thought he was a better actor than this.

Dayle said nothing for long moments. "Some information is dangerous to have, Natches," he finally replied.

"Yeah, so pull the damned trigger next time I step outside, why don't you? That would just solve all our problems."

Dayle chuckled. "That sixth sense of yours has always been good. Come to your aunt Nadine's house, Natches. One hour. Just give me a few minutes to talk to you; that's all I'm asking for. Believe it or not, we might have a few things in common."

Uh-huh. They sure did. His blood and the fact that Natches really wanted to spill it.

But he stayed silent.

"I can't imagine we have anything in common," he finally stated. "And I doubt Nadine would let me in the door."

"One hour, Natches." Dayle's voice gentled, and it sounded sickening. "I'll be there waiting for you."

This time Dayle disconnected.

Natches flipped the phone closed and returned it to the clip on his belt. He checked the clock. It was barely nine and he needed a beer. Hell, whiskey. The bastard was driving him to drink.

He pushed his fingers through his hair and walked upstairs. He buckled the black leather chaps he used for riding the Harley in winter over his jeans and pulled on the heavy boots he wore when riding the powerful machine.

The leather jacket, scuffed and beaten, was pulled from the closet and thrown to the bed as he moved to the dresser. He tucked a knife in the side of his boot. Picking up the jacket, he walked downstairs and pulled a beer from the refrigerator.

Hell, he wished Chaya was here. He'd lie on the couch with her again, hold her, and reinforce the shield. His lips quirked at the thought of that. It had taken him long enough to get beneath *her* shields, but once he had, the woman he found beneath there was more than a match for him. And he liked that; he liked that fine.

He finished the beer, tossed it in the trash, and moved to the couch to wait. He'd wait that hour before he left the houseboat. There was no sense in arriving early, or even on time. He may as well make an entrance when he arrived. He and Dayle Mackay had never pretended to stand on ceremony with each other.

He pushed his fingers through his hair and thought of the team moving into place. They knew where Dayle's spotters were; that would make it easier. Natches knew Alex and his team—they didn't make mistakes. And Dawg and Rowdy were black death when they wanted to be.

He waited. He didn't pace; instead, he sat on the couch and stared around the living room. He thought of the house Dawg had nearly completed farther in the mountains. There was land close to him, and it wasn't but a few miles from the house Rowdy and Kelly were building. He could buy that land, build him and Chaya a home. A place to love and to raise their babies.

Lots of bedrooms, he thought. He wanted to fill her life with babies and with laughter. Both their lives. He wanted to be the husband he'd dreamed of being with her, the father he'd never had.

When the clock showed five minutes past the hour, he stood and left the houseboat. He paused on the deck as though considering turning back, then shook his head and moved to the docks, striding quickly to the small metal building Ray had allowed them to set up to park the Harleys in. He took his time getting it out and checking it over.

Half an hour and he was on the road. He didn't rush, there was no need to. Dark glasses protected his eyes from the cold wind, but it ruffled through his hair, clearing his head.

He pushed thoughts of Chaya and babies as far back in his mind as he could, though he admitted, that wasn't far. Hatred, a child's rage and pain, and the fear of the dark that kid had known. He erased it from his mind. It was just another mission he told himself. Except this time, he wasn't going to kill.

He pulled onto the side of the street before Nadine's driveway forty-five minutes past the deadline and parked the Harley before cutting the motor and stepping off. Far enough away that he'd be surprising them.

He'd passed the dark panel van parked on the street, blending in with the SUVs and pickups it shared space with. Wasn't Nadine nice? Why, she had bought her a nice little place in the middle of town. Made things so much easier. But it didn't make this any easier.

Stepping up to the door, he didn't bother to knock. He pushed open and stepped into the living room before coming to a rocking stop.

"You're determined to make me puke this morning," he stated

as he watched his aunt jump from Dayle's lap and Dayle pull his hand slowly from beneath the silk dress she was wearing.

Nadine didn't even bother to flush. Actually, she let a nervous little smile touch her lips; it was almost welcoming.

What dimension of the twilight zone did he step into? Natches wondered as he lifted his brow and closed the door.

"We thought you weren't arriving." Dayle rose to his feet, adjusting the polo shirt he wore and the creased slacks.

He looked as powerful as he ever had. Six feet plus, wider than Natches, broader. Older, Natches reminded himself as he hooked his thumbs in the top of the chaps he wore and stared at the man who dared call him son.

"I didn't think I was either." He shrugged and stared at Nadine as she twisted her hands together nervously and glanced between Dayle and Natches. "What's her problem?"

Dayle smiled. "She wants to welcome you home."

"Really?" Natches arched his brows. "How interesting. Last I heard, she wanted to gut me for popping Johnny's head off for him. Changed her mind rather fast, didn't she?"

She paled, swaying as Dayle put his arm around her and whispered something in her ear before nodding toward the back of the house. Giving him a grateful look, she accepted his kiss on the lips before moving through the house.

Natches shook his head. "You know, that relationship you have going on there never did make sense to me. She had her brother's kid, and you're not the brother. No wonder Johnny was so screwed up. Now she just wants to welcome me right into the family as though she never hated my guts? You two been doing hard drugs or something?"

"You always were a smart-mouthed little bastard," Dayle snapped irritably.

"Yeah, I do good at that." Natches grinned in pride. "So, what the hell do you want and how do I return things to where you ignore me rather than harass me?"

Dayle grimaced, his lined face tightening into displeasure as he pushed his hair, still thick and barely graying, back from his forehead.

"Little whelp," he muttered. "You don't even look like me. If it wasn't for those eyes of yours I'd swear you weren't even mine."

"Maybe Chandler was my daddy as well as Johnny's," Natches mocked. "From what I remember, it could be possible."

"I thought of that," Dayle snapped. "Even had the paternity test done. No such luck, you're mine. And now it's time we both come to terms with that."

"And how do you suggest we do that?"

"You know what I am, what I'm a part of." Dayle sighed. "I always knew you'd remember it."

"Is that why you hired Linkins to try to kill me in Iraq?"

Dayle shrugged again. "It wasn't an easy order to give. And I have to admit, I wasn't disappointed when it failed."

Natches forced himself to keep from curling his fingers into fists.

"The strike order on the hotel where Chaya's husband and child were?" he asked. "Another attempt?"

Dayle's eyes widened, then narrowed. "That had nothing to do with you or the girl. I didn't find out about your relationship with her until later. And I didn't give that order, that came from one of our founding members based there at the time. Craig Cornwell was working for us. We had no idea he was working for the enemy, too, until then. We couldn't risk his capture. He would have talked."

"I want to know how the hell you managed it. A strike order, authenticated and radioed to the planes. That seems pretty much impossible."

"Orders get messed up sometimes." Dayle shrugged. "The commander only knew the orders he received. We just had to get them through the proper channels. As I said, Iraq wasn't my call. I'm a recruiter, that's all."

"You're not a very good recruiter," Natches informed him. "I've been checking up on you a bit. Dishonorably discharged, malcontents, some of your boys aren't even in the military. Those that are still there are just a breath from being tossed into Leavenworth."

"Because they know where our leaders are taking us," Dayle snarled. "Someone has to pave the way. The revolution is building, Natches. You can be a part of it. You can be at my side as a general and a leader now that you've disassociated yourself from Ray's little bastards."

And here it was. Natches grinned in full-throttled smug triumph. "What makes you think I've done that?"

Dayle tensed. "My reports are that you're arguing over information you're refusing to turn over to DHS. That you're protecting me." Pride flared in his eyes.

Natches let himself chuckle at that one. "Nah, not really. They're just a little ticked off at me right now because I wouldn't let them in on the fun. No, sorry, Dayle, I'm here to bust your ass."

Dayle froze, his eyes narrowed. "You're not serious."

"Yeah, I am." Natches grinned. "Real serious. See, those guys

323

you had targeting me in their gunsights? Dawg and Rowdy have them already. Go ahead. Try to call one of them."

Dayle pulled his cell phone from his belt and punched a number in. Listened. Tried another. Another. Yeah, Dawg and Rowdy were black death when they wanted to be.

"I'd say there's some blood fertilizing a few areas." Natches nodded. "It was a good try though. Too bad you didn't pay attention to the fact that I don't even fucking hate you. I just basically want to see you locked up until hell freezes over, knowing I put you there."

Yeah, this was better than a bullet. He watched Dayle pale, watched his shoulder twitch as he prepared to go for his weapon.

Natches went for his first. He pulled the Glock from the back holster beneath his jacket, holding it comfortably on his father.

"Did you really think you were going to convince me to help you do anything?" Natches asked him. "I ask again, are you on hard drugs?"

Dayle's lips thinned as he watched Natches lean against the wall, the gun held easily, pointing directly at him.

"You can't prove any of this."

" 'Course I can. I'm wired." He shrugged.

Dayle grinned at that. "Not here you aren't, Natches. Any wire you wore was jammed the minute you walked in."

"Cell phones aren't jammed, are they?"

Dayle glanced at his cell. "Yours isn't open though."

"Doesn't have to be." He shrugged. "I got ya. DHS has ya. Busted, old man."

"I don't think so."

Natches swung around, the gun barreling on Nadine's voice as he felt his stomach drop.

Janey. For a moment, fear had nearly paralyzed him, the thought of Chaya uppermost in his mind. But now, the fear nearly burned through his mind. Chaya could have worked with him; she would have known what to do. But it wasn't Chaya Nadine held by long, thick black hair. It wasn't Chaya who stared at him from dazed, confused eyes.

"Insurance." Dayle sighed. "Put the gun down, and hand me the cell phone, please."

Natches watched as Nadine leveled her own gun at Janey's head.

"I'd love to kill her," she told him vindictively. "Pop her little head right off, just like you did Johnny's."

Natches lowered the gun, shifted away from the wall and forced Nadine in a better alignment with the window as he came closer to her.

Be in position, Alex, he prayed. God help them all, he better be in position.

He pulled the cell phone from his belt and tossed it to Dayle. He almost winced as Dayle cracked it against the table, busting the frame before he dropped it into the vase of water that held fresh flowers. So much for Cranston's new toy.

"The gun, Natches." Dayle waggled his fingers demandingly. "Let's not . . ."

Pop.

Nadine went down, dragging Janey with her as Dayle jumped him. The fist that plowed into Natches's jaw felt like a jackhammer. He went backward, the gun flying, clattering to the floor before he righted himself and faced an enraged Dayle.

"Just like Johnny," Natches snarled. "What now, bastard?"

"Now I beat you to fucking death like I should have when you were a snot-nosed kid," Dayle snarled.

Natches laughed as he shed his coat, feeling the blood pump through his body, adrenaline racing through his veins.

"I'm not a kid now, old man," he sneered. "Come and get me. We'll see who ends up with the busted ribs this time."

The second Chaya realized Nadine Grace had a hostage, and who it was, panic nearly flared in her throat.

"We have a hostage situation." She spoke quietly into the mic at her cheek that connected her to the team surrounding the house.

Alex was the closest in position, stretched out on the roof across the street, hidden from view by the branches of an aged oak growing beside it.

"Alex, confirm visual."

"Confirmed. Target acquired."

She heard the pop of the sniper rifle, her eyes widening as Cranston began to curse and order all agents to converge on the house.

"All agents, be advised, don't interfere. Cover only. This is Natches's fight."

"Are you insane?" Cranston turned back to her, his eyes bugging out of his head. "Natches will kill him." He pulled his own mic closer to his mouth. "All agents, detain—"

"No." Before Cranston could stop her she pulled the plug on his communications unit and stared back at him furiously. "Stop fighting me so I can get to Natches. We cover him, that's it. This is his fight, Cranston. No matter what."

"And if his father manages to get a killing blow in? What then, Agent Dane?"

She breathed in roughly. "Then I'll deal with it, Timothy. It's his fight. It's his pride. I won't take it from him."

He cursed again, turned from her, and a second later they were running from the van to the sidewalk, racing to the two-story brick house that sat peacefully amid the residential street.

Neighbors were stepping from their houses as the sheriff's car sped down the street, sirens wailing. And she wondered how Timothy had managed to keep Zeke from coming in sooner.

They rushed the house. Dawg and Rowdy with their black law enforcement vests made it there first. The door splintered as they went through it, and stood blocking the living room, staring back at Natches and Dayle Mackay in shock.

They were brutal. Fists were slamming into faces. Natches's jaw and lip were bleeding; Dayle probably had teeth missing though. He was bleeding profusely from the mouth, stumbling back as Natches buried his fist in his ribs. And from the grunt of pain, it wasn't the first time.

Dayle went to one knee, staggered, and then pulled himself back up. Lowering his head he charged Natches. A second later, he came up on his tiptoes, a wet groan leaving his throat as Natches buried his fist in his stomach and threw him back.

"Have you had enough?" Natches's drawl was lazy, that dangerous sound Chaya swore she was going to make sure he never uttered again.

"Son of a bitch," Dayle wheezed and charged again.

The blow to his ribs took him to his knees.

"We can keep this up all day," Natches informed him, stepping back as Dayle rolled to his side. "Come on, old man; pull your ass back up. I don't think you're bleeding enough."

Nadine was sprawled where Alex's bullet had left her, and as

Chaya watched, Alex stepped into the hall from the back and lifted Natches's sister into his arms. Her eyes met his, and she almost backed up at the emotion in Alex's face.

"She's been drugged, Alex," Natches told him, still watching Dayle as he held his ribs and groaned weakly. "Get her to the hospital, now."

Alex moved as Timothy barked orders into his radio, calling for a unit to meet Alex on the street for the drive into the hospital.

Zeke stepped into the house, and he, too, watched as Natches moved farther back from Dayle Mackay.

"I think his rib is broken, maybe several of them," Natches informed them cheerfully as he gripped Chaya's arm and began to move her back. "Take care of this, boys. We'll see you in a few days."

"She can't leave." Timothy was nearly hyperventilating now. "You need to be debriefed. We have fucking red tape to get through and questions that need answering. Get your ass back here, Natches. Agent Dane."

Natches turned back to him, stared at him, and Timothy went quiet.

"You remember that talk we had last year, Timothy?" Natches asked him.

Timothy glared back at him.

"I see you do. Cut the red tape. You have the damned recording if your phone worked. Debrief him." He shoved his finger in Dayle's direction. "Arrest him, get him the hell out of Somerset and keep him locked up. Because if I have to deal with you one more time, in my town, I might break a promise I made to myself and Chay about no more killing. You don't want that."

"And Timothy." Chaya stood her ground when Natches would

have dragged her out of the house. "Don't forget your promise to me. I did my part. I expect yours as a Christmas present. As we agreed."

He rubbed his balding head, squinted at her, then sighed. "By Christmas."

She nodded, then turned and let Natches lead her from the house. The street was filled with vehicles. He wrapped his jacket around her, lifted her to the back of the Harley, and seconds later they were maneuvering through the crowd converging on the Grace home.

It was over. She wrapped her arms around his waist and leaned against his back as they hit the interstate and headed back to the *Nauti Dreams*.

"You promised me at least a week in that bed of yours," she reminded him. "How are you going to keep your cousins away from us?"

"I have my ways." He turned, flashed her a wicked smile and a wink. "Don't worry, baby. I have my ways."

EPILOGUE

Enter At Your Own Risk
No Knocking
No Visitors
GO AWAY

The sign blocked the entrance to the *Nauti Dreams* for two weeks. It had gone up a week after Dayle Mackay's arrest, and Chaya and Natches stayed secluded.

Rowdy and Dawg shook their heads as they passed by and heard the male laugher, the feminine giggling, from inside. They swore Natches and Chaya were going to starve before they came out, but they both had to admit, the sound of Natches's laughter from inside that houseboat lightened their hearts.

Finally, the sign came down though. As October turned into

November, and the chill wind turned icy on the lake, Natches stepped from the *Dreams*.

Dressed in jeans, zipped only, no shirt, and socked feet, he inhaled the scent of winter coming and wrapped his arms around the real dream in his life as she stood in front of him, bundled in a quilt, drowsy and sated from the early morning loving they had shared.

Excited by the knowledge they carried.

Natches had slipped from the boat the night before and made a trip to the pharmacy. This morning Chaya had taken the pregnancy test he had brought home, and it was positive. She was having his child.

"You're going to teach him to play baseball then?" she asked, a smile teasing her lips as he kissed the curve of her neck.

"Of course," he drawled. A silky, rich, lazy sound that she already loved. "And if we have a daughter, I swear, Chay, I'm locking her up till she's fifty."

"If you lock her up, she won't be able to find a Harley-riding hellion to steal her heart," she teased, laughing.

"My point exactly, sweetheart. My point exactly."

Before Chaya could reply, Dawg stepped out of the *Nauti Nights*, pushed his fingers through his mussed hair, and threw them both an irritated look.

"Take your mushy crap back behind closed doors," he grumbled, the scowl on his face boding ill for daring to get in his way.

Chaya watched him in surprise as Natches arched a brow.

"Problems, Dawg?" he asked.

Dawg grunted. "I'm calling her brother; maybe he can force that hardheaded little minx to listen to reason. She sure as hell isn't listening to me."

"About what?" Chaya asked him.

"She needs to go to the damned doctor," he snarled. "Three weeks now and she's sick more often than not. She's tired all the damned time, and she refuses to go to the doctor. Just looks at me like she wants to rip my head off or something."

Worry strained the thin, tight-lipped expression on his face.

Chaya grinned and he glared at her. "She's sick."

"It's normal." She rolled her eyes at his look.

The thought of it still cracked her up. Crista Mackay had been complaining of her ailment the night she, Kelly, and Maria Mackay had been at the boat.

"The hell it is. She never gets sick."

"She does if she's pregnant."

Natches tensed, but Dawg froze. He stared back at her, his lips parting, then closing a second before she swore he almost stumbled as he stood still staring at her.

"She's what?"

Chaya frowned. "I thought she knew. With the morning sickness—she said it wasn't fair you weren't sick, too." She had known, hadn't she? Chaya asked herself. "Doesn't she know?"

Dawg lifted a hand toward the door, and she swore it was shaking. Then he turned back to her and swallowed tightly.

"Damn." His voice was almost weak. "Are you sure?"

Chaya stared back at him in surprise. "Sure she's pregnant?" She laughed. "No, but Natches bought no less than three of those tests he slipped out last night to get. We won't need the last two. You're welcome to them."

Dawg's gaze sharpened. "You're . . . ?" He couldn't seem to say the words.

"Pregnant?" Natches drawled in amusement. "So the test says."

Dawg looked back inside the houseboat, looked to Chaya, then at Natches, and she swore he paled.

"What if she has a girl?" he almost wheezed. "Oh hell. A Mackay daughter? Natches, what will we do?"

"Lock her up till she's fifty." Natches laughed as Chaya butted her elbow into his tight stomach. "We'll lock them up till they're fifty, Dawg, because I don't think I would survive it."

"A baby?" Dawg shook his head, blinked, then without another word, turned and went back into the houseboat.

"A dollar says she's dressed and headed to the doctor in the next hour." Natches chuckled.

"Two says he borrows the test," she countered.

An hour later, Dawg barged in, ignoring the fact that the door was closed and drapes were drawn. He even ignored Natches's curse as he tried to fix the quilt around Chaya's naked body.

"I need that damned test."

He was definitely pale. And his hands really were shaking.

"Get up, Natches. This ain't no time for that crap." He all but lifted Natches from the couch as Chaya dissolved into laughter. "Get the damned test already."

"You owe me, Natches," she called out as he laughed and headed upstairs for the pharmacy bag. Then she looked at Dawg again.

He was pacing. Dressed in jeans and a dark blue shirt, the ends hanging over his jeans, barefoot and decidedly worried, he paced the living room and stared at the stairs.

"Wish he'd hurry," he growled.

Chaya held the quilt tight around her. She knew Crista had miscarried their first child several years ago, something Dawg hadn't known about until Crista'd returned to Somerset the year before. If

Dawg's demeanor was any indication now, he was terrified. A terrified Nauti Boy. She would have had to see it to believe it.

"She'll be fine," she said softly then.

He turned back to her, his light green eyes pinning her, his expression intense. "Damned right she will be," he snarled. "I'll make sure of it. Hurry, Natches," he yelled. "Damn it, I don't have all day."

Natches was grinning as he came back down the stairs, tossed the bag to his cousin, and watched as Dawg rushed from the houseboat.

"Do you think he'll survive it?" He chuckled, returning to the couch and wrapping her in his arms.

"As long as it's not a girl," she snorted. "You guys deserve girls. A half dozen of them at least."

The wounded-male look he gave her had her giggling. "That's just wrong, Chay. On so many levels." He sighed. "A daughter would make me old before my time."

"That's okay." She nipped his chin and touched his cheek. He was her nauti dream; she wasn't going to allow that. "I promise I'll keep you young."

He smiled at that and caught her lips in a heated, hungry kiss. Because it was the truth. Loving Chaya would always keep him young. And maybe, just maybe, it would give him the strength to survive if God decided to start laughing at the Nauti Boys and actually gave them daughters.

Christmas Day

"Now, you can't look," Chaya reminded Natches firmly as he kept his back to the door of the houseboat, his forest green eyes watching her with amusement and love.

There was nothing she had ever known that had prepared her for the full extent of Natches's love. He could drive her crazy, make her insane with his arrogance and male dominance, but there was always a smile, always a kiss, and he always held her. It was like nothing she could have imagined.

"We could be in bed, cozy and warm," he suggested, his brows waggling. "We could try out those new presents I bought you."

She blushed. He'd bought her a small cedar box and more vibrators than one woman could use in a lifetime.

"Later," she promised, ducking around him to stare out of the door to where two figures were making their way along the dock to the houseboat.

She checked Rowdy's and Dawg's boats. The men were coming out, their wives with them.

Dawg was still in shock that Crista was pregnant and had kept that news from him for over a week before Chaya had unintentionally dropped the bomb. He barely let Crista walk on her own now. The other woman swore it was all she could do to keep him from carrying her every step she needed to make.

Rowdy wasn't much better. It seemed all of the women who belonged to the Nauti Boys were pregnant within weeks of one another. And each one of their men would go pale at the mention of having daughters.

"Now, remember, keep your back turned." Chaya opened the door, the cold wind swirling in as Dawg, Crista, Rowdy, and Kelly stepped inside.

"He looks impatient, Chaya." Kelly laughed, her gray eyes twinkling as she looked at Natches's back.

"Why are they here?" Natches almost turned around, but Chaya was ready for him. She pushed his shoulder back.

"Stay," she ordered laughingly.

"I'm not a dog," he grumped. "It's Christmas day."

"Here are Ray and Maria." Rowdy opened the door, and Ray stepped inside, beaming.

The others knew the surprise coming, just as they knew how hard it had been for Timothy to arrange it. But he had come through, just as he had promised he would.

She looked down the dock again, feeling her hands sweating. They were getting closer.

"Natches?" She turned to him.

"Can I turn around yet?" There was a grin in his voice.

"Not yet." She wiped her hands down the sides of her jeans and looked around at the others helplessly. Maybe she had gone about this the wrong way.

Ray winked at her. "Grandsons are good things to have," he told her.

"Yeah, and you get three of them." Natches laughed. "Come on, Chay. Let me turn around."

The other two guests stepped onto the deck of the boat as Chaya slid the door open to let them in.

Timothy stood beside the young man Natches had been trying so hard to get out of Iraq. Faisal was older now, twenty, but his smile was still bright, if a little nervous.

He was wearing jeans and a white shirt beneath the leather jacket Chaya had asked Timothy to get him. His eyes glittered with warmth and excitement as he stared around the room at everyone.

"Chaya." Natches's voice was a warning now as he felt the tension gathering in the room. "Who's visiting?"

She smiled at Faisal before moving in front of Natches.

"I love you," she told him, staring up at him. "I've loved you forever."

"I'll love you past forever, baby," he said shamelessly. "Now what the hell is going on?"

She breathed in, then nodded to Faisal.

His smile lit up the room. "I wish to you, Natchie, a merry Christmas."

Natches froze. His eyes widened, shock spreading over his face as he turned slowly.

He stared at the young man and saw the boy he remembered. Courage and strength still lined Faisal's face and filled his eyes, and his smile was still wide, friendly. He was a man now, but Natches saw the boy who had aided Chaya's rescue in Iraq. The kid who had risked his own life to protect an American.

"Mr. Cranston. He says I'm an American now." Faisal stared at Natches, that hint of nervousness back. "That you wanted me here."

There was a hint of question in Faisal's voice when Natches didn't speak. He couldn't; his throat was tight, so many emotions tearing through him now. Chaya would have died if this young man hadn't gotten a message out that she had been captured. She and Natches would have both died if Faisal hadn't covered them, if he hadn't helped Natches rescue her.

There would be no light in his world if it hadn't been for this boy. No Chaya, no life growing within her. There would have been nothing but the killer he had been slowly turning into.

Natches blinked back the moisture in his eyes, then moved to the boy. Before he knew his own intentions, he wrapped his arms around the kid and hugged him quickly and tightly before grasping his shoulders and pushing him back.

"Hell, Faisal, you grew up on me, kid," he said huskily. "Why the hell did you go and do that?"

Faisal's grin was filled with warmth. "Timothy Cranston. He says you have a baby coming. Maybe a little girl that will need a brother such as I. I could be a very good brother, Natchie."

A little girl. Natches felt his stomach clench in fear.

"Nah, a boy. You'll have to help me teach him how to fight."

"This I can do." Faisal nodded, clapping Natches on the shoulder, his nerves receding. "I will do this, Natchie. I . . ." He looked around. "This is your family that you told me of? Damned Dawg and Fucking Rowdy?"

Dawg and Rowdy glared at Natches as he cleared his throat. "Just Dawg." Natches almost laughed as he nodded to his cousin. "His wife, Crista. Rowdy and his wife, Kelly. And Uncle Ray and Aunt Maria."

"Your uncle Ray, too, son." Ray stepped forward and shook the boy's hand before patting him on the back. "We're all your family."

Faisal's expression clenched then, emotion working through him as it was through Natches. Hell, Natches'd come to think of Faisal as an adopted cousin, or even a son. He hadn't imagined the young man he had turned into, but that would work, too.

"My family?" Faisal asked, turning back to Natches to be certain. "They are my family as well?"

"Adoption papers." Timothy slapped them into Natches's hand. "We began the process when you first started harassing me for it. I'm on suspended leave, I'll have you know, for pushing this through."

"For this and several rules he broke in a certain arrest." Chaya glared at him. "Timothy, you need to settle down and stop making everyone crazy."

Timothy's smile was all teeth. "Maybe I'll move to Somerset. Fine little town. I could have a hell of a lot of fun here."

Natches ignored the sniping as he stared at the papers.

"Faisal Mackay," he said, looking up at the boy. "This works for you?"

Faisal's smile was filled with excitement. "Mackay, it is a good name. Strong. And filled with family." There was hunger in the boy's eyes as he stared around the room. The hunger for family, for roots. "If it pleases you, Natchie, it pleases me."

"Hell, I got a nephew." Dawg grinned. "He can work at the lumber store."

"The marina would be better," Ray argued. "He'll like the lake."

"He can make up his own mind." Natches clasped the boy's arm and felt Faisal's fingers curl around his, too, as he grinned down at him. "But he gets to work in a garage first."

Natches turned to Chaya, pulled her to his side, and felt the warmth of family surround him. Even Timothy, the rabid little fucker, was grinning.

"I hid your presents in the back," Chaya told Faisal. "Both of your presents." She looked to Timothy. "Merry Christmas, Timothy."

He scratched his cheek and frowned at her. "I didn't get you anything." Out of sorts, that was Timothy, clear to the bone.

"Yeah, you did." She smiled softly and looked around the room at the family she had. "You gave me everything, Timothy."

She surprised him with a kiss to his cheek, then moved from the room to the back of the boat, where she had hidden the other presents from Natches. The rest of the family's were beneath the tree, and now it was time to add to that family.

She turned back when she reached the hall, a grin touching her lips as the cousins began to argue around Faisal again about where he could work. The young man looked ecstatic, excited, nervous, and filled with hope.

With hope. That was what they all had now, what Timothy had given to them.

As the agent turned to her helplessly, she winked at him and smiled before entering the room that held the presents.

Life was exceptionally good. Natches's sister would be here within the hour to open presents, then they would move to Dawg's and Rowdy's boats, and eventually to Ray and Maria's for a family dinner and more presents.

Janey was settling in slowly, finally finding a balance, and Faisal was now safe and where he belonged. With the family that would ensure his future. She and Natches had a life now. Warmth. Family.

Finally, Chaya had found home.

Look for
Lora Leigh's sexy new book

Nauti Intentions

Coming Winter 2009 from Berkley Sensation